ROGUES AND VAGABONDS
COMPTON MACKENZIE

By COMPTON MACKENZIE

ROGUES AND VAGABONDS

By

COMPTON MACKENZIE

GEORGE H. DORAN COMPANY
ON MURRAY HILL　：　：　NEW YORK

To A. H.

CONTENTS

ROGUES AND VAGABONDS

ROGUES AND VAGABONDS

SUPERIOR
FIRE WORKS
at the
NEPTUNE'S GROTTO
Tavern and Tea Gardens
PIMLICO
on Thursday Evening, 20th, July, 1829.

By
MADAME ORIANO
The Celebrated Pyrotechnic to HIS MAJESTY
The Exhibition will include
A Grand Display of various kinds of

WATER FIRE WORKS
On the Grosvenor Basin.

ORDER OF FIRING

1. A Battery of Maroons, or imitation Cannon
2. A Bengal Light
3. Sky Rockets
4. A Saxon Wheel

5. Tourbillions
6. Phenomenon Box and Mime
7. Line Rockets
8. A Metamorphose with alternate changes, and a beautiful display of Chinese Lattice Work
9. Sky Rockets
10. Horizontal Wheel with Roman Candles and Mine
11. Tourbillions
12. A regulating piece in two mutations, displaying a Vertical Wheel changing to five Vertical Wheels and a figure piece in Straw and brilliant fires
13. Grand Battery of Roman Candles & Italian Streamers
14. A regulating piece in four mutations displaying a Vertical Wheel changing to a Pyramid of Wheels, a Brilliant Sun, and a superb shower of fire
15. Sky rockets

GRAND FINALE

MADEMOISELLE LETIZIA ORIANO

Will with a temerity hitherto unknown in the blazing annals of her profession slide down an inclined rope 350 feet high, erected on the firework platform, wreathed in Fizgigs and Fiery Serpents and accompanied by the awful thunder of a Battery of Maroons.

Admission 1s each

Gardens open at half-past seven, and commences at Nine o'clock precisely.

"Neptune's Grotto" was one of the many pleasure-gardens that in the days when the Londoner was comparatively a free man helped to amuse his leisure. Yet even by the ninth year of the reign of King George IV

most of the famous resorts of the preceding century had
already been built over, and now that Lord Grosvenor
was developing the Manor of Ebury (Buckingham Palace
appearing fixed as the metropolitan abode of the Sovereign) "Neptune's Grotto" was likely to vanish soon and
leave no more trace of its sparkling life than the smoke
of a spent rocket.   Indeed, change was already menacing.
For two years Cubitt, the famous builder, had been filling
up the swampy land between Vauxhall Bridge Road and
Ranelagh with the soil he had excavated in the construc-
tion of St. Katharine's Docks.   His cadaverous grey plas-
tered terraces were creeping nearer every week.   Willow
Walk, a low-lying footpath between the cuts of the Chelsea
Water Works, in a cottage hard by which Jerry Abershaw
and Gentleman James Maclaine the highwaymen once
lodged, would soon be turned into the haggard Warwick
Street we know to-day.   The last osier bed would ultimately be replaced by the greasy aucubas of Eccleston
Square, and Lupus Street would lie heavy on ancient
gardens.   The turnpike at Ebury Bridge had been gone
these four years; the old country road to Chelsea would
within a lustrum be lined by houses on either side and
become Buckingham Palace Road.   Even the great basin
of the Grosvenor Canal would run dry at last and breed
from its mud Victoria Station.

However, in 1829 "Neptune's Grotto" still remained
much as it had been for over a century.   The house of
mellow red brick was covered with lattice-work, which on
this warm July evening was all fragrant and ablow with
climbing roses.   Only the box trees had changed the pattern
of their topiary.   In place of earlier warriors or statesmen
you would have found Lord Nelson and the Duke of
Wellington at this date, the general more freshly trimmed
than the admiral, but likely to go unpruned in the years
of his unpopularity that were coming.   His sacred
Majesty King George III had been allowed to sprout into
the rounder bulk of his sacred Majesty King George IV,
but the new portrait was hardly more attractive than the

blowsy original. The garden paths were bordered with
stocks and hollyhocks. There were bowling-greens and
fishponds, and a dark alley in emulation of the notorious
dark alley of Vauxhall. Most of these amenities, however, had been made familiar by a score of other pleasure-
gardens all over London. What gave "Neptune's Grotto"
its peculiar charm was the wide green lawn running down
to the edge of the great reservoir. In the middle of this
was the grotto itself, under the ferny arches of which an
orchestra of Tritons languorously invited the little world
of pleasure to the waltz, or more energetically commanded
it to the gallopade. The firework platform was built out
over the water on piles; and the lawn was surrounded
on three sides by small alcoves lined with oyster shells, in
some of which the lightest footstep on a concealed
mechanism would cause to spring up a dolphin, or a mer-
maid, a harlequin or a Mother Shipton, startling intruders
for the maiden who first encountered them, so startling
that she would usually fling herself into the arms of the
beau in escort and require to be restored with various
liquors much to the satisfaction of Mr. Seedwell, the
owner of the gardens.

High tortoiseshell combs and full curled hair, wide
skirts of Gros de Naples flounced and pinked and scal-
loped and fluted, white stockings and slippers of yellow
prunella, Leghorn hats of transparent crape bound with
lavender sarsenet or puffed with small bouquets of mar-
about, bonnets of jonquil-yellow with waving ostrich
plumes, bonnets of marshmallow-rose with ribbons of
lilac and hortensia floating loose, double Vandyke collars
of Indian muslin, grass-green parasols and purple reti-
cules, leg-of-mutton sleeves and satin roulades, pelisses
and pèlerines most fashionably of camelopard-yellow,
ivory shoulders, Canezon spencers and gauze capotes,
fichus of ethereal-blue barège, laughter and whispers and
murmurs and music (ah, yes, no doubt and plenty of
simpers too), where now trains thunder past filled with
jaded suburbans, whose faces peep from the windows as

their owners wonder if the new film at the picture-theatre will be worth the trouble of visiting after tea in our modish contemporary shades of nude, French nude, sunburn, and flesh. Would that Stephenson had never cursed humanity with his steam-engine, and would that this tale might never creep nearer to the present than that July night of 1829! Alas, it has more to do with the grandchildren and great-grandchildren of those who fluttered out like moths in that summer dusk to watch Madame Oriano's fireworks; and these at whom you gaze for the moment are but creatures in a prologue who will all be ghosts long before the last page is written.

However, here come those ghosts, still very much alive and shilling in hand, some from Knightsbridge, some from Chelsea, some from Westminster. "Strombolo House," which used to charge half-a-crown for its fireworks, so famous were they, is closed. To be sure the "Monster" is still open, but there are no fireworks in the entertainment there to-night; a performing bear is all that the "Monster" can offer to-night. The "Orange Tea Gardens" are gone for good: St. Barnabas' Pimlico, will occupy their site, and on it cause as much religious rowdiness in another twenty years as ever there was of secular rowdiness in the past. "Jenny's Whim" hard by the old turnpike has already been covered with builder Cubitt's beastly foundations. There is no longer much competition with "Neptune's Grotto" in the manor of Ebury. A few pause in Vauxhall Bridge Road when they see the hackney-coaches filled with merry parties bound for the most famous gardens of all; but they decide to visit them another evening, and they cross the road to Willow Walk, where one remembers seeing Jerry Abershaw's body swinging from the gibbet on Putney Common and that scarcely thirty years ago, and another marvels at the way the new houses are springing up all round. Some shake their heads over Reform, but most of them whisper of pleasure and of love while ghostly moths spin beside the path, and the bats are seen hawking against the luminous west and the dog-star which was glimmering long before his fellows is already dancing like a diamond in the south.

While the public was strolling on its way to "Neptune's Grotto," within the gardens themselves Mr. Seedwell, the proprietor, and Madame Oriano made a final inspection of the firework platform.

" You think she can do it?" he was saying.

"Offa coursa she can do it," Madame replied sharply.

Mr. Seedwell shook his head in grave doubt. Weighing eighteen stone and a bit over he found it hard to put himself in Mademoiselle Letizia's place.

"I don't want an accident," he explained. "The magistrates are only too glad of an excuse to close us down these days."

"Dere willa not be no accident," Madame Oriano assured him.

And Mr. Seedwell, looking at the raven-haired and raven-beaked and raven-eyed woman beside him, took her word for it and went off to see that all was ready inside the house for the entertainment of his guests.

Madame Oriano squeezed a handful of her yellow satin gown.

"*Bagnato!*" [1] she murmured to herself. Then looking across to one of the alcoves she called out in a shrill harsh voice, "Caleb! Caleb Fuller!"

A beetle could not have left his carapace more unwillingly than Caleb Fuller that alcove. He was a young man—certainly not more than twenty-five, perhaps not as much—whose lumpish and pasty face suggested at first an extreme dulness of mind until one looked a little closer and perceived a pair of glittering granite-grey eyes that animated the whole countenance with an expression that passed beyond cunning and touched intelligence. Beside the dragon-fly vividness of his employer he appeared, as he shambled across the lawn to hear what she wanted of him, like an awkward underground insect, with his turgid

[1] Wet.

rump and thin legs in tight pantaloons and his ill-fitting
tail-coat of rusty black.

"Dissa English cleemat *non è possibile,*" Madame
shrilled. "Everyting willa be wet before we beginna to
fire."

"It's the heavy dew," said Caleb.

"Oh, *diavolo!* What do it matter which it is, if de fireworks will alla be—how you say—spilt?"

"Spoilt," he corrected gloomily.

"Che lingua di animali, questa English linguage!
Where issa John Gumm?"

"In the tap-room," Caleb informed her.

"Drinking! Drinking," she shrilled. "Why you don'ta
to keep him notta to drink before we are finished?"

John Gumm who was Madame's chief firer had already
imperilled by his habits several of her performances.

"Somebody musta go and putta clothes on de fireworks.
Non voglio che abbiamo un fiasco,[2] I don'ta wish it. You
hear me, Caleb?"

Caleb was used to these outbursts of nervous anxiety
before every display, and on most evenings he would have
humoured Madame by bullying the various assistants and
have enjoyed giving such an exhibition of his authority.
But this evening he would not have been sorry to see the
damp air make the whole display such a fiasco as Madame
feared, for he bitterly resented the public appearance of
Letizia Oriano, not so much for the danger of the proposed feat, but for the gratification the sight of her shapely
legs would afford the crowd. In fact when Madame had
summoned him to her side, he was actually engaged in a
bitter argument with Letizia herself and had even gone
so far as to beg her to defy her mother and refuse to
make the fire-clad descent.

"There won't be enough dew to prevent the firing,"
he argued. "And more's the pity," he added, gathering
boldness as jealousy began once more to rack him.
"More's the pity, I say, when you're letting your only

[2] "I do not want us to have a fiasco."

child expose her—expose herself to danger." He managed to gulp back the words he just lacked the courage to fling at her, and though his heart beat "Jezebel! Jezebel!" he dared not say it out.

"Dere is nottings dangerous," she snapped. "She has walked the slacka rope and the tighta rope since she was a *bambina*. Her fazer has learnt her to do it."

Caleb groaned within himself. Letizia's father was as mythical and as many-sided as Proteus. Italian prince, English nobleman, play-actor, ballet-master, acrobat, with as many aliases as a thief, he was whatever Madame chose he should be to suit her immediate argument. Nobody knew his real name or his real profession. Once, when Caleb had remonstrated with her for being apparently willing to sell Letizia to a rich and snivelling old rake, she had actually dared to argue that she was better capable of guarding her daughter's virtue than anybody else because the father of her had been a cardinal. Caleb, who was sick with love for Letizia and sick with hate for Popery, was near losing his reason. Luckily, however, the old suitor fell into a hopeless palsy, and since then Madame's financial affairs had prospered sufficiently to make her independent of Letizia's cash value. That her affairs had prospered was largely due to Caleb himself, who, entering her service as a clerk when he was hardly nineteen, had lost no time in gathering into his own plump white hands the tangled skeins of the business so that he might unravel them at his own convenience without ever again letting them go.

Madame Oriano had been glad enough to put the financial side of the business in Caleb's hands, for, having inherited from her father, Padua's chief artist in pyrotechny, a genuine passion for inventing new effects, she devoted herself to these with renewed interest, an interest moreover that was no longer liable to be interrupted by amours. She had grown gaunt and her temper, never of the sweetest, had long made her an impossible mistress for any man however young be might be. At the age of

sixteen she had eloped from her father's house in Padua
with an English adventurer. After a year of doubtful
bliss he had left her stranded in a Soho garret with a cageful of lovebirds and twenty pairs of silk stockings—he
had intended these as a present for the schoolgirl he was
planning to abduct, but in the confusion of escaping from
his old sweetheart he had left them behind him. Maria
Oriano entered upon a period of fortune-telling, then went
into partnership with an Italian pyrotechnist to whom
with intervals of amorous escapades she remained loyal
for ten years, in fact till he died, after which she carried
on the business in her own name. Letizia was born when
her mother was approaching forty, and since neither Letizia nor anybody else ever discovered who the father was,
it may safely be assumed that Madame really did not
know herself which of her lovers might be congratulated.
She had a dozen in tow about this time. No solution of
the mystery had ever been provided by Letizia herself,
who now, at seventeen, was the image of her own mother
when she, a year younger, ran away from Padua, a dark
and slim and supple and lustrous-eyed young termagant.

There she was now, fretfully tapping the floor of the
alcove with her dainty foot and wondering what her
mother could want with Caleb. It was not that she wanted
Caleb so much for herself, not at any rate for the pleasure of his conversation. But she was used to quarrelling
with him, and she missed his company much as a child
might miss a toy that it could maltreat whenever it was
in the mood to do so. She might laugh at his awkward
attempts to make love to her, but she would have been
piqued by his indifference, piqued and puzzled by it as
she would have been puzzled by the failure of her spaniel
to wag its tail when she entered a room. There was Caleb
bowing and scraping to her mother (who looked a pretty
sight in that yellow satin gown) while she who after all
was this evening indubitably *the* attraction was left alone
in this dull alcove without so much as a glass of champagne to sip. How much would her mother worry about

the dampness of the fireworks, were she to announce that she could not make the descent that was to bring the display to such a grand conclusion? It would serve them all right if she did rebel. They would appreciate her much more were she sometimes to assert herself. Letizia pulled open the cloak of light blue velvet that she was wearing over her costume and contemplated her slim legs and the beautifully unwrinkled tights. The upper part of her dress consisted of an abbreviated tunic of asbestos round which the unlit fireworks coiled like blue snakes.

"Or sausages," murmured Letizia resentfully. "If I did not look like Guy Fawkes and if it were a little darker, I'd put on a mask and have such fun amongst the crowd. Oh gemini, wouldn't I just!"

She jumped up in a fit of impatience. Her foot pressed the concealed mechanism in the floor of the alcove, and immediately there sprang up before her a life-size Mother Shipton, quivering all over and shaking her steeple hat, and seeming in the twilight most horribly real.

"Gesù Maria, Giuseppe!" she shrieked, crossing herself in an agony of terror.

Caleb, whose first thought was that some young buck was trying to kiss Letizia, paid no more attention to Madame Oriano's complaints of Gumm's drunkenness and the dewy nightfall, but plunged off to the rescue, splitting the seat of his pantaloons in an effort to move his clumsy legs really fast.

"Oh gemini, Caleb, the Devil's been sitting beside me all the time and I never knew it," Letizia cried, when she saw him.

"I make no doubt he has," said Caleb in lugubrious agreement. "But this ain't him. This ain't no more than one of those fortune-telling figures you'll see at fairs. That's what they call fun, that is," he groaned.

"It sprang up so sudden, Caleb. The Devil couldn't have sprung up no faster. Oh gemini, it set me off praying, Caleb."

"Praying!" he scoffed. "I wouldn't give much for you

if the Devil did come to take you, and you had to trust to *your* prayers."

"It's made my heart thump, Caleb. Only feel how fast it beats."

The young man snatched his hand away from her.

"Hussy! Nought would please you so well as to lead me on into sin."

It was Caleb's heart that was beating now, so fast indeed that he turned in desperation to strike down the puppet that seemed to be leering at him like an old bawd in a dark entry.

"Oh, you sicken me," she pouted. "I'll surely never have the courage to mount to the top of the mast now. At least, I won't unless I have some champagne, Caleb."

There was no answer.

"Did you hear me, Caleb?" she pressed softly. "I said champagne."

He turned his back and feigned not to hear. But a passing waiter heard and came into the alcove, rubbing his hands in anticipation of serving them.

"Champagne, Caleb."

"Yes, ma'am. Certainly, ma'am."

"No," Caleb shouted.

The waiter inclined his head in sarcastic acknowledgment.

"And light the lamp," Caleb told him.

Above the circular stone hung a great green globe painted over with fish, which when lighted up shed a kind of subaqueous sheen upon the alcove.

"And the champagne, sir?" the waiter asked.

"Bring a bottle quickly," Letizia commanded with a laugh of mockery.

"Bring nothing at all," cried Caleb, swinging round on his heels in a rage.

"Oh gemini, Caleb," Letizia cried. "Your handkerchief's falling out of your pocket."

She grabbed at it, and pulled out the tail of his shirt. Letizia flung herself into a chair, clapping her hands and throwing her legs into the air in a very ecstasy of delight.

"Oh gemini, Mr. Waiter; bring two bottles," she cried. "And a needle and a thread, for I'll burst my own trunks next and never dare stand on a chair, let alone come sliding down to the ground from a mast."

The waiter departed to obey her commands, a wide grin on his insolent face.

"Listen to me, Letizia," Caleb cried in a rage, seizing her wrist. "I'll pay for not one drop of champagne, d'ye hear me? Little Jezebel that you are! You love to make me suffer for your wantonness. I was pure till your Popish gipsy eyes crossed mine and turned them to thoughts of sin. Isn't it enough that you're going to mount that accursed firework platform for every gay young sprig to stare at you carnally and gloat on your limbs and lust after you? Isn't it enough, I say, for one evening?"

"You're a fine one to accuse me of making myself a show," she retorted, wresting herself from his grasp. "And you with the tail of your shirt sticking out of your breeches! You'd better call it your flag of truce, Caleb, and cry peace."

"I'll make no peace with you, young Jezebel, in this wanton humour."

"Why then, catch me if you can, Mr. Preacher, for I'll have my champagne, and Mr. Devil can pay for it, if you won't."

With this she stood mocking him from the lawn outside.

"Come back," he groaned, the sweat all beady on his forehead.

"I won't come back neither," laughed Letizia, pirouetting.

"Pull your cloak round you, shameless minx."

"No, and I won't do that, neither."

She flung it farther from her and taunted him with the

sight of her legs so slim and so shapely in the light blue silk.

"You dursn't run after me, Caleb, or you'll be taken to Bedlam for a lunatic when the people see you running after me like a draggle-tailed duck. Quack-quack, Caleb! I'm the grand finale to-night, and if you won't give me champagne I'll find some one who will, and he'll have the grandest finale of all."

Unfortunately for Letizia when she turned round to run away she ran into her mother, who caught her by the ear and led her back into the alcove.

"*Sei pazza?*" she demanded.

"If I am mad, it's his fault," protested Letizia angrily. "Let go of my ear, mamma! You're hurting me."

"*Vuoi far la putanella, eh?*" [3] cried Madame Oriano furiously, squeezing her daughter's ear even harder.

"Eh, *basta,*[4] mamma! Or I'll be no grand finale to-night for you or nobody else. I only asked for champagne because that old witch jumped up out of the floor and frightened me. If you hadn't been screaming so loud yourself, you might have heard me scream."

"*Insolente,*" cried Madame, making coral of her daughter's ivory cheeks with several vicious slaps.

Luckily for Letizia the waiter came back at this moment with a tray on which were glasses and the bottle of champagne. This gave Madame Oriano a real opportunity. Picking up her skirt as if she were going to drop a curtsey, she raised one foot and kicked the tray and its contents up to the oyster-inlaid ceiling of the alcove. She might have been giving the signal for the fireworks to begin, for just as the contents of the tray crashed to the ground the thunder of the maroons reverberated about the pale sapphire of the nine o'clock sky.

Madame hurried out into the excited crowd of spectators, clapping her skinny hands and crying, "*Bravo!*

[3] "You want to play the little wanton, eh?"
[4] Enough.

Bravimissimo!" at the top of her voice. She believed in
the power of the claque and always led the applause of her
own creations. Immediately after the maroons the Bengal
light flared and turned the upturned faces of the crowd to
a lurid rose, the glassy waters of the basin to garnets.
Letizia, who had been sobbing with pain and fury while
the maroons were exploding, responded with all her being
to the excitement of the Bengal light. She forgot her
pain, her rage, her disappointment. She quivered like the
Mother Shipton, became like the puppet a mere dressed-up
spring. She longed for the moment when she should be
summoned to ascend the platform and climb the mast to
the crow's-nest on the summit, and most of all for the
moment she should hear the sausages round her asbestos
tunic fizz and cackle and spit, and when wreathed in
flames, balancing herself with a flashing Italian streamer
in each hand, she should slide down the long rope into
the tumultuous cheers of the public below.

Caleb was aware of her eagerness and, having in himself nothing of the mountebank, supposed that she was
merely longing to display her legs to the mob. He vented
the bile of his jealousy upon the waiter.

"I'll report you to Mr. Seedwell," he stormed. "How
dare you bring champagne without an order?"

"Madame . . ."

"Get out of here," Caleb shouted. "This is no madam,
you lousy wretch. I'll have no rascals like you come
pimping round this young lady."

Sky rockets were shedding their fiery blossoms upon the
air, and the water below was jewelled with their reflec-
tions. Tourbillions leapt up to tremble for a moment in
golden spirals. Mutation followed mutation as shivered
wheels of rubies turned to fountains of molten emeralds
and amethysts and blazing showers of topaz. Above the
explosions, above the applause, the shrill voice of Madame
Oriano rang out continually, *"Bravo! Bravissimo! An-
cora! Bene! Benissimo! Che splendore! Che mag-
nificenza!"*

Letizia stood rapt like a saint that expects a corporeal assumption to the seventh heaven.

"It's time I went up," she breathed.

"Not yet," Caleb pleaded, in horror of the moment when that lewd and accursed mob should gloat upon her slim form.

"It is. It is! Let me go, Caleb! Gemini, you crazy fool, you'll make me late."

Letizia sprang away from his detaining arms.

"Why don't you set fire to your shirt, Caleb, and slide down behind me?" she called back to him in mockery.

There were shouts of enthusiasm when the figure of Letizia stood up dimly against the stars. Followed a silence. Old John Gumm fired the fizgigs and the serpents. With a shriek of triumphant joy Letizia launched herself from the mast. High above the wondering murmurs of the crowd her mother's voice resounded.

"Che bella ragazza! [5] *Brava! Bravissima! Avanti, figlia mia! Che forma di Venere!"* [6]

"Almighty God," Caleb groaned. "She might be naked."

When the flaming vision touched earth, he rushed forward to recapture it; but Letizia, intoxicated with success, flung herself into the arms of three or four young bucks who were waiting to carry her off to champagne, while from the grotto in the middle of the lawn the Triton orchestra struck up Weber's seductive *Invitation to the Waltz.*

[5] "What a lovely girl!"
[6] "Forward, my daughter! What a figure of Venus!"

CHAPTER II

THE FACTORY

Caleb was in such a turmoil of jealous agitation for several hours after the grand finale as to be almost beside himself; and although Madame Oriano, in high good humour over the success of the fireworks, offered to sew up the split in his pantaloons, she could not sew up the rents that Letizia's behaviour was tearing in her manager's peace of mind. Once he ventured to approach the alcove where she sat drinking and flirting with half-a-dozen hopeful courtiers, and asked her to come with him. Letizia shrieked with laughter at such a notion and shrieked louder when her companions began to pelt Caleb with crusts of bread; and maybe she would not have laughed much less loudly if they had gone on to pelt him with bottles as they threatened they would do unless he quickly took himself off and ceased to annoy them. Caleb, to do him justice, would not have cared a jot if he could have rescued Letizia from their company at the cost of a broken crown; but he did not want to expose himself to the mortification of being vanquished and, since he felt positive that this could be the only result of his intervention, he retreated to brood over his wrongs in a secluded arbour, from which he had the minor satisfaction of driving away the amorous couples that in turn hopefully sought its dark protection throughout that warm and starry July night.

Was Madame Oriano dependent enough yet upon his help in the business to insist on her daughter's marrying him? That was the question. Caleb felt convinced that she would not object, but if the little hussy herself refused, would her mother compel her? Brought up in the

26

egocentric gloom of an obscure Protestant sect known as the Peculiar Children of God, Caleb's first thought was always the salvation of his own soul. This, as often happens, had become a synonym for the gratification of his own desires. He desired Letizia. Therefore he must have her, or his soul would be imperilled. What she felt about it was of little importance. Besides, she so clearly had in her the makings of a wanton that it was his duty to save her soul as well, which he had every reason to suppose he should be able to do could he but safely secure her for a wife. The state of affairs could not continue as it was at present. His imagination must not remain for ever the tortured prey of carnal visions. Letizia's white neck . . . Letizia's girlish breasts . . . Letizia's red alluring lips . . . Letizia's twining fingers . . . and at this moment in the alcove those drunken sons of Belial were gloating upon her. . . . No, it could not go on like this! She must be his with God's benign approval. Caleb sat for an hour, two hours, three hours maybe, in a dripping trance of thwarted passion, burning as fiercely with the hot itch of jealousy as if he had actually been flung into a steaming nettle-bed.

Dawn, a lucid primrose dawn, was bright beyond the towers of Lambeth Palace when the hackney-coach with Madame Oriano, Letizia, and Caleb went jogging homeward over Westminster Bridge. Even now, though Letizia had fallen deliciously asleep on his shoulder, Caleb was not at peace, for the semioctagonal turrets which were set at intervals along the parapet to serve as refuges for the homeless, reminded him of the alcoves at "Neptune's Grotto," and his mind was again tormented by the imagination of her behaviour that night. She reeked too, of wine, in this fresh morning air. He shook her roughly:

"Wake up! We're nearly home."

Madame Oriano was snoring on the opposite seat.

"Why don't you poke mamma like that?" Letizia cried out resentfully.

An impulse to crush her to his heart surged over Caleb,

but he beat off the temptation, panting between desire of
her and fear for himself. Kisses would forge no chain
to bind this wanton, and he, should he once yield to kiss-
ing her, would be led henceforth by a Delilah. The hackney-coach jogged on into the Westminster Road.

Madame Oriano's factory consisted of the unused rooms
in an ordinary York Street dwelling-house. Special precautions to isolate the dangerous manufacture were practically unknown at this date. All firework-making by an
Act of Dutch William was still illegal, and from time to
time prosecutions of pyrotechnists were set on foot at the
instigation of the magistrates when the boys of a neigh-
bourhood became too great a nuisance on the Fifth of November. Inasmuch, however, as firework displays were
a feature of coronations, peace declarations, births of
royal heirs, and other occasions of public rejoicing, the
Law adopted then as ambiguous an attitude as it does now
in this early twentieth century, toward betting. Until
Caleb arrived in London from the Cheshire town where
he had been born and bred, Madame Oriano produced her
fireworks in fits and starts of inventive brilliance that were
symbolical of the finished product. Most of her workmen
were habitual drunkards. No kind of attempt was made
to run the business side with any financial method. From
time to time the proprietress put a card in the window
advertising her need for an accountant. Clerks came and
clerks went until she began to look on the whole class as
no better than predatory nomads. It was in answer to
one of these cards in her window that Caleb presented
himself. His conscience troubled him at first when he
found with what mountebank affairs firework-making was
likely to bring him into contact, but he was seized by a
missionary fervour and began to devote all his energy to
making the business respectable. Only John Gumm, the
chief firer, managed to survive Caleb's cleansing zeal. The
rest of the drunken workmen were sacked one after another, and their places taken wherever it was possible by
young lads and girls that Caleb procured from the poor-

house. The long hours and bad food he inflicted upon these apprentices seemed to bring the business nearer to genuine respectability. It showed sound economy, and the most censorious Puritan could not discover in those workrooms filled with listless children anything that pandered to the gratification of human pleasure. One could feel that when the fireworks left the factory there was nothing against their morality. Their explosion under the direction of Madame Oriano and drunken John Gumm was of course regrettably entertaining, but the rest of the business was impeccably moral. Not only did Caleb attend to the accounts, to the management of the workers, and to the judicious purchase of materials, but he also studied the actual art of pyrotechny, and early this very year he had discovered how to apply chlorate of potash to the production of more brilliant colours than any that had hitherto been seen. He had not yet revealed this discovery to Madame Oriano, because he was planning to use the knowledge of it as a means of persuading her to insist on Letizia's marrying him. She would be so much astonished by the green he had evolved by combining nitrate of baryta with chlorate of potash that she would give him anything he demanded. And as for the red he could now produce by adding nitrate of strontia to his chlorate of potash, why, if such a red could only be bought in the ultimate depths of Hell, Madame would have to buy.

The hackney-coach drew up in front of the dingy house in York Street, and by the time Caleb had done arguing with the driver about his fare mother and daughter had tumbled into bed. In spite of the nervous strain he had been enduring all night Caleb could not make up his mind to go to sleep himself. He was indeed feeling very much awake. It was now full day. The sunlight was glinting on the grimy railings of the area, and the footsteps of early workers shuffled past along the pavement at intervals. Caleb looked round the room and frowned at the tools lying idle on the tables and benches. He was filled with indignation at the thought that all those misbegotten

apprentices should be snoring away these golden hours of
the morning in their garret. He was too lenient with
them, far too lenient. It would do the brats good to be
awakened a little earlier than usual. He was up and
dressed; why should they still be snoring? The back of
his mind, too, itched with an evil desire to make somebody pay for what he had suffered last night. Caleb set
off upstairs to rouse the apprentices. As he drew near
the bedroom where Madame Oriano and Letizia slept together in that gilded four-poster which so much revolted
his sense of decency, Caleb paused, for the door was wide
open. He tried to keep his face averted while he hurried
past; but his will failed him and, turning, he beheld the
vision of Letizia, so scantily wrapped in her cloak of sky-
blue that her white body appeared as shamelessly unclad
as the vicious little Cupids that supported the canopy of
the bed. Caleb staggered back. Had there been a knife
in his hand, he might have cut Letizia's throat, such an
intolerable loathing of her beauty seized him. He rushed
madly past the open door, and a moment or two afterwards he stood in the garret, surveying with hate the
sleeping forms of the apprentices. A sunbeam glinting
through the broken lattice of the dormer lit up the four
flushed faces, spangled the hair of the youngest and fair-
est, and for Caleb pointed at the spectacle of brazen sloth.

"Get up, you charity brats," he shouted, pulling off the
dirty coverlet. "Get up and work, or I'll report you to
the overseers for incorrigibles."

The children sat up in bed dazed by this sudden awak-
ening.

"Don't loll there, rubbing your eyes and staring at me,"
Caleb snarled. "If you aren't downstairs and hard at
work on those composition stars in five minutes, I'll see
what a good flogging will do for you."

From the boys' garret Caleb went across to visit the
girls'.

"Get down to your scissors and paste, you lazy hussies,"
he bellowed in the doorway.

The little girls, the eldest of whom was hardly twelve, sat up in a huddle of terror. The shift of the youngest, who might be ten, was torn so that her bare shoulder protruded to affront Caleb's gaze. He strode into the room and struck the offending few inches of skin and bone.

"Will nothing teach you modesty?" he gibbered. "Aren't you afraid of burning in Hell for your wickedness? Shame on you, I say. Have you no needle and thread, Amelia Diggle? You ought to be whipped, and I hope Madame will whip you well. Now stop that blubbering and dress yourself, and in five minutes let me find you all hard at work."

Caleb retired to his own bedroom, where after a miserly use of soap and water he changed out of his rusty black evening clothes into the drab of daily life. He was then able to bend down and say his prayers, partly because the drab breeches were not as tight as the black pantaloons and partly because they did not show the dust so easily.

In contemplating Caleb while he is kneeling to ask his savage deity to give him Letizia and to bless his discovery of chlorate of potash as a colour intensifier and to fructify his savings and to visit His wrath upon all unbelievers, one may feel that perhaps it was being unduly sentimental last night, a trifle wrought upon by music and starshine and coloured lamps, to wish that this tale might remain in the year of grace 1829.

Caleb rose from his knees and, fortified by his prayers, succeeded this time in passing the open door of Letizia's bedroom without so much as one swift glance within. He came down to the basement and with a good deal of complacency gloated over the sight of those children all so beautifully hard at work. He would have liked to tell them how lucky they were to be in the care of somebody who took all this trouble to rouse them early and teach them the joys of industry. The thought of how many more composition stars would be made to-day than were made yesterday was invigorating. He regarded the tousled heads of the apprentices with something like good-will.

"That's the way, boys, work hard and well and in three hours you'll be enjoying your breakfast," he promised. Then suddenly he looked sharply round the room. "Why, where's Arthur Wellington?"

At this moment the foundling thus christened, a fair-haired child of eleven, appeared timidly in the doorway, and shrank back in terror when his master demanded where he had been.

"Please, Mr. Fuller, I was looking for my shoe," he stammered, breathing very fast.

"Oh, you were looking for your shoe, were you, Arthur Wellington? And did you find your shoe?"

"No, Mr. Fuller," the boy choked. "I think it must have fell out of the window."

His blue eyes were fixed reproachfully, anxiously, pleadingly, on Joe Hilton the eldest apprentice who bent lower over his task of damping with methylated spirit the composition for the stars, the while he managed to scowl sideways at Arthur.

"So you've been loitering about in your room while your companions have been hard at work, Arthur Wellington?"

"I haven't been loitering. I've been looking for my shoe."

"Contradict me, will you, Arthur Wellington?" said Caleb softly. "Show me your other shoe. Come nearer, Arthur. Nearer. Take it off and give it to me."

The boy approached, breathing faster; but he still hesitated to take off the shoe.

"Don't keep me waiting, Arthur," Caleb said. "You've kept me waiting long enough this lovely summer morning. Give me the shoe."

Arthur did as he was told.

"Don't go away, Arthur Wellington. I'm talking to you for your good. This lovely summer morning, I said. Perhaps you didn't hear me? Eh? Perhaps you're deaf? Deaf, are you, you workhouse brat?"

Caleb gripped the boy's puny shoulder and banged him several times on the head with the shoe.

"Perhaps you won't be so deaf when I've knocked some of the deafness out of you," he growled. "Blubbering now, eh, you miserable little bastard? Look up, will you! Look up, I say! Oh, very well, look down," and Caleb pushed the boy's head between his own legs and thrashed him with the first weapon that came to hand, which was a bundle of rocket-sticks.

"Button yourself up, Arthur Wellington," said Caleb, when he had finished with him and flung him to the floor where he lay writhing and shrieking and unbraced. "If I were you, Arthur Wellington, I'd be ashamed to make such an exhibition of myself in front of girls. That's enough! Stop that blubbering. Do you hear? Stop it, and get to work. Stop it, will you, Arthur Wellington, unless you want another thrashing twice as bad."

One of the apprentices was placing the stars on the fender to dry them before the fire which Caleb had lighted to make himself the tea.

"Be careful, Edward Riggs, not to put those stars too close, or you'll be having an accident."

"They're all right where they are, aren't they, Mr. Fuller?"

"Yes, as long as you're careful," said Caleb. "Now I'm going upstairs to my office to work. We all have our work to do, you know. And if I hear any laughing or chattering down here, I'll make some of you see more stars than you'll ever make in a week."

One of the girls managed to titter at this and was rewarded by one of Caleb's greasy smiles. Then he left the apprentices to their work and went into the question of accounts, hidden in his sanctum, which was on the first floor and hardly bigger than a powder-closet. Indeed, Caleb's high stool and desk with two ledgers and an iron box chained to a staple in the floor filled it so nearly full that when the manager was inside and hard at work nobody could get in unless he squeezed himself into the corner. Caleb's expressed object in keeping Madame Oriano's books so meticulously was that if at any moment a purchaser came along with a firm offer for the business, lock, stock, and barrel, he would obtain a better price for it. It was useless for the owner to protest that no inducement or offer of any kind would tempt her into a sale, Caleb insisted. He was as always outwardly subservient to his mistress, but he insisted. And she would tire of arguing with him when she had fired off a few Italian oaths and shrugged her shoulders in contempt of such obstinacy.

"Besides," Caleb used to point out, "so long as I keep my books properly, anybody can see my honesty. If I kept no books, people would be saying that I was robbing you."

"I would notta believe them."

"No, you mightn't believe them until you were angry with me about something else; but you might believe it then, and I shouldn't care to be accused of robbing you. It would hurt me very deeply, ma'am."

As a matter of fact Caleb had robbed Madame Oriano with perfect regularity for the last five years. The humble savings, to which from time to time with upturned eyes he would allude, were actually the small clippings and parings he had managed to make from her daily profits. He did not feel the least guilt in thus robbing her, for not merely could he claim that he was the only person who did rob her nowadays, but he could also claim that these robberies practically amounted to the dowry of her daughter. It was not as if the money were going out of the family. Whether, in the event of his failing to marry Letizia, Caleb would have made the least reparation is doubtful. He would have found another excuse for his behaviour. One of his principles was never to admit even to his tribal deity that he had been or was wrong. He could imagine nothing more corruptly humiliating than the Popish habit of confession. On the other hand, he was always willing to admit that he was liable to err, and he always prayed most devoutly to be kept free from temptation.

In his dusty little office that morning the various emotions to which he had been subjected since yesterday began to react at last upon Caleb's flabby body. Leaning forward upon his desk, he put his head down upon his folded arms and fell into a heavy sleep.

He was awakened by a series of screams, and jumping off his stool he hurried out into the passage just as one of the girl apprentices enveloped in flames came rushing up the stairs from the basement. He tried to stop her from going higher, but she eluded him, and as she went flashing up the stairs toward the upper part of the house she screamed:

"It was Arthur Wellington done it! Don't laugh at him, Joe Hilton. Don't laugh at him no more, or he'll throw the stars on to the fire. Where's a window? Where's a window?"

The wretched child vanished from sight, and the moment after a ghastly scream announced that she had found a window and flung herself from it into the street.

Letizia's spaniel came barking down from the room above. Simultaneously there was a frenzied knocking on the front door, flashes and crashes everywhere, smoke, more shrieks of agony, and at last a deafening explosion. It seemed to Caleb that the whole house was falling to pieces on top of him, as indeed when he was dragged out of the ruins he found that it had.

CHAPTER III

THE PROPOSAL

Accidents in firework factories occurred so often in those days, when the law had not yet recognised gunpowder as a means to provide popular diversion and taken steps in the Explosives Act to safeguard its employment, that for six poorhouse children to lose their lives and for two others to be permanently maimed was hardly considered as serious as the destruction of two comparatively new houses in York Street. Madame Oriano's own escape was voted miraculous, especially when it was borne in mind that both her legs had to be amputated; and while some pointed out that if she had not been sleeping in that florid four-post bed she need not have had her legs crushed by the canopy, others were equally quick to argue that it was precisely that canopy which saved the rest of her body from being crushed as completely as her legs. The bed certainly saved Letizia.

The accident was attributed to the inhuman carelessness of a parish apprentice known as Arthur Wellington, whereby he had placed a composition star on the hob of a lighted fire in order to dry it more expeditiously before being rammed into the casing of a Roman candle. Caleb in his evidence suggested that parish apprentices were inclined to make up for lost time in this abominable way. Everybody shook his head at the wickedness of parish apprentices, but nobody thought of blaming Caleb for the arrangement of a workroom that permitted such a dangerous method of making up for lost time. As for Caleb himself, when he had recovered from the shock of so nearly finding himself in Heaven before he had planned to retire there from the business of existence, he began to realise that the destruction of the factory was the best thing that could have happened for an earthly future that he hoped long to enjoy. He took the first opportunity of laying before Madame Oriano his views about that future. Should his proposal rouse her to anger, he could feel safe, inasmuch as she could certainly not get out of bed to attack him and was unlikely to leave the hospital for many weeks to come.

"Well, I willa always say dissa one ting, my friend, and datta is I have never had no *esplosione* in alla my life before dissa one. Such *fortuna* could never last for ever, I am secure. My legs, they makka me a little bad, datta is all."

Caleb regarded his mistress where she was lying in bed looking like a sharp-eyed bird in tropical vegetation, under the gaudy satin coverlet of her four-poster which she had insisted on having mended and brought to the hospital.

"I'm sure we ought all of us to be very thankful to our Father Who put His loving arms around us and kept us safe," he oozed.

Madame Oriano, become an old lady since her accident, smiled grimly.

"*Peccato che Nostro Padre non ha pensato per mie povere gambe!*" she muttered.

"What did you say?" Caleb asked timidly. He could never quite rid his mind of the fancy that the Italian language had a dangerous magic, an abracadabral potency which might land him in Hell by merely listening to it.

"I say it issa damn pity He does not putta His arms around my legs. Dat is what I say, Caleb."

"He knows best what is good for us," Caleb gurgled, turning up his eyes to the ceiling.

"*Può essere,*" the old lady murmured. "Perraps He do."

"But what I've really come to talk about," Caleb went on, "is the future of the business. Your presence, of course, will be sadly missed; but you'll be glad to hear

that I have managed to fulfil all our engagements up to
date, though naturally with such a terrible loss of material
the profits will be small—dreadfully small."

No doubt Caleb was right, and even what profit there
was he probably put in his iron box which had comfortably survived the destruction of the factory.

"I don'ta aspect no profit," said Madame Oriano.

"But I have been turning things over in my mind,"
Caleb pressed, "and I hope very much that you will be
pleased with the result of my—er—turnings. Yes, I'm
hoping that very much indeed." Caleb took a deep gulp
before he went on, staring away out across the chimney-
stacks to escape the old lady's arched eyebrows.

"Madame Oriano, when I came to London six years
ago and entered your service, you were a mother to me.
I can never forget your beautiful maternal behaviour,
ma'am, and, oh, ma'am, I am so anxious to be a son to
you now in the hour of your trouble—a true son."

"You never could notta be a son for me, Caleb. *Siete
troppo grasso, caro.* You are too big. How you say?
Too fat."

"Ah, Madame Oriano, don't say you won't let me be
a son to you till you've heard all I have to tell you. I
want to marry your daughter, ma'am. I want to marry
your Letizia. I loved her from the first moment I set
eyes on her, although of course I knew my position too
well to allow myself to indulge in any hopes that would
have been wanting in respect to my employer. But I
have worked hard, ma'am. Indeed, I venture to think
that my love for your daughter is not near so presumptuous at this moment as it would have been when I first
entered your service."

"*Sicuro!* She hassa seventeen years old now," said
Madame Oriano sharply. "She hadda only eleven years
then."

"Sweet seventeen!" Caleb sighed.

"*Non credo che sia tanto dolce.*"

"Oh, I do wish that I understood Italian a little better," Caleb groaned unctuously.

"I say I do notta tink she issa so very damn sweet. I tink she issa—how you say in English—one beech."

No doubt, Caleb profoundly agreed with this characterisation of Letizia, held he up never so plump a protestant hand.

"Oh, do give your consent to our marriage," he gurgled. "I know that there is a difference of religion. But I have ventured to think once or twice that you could overlook that difference. I have remarked sometimes that you did not appear to attach very great importance to your religion. I've even ventured to pray that you might come in time to perceive the errors of Romanism. In fact, I have dreamed more than once, ma'am, that you were washed in the blood of the Lamb. However, do not imagine that I should try to influence Letizia to become one of the Peculiar Children of God. I love her too dearly, ma'am, to attempt any persuasion. From a business point of view—and, after all, in these industrious times it is the business point of view which is really important—from a business point of view the match would not be a very bad one. I have a few humble savings, the fruit of my long association with you in your enterprises."

Caleb paused a moment and took a deep breath. He had reached the critical point in his temptation of Madame Oriano, and he tried to put into his tone the portentousness that his announcement seemed to justify.

"Nor have I been idle in my spare time, ma'am. No, I have devoted much of that spare time to study. I have been rewarded, ma'am. God has been very good to me and blessed the humble talent with which he entrusted me. Yes, ma'am. I have discovered a method of using chlorate of potash in combination with various other chemicals which will undoubtedly revolutionise the whole art of pyrotechny. Will you consider me presumptuous, ma'am, when I tell you that I dream of the moment when Fuller's Fireworks shall become a byword all over Great Britain for all that is best and brightest in the world of pyrotechny?"

Madame Oriano's eyes flashed like Chinese fire, and Caleb, perceiving that he had made a false move, tried to retrieve his position.

"Pray do not suppose that I was planning to set myself up as a manufacturer of fireworks on my own. So long as you will have me, ma'am, I shall continue to work for you, and if you consent to my marrying your Letizia I shall put my new discovery at your service on a business arrangement that will satisfy both parties."

Madame Oriano pondered the proposal in silence for a minute.

"Yes, you can have Letizia," she said at last.

Caleb picked up the hand that was hanging listlessly over the coverlet and in the effusion of his gratitude saluted it with an oily kiss.

"And you'll do your best to make Letizia accept me as a husband?" he pressed.

"If I say you can have Letizia, *caro*, you willa have her," the mother declared.

"You have made me the happiest man in England," Caleb oozed.

Whereupon he walked on tiptoe from the room with a sense even sharper than usual that he was one of the Lord's chosen vessels, a most peculiar child even among the Peculiar Children of God.

Just when the hot August day had hung two dusky sapphire lamps in the window of the room, Madame Oriano, who had been lying all the afternoon staring up at the shadows of the birds that flitted across the ceiling, rang the bell and demanded her daughter's presence.

"*Letizia, devi sposarti,*" she said firmly.

"Get married, mamma? But I don't want to be married for a long time."

"Non ci entra, cara.   Devi sposarti.   Sarebbe meglio— molto meglio.   Sei troppo sfrenata." [1]

"I don't see why it should be so much better.   I'm not so harum-scarum as all that.   Besides, you never married at my age.   You never married at all if it comes to that."

"Lo so.   Perciò dico che tu devi sposarti." [2]

"Thanks, and who am I to marry?"

"Caleb."

"Caleb?   Gemini!   Caleb?   Marry Caleb?   But he's so ugly!   And he don't wash himself too often, what's more."

"Bello non è . . . ma che importa?   La bellezza passa via."

"Yes, I daresay beauty does pass away," said Letizia indignantly.   "But it had passed away from Caleb before ever he was born."

"Che importa?"

"I daresay it don't matter to you.   But you aren't being expected to marry him.   Besides, you've had all the beaux you wanted.   But I haven't, and I won't be fobbed off with Caleb.   I just won't be, and you may do what you will about it."

"Basta!" Madame Oriano exclaimed.   "Dissa talk is enough."

"Basta yourself and be damned, mamma," Letizia retorted.   "I won't marry Caleb.   I'd sooner be kept by a handsome gentleman in a big clean cravat.   I'd sooner live in a pretty house he'd give me and drive a crimson curricle on the Brighton Road like Cora Delaney."

"It does not import two pennies what you wish, *figlia mia.*   You willa marry Caleb."

"But I'm not in love with him, the ugly clown!"

"Love!" scoffed her mother.   *"L'amore!   L'amore!* Love is mad.   I have hadda so many lovers.   *Tanti tanti*

---

[1] "That doesn't come into it, my dear.   You must get married.   It vould be better—much better.   You are too harum-scarum."

[2] "I know that.   That's why I say that you must get married."

amanti! Adesso, sono felice? No! Ma sono vecchia assai. Yes, an old woman—*una vecchia miserabile senza amanti, senza gambe—e non si fa l'amore senza gambe, cara, ti giuro—senza danaro, senza niente."*

Sans love, sans legs, sans money, sans everything, the old woman dropped back on her pillows utterly exhausted. A maid came in with candles and pulled the curtains to shut out the dim grey into which the August twilight had by now gradually faded. When the maid was gone, she turned her glittering, sombre eyes upon her daughter.

"You willa marry Caleb," she repeated. "It willa be better so—*molto meglio cosi. Gli amanti non valgono niente.* All who I have been loving, where are dey now? *Dove sono? Sono andati via.* Alla gone away. Alla gone. You willa marry Caleb."

Letizia burst into loud sobs.

"But I don't want to marry, mamma."

"Meglio piangere a diciasette che rimpiangere a sessanta," [3] said Madame Oriano solemnly. "You willa marry Caleb."

Letizia felt incapable of resisting this ruthless old woman any longer. She buried her head in the gaudy satin coverlet and wept in silence.

"Allora dammi un bacio."

The obedient daughter leaned over and kissed her mother's lined forehead.

"Tu hai già troppo l'aria di putana, figlia mia. Meglio sposarti. Lasciammi sola. Vorrei dormire. Sono stanca assai . . . assai." [4]

Madame Oriano closed her eyes, and Letizia humbly and miserably left her mother, as she wished to be left, alone.

---

[3] "Better to weep at seventeen than to repine at sixty."

[4] "You have already too much the air of a wanton, my daughter. Better to get married. Leave me alone. I want to sleep. I'm very tired."

CHAPTER IV

MARRIED LIFE

So, Caleb Fuller married Letizia Oriano and tamed her body, as without doubt he would have succeeded in taming the body of any woman of whom he had lawfully gained possession.

Madame Oriano did not long survive the marriage. The effort she made in imposing her will upon her daughter was too much for a frame so greatly weakened. Once she had had her way, the desire to live slowly evaporated. Yet she was granted a last pleasure from this world before she forsook it for ever. This was the satisfaction of beholding with her own eyes that her son-in-law's discovery of the value of chlorate of potash as a colour intensifier was all that he claimed for it. That it was likely to prove excessively dangerous when mixed with sulphur compounds did not concern this pyrotechnist of the old school. The prodigious depth and brilliant clarity of those new colours would be well worth the sacrifice of a few lives through spontaneous ignition in the course of manufacturing them.

The first public demonstration that Caleb gave was on the evening of the Fifth of November in a Clerkenwell tea-garden. It is unlikely that Madame Oriano ever fully comprehended the significance of these annual celebrations. If she ever did wonder who Guy Fawkes was, she probably supposed him to be some local English saint whose martyrdom deserved to be commemorated by an abundance of rockets. As for Caleb, he justified to himself some of the pleasure that his fireworks gave to so many people by the fact that the chief festival at which

43

they were employed was held in detestation of a Papist conspirator.

On this particular Fifth of November the legless old lady was carried in an invalid's chair through the press of spectators to a favourable spot from which she could judge the worth of the improved fireworks. A few of the rabble jumped to the conclusion that she was a representation of Guy Fawkes himself, and set up the ancient chorus:

> Please to remember the Fifth of November
> Gunpowder treason and plot;
> We know no reason why gunpowder treason
> Should ever be forgot!
> A stick and a stake for King George's sake,
> A stick and a stump for Guy Fawkes's rump
> Holla, boys! holla, boys! huzza-a-a!

Madame Oriano smiled grimly when Caleb tried to quiet the clamour by explaining that she was flesh and blood.

"Letta dem sing, Caleb. *Non fa niente a me.* It don'ta matter notting to me."

A maroon burst to mark the opening of the performance. This was followed by half-a-dozen rockets, the stars of which glowed with such greens and blues and reds as Madame Oriano had never dreamed of. She tried to raise herself in her chair.

"Bravo, Caleb! *Bravissimo! Ah dio, non posso più!* It is the besta *colore* I havva ever seen, Caleb. *E ottimo! Ottimo, figlio mio.*"

She sat entranced for the rest of the display; that night, like a spent firework, the flame of her ardent life burnt itself out.

The death of his mother-in-law allowed Caleb to carry out a plan he had been contemplating for some time. This was to open a factory in Cheshire on the outskirts of his native town. He anticipated trouble at first with the Peculiar Children of God, who were unlikely to view

with any favour the business of making fireworks. He
hoped, however, that the evidence of his growing prosperity would presently change their point of view. There
was no reason to accuse Caleb of hypocrisy, or to suppose
that he was anything but perfectly sincere in his desire
to occupy a high place in the esteem of his fellow be-
lievers. Marriage with a Papist had in truth begun to
worry his conscience more than a little. So long as Letizia had been a temptation, the fact of her being a daughter of Babylon instead of a Peculiar Child of God had
only made the temptation more redoubtable, and the satisfaction of overcoming it more sharp. Now that he was
licensed to enjoy her, he began to wonder what effect
marriage with a Papist would have on his celestial patron.
He felt like a promising young clerk who has imperilled
his prospects by marrying against his employer's advice.
It began to seem essential to his salvation that he should
take a prominent part in the prayer-meetings of the Peculiar Children of God. He was ambitious to be regarded
himself as the most peculiar child of all those Peculiar
Children. Moreover, from a practical standpoint the
opening of a factory in the North should be extremely
profitable. He already had the London clients of Madame
Oriano; he must now build up a solid business in the
provinces. Fuller's Fireworks must become a byword.
The King was rumoured to be ill. He would be succeeded
by another king. That king would in due course have
to be solemnly crowned. Liverpool, Manchester, Sheffield, Leeds, and many other large towns would be wanting to celebrate that coronation with displays of fireworks. When the moment arrived, there must be nobody
who would be able to compete with Fuller and his chlorate of potash.

So to Brigham in Cheshire Caleb Fuller brought his
wife. In some fields on the outskirts of the town in
which he had spent a poverty-stricken youth he built his
first sheds, and in a dreary little street close to Bethesda,
the meeting-house of the Peculiar Children of God, he

set up his patriarchal tent. Here on a dusty September dawn just over two years after her last public appearance at "Neptune's Grotto," Letizia's eldest daughter was born. The young wife of Caleb was not yet thoroughly tamed, for she produced a daughter exactly like herself and called her Caterina in spite of the father's objection to a name associated with the wheels of which he made so many. Not only did she insist on calling the child Caterina, but she actually took it to the nearest Catholic chapel and had it baptised by a priest.

It happened about this time that one of the apostles of the meeting-house was gravely ill, and Caleb, who had designs on the vacant apostolic chair, decided that his election to it must not be endangered by the profane behaviour of his young wife. When he remonstrated with her, she flashed her eyes and tossed her head as if he were still Caleb the clerk and she the spoilt daughter of his employer.

"Letizia," he said lugubriously, "you have destroyed the soul of our infant."

"Nonsense!"

"You have produced a child of wrath."

"My eye!" she scoffed.

Caleb's moist lips vanished from sight. There was a long silence while he regarded his wife with what seemed like two pebbles of granite. When at last he spoke, it was with an intolerable softness.

"Letizia, you must learn to have responsibilities. I am frightened for you, my wife. You must learn. I do not blame you entirely. You have had a loose upbringing. But you must learn."

Then, as gently as he was speaking, he stole to the door and left Letizia locked behind him in her bedroom. Oh, yes, he tamed her body gradually, and for a long time it looked as if he would tame her soul. She had no more daughters like herself, and each year for many years she flashed her eyes less fiercely and tossed her head less defiantly. She produced several other children, but they all took after their father. Dark-eyed Caterina was followed by stodgy Achsah. Stodgy Achsah was followed by podgy Thyrza. These were followed by two more who died almost as soon as they were born, as if in dying thus they expressed the listlessness of their mother for this life. Maybe Letizia herself would have achieved death, had not the way Caleb treated little Caterina kept her alive to protect the child against his severity.

"Her rebellious spirit must be broken," he declared, raising once more the cane.

"You shall not beat her like this, Caleb."

"Apostle Jenkins beat his son till the child was senseless, because he stole a piece of bread and jam."

"I wish I could be as religious as you, Caleb," said his wife.

He tried to look modest under the compliment.

"Yes," she went on fiercely, "for then I'd believe in Hell, and if I believed in Hell I'd sizzle there with joy just for the pleasure of seeing you and all your cursed apostles sizzling beside me."

But Letizia did not often break out like this. Each year she became more silent, taking refuge from her surroundings in French novels which she bought out of the meagre allowance for clothes that her husband allowed her. She read French novels because she despised the more sentimental novelists of England that were so much in vogue at this date, making only an exception in favour of Thackeray, whom she read word for word as his books appeared. She was learning a bitter wisdom from literature in the shadows and the silence of her wounded heart. After eight years of married life she bore a son, who was called Joshua. There were moments when Letizia was minded to smother him where he lay beside her, so horribly did this homuncule reproduce the lineaments of her loathed husband.

Meanwhile, the factory flourished, Caleb Fuller became the leading citizen of Brigham and served three times as Mayor. He built a great gloomy house on the small hill that skirted the mean little town. He built, too, a great gloomy tabernacle for the Peculiar Children of God. He was elected chief apostle and sat high up in view of the congregation on a marble chair. He grew shaggy whiskers and suffered from piles. He found favour in the eyes of the Lord, sweating the poor and starving even the cows that gave him milk. Yes, the renown of Fuller's Fireworks was spread far and wide. The factory grew larger year by year. And with it year by year waxed plumper the belly and the purse of Caleb himself, even as his soul shrivelled.

In 1851 after twenty years of merciless prosperity Caleb suffered his first setback by failing to secure the contract for the firework displays at the Great Exhibition. From the marble chair of the chief apostle he called upon the Peculiar Children of God to lament that their Father had temporarily turned away His countenance from them. Caleb beat his breast and bellowed and groaned, but he did not rend his garments of the best broadcloth, because that would have involved his buying new ones. The hulla-balloo in Bethesda was louder than that in a synagogue on the Day of Atonement, and after a vociferous prayer-meeting the Peculiar Children of God went back to their stuffy and secretive little houses, coveting their neighbours' wives and their neighbours' maids, but making the best of their own to express an unattainable ideal. Horrid stuffy little bedrooms with blue jets of gas burning dimly through the night-time. Heavy lumps of humanity snoring beneath heavy counterpanes. Lascivious backbiting of the coveted wives and maids on greasy conjugal pillows. Who in all that abode of prurient respectability and savage industrialism should strip Caleb's soul bare? Who should not sympathise with the chief apostle of the Peculiar Children of God?

Yet, strange to say, Caleb found that God's countenance continued to be averted from his own. He was still licking the soreness of his disappointment over the Exhibition fireworks when one morning in the prime of June his eldest daughter left the great gloomy house on the hill, never to return. While Caleb stormed at his wife for not taking better precautions to keep Caterina in bounds, he was aware that he might as well be storming at a marble statue. He lacked the imagination to understand that the soul of Letizia had fled from its imprisonment in the guise of Caterina's lissom body. But he did apprehend, however dimly, that henceforth nothing he might say or do would ever again affect his wife either for good or for ill.

Cold dark eyes beneath black arched brows surveyed him contemptuously. He had never yet actually struck Letizia; but he came near to striking her at that moment.

"She wanted to go on the stage."

"A play-actress! My eldest daughter a play-actress!"

"Alas, neither she nor I can cup those drops of blood she owes to you. But her soul is hers and mine. You had no part in making that. Even if you did crawl over my body and eat the heart out of me, you slug! Do what you like with the others. Make what you can of them. But Caterina is mine. Caterina is free."

"As if I had not suffered enough this year," Caleb groaned.

"Suffered? Did you say that you had suffered?" His wife laughed. "And what about the sufferings of my Caterina all these years of her youth?"

"I pray she'll starve to death," he went on.

"She was starving to death in this house."

"Ay, I suppose that's what the Church folk will be saying next. The idle, good-for-nothing slanderers! Not content with accusing me of starving my cows, they'll be accusing me of starving my children now. But the dear Lord knows . . ."

"You poor dull fool," Letizia broke in, and with one more glance from her cold dark eyes she left him.

Caterina had as dissolute a career as her father could have feared and as miserable an end as he could have hoped, for about twelve years later, after glittering with

conspicuous shamelessness amid the tawdry gilt of the
Second Empire, she died in a Paris asylum prematurely
exhausted by drink and dissipation.

"Better to die from without than from within," said
her mother when the news was brought to Brigham.

"What do you mean by that?" Caleb asked in exas-
perated perplexity. "It's all these French novels you read
that makes you talk that high-flown trash. You talk for
the sake of talking, that's my opinion. You used to talk
like a fool when I first married you, but I taught you at
last to keep your tongue still. Now you've begun to talk
again."

"One changes in thirty-four years, Caleb. Even you
have changed. You were mean and ugly then. But you
are much meaner and much uglier now. However, you
have the consolation of seeing your son Joshua keep pace
with you in meanness and in ugliness."

Joshua Fuller was now twenty-six, an eternal offence
to the eyes of his mother, who perceived in him nothing
but a dreadful reminder of her husband at the same age.
That anybody could dare to deplore Caterina's life when
in Joshua the evidence of her own was before them en-
raged Letizia with human crassness. But Joshua was
going to be an asset to Fuller's Fireworks. Just as his
father had perceived the importance of chlorate of potash
in 1829, so now in 1863 did Joshua perceive the importance of magnesium, and the house of Fuller was in
front of nearly all its rivals in utilising that mineral, with
the result that its brilliant fireworks sold better than
ever. The Guilloché and Salamandre, the Girandole and
Spirali of Madame Oriano, so greatly admired by old
moons and bygone multitudes, would have seemed very
dull affairs now. Another gain that Joshua provided for
the business was to urge upon his father to provide for
the further legislation about explosives that sooner or
later was inevitable. With an ill grace Caleb Fuller had
complied with the provisions of the Gunpowder Act of
1860; but, when the great explosion at Erith occurred a

few years later, Joshua insisted that more must be done to prepare for the inspection of firework establishments that was bound to follow such a terrific disaster. Joshua was right, and when the Explosives Act of 1875 was passed the factory at Brigham had anticipated nearly all its requirements.

By this time Joshua was a widower. In 1865, at the age of twenty-eight, he had married a pleasant young woman called Susan Yardley. After presenting him with one boy who was christened Abraham, she died two years later in producing another who was christened Caleb after his grandfather.

The elder of these two boys reverted both in appearance and in disposition to the Oriano stock, and old Mrs. Fuller—she is sixty-three now and may no longer be called Letizia—took a bitter delight in never allowing old Mr. Fuller to forget it. She found in the boy, now a flash of Caterina's eyes, now a flutter of Madame Oriano's eyelids. She would note how much his laugh was like her own long ago, and she would encourage him at every opportunity to thwart the solicitude and defy the injunctions of Aunt Achsah and Aunt Thyrza. When her son protested against the way she applauded Abraham's naughtiness, she only laughed.

"Bram's all right."

"I wish, mamma, you wouldn't call him Bram," Joshua protested. "It's so irreverent. I know that you despise the Bible, but the rest of us almost worship it. I cannot abide this irreligious clipping of Scriptural names. And it worries poor papa terribly."

"It won't worry your father half as much to hear Bram called Bram as it'll worry poor little Bram later on to be called Abraham. That boy's all right, Josh. He's the best firework you've turned out of this factory for many a day. So, don't let Achsah and Thyrza spoil him."

"They try their best to be strict, mamma."

"I'm talking about their physic, idiot. They're a pair of pasty-faced old maids, and it's unnatural and unpleas-

ant to let them be for ever messing about with a capital
boy like Bram.   Let them physic young Caleb.   He'll be
no loss to the world.   Bram might be."

Joshua threw his eyes up to Heaven and left his unaccountable mother to her own unaccountable thoughts.
He often wondered why his father had never had her
shut up in an asylum.   For some time now she had been
collecting outrageous odds and ends of furniture for her
room to which none of the family was allowed access
except by special invitation.   Ever since Caterina had run
away old Mrs. Fuller had had a room of her own.   But
she had been content with an ordinary bed at first.   Now
she had procured a monstrous foreign affair all gilt and
Cupids and convolutions.   If Joshua had been his father
he would have taken steps to prevent such a waste of
her allowance.   He fancied that the old man must be
breaking up to allow such furniture to enter the house.

Not long after the conversation between Joshua and
his mother about Bram, a travelling circus arrived at
Brigham on a Sunday morning.   The Peculiar Children
of God shivered at such a profanation of the Sabbath,
and Apostle Fuller—in these days a truly patriarchal figure with his long white food-bespattered beard—preached
from the marble chair on the vileness of these sacrilegious
mountebanks and the pestilent influence any circus must
have on a Christian town.   In spite of this denunciation
the chief apostle's own wife dared to take her elder grand-
child on Monday to view from the best seats obtainable
the monstrous performance.   They sat so near the ring
that the sawdust and the tan were scattered over them by
the horses' hoofs.   Little Bram, his chin buried in the
worn crimson velvet of the circular barrier, gloated in an
ecstasy on the paradisiacal vision.

"Brava! Bravissima!" old Mrs. Fuller cried loudly
when a demoiselle of the *haute école* took an extra high
fence.   "Brava! Bravissima!" she cried when an eques-
trienne in pink tights leapt through four blazing hoops

and regained without disarranging one peroxide curl the shimmering back of her piebald steed.

"Oh, grandmamma," little Bram gasped when he bade her good night, "can I be a clown when I'm a man?"

"The difficulty is not to be a clown when one is a man," she answered grimly.

"What *do* you mean, grandmamma?"

"Ah, what?" she sighed.

And in their stuffy and secretive little bedrooms that night the Peculiar Children of God talked for hours about the disgraceful amount of leg that those circus women had shown.

"I hear it was extremely suggestive," said one apostle, smacking his lips with lecherous disapprobation.

"Was it, indeed, my dear?" the dutiful wife replied, thereby offering the man of God an opportunity to enlarge upon the prurient topic before he turned down the gas and got into bed beside her.

"Bram was very naughty to go to the circus, wasn't he, Aunt Achsah?" young Caleb asked in a tone of gentle sorrow when his pasty-faced aunt leaned over that Monday night to lay her wet lips to his plump pink cheeks.

"Grandpapa was very cross," Aunt Achsah mournfully replied, evading the direct answer, but implying much by her expression.

"Gran'papa's not cross with me, is he, auntie?" young Caleb asked with an assumption of fervid anxiety.

"No, my dear child, and I hope that you will never, never make your dear grandfather cross with you."

"Oh, I won't, Aunt Achsah," young Caleb promised, with what Aunt Achsah told Aunt Thyrza was really and truly the smile of one of God's most precious lambs.

"Thyrza, Thyrza, when that blessed little child smiles like that, nobody could deny him anything. I'm sure his path down this vale of tears will always be smoothed by that angelic smile."

She was talking to her sister in the passage just outside young Caleb's bedroom—he had already been separated from his elder brother for fear of corruption—and he heard what she said.

When the footsteps of his aunts died away along the passage, the fat little boy got out of bed, turned up the gas, and smiled at himself several times in the looking-glass. Then he retired to bed again, satisfied of his ability to summon that conquering smile to his aid whenever he should require it.

CHAPTER V

TINTACKS IN BRIGHAM

On a wet and gusty afternoon in the month of March, 1882, Bram Fuller, now a stripling of sixteen, sat in one of the dingiest rooms of that great gloomy house his grandfather had begun to build forty years before. It looked less stark, now that the evergreen trees had grown large enough to hide some of its grey rectangularity; but it did not look any more cheerful in consequence. In some ways it had seemed less ugly at first, when it stood on top of the mean little hill and was swept clean by the Cheshire winds. Now its stucco was stained with great green fronds and arabesques of damp caused by the drip of the trees and the too close shrubberies of lanky privet and laurel that sheltered its base. Old Mr. Fuller and his son were both under the mistaken impression that the trees planted round Lebanon House—thus had the house been named—were cedars. Whereas there was not even so much as a deodar among the crowd of starveling pines and swollen cryptomerias. Noah's original ark perched on the summit of Ararat amid the surrounding waters probably looked a holier abode than Lebanon House above the sea of Brigham roofs.

The town had grown considerably during half a century, and old Mr. Fuller had long ago leased the derelict pastures, in which his cows had tried to eke out a wretched sustenance on chickweed and sour dock, to accommodate the enterprising builder of rows of little two-storied houses, the colour of underdone steak. The slopes of the hill on which the house stood had once been covered with fruit-trees, but the poisoning of the air by the various chemical factories, which had increased in number every year, had long made them barren. Joshua had strongly advised his father to present the useless slopes to Brigham as a public recreation ground. It was to have been a good advertisement both for the fireworks and for the civic spirit that was being fostered by the Peculiar Children of God. As a matter of fact, Joshua himself had some time ago made up his mind to join the Church of England as soon as his father died. He was beginning to think that the Bethesda Tabernacle was not sufficiently up-to-date as a spiritual centre for Fuller's Fireworks, and he was more concerned for the civic impression than the religious importance of the gift. On this March afternoon, however, the slopes of Lebanon were still a private domain, for old Mr. Fuller could never bring himself to give away nine or ten acres of land for nothing. He was much too old to represent Brigham in Parliament himself, and it never struck him that Joshua might like to do so.

So, Bram Fuller was able to gaze out of the school-room window, to where, beyond the drenched evergreens hustling one another in the wind, the drive ran down into Brigham between moribund or skeleton apple-trees fenced in on either side by those raspberry-tipped iron railings that his grandfather had bought so cheaply when the chock-a-block parish churchyard was abolished and an invitingly empty cemetery was set apart on the other side of the town for the coming generations of Brigham dead. Bram was still a day-boy at the grammar school, and as this afternoon was the first half-holiday of the month he was being allowed to have a friend to tea. Jack Fleming was late, though. There was no sign of him yet coming up the slope through the wind and wet. Bram hoped that nothing had happened to keep him at home. He was so seldom allowed to entertain friends that Jack's failure to appear would have been an overwhelming disappointment. He looked round the schoolroom dejectedly. Never had it seemed so dingy and comfortless. Never had that outline portrait of Queen Victoria, filled in not with the substance of her regal form, but with an account of her life printed in minute type, seemed such a futile piece of ingenuity; never had the oilcloth seemed infested with so many crumbs, nor the table-cloth such a kaleidoscope of jammy stains.

Old Mrs. Fuller had been right when she recognised in the baby Bram her own race. She and he had their way, and Abraham was never heard now except in the mouth of the grandfather. Yes, he was almost a perfect Oriano, having inherited nothing from his father, and from his mother only her pleasant voice. He was slim, with a clear-cut profile and fine dark hair; had one observed him idling gracefully on a sunsplashed *piazza,* he would have appeared more appropriate to the setting than to any setting that Brigham could provide. He was a popular and attractive youth with a talent for mimicry, and a gay and fluent wit. His young brother, who fortunately for the enjoyment of Bram and his friend had been invited forth himself this afternoon, was a perfect Fuller save that he had inherited from his mother a fresh complexion which at present only accentuated his plumpness. All the Fuller characteristics were there—the greedy grey eyes, the podgy white hands, the fat rump and spindle legs, the full wet lips and slimy manner. To all this young Caleb could add his own smile of innocent candour when it suited his purpose to produce it. At school he was notorious as a toady and a sneak, but he earned a tribute of respect from the sons of a commercial community by his capacity for swopping to his own advantage and by his never failing stock of small change, which he was always willing to lend at exorbitant interest on good security. Bram was badly in debt to his young brother at the present moment, and this added something to the depression of the black March afternoon, though that was lightened at last by the tardy arrival of his expected friend with the news that Blundell's Diorama had arrived in Brigham and would exhibit itself at seven o'clock.

"We must jolly well go, Bramble," Jack declared.

Bram shook his head despondently.

"No chink!"

"Can't you borrow some from young Caleb?"

"I owe him two and threepence halfpenny already, and he's got my best whalebone-splice bat as a security till I pay him back."

"Good Lord, and I've only got sixpence," Jack Fleming groaned.

"Anyway, it's no use," Bram went on. "The governor wouldn't let me go into Brigham on a Saturday night."

"Can't you find some excuse?"

Bram pondered for a few seconds.

"I might get my grandmater to help."

"Well, buck up, Bramble. It's a spiffing show, I hear. They've got two girls with Italian names who play the guitar or something. We don't often get a chance of a decent evening in Brigham."

"You're right, Jack. All serene! Then I'll have a try with the grandmater. She's such an old fizzer that she might manage it."

Bram went up cautiously to old Mrs. Fuller's room. She was seventy now, but still able to hate fiercely her octogenarian husband who was for ever browsing among dusty commentaries on the Old Testament nowadays, and extracting from the tortuous fretwork of bookworms such indications of the Divine purpose as the exact date and hour of the Day of Judgment. He was usually clad in a moth-eaten velveteen dressing-gown and a smoking cap of quilted black silk with a draggled crimson tassel. The latter must have been worn as a protection to his bald and scaly head, because not a puff of tobacco smoke had ever been allowed to contend with the odour of stale food that permeated Lebanon House from cellar to garret.

The old lady was sitting by the fire in her rococo parlour, reading Alphonse Daudet's new book. Her hawk's face seemed to be not so much wrinkled as finely cracked like old ivory. Over her shoulders she wore a wrap of rose and silver brocade.

"Why, Bram, I thought you were entertaining visitors this afternoon."

"I am. He's downstairs in the schoolroom. Jack Fleming, I mean."

"Is that a son of that foxy-faced solicitor in High Street?"

Bram nodded.

"But Jack's rather decent. I think you'd like him, grandmamma."

"Ah, I'm too old to begin liking new people."

Bram kicked his legs together, trying to make up his mind what line to adopt for enlisting the old lady's sympathy.

"Blundell's Diorama is here," he announced at last.

"What's that? A new disease?"

The boy laughed.

"It does sound rather like a disease, doesn't it? No, it's the same sort of thing as Poole's Myriorama."

"I'm no wiser."

"Well, it's a set of large coloured pictures of places in foreign parts. And there are some singers with guitars. Italian perhaps." Ah, cunning Bram!

"Italian, eh? And you want to gaze into their liquid and passionate orbs, eh?"

"I would rather like to—only as a matter of fact I haven't got any chink. Caleb lent me some, but he won't lend me any more till I pay him back. I've had to give him my best bat till I do."

"How much do you owe the little alligator?"

"Two and threepence halfpenny, and sixpence interest up to date, and twopence for the linseed oil for oiling the bat, because he said he'd have to keep it in good condition during the winter. Two and elevenpence halfpenny altogether."

Mrs. Fuller grunted.

"And anyway papa won't let me go down into Brigham unless I can get a good excuse."

"And so you want an excuse from me? *Ho capito.*
Well, Bram, it's a strange thing, but my rheumatism has
suddenly become very bad and I'd be much obliged if
you'd go down into Brigham and buy me a bottle of embrocation. Here's five shillings. I don't want the change.
St. Jumbo's Oil is the name of the embrocation. It'll
probably take you all the evening to find it, and if you
don't find it I shan't really mind, because my rheumatism
is bound to be much better by the time you come back."

"I say, grandmamma, you are . . . you are . . ."

But Bram could not find any word to describe her
suitably without blushing too deeply to attempt it.

Blundell's Diorama which filled the Brigham Corn Exchange (not much corn was sold there by this date) was
an entertainment at which the least sophisticated would
scoff in these cinematographic days. It consisted of a
series of crude and highly coloured views of the world's
beauty spots treated in the panoramic manner of the drop-
curtain. The lighting was achieved by gas footlights
and floats with occasional assistance from amber, green,
and crimson limes. Mr. Blundell himself, a gentleman
with a moustache like an Aintree hurdle, and dressed in
a costume that was something between a toreador's, a
cowboy's, and an operatic brigand's, stood in front to
point out with a stock-rider's whip the chief objects of
interest in each picture that was unrolled for an absorbed
audience.

"This scene to which I now have the pleasure of inviting your earnest attention represents the world-famous
Bay of Naples. 'Veedy Napowly ee poy morry,' as Dante
said. Dante, I may remind you was the Italian equivalent
of our own William Shakespeare, the world-famous dramatic genius at whose house in Stratford-on-Avon we
have already taken a little peep this evening. Yes, 'See
Naples and die,' said the Italian poet. In other words,
'Don't waste your time over sprats when there's whales
to be caught.' The world-famous fir-tree, on the extreme
right of the picture as I stand, is reputed to be two thou-

sand years old, and under its hoary branches it is said that the Emperor Nero held many of his most degraded orgies, which I shall not sully your eyes by exhibiting at an entertainment to which I flatter myself the youngest infant in Brigham can come without a blush. The waters of the Bay of Naples as you will note are always blue, and the inhabitants of the gay city are renowned for macaroni and musical abilities. With your kind permission the Sisters Garibaldi will now give you a slight impression of the atmosphere of Beller Napowly as it is affectionately called."

Two young women dressed in ribbons and sequins immediately pranced on to sing *Santa Lucia,* while the lecturer beat time with his stockwhip, rolling occasionally a sentimental eye at the audience. When the music was over, he invited their attention to various architectural features in the landscape, and then, assuming a tragic profundity of tone, he continued:

"Hitherto all has been fair, but the words 'See Naples and die' have sometimes been fraught with a much deeper significance. On the extreme left as I stand you will observe towering above the unconscious city the mighty peak of Vesuvius, the world-famous volcano which from time to time commits the most horrible eruptions and threatens to overwhelm with boiling lava the gay city at its base. With your kind permission I shall now have the pleasure of giving you a realistic representation of the city of pleasure when threatened by one of the burning mountain's all too frequent outbursts."

He signalled with his whip to the limelight man at the back of the hall. Whereupon after a loud preliminary fizzing a crimson glow suffused the whole picture, while the orchestra, consisting of a piano, a flageolet, and a double-bass, played the "Dead March" from *Saul.*

"Our next picture shows you the world-famous Alhambra of Granada by moonlight. . . ."

No tragedy here, but a transparency moon and a *pas de deux* by the Sisters Garibaldi accompanied by castanets, which on the authority of Mr. Blundell was a lifelike rendering of the world-famous Spanish fandango. . . .

When the performance was over, Bram emerged from his circumgyration of the illustrated world feeling that something must be done about Brigham. After the sequins and ribbons and cobalt seas, after bullfights and earthquakes, juggernauts, pagodas, and palms, Brigham in the wind and wet of a Saturday night in March was not to be endured without some kind of protest. To go meekly back to Lebanon House and a long jobation from his father on the sin of attending a public performance in which female dancers actively participated was unimaginable in this elated mood. If there had to be a row, why couldn't there be a row over something that really deserved it?

"My gosh, Jack, I'm just itching to do something," he confided to his chum. "Don't you wish we had wings and could fly right away to the other end of the world now?"

"What's the use of wishing for wings?" objected young Fleming, who had enjoyed the entertainment, but was not prepared to be mentally extravagant in its honour.

"Well, of course I don't mean real wings," Bram explained. "Only, I simply can't stick Brigham much longer. I couldn't stick it even if I left school."

They were passing Bethesda as Bram was speaking, and the sight of its hideousness looming up in the empty wet gaslit street revolted the boy.

"I wish I could burn that down," he exclaimed savagely.

"Well, you can't do that either," said his friend. "So what's the good of wishing?"

"I say, Jack, there's a window open! I believe I could climb in," declared Bram in sudden excitement.

Jack Fleming was not one of the Peculiar Children of God, nor had he any clear notion how severe a penalty was entailed by sacrilege; but the idea of climbing into any place of worship by night—church, chapel, or meeting-house—filled him with superstitious dread, besides alarming him in its legal aspect.

"Don't be a mad ass," he adjured his friend. "What would you do if you did climb in?"

"Oh, I don't know. Just mess it up," said Bram.

"But supposing you were caught?"

"Well, it would be worth a row. You don't know my governor, Jack. If you knew him, you'd do anything that was worth while getting pi-jaws for. I get pi-jaws now for nothing. If you funk it, don't stay with me. But I'm going to climb into that rotten old tabernacle, and if I can burn it up, I jolly well will burn it up."

Jack Fleming was seized with panic. Bram was always a mad sort of chap, but this project was far madder than anything of which he had fancied him capable.

"Look here, I've got to be in soon," he protested. "And you've farther to go than I have. Don't play the giddy goat."

But Bram's mind was dancing with the brightness of Blundell's Diorama. He had no patience with the dull brain of his friend.

"I tell you I'm going to climb in," he insisted.

"Well, I tell you I'm going home," said Jack.

"All right then, go!" Bram could not forbear shooting a poisoned shaft. "Only if there's a row, don't peach, that's all I ask."

"You needn't sneer at a fellow just because he doesn't happen to be quite such a giddy goat as yourself," said Jack.

But Bram was riding over the deserts of Arabia: he was away on the prairies farther than Fenimore Cooper or Mayne Reid had ever taken him; Chimborazo towered above his horizon, not the chimney-pots of Brigham.

"See you on Monday as usual," he called back cheerfully to his friend as he leapt up and caught hold of the sill. A moment later his lithe shape had vanished in the darkness of Bethesda. Jack Fleming hesitated a moment: but after all he was not one of the Peculiar Children of God, and if it became a case for the magistrates, they might take a more serious view of his behaviour as the son of a church-going solicitor than of Bram's, who was the grandson of a chief apostle. Jack turned his face homeward.

Meanwhile, inside the tabernacle Bram was wondering what he should do with the beastly place. He struck a match, but the shadows it conjured all over the great gaunt building made him nervous, and he soon abandoned the project of burning the whole place to the ground. He thought and thought how to celebrate his adventure at the expense of the worshippers when they gathered together to-morrow morning to groan loudly over their own sins and louder still over the sins of other people. He could think of nothing. Inspiration was utterly lacking. Had he known beforehand that he was going to break into Bethesda like this, what a multitude of tricks he would have been ready to play. As it was, he would just have to climb out again and be content with the barren triumph of having climbed in. He had struck another match to light his path out among the benches without barking his shins as he had barked them feeling his way in from the window, and it illuminated a cardboard packet of tintacks evidently left there by the caretaker, who must have been renovating something or other in honour of the approaching Sabbath. Bram did not hesitate, but forthwith arranged four tintacks on each of the pitch-pine chairs of the eleven apostles and actually half-a-dozen, and these carefully chosen for their length and sharpness, on the marble chair of the chief apostle himself. For once in a way he should look forward to Sunday morning; for the first time in his life he should be able to encounter with relish the smell of veils and varnish in Bethesda. Of course, it would be too much to hope that all the fifty tintacks would strike home, but the chances were good for a generous proportion of successes, because it was the custom of the twelve apostles to march in from the apostolic snuggery and simultaneously take their seats with the precision of the parade-ground.

While Bram was having to stand up and listen to a

long pi-jaw that night on his return, he nearly laughed aloud in thinking that to-morrow morning in Bethesda his father who occupied at present the chair of James the Less would wish that he was standing too. Before going to bed Bram went to wish good night to his grandmother and thank her for the way she had helped him.

"I wish I could travel round the world, grandmamma."

"Ah, child, be glad that you can still have wishes. It's when all your wishes turn to regrets that you can begin sobbing. Here am I, with only one wish left."

"What's that?"

"The grave," said the old lady.

Bram was startled when his grandmother said this with such simple earnestness. Death presented itself to his young mind as something so fantastically remote that thus to speak of it as within the scope of a practical wish seemed to demand some kind of distraction to cure such excitability.

"You never go to Bethesda, do you, grandmamma?" She laughed and shook her head.

"I wish you'd come to-morrow morning."

"What, at seventy become a Peculiar Child of God? No, Bram, I may be in my second childhood, but it's not going to be a peculiar second childhood."

"All the same, I wish you would come. I think you'll laugh."

Bram's dark eyes were twinkling so brightly in anticipation of the scene to-morrow morning that his grandmother's curiosity was roused. However, he would not tell her why he advised her to sample the meeting-house for the first time in her life to-morrow. He still retained enough of the child's suspicion of the grown-up's theory of what is and what is not a good joke to make him cautious even with her, though he was extremely anxious to give the old lady the benefit of the diversion he had prepared. He was so urgent indeed that in the end she actually promised to come if she felt able to stand the prospect in the morning.

Before going to bed Bram went into his brother's room and paid him back the loan with interest.

"And I'll have my bat to-night, thank you very much," he said.

Caleb did not play cricket himself, but he was much disgusted at losing the bat, because he had planned to sell it for at least five shillings at the beginning of the summer term.

"Look here, I'll give you three shillings for it, if you don't want to pay me back the money, Bram."

"No, thanks."

Caleb tried his last resource. Sleep was heavy on his eyelids, yet he managed to suffuse his pink podgy countenance with that bland, persuasive smile.

"It isn't really worth more than two shillings, Bram, but as you're my brother I don't mind giving you three for it."

Bram had one tintack left in his pocket. This he dug into Caleb's fat leg.

"Ouch! You cad," Caleb squealed. "You cad! You cad! What is it?"

"A tintack," said Bram coolly. "Want it in again? No? All serene. Then hand over the bat."

He retired with his rescued treasure to his own room, and for five minutes in the joy of repossession he practised playing forward and back to the most devilishly tricky bowling until at last he caught the leg of the bedstead a whack which clanged through the nocturnal quiet of Lebanon House like an alarm bell. Whereupon Bram hurriedly put out the gas and jumped into bed. People were right when they said he was very young for his age and wondered how Joshua Fuller ever produced such a flipperty-gibbet of a son.

The next morning was fine, and old Mrs. Fuller's announcement that she was going to visit Bethesda threw the household into consternation.

"Mamma!" the eldest daughter gasped. "Why, you've never . . ."

Mrs. Fuller quelled poor Achsah instantly.

"Thank you, my dear, I am not yet in my dotage. I know precisely what I have done and what I have not done in my life."

"You don't think you'll catch cold?" suggested Thyrza.

"Not if your father preaches about Hell," said the old lady.

"If you're coming to mock, mamma," her son interposed, "I can't help feeling it would be better if you stopped away."

"Hoity-toity, Master Joshua," the old lady chuckled.

What the chief apostle thought about his wife's intention did not transpire, for he was so deaf nowadays that his family considered it wiser not to apprise him of the sensational news. He would probably never understand what they were trying to tell him, but if he should, the nervous shock might easily render him as mute as he was deaf, to the detriment of his weekly discourse, which was the delight of the older Peculiars, flavoured as it was with the brimstone and sulphur of the sect's early days. The chief apostle, no doubt partly on account of his pyrotechnical knowledge, could conjure hellish visions against any preacher in the land.

There was some discussion about who should drive to chapel in the Fuller brougham, a dreadful old conveyance looking like a large bootblack's box, which had been picked up cheap at the sale of a deceased widow's effects. Either Achsah or Thyrza usually accompanied their father. There was no room for a third person when Mr. Fuller and his beard were inside.

"Don't disturb yourselves," said Mrs. Fuller. "I've sent the boy to fetch a fly from the hotel. Bram can be my beau."

When she and her grandson were driving off together, she turned to him and said:

"Now what is the reason for having dragged me out in this musty fly on a Sunday morning?"

Her regard was so humorous and candid that the boy

surrendered his suspicion and confided to her what he had prepared for the apostles.

"I'll give you sixpence for every tintack that goes hard home," the old lady vowed. "I'd give you a sovereign apiece, if I had the money."

The congregation of Bethesda seemed to be composed of candle-faced men and fiery-nosed women. The atmosphere literally did stink of respectability, for even scented soap was considered a diabolic weapon. However, in spite of the discouragement that the male Peculiars accorded to the vanity of female dress, the female Peculiars were as well equipped with panniers and bustles as the fashionable females of other sects. In view of what was waiting for them, it was unfortunate for the men that they too did not wear bustles. Bram cast an eye on the apostles' chairs and whispered to his grandmother that the tintacks were undisturbed. She emitted a low chuckle of approbation such as that with which a parrot welcomes some special effort of ventriloquism by a human being.

The door of the apostolic snuggery opened. Shambling along with an exaggeration of the way he used to shamble as a young man, followed by a trail of dismal men, most of whom had mutton-chop whiskers, came Caleb Fuller making for the chair of Simon Peter—oblivious presumably of the Popish claims thereby implied. The sons of Zebedee were represented by two grocers in partnership —Messrs. Giddy and Dopping. Andrew suitably had an expatriated Scotsman in the person of Maclozen the chemist. Philip, Bartholomew, Matthew, and Thomas were earthily represented by Mr. Hunnybum, Mr. Rabjohn, Mr. Campkin, and Mr. Balmey. The seat of James the Less was Joshua Fuller's. Simon and Jude found their types of apostolic virtue in Mr. Pavitt and Mr. Pead, and finally Mr. Fricker, a sandy-haired young man who walked the shop of Mr. Rapjohn the draper, followed humbly in the rear as the coopted Matthias, hoping no doubt one day to lead the lot as patriarchally as Mr. Fuller was leading them this morning.

"Brethren," the chief apostle groaned. "I am four score years and two in the sight of the Lord, and my sins are as scarlet."

"Made with chlorate of potash," muttered Mrs. Fuller, "so bright a scarlet are they."

"Brethren, groan with me."

The Peculiar Children of God groaned lustily.

"Brethren, we will now be seated until one of us shall be moved by the Spirit of the Lord to testify."

The congregation rustled down into their seats. The apostles sat down firmly and austerely as became leaders of religion. The congregation remained seated. The apostles rose with a unanimous howl, moved not by the Spirit, but by the fifty tintacks, every one of which, by old Mrs. Fuller's reckoning when she paid over twenty-five shillings to Bram, must have struck hard home.

Of course, there was an investigation into the lamentable affair by the apostolic body of the Peculiar Children of God. The caretaker was invited to explain the presence of all these tintacks on the apostolic chairs. It was idle for the caretaker to deny all knowledge of tintacks, because in the chapel accounts there was an item against her, proving that she had only this week purchased for use in Bethesda a large packet of tintacks. This purchase of tintacks she made no attempt to deny, but she maintained, without her evidence being in the least shaken, that when she last saw the tintacks the bulk of them remained in the cardboard box from which she had taken only two or three to nail down the strips of carpet on the benches where they had come loose. It seemed equally idle for the apostles to accuse such a ramshackle old woman of having deliberately arranged the tintacks as weapons of offence, nor could it seriously be argued that mere carelessless was responsible for leaving them about point upward in groups of four. Some of the older apostles were inclined to blame the Devil for the assault;

but the younger members of the apostolic body, reacting to the spirit of intellectual progress that was abroad, could not accept the theory of so literally diabolic a practical joke. Mr. Fricker, the junior apostle, put forward an opinion that the outrage had been committed by members of the Salvation Army, a body which was making considerable and most unwelcome progress in Brigham. The result of the investigation, however, was to leave the horrid business wrapt in mystery, in which costume it would doubtless have remained for ever if that afternoon young Caleb Fuller had not said to his father with a smile of radiant innocence:

"Papa, how funny it should have been tintacks on your chair."

"What do you mean by 'funny,' my boy?" demanded Joshua angrily. "What are you grinning at?"

"I didn't mean to grin, papa," said Caleb, turning out his smile as swiftly as if it were a flaring gas-jet. "What I meant was 'funny' was that last night Bram had a tintack in his pocket, because he ran it into my leg."

"Bram had a tintack?" repeated the father.

"Yes, and he was out late last night, and Mrs. Pead was saying outside Bethesda that she'd noticed one of the windows in the chapel was left open all last night."

Joshua Fuller's pasty face pulsed and sweated like a boiling beefsteak pudding.

"Where's Bram now?"

"He's upstairs in grandmamma's room, and they were laughing, papa. I thought it funny they should be laughing like that on a Sunday afternoon."

"You thought it funny, did you?" Joshua growled. "If you don't look out for yourself, my boy, I'll thrash you soundly when I've finished with your brother."

"What have I done, papa?" Caleb began to blubber. "I thought you wanted to find out who put the tintacks on the apostles' chairs."

But his father did not stop to listen. His only idea was to punish Bram. The threat to Caleb was really nothing more than the effervescence of his rage. In the hall he picked out from the umbrella-stand a blackthorn stick, armed with which he entered his mother's parlour, where he found her feeding Bram with crumpets.

"So it was you, was it?" he chattered. "Go up to your bedroom and wait for me."

"What are you going to do to the boy?" old Mrs. Fuller demanded.

"What am I going to do to him? I'm going to teach him a lesson with this." He banged the floor with the blackthorn.

"You'll never use that on him, Joshua," said his mother.

"Won't I?"

"Never! Bram, don't let your father touch you with that stick. If he strikes you, strike him. You're as good a man as he is in a fight. Strike him hard, hard, d'ye hear?"

"Are you mad, mamma, to encourage the young ruffian in this way?"

"He'll be mad if he lets you strike him."

While the other two were talking, a very white Bram was settling his future as rapidly as a drowning man is supposed to review his past. Fifty tintacks at sixpence apiece? Twenty-five shillings in his pocket. The only time he had ever been rich in the whole of his life! This would mean leaving the grammar school. He would have to work in the factory. "The bottom of the ladder, my boy; that's the way to begin." No pocket money. Sticking at accounts, Brigham, eternally, hopelessly. Always Brigham. And Lebanon House. And the flogging. The pain wouldn't matter. But the disgrace of it at his age! And begging grandpapa's pardon. Shouting his apologies in those hairy ears. Coming always a little closer and trying to make himself understood, closer still. So close that he would be sick with the smell of stale food on that filthy old white beard. Apologising to the rest of them. To Giddy and Dopping and Hunnybum and Pead.

Apologising to that horrible brute Fricker? No! Prayed for publicly by the Peculiars as last Sunday they prayed for that girl who had a baby? No!

"How did you find out, papa?" Bram heard himself saying from an infinitely remote distance. He was shivering lest he should hear that Jack Fleming had betrayed him.

"Because, thank the dear Lord, I have one son who knows his duty as a Christian," his father was saying.

Of course! Caleb had had a taste of tintack last night. No! No! No! He could not give that little sneak the pleasure of gloating over his punishment. No! The pictures of Blundell's Diorama rolled across his memory. Cobalt seas and marble halls, pagodas, palms . . . twenty-five shillings in his pocket and the world before him if he could only make up his mind.

"Did you hear me tell you to go up to your bedroom, my boy?"

"Grandmamma, grandmamma, let me kiss you good-bye," Bram cried by the door.

The old lady drew near.

"Grandmamma," he whispered as she folded him to her withered breast, "I'm going to run away. Can you keep him in?"

Bram heard the key turn in the lock and a loud chuckle beyond the closed door. Then he heard the sound of his father's voice raised in anger. Bram paused. Surely he would not strike grandmamma. He listened a moment at the keyhole, smiled at what he heard his father being called, and, blowing back a kiss to reach through the closed door the old lady's heart, hurried up to his room. But not to wait there for his father to come with the blackthorn. No, just to throw a few clothes into an old carpet-bag and a minute or two later to go swinging out of Lebanon House for ever. On his way down the drive he remembered that he had not licked Caleb for peaching. It was a pity to let the little brute escape like that. He hesitated, decided that it was no' worth while to run the risk of being caught merely in order to lick Caleb, and swung on down the drive. He had no plans, but he had twenty-five shillings in his pocket, and there was a train to Liverpool in half-an-hour. As a dissipation he had sometimes watched its departure on the Sunday afternoons when he managed to escape from Lebanon House and Bible readings, which was not often. Of course, there would be plenty of people to tell his father where he had gone. But Liverpool was a larger place than Brigham, and, if he could not get taken on by the captain of an outward-bounder, he would be a stowaway. Something would turn up. Bram hurried on. It was a good mile from Lebanon House to the railway station. The booking-clerk stared through his pigeon-hole when Bram asked for a single to Liverpool. The idlers on the platform stared when they saw Bram Fuller, the grandson of the great Caleb, shoulder his carpet-bag and enter the Liverpool train. But Bram himself stared hardest of all when he found himself in a compartment with Mr. Blundell of Blundell's Diorama and the Sisters Garibaldi.

CHAPTER VI

THE DIORAMA

Mr. Blundell did not believe in allowing the public to suffer in ignorance of who he was. This was not merely due to a desire to advertise himself and his goods. He was genuinely anxious to give the public a treat, and his progress from town to town was a kind of unlimited extension of the free-list. There he sat opposite Bram as if the wooden seat of the third-class compartment were a Mexican saddle, the train a bronco. On the other hand, the Sisters Garibaldi had lost most of their exotic charm now that they were dressed like other women in panniers and bustles instead of the ribbons and sequins of Southern romance. What was left of it vanished for Bram when he heard one of them say to the other in an unmistakably cockney accent:

"Did that masher in front send you the chocolates he promised, dear?"

"No, he didn't, the wretch."

"I told you he'd have to pawn his trousers before you ever saw those chocolates, didn't I, dear?"

"I wouldn't like to say what you've told me and what you haven't told me, dear. You wag your tongue a good deal faster than what a dog wags its tail."

Mr. Blundell doffed his sombrero and revealed a head of hair that was ridiculously out of keeping with that haystack of a moustache, for it looked as if somebody had unwound the shining black twine from the handle of a cricket bat and tried to wind it again with less than half the quantity.

"Now, girlies," he remonstrated in a fruity voice, "don't make things uncomfortable all around by arguing.

Us men don't like to see little birdies pecking at one another. That's right, isn't it?"

This appeal was addressed to Bram, who smiled as politely as he knew how and received in exchange a wink from Mr. Blundell so tremendous as almost to give the impression that he had pulled down the curtain of the compartment window and let it go up again with a snap.

"Going far?" he continued genially.

"Liverpool."

"By thunder, so are we. The long arm again! You can't get away from it in this world. My name's Blundell."

This information was vouchsafed with an elaborate nonchalance.

"Unwin U. Blundell," he added.

"I was enjoying the Diorama last night," Bram said. "It was simply splendid."

"Ah, you were in front? Dainty little show, isn't it? Instructive, yet at the same time trees amusong as the Froggies say. Bright, but never coarse. Rich, but never ostentatious. Funny thing, I suppose I've knocked about the world more than most of us have, and yet I've always set my face against anything the teeniest tottiest little bit coarse. Did you notice I said my name was Unwin U. Blundell? Got me, as our cousins the Americanos say? The initials by themselves would be coarse, and my entertainment is refined from start to finish."

One of the Sisters Garibaldi giggled.

"Now, Clara," he said severely. "By the way, permit me, Miss Clara Garibaldi, Miss Mona Garibaldi, Mr. . . ."

"Bram Fuller."

"No relation to Fuller's Fireworks, I suppose?"

Bram explained that he was.

"By Jenkins, the long arm again! Why, only last week at Burton-on-Trent I used a packet of Fuller's squibs for the eruption of Mount Vesuvius. But I had to give it up. Yes, I found it frightened the women and children too much. They were so shook by the effect that when the moon rose behind the Alhambra they thought *that* was going off with a bang and started screaming again, so the fandango went rotten."

"It certainly did," the Sisters Gairbaldi agreed in a huffy chorus.

"Coming back to my name," said Mr. Blundell. "What do you think my second name is? I'll give you a sovereign if you can guess it in three. That offer's on tap to any stranger with who I have the pleasure of a heart to heart. Give it up? I thought you would. Ursula!"

"But that's a girl's name, isn't it?" Bram said in astonishment.

"Of course it is. But my dear old mother got it into her head that it was a boy's name. The parson argued with her. The sexton argued. The godfathers and godmothers argued. The only one that didn't argue was my poor old dad, who knew better. So, Ursula I was christened, by thunder. Unwin Ursula Blundell."

The confidential manner of the showman invited confidence in return, and before the train had puffed out of more than two of the stations between Brigham and Liverpool he was in possession of Bram's history.

"So you're thinking of going to sea? It's a hard life, my young friend. Can't you think of a better way of earning a living than rolling down to Rio? What about the boards?"

Bram looked puzzled.

"The stage. The profession. Tragedy! Drama! Comedy! Farce!"

"Well, I'd like to be an actor," said Bram eagerly. "But could I act? My grandmater said I was a jolly good mimic."

"There you are! What more do you want?"

"But aren't I rather young?" Bram asked, in a sudden panic that he was making a fool of himself. "I mean, who would give me anything to act?"

"That's where Unwin U. Blundell enters, my young

friend. Let's figure out your case. You want to keep
out of the way of your father. You don't want to be
hauled back to Brigham and set to work in an office. Am
I right?"

Bram nodded.

"So far, so good. Now we're up against the long arm
again. *I* want a young cannibal chief as an extra attraction for the Diorama. Why shouldn't you take on the
job? It'll mean staining yourself brown and talking some
kind of gibberish when I give the cue. I'll stand you in
board and lodging and pay you five shillings a week for
yourself. What's more, I'll teach you how to look like a
cannibal chief, and how to act like a cannibal chief. I'd
want a short war dance every night. The girls will fake
up something tasty there. Then before the show begins
you could shake hands with the audience at twopence a
head. Mind you don't forget to shiver all the time.
That'll make the women take an interest in you. But
you mustn't forget you're a cannibal. If anybody with
a bit of ombongpong comes in to take a peep at you, you'll
want to gloat some. You know what I mean? Look as
if you was thinking which was the best slice. That'll go
great. I *was* thinking of touring a big baboon, but a
cannibal chief's worth two baboons. Nothing derogatory,
if you follow my meaning. We'll make you a prince, so
as you'll be treated with respect. Prince Boo Boo. You
want to give 'em a nice easy name so as they can talk
about it to their friends without thinking that some Mr.
Knowall in the corner's going to jump up and correct
them all the time. Nobody could go wrong over a name
like Boo Boo. An infant in arms could say it. Prince
Boo Boo, the world-famous cannibal chief from the savage Solomon Islands. The youngest son of the world-
famous King Noo Noo who boasts of having eaten
twenty-three missionaries, nine traders, and fourteen ship-
wrecked mariners since he ascended the throne. Prince
Boo Boo himself was taken as a hostage for the lives of
three French sailors who had been captured by his father.

Unfortunately the king's appetite was so ferocious and
the sailors were so fat that without thinking about his
youngest son he went and ate the lot. Prince Boo Boo
was carried off to Europe where Unwin U. Blundell,
always on the quee vyve for novelties that will attract his
many patrons all over the civilised world, secured his ex-
clusive services. Come on, say the word, and we'll get the
bills printed and the costume made in Liverpool, and on
Monday week we'll show 'em what's what when we open
in St. Helens."

The runaway did not hesitate. Mr. Blundell's offer
solved the problem of his immediate future far more
swiftly and far more easily than he would ever have dared
to hope.

Bram was a great success as a young cannibal chief.
His natural shivers during the excesses of an English
summer filled the hearts of all the women with the warm-
est sympathy, and a moment later the way he gloated over
imagined titbits of their anatomy made them shiver as
realistically as himself.

"It's going great, laddie," Unwin U. Blundell declared.
"To rights, it's going. Props at the Royalty, Blackburn,
who's an old pal of mine, is making me a two-pronged
wooden fork, which was used by your dad, King Noo
Noo. With a bit of bullock's blood we'll have the ladies
of Bolton in a state of blue horrors next week. And if
one of 'em faints, laddie, there's a shilling onto your
salary when the ghost walks next Friday night."

The Sisters Garibaldi were inclined to be jealous of
Bram at first, but their feelings were appeased by being
given a special new dance in which they were dressed in
costumes that looked like rag mats trimmed with feather
dusters, a dance that began with a seated swaying movement and ended with wild leaps into the air to the accompaniment of cannibalistic whoops.

Bram stayed with Unwin U. Blundell for nearly two
years; but he did not remain a young cannibal chief to
the exclusion of everything else.

"It's not good for any actor to play one part too long. My old granddad was considered the finest Hamlet ever seen on the Doncaster circuit. Well, I give you my word, after you'd heard him in 'To be or not to be,' you didn't know yourself if you were or if you weren't. But he played it too often, and he thought he'd vary things a bit by playing Richard III and Macbeth on the Shakespeare nights. But it was too late. He knew he'd waited too long the very first night he played Macbeth, because instead of saying 'Is this a dagger that I see before me?' he started off 'Is this a bodkin that I see before me?' It humiliated him, poor old chap, and he gave up tragedy and took to farce, and that killed him. Yes, it's a mistake to get into a groove."

So one day Prince Boo Boo disappeared from the programme of Blundell's Diorama and was succeeded by Wo Ho Wo, a Chinese philosopher. The Celestial did not prove an attraction, and Wo Ho Wo soon gave place to Carlo Marsala, the boy brigand of Sicily, a part which suited Bram to perfection, so well indeed that the Sisters Garibaldi could not bear it and were only persuaded to stay on with the Diorama by turning Bram into a young Red Indian brave, and featuring him in a dance with his two squaws before the tableau of Niagara.

In addition to the various geographical rôles he enacted with Unwin U. Blundell, Bram learnt something about theatrical publicity, and no doubt, if he had cared, he might have learnt from Mona and Clara Garibaldi a good deal about love. Although their obvious inclination to make him a bone of contention did not give Bram the least pleasure or even afford him the slightest amusement, Mr. Blundell, who had evidently been observing the pseudo-sisters becoming quite like real sisters in the fierceness of their growing rivalry, ventured to utter a few words of worldly admonition to the endangered swain.

"Don't think I'm trying to interfere with you, laddie. But I've had so much of that kind of thing myself, and I'd like to give you the benefit of my experience. Never

try and drive women in double harness. You might as
well try and drive tigers. They'll start in fighting with
each other, but it's *your* head that'll get bit off, that's a
cinch. I wouldn't be what I am now—Unwin U. Blundell of Blundell's world-famous Diorama—if I'd have let
myself go galloping after the ladies. Two whiskies, and
a man's a man. Two women, and he's a miserable slave.
What does Bill Shakespeare say? 'Give me the man
that is not passion's slave.' Take it from me, laddie, if
Bill said that, he meant it. He'd had some. That's
what I like about the One and Only. He's had some of
everything."

Bram assured Mr. Blundell that he well understood
how easily a young man could make a fool of himself
and thanked him for his good advice, which he followed
so well during the whole of the time he was travelling
round Great Britain with the Diorama, that when at the
end of it he left to tread the legitimate boards he found
that the Sisters Garibaldi, if not sisters to each other,
were wonderful sisters to him.

"I'm sorry to lose you, Bram," said the showman when
he was told of his assistant's engagement in a melodrama
called *Secrets of a Great City*. "But I won't try and persuade you to stop. You've got the sawdust in you, laddie.
You're likely to go far, if you stick to your work."

"You've been a good friend to me, Mr. Blundell," said
Bram warmly.

"No man can wish to hear sweeter words than those,"
the showman replied: "You've listened to me every
night spouting on antiquities, old man. But the best
antiquities in the whole blooming world are old friends."

The Sisters Garibaldi wept; Mr. Blundell blew his nose
very hard; the young actor passed into another sphere
of theatrical life.

During the last two years Bram had written to his
grandmother from time to time, and had had from her an
occasional letter in return, in which he heard no news of
Lebanon House beyond an occasional assurance of its

eternal sameness. However, just before he left Blundell
to join the melodrama company he did receive a letter, in
which her large spidery handwriting crossed and sometimes recrossed was spread over several sheets of notepaper.

Lebanon House
Brigham.
April 20th, 1884.

Dear Bram,

I thought it might interest you to hear that your grandfather died last week. Please don't write and tell me that
you are sorry, because that would not be true and there is
no need to make the death of a relation an occasion for an
insincere piece of politeness. You will notice that there is
no black edge to this notepaper. Remember that, when you
next write to me. What is more, if there were any red ink
in the house I would use it. Your brother is leaving school
to take up a chair in your father's office. There will not
be room on the seat of that chair for anybody else. You
need not worry that anybody in this house will ever try to
kill the fatted calf for you. They wouldn't give you a slice
of cold mutton if you came back to-morrow. They wouldn't
give you a pickled onion. So stay where you are, and write
sometimes to that withered leaf,

Your loving
Grandmother.

Bram made rapid strides in his profession—too rapid
really, for by the time he was twenty-three he already had
a reputation in the provinces as what was, and no doubt
still is, known as a utility man. Such a reputation, serv-
iceable enough in the provinces, is likely to prove a barrier to ultimate success. Paradox though it be, the better
actor all round a man is, the less likely he will be ever to
achieve success in London. It is the old tale of the
general practitioner and the Harley Street specialist.
However, to be playing good parts at so early an age was
enough for Bram. He had no ambition to become
famous for a novel mannerism, and he was always ready

to act anything—low comedy, light comedy, heroes, villains, heavy fathers, and walking gentlemen. He was never out of an engagement, and as he would have starved rather than ask help of his relations, this was his chief concern. To fame and fortune on a grand scale he did not aspire.

CHAPTER VII

TRUE LOVE

It was when Bram was twenty-three that he first found himself in the same company as Nancy O'Finn. She was then a tall dark-haired girl of eighteen with misted blue lakes for eyes and cheeks rose-burnt to the sharp crimson of a daisy's petals. Her voice with just a touch of a brogue in it had the rich tones of a violoncello; her figure was what was called fine in those days when women were not anxious to look as if a steam-roller had passed over their bodies during the night. She was with her father, Michael O'Finn, who had been supporting Mrs. Hunter-Hart in heavies for fifteen years—ever since Mrs. Hunter-Hart had set out to tour the provinces with a repertory of Shakespeare's comedies. Mrs. Hunter-Hart was now nearly fifty—some declared she was several years over—but her Portia, her Viola, her Rosalind, her Beatrice, and her Katherina, were ageless. This admirable veteran did not fear the rivalry of youth. So here was Bram at twenty-three playing Gratiano, Sir Andrew Aguecheek, Corin, Verges, and Biondello, and Nancy O'Finn at eighteen playing Nerissa, Maria, and Audrey. Indeed most of Mrs. Hunter-Hart's company, with the exception of Michael O'Finn and herself, were under thirty. Bram was enjoying himself so much that out of sheer good-will toward life he fell deep in love with Nancy. For a while, everybody in the company watched the affair sympathetically. Even Miss Hermione Duparc, the second lady, who had never understood why Mrs. Hart had cast Nancy for the part of Nerissa and herself for Jessica, was heard to murmur intensely that the little affair lent quite a sparkle of romance to Spring in the

Black Country and that it was pretty to see the way those two children were enjoying themselves. However, the affair presently became serious when the young lovers announced that they were going to be married and Michael O'Finn woke up to the fact that he was in danger of losing his only daughter.

"But, O'Finn, you've only had Nancy touring with you for a few months," Bram protested, when the heavy father, one hand thrust deep into his buttoned frock-coat, strode up and down the unusually spacious sitting-room he and Nancy were sharing that week in Birmingham, and proceeded to give a performance of a character that had slipped between King Lear and Shylock and fallen into melodrama.

"I had dreamed," the old actor declaimed in a voice that rustled with Irish foliage and was at the same time fruity with pompous tragic tones, "I had dreamed of many harpy yeers before us, harpy, harpy yeers in which I would behold my only daughter growing more like her beloved mother whose loss has darkened the whole of my existence, since I laid her to rest to wait for the last trump to ring out above the moil and toil of Newcastle-on-Tyne. Young man, you have wounded a father in his tenderest spot. You have shattered his hopes. You have torn the fibres of his heart. In my mind's eye I perceive my little daughter still clutching at the dear maternal breast, and you blast that sacred vision by proposing to commit matrimony with this tender suckling."

"But, O'Finn, you didn't object to her acting in other companies till she was twelve years old; and for four years after that she lived with an aunt in Dublin, so that you hardly ever saw her."

"Young man, do not taunt an unhappy parent with what he has missed. She and I were clutched by the iron hand of circumstance. The practical considerations of finance ruled that we should live sundered until now; but now, now at the very moment when the clouds are breaking to a glorious day, you descend upon us like a thun-

derbolt out of a clear sky and propose to marry this moth-
erless child and drench the cheeks of a stricken father
with tears, idle tears."

"But, O'Finn, Nancy isn't as young as all that," Bram
protested.

"Spare your taunts, young man. I charge you, spare
them. Be content with the havoc you have wrought, but
do not gloat like a vulture upon the reeking ruins."

"Look here, O'Finn, can't we discuss this matter sensibly?"

"Sensibly?" cried the heavy father, throwing up his
arms as a suppliant at the throne of Heaven. "Sensibly?
Ha-ha! Tarquin's loathly form steals into my domestic
hearth and ravishes my daughter's love, and I, I the
broken-hearted parent, am invited by the ravisher himself
to discuss the matter sensibly! Tempt me not to violence,
young man. Do not tempt me, I say. For twenty years,
whenever I have had occasion to visit the metropolis of
the Midlands, I have stayed in Mrs. Prattman's comfortable lodgings without ever breaking so much as a humble
egg-cup. Do not tempt me to bring the whole house about
my ears in the wild and uncontrollable fury of despair."

Bram began to laugh.

"He laughs! Ha-ha! He laughs! He surveys the
havoc he has made and laughs! A hyena wandering in
a desert might abstain from laughter at such a moment,
but not this young man. No, no! *He* laughs."

"I'm really very sorry, O'Finn, but if you will go on
talking like that, I simply can't help laughing."

At this moment Nancy herself entered the sitting-
room.

"Hello, boys, what's the joke? Do tell a pal," she
cried in a radiance of good-fellowship.

The heavy father sank down into one of Mrs. Prattman's armchairs and buried his head in his knees.

"It isn't a joke at all, Nancy. It's very serious. Your
father won't hear of letting us get married, he says we're
too young."

"The dear old duffer," said Nancy. "Why, then we'll just have to get married without saying any more about it."

"Never!" thundered the heavy father, springing to his feet.

"Then I'll go back to Aunt Kathleen," Nancy vowed. "If I'm old enough to make love on the stage, I'm old enough to make love off it."

Michael O'Finn, having taken up this attitude in his lodgings, could not resist elaborating it before the performance in the cosy little saloon bar of the "Saracen's Head" just round the corner from the stage-door. The result was that his delivery of Jacques's great speech in the Forest of Arden lost much of its austere melancholy and most of its articles definite and indefinite. A pronounced thickening of all the sibilants with a quantity of unnecessary tears left Jacques himself, at the end of that strange eventful history, in a state of mere oblivion and apparently sans teeth, sans eyes, sans taste, sans everything. When the curtain fell on the second act, Mrs. Hunter-Hart, who had been watching him from the wings, invited her heavy man to step up to her dressing-room and explain what he meant by it.

"I am ecsheedingly dishtreshed, Mrs. Hart, but a domeshtic mishfortune overtook me thish afternoon and I'm afraid that I drank rather more than wash good for me in the 'Sharashen's Head.'"

He proceeded to give Mrs. Hunter-Hart an account of the shock which had led him into such unprofessional conduct.

"O'Finn, I'm astonished at you! I would not believe that a man of your age could make such an unmitigated ass of himself. Come, let me try you with your cues. *Even a toy in hand here, sir: nay, pray be covered.*"

"*Will you be married, motley?*" O'Finn muttered thickly.

"*As the ox hath his bow, sir,*" Mrs. Hart went on, "*the horse his curb, and the falcon her bells, so hath man*

his desires; and as pigeons bill, so wedlock would be nib-
bling."

"Yes, I perceive the point you're making, ma'am," the
old actor admitted. "But with your permission I
would . . ."

"Beginners third act," cried the junior member of the
company, hurrying along the stone corridors past the
dressing-room doors.

Perhaps if the interval had been longer, Mrs. Hunter-
Hart might have persuaded Michael O'Finn that he was
behaving unreasonably and absurdly. As it was, he recovered his sense of outraged paternity, and on the following night he worked up his feelings in the bar of the
"Saracen's Head" to such a pitch that several members of
the company began to think that Bram really must have
been behaving rather badly with Nancy. O'Finn played
Sir Toby Belch that night, and, as the *Birmingham Daily
Post* said, it was probably as ripe a performance as had
ever been seen on any stage.

However, what had begun not exactly in jest, but to
some extent as a piece of play-acting, became serious; for
Michael O'Finn, who had nearly ruined his youthful
career by hard drinking, seemed inclined to revert to the
wretched habit in his maturity. Bram began to feel thoroughly upset, in spite of Nancy's protestations of undying
love and her promise to run away and be married to him
the moment he gave the word. Mrs. Hunter-Hart herself
continued to be kind, and was always assuring them of
her great influence over the intransigent father and of
the certainty that he would soon come to his senses. The
rest of the company was on the whole unfavourable to the
lovers, so sad was the picture that O'Finn drew of a deso-
late future bereft of his only daughter and doomed for
ever to tour the provinces in lonely lodgings without being
allowed to buy that little cottage in the country, where
with Nancy in affectionate ministration he was to rest
during the rose-hung Junes of conventional idealism, and
to which he was ultimately to retire on his savings for a

peaceful pipe-smoking old age. As a matter of hard fact, Michael O'Finn had exactly two weeks' salary in his bank, barely enough to pay the lawyer for the conveyance of a two-roomed bungalow on the banks of the Thames.

A week or two later in the middle of this situation Bram received a letter from his grandmother:

> Lebanon House
> Brigham.
> May 31st, 1889.

DEAR BRAM,

Your father is dead. He was humbly presenting a loyal address to the Duke of Edinburgh and having always had, as you know, a wretched crop of hair, he caught a cold which developed into pneumonia, and that's the end of my son Joshua. I understand that Caleb is the sole heir subject to certain annuities payable to your aunts and an injunction not to let his mother starve. You are not mentioned in the will. However, since Caleb won't come of age for a month or two, the executors (neither of whom are Peculiars) think that, if you were to return home immediately, pressure could be brought to bear on your brother to come to an equitable arrangement by which, if you consented to devote yourself to the business, you should be made a partner in the firm. It lies with you, my dear boy. Is it worth while to make yourself pleasant to that sleek Jacob for the sake of perhaps a thousand pounds a year (I don't think you'd get more out of it), or would you prefer to remain poor, free, and honest? I know which I should choose if I were you. You know that I would like to see you before I die, though I'm bound to say that at the present there is no sign of my dying. More's the pity, for I am heartily sick of this life, and though I admit I am now faced with the dread of another much longer one hereafter, I'm hoping that the rumour prevalent about eternity has been grossly exaggerated. I rarely leave my own room nowadays, and my eyes have been giving me a good deal of trouble, so that I find it almost impossible to read. However, luckily I have unearthed in Brigham a pleasant young woman with a respect for commas and

colons who reads aloud to me in a not quite intolerable
French. She winces at Zola, but then so do I, for he's such
a rank bad writer. Nevertheless, I cannot resist the rascal
just as once upon a time I could never resist staring into
shop windows. How your grandfather hated that habit of
mine! He never knew what it might lead to. People feel
the same about Zola, I suppose. Strange your father dying
abruptly like this. I had figured him as a perpetual phenomenon like the smoke of the Brigham chimneys. If you *do*
decide to come home, you should come quickly.

Your loving
GRANDMOTHER.

Bram contemplated the sheets of sprawling spidery
handwriting and wondered what he ought to do. His
grandmother did not know what a problem she was putting before him. It was not so easy to laugh at the idea
of a thousand pounds a year, now that he was engaged
to Nancy. A settled prospect was likely to make her
father take another view of their marriage. It would
be deuced hard to eat humble-pie to Caleb, but with
Nancy as a reward he could achieve even that. And
life in Brigham? Ugh! Well, even life in Brigham with
Nancy laughing beside him would be sweeter and lovelier
than life in Paradise without her.

He showed the letter to his sweetheart and asked her
advice. Afterwards, he used to wonder how he could
ever have doubted for a moment what her answer would
be.

"Go home?" she exclaimed. "Why, Bram darling,
you must be mad to think of such a thing. What's a
thousand a year compared with your self-respect?"

"I thought your father might take a more reasonable
view of our marriage, if I could be doing something more
solid than acting in the provinces."

"Has *he* ever done anything more solid himself?
Never in his life. Well, listen to me, Bram, if you go
back home and crawl to that brother of yours, I swear

I'll break off our engagement. Now there it is straight."

"You know there's only one reason would make me go home."

"Well, you'll have to marry a squib, my dear, for you'll certainly never marry your Nancy if you do."

"There doesn't seem much chance of my ever marrying you as things are now," Bram sighed.

"Will you elope? Now listen to me, I'm serious. I'm after thinking that an elopement is the only solution for us. What is it Touchstone sings to Audrey:

Come, sweet Audrey:
We must be married, or we must live in bawdry!

At least he doesn't sing it in our version, because dear old Ma Hart is so damned genteel she wouldn't have such a sentiment uttered by a member of her pure company. But it's in Shakespeare, for I read it when I was studying the part."

"But your father, you lunatic?"

"Och, my father! He can't drink any more than he's drinking now, and it would give him a gentlemanly excuse for getting drunk if he was to celebrate his daughter's wedding. Listen. You've enough money to buy the ring and the license?"

"Oh, I've saved twelve pounds this tour already."

"Next week's Leamington and Coventry, and the week after's Leicester. Let's be married in Leicester on Saturday week. That's the only way to deal with father, and indeed it's a kindness to the man, for he's getting tired of playing the ill-used father, and a little bit of geniality for a change will do him all the good in the world."

Bram caught her to him.

"You won't regret it, Nancy?"

"Why should I regret it?"

"You shan't, you shan't, dear Nancy. Listen, I haven't said anything about this before, because I didn't want to give you the idea that I was trying to make a bargain over you. But I don't believe in mixed marriages, and

I think I'd like to be a Catholic. My grandmother's a Catholic, you know, and she's the only creature in the world I really care for, except you, my sweetheart."

"Ah, now, don't think it's so easy to become a Catholic. You'll have to have the devil's own amount of instruction first. You can be married without knowing a thing at all about it. But the priest won't baptise you so easy as he'll marry you. Conversion can wait till we have a little more time to ourselves."

So, on the sixteenth of June at Leicester Bram and Nancy were married. The ceremony achieved, they went for a long drive in a fly through the not very beautiful Leicestershire country and arrived back at Michael O'Finn's lodgings about five o'clock to announce the state of affairs at the favourable hour when he should be digesting his dinner over a cigar. It was the last evening of the tour and *Twelfth Night* was in the bill, so that, if he should go out and get drunk before the performance, he was less likely to disgrace himself as obviously as in any of his other parts.

"Well, we've done it, father," Nancy began.

"Done what?" he demanded, crackling the leaves of *The Stage* and scowling at Bram over the top of it.

"We're married. Yes, we were married in St. Aloysius' Church this morning at twelve o'clock. There's nothing to be done about it, father."

"Nothing to be done about it?" repeated O'Finn. "There is a very great deal to be done. Come to my arms, my beloved child. Weep upon my shoulder in the excess of your new-found happiness. Weep, I say. Spare not one single tear. Weep, weep. Young man, give me your hand. I have entrusted you with the guardianship of the being I hold most sacred of earth's creatures. Honour that trust, young man. Rejoice a father's heart by your devotion. God bless you both, my children. And now let us make arrangements to celebrate this auspicious event by a supper to our friends and intimates at that best of hostelries, the old 'Blue Boar.' There is not a

moment to be lost. Mine host will want to make his
arrangements with the authorities for an extension of the
license to some seasonable small hour that will suitably
hallow the occasion. I will leave you here to bill and
coo. Did you see what *The Stage* said about my Tranio
this week? Read it, my boy. You'll be delighted with
the way the notice is written. Judicial—very, very judicial."

With this O'Finn, humming the *Wedding March* in his
rich bass, left the newly wed pair to themselves.

"Well, I'm bothered," Bram gasped. "He's completely
turned round."

"I rather thought he would," Nancy said. "I've never
known him refuse a fat part. He was getting tired of
gloom."

When Nancy and Bram went down to the theatre that
night, O'Finn met them at the stage-door, beaming with
good-will.

"I've seen my dear old manageress. She has consented
to grace the festivity in person, and the acting-manager
of the theatre has insisted on our using the green-room.
The supper is being sent in from the 'Blue Boar.' Ham.
Chicken. Lobster. All the appropriate delicacies. Several of the orchestra are coming. Very jolly fellows.
We'll have some capital fiddling. My dear old pal
Charlie Warburton will give us Hood's *Bridge of Sighs,*
and I daresay we can persuade him into *Eugene Aram* as
well. I've asked Mrs. Hart to recite us one of her gems.
In fact, the whole crowd will oblige. We are going to
make a memorable night of it. You couldn't have chosen
a better time to get married. We've had a splendid Whit-
week, and that showery Whit Monday put Mrs. H.-H.
into such a delightful humour. The last day of the tour.
By gad, girl, I'm proud to be your poor old father. And
the booking to-night is splendid, I hear. We shall have
a bumper house for *Twelfth Night.*"

It was a merry evening in the old green-room of the
Opera House, Leicester, now, alas! fallen from its com-

panionable status and turned to some practical and business-like purpose. Gilded mirrors on the walls, glittering gasoliers, bright silver, and shining faces, warmth and happiness of careless human beings gathered together for a few hours in fellowship, all are vanished now. Files and dockets and roll-top desks have replaced them.

There is no doubt that the central figure on that genial night was Michael O'Finn. The bride and bridegroom were teased and toasted, but the central figure was the erstwhile dejected father. How many speeches he made it would be hard to say, but he certainly made a very great many. He proposed everybody's health in turn, and when everybody's health had been proposed and drunk, he proposed corporate bodies like the theatre orchestra, the town council of Leicester, and Mrs. Hunter-Hart's Shakespearian Company. And when he had exhausted the living he sought among the dead for his toasts, raising his glass to the memory of Will Shakespeare, Davy Garrick, Ned Kean, and Mrs. Siddons. When the mighty dead were sufficiently extolled he proposed abstractions like Art and the Drama. His final speech was made about four o'clock in the morning—to the memory of the happy days, old friends, and jolly companions.

"Ladies and gentlemen, I am sure that you will agree with me that we have all spent a very enjoyable and—er—delightful evening. Those who have not, hold up their hands. As I suspected *nemine contradicente,* carried unam . . . But there is one more toast to which I will invite you to raise your glasses. Ladies and gentlemen, another night of our earthly pilgrimage has waned. The sun of to-morrow already gilds the horizon, though we may still seem to be living in to-night. We have all wished long life and happiness to my beloved daughter and the excellent young man—may I add excellent young actor—who has—er—joined his future with hers, in short, who has married her. But there is yet another toast to which I must bid you raise your glasses. Ladies

and gentlemen, we have reached the end of a happy tour
with my dear old friend and manageress, Mrs. Hunter-
Hart. Some of us will meet again under her banner in
the last week of July on the sunny South Coast; others
will not. We shall probably never find ourselves all together at the same festive board. Let me beg you therefore to drink all together, for perhaps the last time in
this mortal life, to the toast of happy days and sweet
memories, old friends and jolly companions. Ladies and
gentlemen, I confess without shame that a teardrop lurk-
ing in the corner of my eye has coursed down my cheek
and alighted upon the lapel of my coat as I give you this
solemn toast. Happy memories! What a world of
beautiful images those two words conjure up! I see again
the little cradle in which my mother rocked me to sleep.
I kneel once more by her knees to say my childish prayers.
Anon I am a happy urchin tripping and gambolling down
the lane to the village school. Anon I stand before the
altar with my dearly beloved and alas! now for ever
absent wife beside me. I hear once more the vociferous
plaudits of the crowded pit as I cry to Macbeth, 'Turn,
hell-hound, turn.' I live again through the delightful
moments of first meeting my dear old friend and manageress, Emmeline Hunter-Hart, who has upheld the banner of the legitimate drama against odds, ladies and gentlemen, odds, fearful, tremendous, overwhelming odds.
She has seen on all sides the hosts of evil in the shape of
these vile problem plays that have degraded, are degrad-
ing, and will continue to degrade the sacred fane of
Thespis. Happy memories, ladies and gentlemen! And
surely I may ask you to count this night as one of your
happiest memories. To the young couple who this morning resolved to face the storms of life together, surely
this night will be a happy memory. Happy memories
and—let us not forget them—old friends, for are not all
our happiest memories bound up with old friends?
Ladies and gentlemen, I give you the double toast to
which I hope you will accord full musical honours by

joining with me in singing friendship's national anthem, the moving song of the immortal Robbie Burns, *Should Old Acquaintance Be Forgot.*"

The party broke up. The footsteps of the company died away along the cobbled streets of Leicester. The night became a happy memory. The bride and bridegroom went dreaming homeward, life before them, the dewy freshness of June around them, and overhead the faded azure of the empty morning sky.

CHAPTER VIII

ROGUES AND VAGABONDS

The first thing that Bram and Nancy vowed to each other was that they would never accept anything but a joint engagement. It sounded so easy at first, but during the next four years many anxious moments were caused by that rose-flushed resolution of early married life. However, they did manage it, and not only that but they managed somehow to take with them on tour the baby girl who was born on the sixteenth of July, just a year and a month after they were married.

Letizia was born in a tiny cottage buried among the cherry orchards of Kent. The original Letizia's letter on being informed of the proposed tribute to herself was characteristic:

> Lebanon House
> Brigham.
> July 20th, 1890.

DEAR BRAM,

Why you should burden your wretched infant with the name that nearly eighty years ago was so unsuitably bestowed upon her great-grandmother I cannot imagine. I hope that the challenge you offer to Fate by calling any child Gladness will not be vented on her head.

Lying here in bed, for I am become a bedridden old bag of bones, I look back at my wasted life and wonder why it should be prolonged in this unreasonable manner. Letizia! Did either of you young people realise that Letizia means gladness? However, as you insist on an exchange of compliments between this poor infant and myself, why, let your wife kiss her with her own fresh lips and tell her that once the lips of another Letizia were as fresh. I have just picked up the mirror and looked at myself. When I die, ah, *mon dieu*, when, when . . . let me be crumpled up and flung into the nearest wastepaper basket.

Your affectionate ancestor,

LETIZIA THE FIRST.

By the way, I don't think I've written since Master Caleb celebrated his coming of age by sacking all of the older workmen in the factory three months after they presented him with a token of esteem and respect. I understand they were informed that he only took this step for their own good, because he was afraid that they were getting too old for the dangerous trade of making rockets! The Peculiars made an attempt to recapture him from the Church of England (in which your father had recently invested) by offering him a vacant apostolic seat. Caleb replied that he could not see his way to occupy such a position satisfactorily. True enough, for his behind has swollen like a pumpkin in the sun. The pleasant-faced young woman who reads aloud to me is a most capable gossip. I am getting a new insight into local affairs.

Nancy wished that she could meet this strange old woman whose fierce blood ran in the veins of the raspberry-coloured monkey at her breast that was growing daily so much more like a human being. But she and Bram agreed that it would be foolish to involve themselves in the domesticity either of his family or of hers. They must only have one aim, and that must be the joint engagement.

"Once we separate, things will never be the same again," Nancy said.

"Oh, don't I know it, dearest! But we won't separate."

Nor did they. Difficult though it was sometimes, they did always manage to keep together, those rogues and vagabonds, and what is more they did manage to keep Letizia with them.

"I wonder you don't let your little girl stay with some relation while you're on tour," a jealous mother would observe.

"I like to have her with me during these first years. Time enough to lose her when she goes to school," Nancy would reply.

"But surely the continual change and travelling cannot be good for so young a child?" the critic would insist.

"I think change of air is good for everything," Nancy would reply firmly.

So, up and down the length of England, in and out of Wales, across to Ireland and over the border to Scotland, for the next four years Bram and Nancy wandered. In every new company the first thing they pitched was Letizia's canvas travelling-cot with its long poles and short poles and cross pieces and canopy which all fitted ingeniously together until the final business of lacing up the back like a pair of stays was finished and Letizia was tucked away inside. Always the same luggage—the tin bath packed so full of Nancy's clothes that it was a great struggle to fasten it—Bram's second-hand portmanteau with its flap like an elephant's ear and bulging middle—the trim wicker luncheon-basket, and big wicker theatrical-basket smelling of grease paint and American cloth and old wigs. Endless journeys on Sundays in trains without corridors and on some lines still lighted with oil-lamps so that the baby Letizia, lying on the horsehair cushions of the railway-carriage, would drop asleep to the rhythmic movement of the oil swaying to and fro in the glass container. Long waits at stations like York and Crewe, where the only Sabbath traffic in those days seemed to be touring companies and all the compartments in all the trains were labelled engaged. Long waits while stout men with red noses and blue chins greeted old pals and ran up and down the length of the train, and cracked jokes over flasks of whisky or brandy. Long waits in big smoky junctions, sometimes catching sight of the *Dorothy* company with its pack of hounds—to the great excitement and joy of Letizia, who would be held up to admire the barking of the bow-wows. Late arrivals in smoky northern towns when the only fly at the station would be collared by the manager and the humbler members of the company would have to shoulder their light luggage and walk to their lodgings. Late arrivals in snowstorm and rainstorm, in fog and frost, when the letter ordering the meal had miscarried and the landlady was a gaunt stranger who thoroughly enjoyed telling the weary vagabonds that, not having heard from them, she had *not* lighted the fire in the sitting-room. Late arrivals when the landlady was an old friend and came down the steps to embrace both her lodgers and lead them into a toasting, glowing room with the table laid and a smell of soup being wafted along the little passage from the kitchen. Early morning starts when every lady in Nancy's carriage wanted a different corner and signified her choice with an exaggerated and liverish politeness. Early morning starts when some familiar little thing was left behind and the next lodgings did not look like home until the missing article was forwarded on from the last town. Every week a new town, and sometimes two or three small towns in one week. Every Monday morning at eleven a music call, and after that a walk round the new town to discover the best and cheapest shops. Every day dinner at three o'clock and tea at six. Every evening Letizia left to the guardianship of the landlady while Bram and Nancy set out arm-in-arm to the theatre. Every night except Sunday the swing of a dingy door and the immemorial smell of the theatre within. Our modern young actors and actresses do not know that smell. It vanished in its perfection when electric light took the place of gas, and unretentive encaustic tiles lined the corridors instead of bare stone or whitewashed bricks. It requires something more than the warmth of hot-water pipes to ripen and conserve that smell. It may have lost some of its quintessential peculiarity when gas supplemented candles; but those gas-jets covered with wire guards, on which the ladies and gentlemen of visiting companies were requested by the management not to boil kettles, must have added a beautiful richness of their own.

Thou glorious ancient smell of the theatre, thou sublime pot-pourri of grease-paint, wig-paste, vaseline, powder, perspiration, old clothes, oranges, tobacco, gas, drains, hair, whitewash, hot metal, and dusty canvas, where mayest thou still be savoured instead of that dull odour of Condy's fluid and fire extinguishers which faintly repels us as we pass through the stage-doors of our contemporary palaces of amusement?

Our particular vagabonds found it easier to obtain joint engagements in musical shows. Nancy's contralto voice, untrained though it was, grew better and better each year, and Bram had developed into a capital comedian. In the third and fourth winters after they were married they played together in pantomime, and for the Christmas season of 1894 they were engaged at the Theatre Royal, Greenwich—Bram as Idle Jack in *Dick Whittington* and Clown in the Harlequinade, Nancy as Fairy Queen and Columbine. It was a pity that by now the Harlequinade was already a moribund form of entertainment, for Bram had a genuine talent for getting that fantastic street-life over the footlights. One may be allowed a fleeting suspicion that the English stage has lost more than it has gained by its banishment of the clown from its boards. The French, who are dramatically so much superior, have preserved their clowns.

Bram and Nancy found exceptionally pleasant lodgings in Greenwich. Starboard Alley was a row of diminutive Georgian houses running down to the river and overlooking at the back the grounds of the Trinity Hospital. The bow windows which gave just such a peep of the wide Thames as one may get of the sea itself in little streets that lead down to ancient harbours, had no more than a genteel and unobtrusive curve; it was the very place in which an outward-bound mariner would have felt safe in leaving his wife to wait for his return. Starboard Alley was too narrow for vehicles, so that there was never any sound there but of the footsteps of people walking past on their way to stroll along the embankment above the river— a pleasant place, that embankment, even in this cold December weather, with the seagulls wheeling and screaming overhead and the great ships coming home on the tide, coming home for Christmas on the flowing tide. Not only was the house in Starboard Alley itself attractive, but Mrs. Pottage, the landlady, was as much a feature of it as the bow window, though, to say truth, she had a more obtrusive curve. She was a widow of forty years' standing, her husband, a gunner in one of Her Majesty's ships having been killed off Sebastopol; but she was still comely with her fresh complexion and twinkling eyes, and her heart was young.

"I was hardly eighteen at the time my poor husband vanished out of this world," she told her lodgers, "and the offers of marriage I've had since—well, I assure you the men have always been round me like flies after sugar. But I've never melted like sugar does in the heat. I said 'no' to the first in 1855 within four months of my pore William's death—well, it was death and burial all in one as you might say, because he'd been talking to his mate as cheerful as a goldfinch the moment before and the next moment there was nothing of him left. It was his mate I said 'no' to, four months later, when he was inva- lided home with a wooden leg. He was the first, and I said 'no' to the last only yesterday afternoon just before tea—a Mr. Hopkins he is, a ship's chandler in a small style of business with a head like the dome of the Ob- servatory, but no more in it than an empty eggshell. Oh, I ashore you I gave him a very firm 'no,' and he went back to his chandling as dumb as a doornail. Yes, you might really call it quite a hobby of mine refusing eligi- bles. I used to put the dates down in the butcher's book or the baker's book as the case might be, but I got charged for them one year as extra loaves and ever since then I've kept the dates in my head. Off to rehearsal now, are

you? Well, fancy them having a rehearsal on Christmas
Eve. I call that making a great demand on anybody's
good nature. In fact, if anybody didn't mind being a
bit vulgar, it's what they might call blooming sauce.
And you'll leave your little girl with me? What's her
name, Letishyer? Said with a sneeze, I suppose? Never
mind, I'll enjoy having her hanging on to my skirts. I
never had no children myself. Well, I was just getting
over the first shyness and beginning to enjoy married life
when all of a sudden that Crimeen war broke out and my
poor William had to leave me. Well, it was a mean
crime, and no mistake. Got to start off to the theatre
now? Wrap yourselves up well, for it's biting cold to-
night. It's my opinion we're in for a real old-fashioned
Christmas. Good job, too, I say, the size women are
wearing their sleeves nowadays. Balloon sleeves they
call them. Balloonatic sleeves I should say. Well, toora-
looral! I'll pop your little girl into her cot and have the
kettle on the boil for you when you come back. Ugh!
What a perishing evening!"

The vagabonds arm-in-arm set out toward the theatre,
the north wind blowing fiercely up Starboard Alley across
the Thames from Barking Flats—a searching wind, fierce
and bitter.

The *Dick Whittington* company had been rehearsing
hard during the previous week, and now two days before
the production on Boxing Day it was seeming incredible
that the management would ever have the impudence to
demand the public's money to see such a hopelessly inadequate performance.

"We've been in some bad shows, my dear," Bram said
to Nancy on their way to the theatre, "but I think this
is the worst."

"I'm too tired to know anything about it. But your
songs will go all right, I'm sure."

He shook his head doubtfully.

"Yes, but that fellow Sturt who plays the Dame is a
naughty actor. He really is dire. I simply cannot get

him to work in with me. That's the worst of taking a
fellow from the Halls. He hasn't an elementary notion
how to help other people. He can't see that it takes two
people to make a scene funny."

"Never mind," said Nancy, yawning. "It'll all be
splendid, I expect, on Wednesday. Oh, dear, I am tired.
They've given you a good trap-act in the Harlequinade."

"Yes, that's all right. But do you know, Nancy, it's a
queer thing, but I funk trap-acts. I'm never happy till
I've gone through the last one." He stopped short and
struck his forehead. "Great Scott!"

"What is the matter?"

"We haven't got anything for Letizia's stocking?"

"Bram!"

"What time were we called again?"

"Six o'clock."

"Look here," he said, "you go round and collect some
toys from a toyshop. I'll make an excuse to Worsley if
by any chance he wants the Fairy Queen at the beginning.
But he won't. He wants to get the shipwreck right. We
shall probably be on that till nearly midnight."

So Nancy left Bram at the stage-door and went on to
do her shopping. The streets were crowded with people,
and in spite of the cold wind everybody was looking
cheerful. The shops, too, with their brightly lit windows
all decorated with frosted cotton-wool and holly, exhaled
that authentic Christmas glow, which touches all but
hearts too long barren and heads too long empty. The
man who sneers at Christmas is fair game for the Father
of Lies.

Nancy revelled in the atmosphere, and for a while she
allowed herself to drift with the throng—hearing in a
dream the shrill excited cries of the children, the noise
of toy instruments, the shouts of the salesmen offering
turkeys and geese; smelling in a dream that peculiar odour
of hung poultry mixed with crystallised fruit, oranges,
and sawdust; and perceiving in a dream the accumulated
emotion of people who were all thinking what they could

buy for others, that strange and stirring emotion which long ago shepherds personified as a troop of angels crying, "Peace, good-will toward men." She felt that she could have wandered happily along like this for hours, and she was filled with joy to think that in a short while she should be welcomed by some of these children as the Spirit of Good. The part of the Fairy Queen had never hitherto appealed to her; but now suddenly she was seized with a longing to wave her silver wand and vanquish the Demon King. She passed four ragged children who were staring at a heap of vivid sweets on the other side of a plate-glass window. She went into the shop and bought a bagful for each. It was wonderful to pass on and leave them standing there on the pavement in a rapture of slow degustation. But her time could not be spent in abandoning herself to these sudden impulses of sentimental self-indulgence. She entered a bazaar and filled her bag with small toys for Letizia's stocking— a woolly lamb, a monkey-on-a-stick, a tin trumpet, a parti-coloured ball—all the time-honoured cargo of Santa Claus. She had already bought a case of pipes for Bram's Christmas present. But now she was filled with ambition to give him some specially chosen gift that would commemorate this cold Greenwich Yuletide. What should it be? She longed to find something that would prove to him more intimately than words all that he had meant to her these years of their married life, all that he would mean to her on and on through the years to come. Bram was such a dear. He worked so hard. He was never jealous. He had nothing of the actor's vanity, and all the actor's good nature. What present would express what she felt about his dearness? Ash-trays, cigarette-holders, walking-sticks—what availed they to tell him how deep was her love? Pocket-books, card-cases, blotters—what eloquence did they possess? Then she saw on the counter a little silver key.

"Is this the key of anything?" she asked the shopman.

"No, miss, that is what they call a charm. We have a

large assortment this season. This silver puppy-dog, for
instance. You'd really be surprised to know what a quantity of these silver puppy-dogs we've sold. They're worn
on bracelets or watch-chains. Quite the go, miss, I can
assure you."

"No, I like this key better. Could you let me have
a box for it?"

"Certainly, miss."

"And I want to write something on a card and put it
inside if you'd kindly seal it for me."

"With pleasure, miss."

Nancy leant over the counter and wrote, with a blush
for her folly: *This is the key of my heart. Keep it always, my darling.*

The key and the card were put inside the box; and she
hurried off to the theatre, laughing to herself in an
absurdly delicious excitement at the thought of hiding it
under Bram's pillow to-night.

The dress rehearsal was not over till three o'clock on
Christmas morning. The ladies and gentlemen of the
company were all so tired when at last they were dismissed that when they came out of the theatre and found
Greenwich white and silent under a heavy fall of snow,
not even the comedians had any energy to be funny with
snowballs.

"What time's the call to-morrow, dear?" one of the
chorus called back to a friend in a weary voice.

"There's no call to-morrow, duck. It's Christmas
Day."

"Gard, so it is!"

"Don't forget the curtain goes up for the matinée on
Boxing Day at half-past one, dear."

"Right-o!"

"Queenie's got her boy staying at the 'Ship,'" the
chorus girl explained to Nancy. "And she's the limit for
forgetting everything when he's about. She's potty on
him. Merry Christmas, Miss O'Finn."

"Merry Christmas to you."

All the way back up the court, at the end of which was the stage-door, the Christmas greetings of one to another floated thinly along the snowy air.

"A merry Christmas! A merry Christmas."

Bram took Nancy's arm, and they hurried away back as fast as they could to Starboard Alley, where they found Letizia safe in her cot, one of Mrs. Pottage's stockings hanging like a coal-sack over the foot of it.

"You never told me which stocking to put out," said the landlady. "So I hung up one of my own. Of course, I hung up one of hers as well, pore mite, but hers wouldn't hold more than a couple of acid-drops. Mine is a *little* more convenient."

"How kind of you to sit up for us, Mrs. Pottage," the two vagabonds exclaimed.

"Oh, I've been thinking over old times. You know. On and off the doze, as you might say. My friend Mrs. Bugbird didn't hop it till past midnight. She generally comes in for a chat of a Monday evening, and being Christmas Eve she stayed on a bit extra. She's a real comic, is Mrs. Bugbird; but she had to be a bit careful how she laughed to-night, because last week she ricked the plate of her teeth laughing over a story I told her. Yes, the soup's lovely and hot. But I did let the fire out in your sitting-room. So if you wouldn't mind coming into my kitchen . . ."

"Was Letizia good?" the mother asked.

"She hasn't moved an inch since I put her to bye-bye. I've popped up to look at her several times. In fact, Mrs. Bugbird and me both popped up, and Mrs. B. said a more sweetly pretty infant she never did wish to see. 'Well,' I said, 'Mrs. Bugbird,' I said, 'that's something for you to say with the fourteen you've had.' Fancy, fourteen! Tut-tut-tut! Still if I'd accepted half my proposals, I'd have had more like forty by now."

A canary stirred upon his perch and chirped.

"Hear that?" said Mrs. Pottage. "That blessed bird understands every word I say. Don't you, my beauty?

Now come along, drink up your soup, and do eat a littl
bit of the nice cold supper I've put out for you.

While her lodgers were enjoying the cold roast beef,
Mrs. Pottage examined the purchases made for Letizia's
stocking.

"Oh, dear, how they do get things up nowadays!" she
exclaimed, holding at admiring arm's length the monkey-
on-a-stick. "Lifelike, isn't it? You'll want an orange
and an apple, don't forget. And I wouldn't put in too
many lollipops if I was you, or she won't be able to eat
any turkey. I got you a lovely little turkey. Nine
pounds. Well, you don't want to sit down to an elephant.
I remember one Christmas I invited my sister to come up
from Essex, and I thought she'd appreciate some turkey,
so I told the fishmonger to send in a really nice dainty
little one. Well, by mistake his boy brought round one
that weighed thirty-two pounds and which had won the
prize for the biggest turkey in Greenwich that year.
In fact, it come round to me with a red and white rosette
stuck in its how-d'ye-do as big as a sunflower. Well, it
didn't arrive till past eleven o'clock on Christmas Eve,
and I was down at the 'Nelson's Head' with my sister
till closing time, and there it was waiting for us when we
got back, tied onto the knocker. It gave me a bit of a
start, because I'd had one or two for old sake's sake, and
I thought for the minute some pore fellow had gone and
suicided himself on my front door. Well, there was nothing to be done but cook it, and my sister's a small-made
woman, and when we sat down to dinner with that turkey between us she might have been sitting one side of
St. Paul's and me the other. I give you my word that
turkey lasted me for weeks. Well, the wish-bone was as
big as a church window, and I could have hung my wash-
ing out on the drumsticks. It *was* a bird. Oh, dear, oh,
dear! Well, I know when I threw the head out to the
cat the pore beast had convulsions in the backyard, and
as for the parson's nose, well, as I said to my sister, the
parson as had a nose like that must have been a Jewish

rabbit. What a set out it was, to be sure! And my turkey which I ought to have had was sent up to a large family gathering in the Shooter's Hill Road, and half the party never tasted turkey at all that Christmas."

Mrs. Pottage continued in a strain of jovial reminiscence until her lodgers had finished supper, after which she wanted to accompany them upstairs to their room that she might help in the filling of Letizia's stocking.

"The fact is," she whispered hoarsely, "I put that stocking of mine out, because I'd bought a few odds and ends for her myself."

She dived into the pockets of her voluminous skirt. "Here we are, a bouncing dog with a chube at the end of it to squeeze. She can't swallow it unless she swallows the dog too, and I don't think she'll do that. The *Story of the Three Bears,* warranted untearable, which it isn't, for I tore up two in the shop with my own hands just to show the young man he didn't know what he was talking about. A toy violing. She won't be able to play on it, but the varnish won't hurt her. A drum—well, it was really that drum which decided me to use one of my own stockings. My calves have grown whopping. In fact, I've often said jokingly to Mrs. Bugbird that I ought to call them cows nowadays. That's the lot, I think. Well, I shan't wake you in the morning till you ring. Just one tinkle will be enough. There's no need to turn it round as if you was playing a barrel organ, which is what the fellow who played the villain in *His Life for Her* did last November. He wound up all the wire somewhere inside the wall. A nice set out we had, and then he grumbled because I charged him in the bill for the work the plumber did to get it right again. Well, good night, and a merry Christmas."

When the sound of Mrs. Pottage's hoarse whispering had departed, the little candlelit room glowed in the solemn hush of the great white world, of which it seemed to be the warm and beating heart. Mother and father bent low over the cot and listened to the faint breathing of Letizia, watching lovingly those dark tangled curls and red-rose cheeks. The father bent lower to touch them with his lips.

"No, no, don't kiss her, boy," said the mother. "You might wake her, and she'll be having such an exciting day to-morrow."

Nancy blew out the candle on the table by the bed, and slipped her silver key beneath Bram's pillow. A shaft of moonlight pierced the drawn curtains and struck the canopy of Letizia's cot. The radiance vanished as gathering snow-clouds obscured the face of the moon. Nancy fell asleep to the sound of Bram's watch carrying on a fairy conversation amid the echoes of Mrs. Pottage's absurd stories.

CHAPTER IX

The snowy air had painted the ceiling of the room a lurid grey when Letizia woke her father and mother next morning. She was standing up in her cot, holding the footrails of the big bed with one hand and waving the toy dog in the other.

"Look, muvver, look at my dog? I've got a dog, muvver! Look, faver, I've got a dog! Look, I say! Look, look!"

Her parents had just focussed their sleepy eyes on the dog when it was flung on the floor, and the monkey was being waved in its place.

"Look, muvver, I've got a monkey! And he's climbing up and down. Look, faver, look at my monkey. Oh, do look!"

The monkey's triumph was brief, his degradation swift. The fickle mob had found another favourite.

"Oh, muvver, look at my baa-lamb. I've got a little baa-lamb, faver. Look at my pretty little woolly baa-lamb, faver," she shouted imperiously.

But the lamb immediately followed his colleagues to the floor.

"And I've got a rub-a-dub-dub and a wheedle-wheedle and an apple and an orange. And I saw Santy Claus come down the chiminy, and had a most anormous beard you ever saw and he said, 'How d'ye do, Tizia, will you give me a nice kiss?' And I said, 'Yes,' and he gived me a kiss, and he put fousands and fousands of lovely fings into my stocking. Wasn't Mrs. Porridge kind to give me her stocking because it was so anormous? And please can I

110

come and get into bed with you and bring my trumpet?"

"Come along, darling," invited Nancy, holding out her arms.

Letizia climbed very cautiously out of her cot and was lifted up on the bed and deposited between her father and mother, where she sat and blew her trumpet without a stop until her father picked up his pillow and pretended to smother her.

"Hullo," Bram exclaimed, looking at the little box which was thus uncovered. "Here's something of mother's under father's pillow."

Nancy smiled and shook her head.

"No, boy, that's yours."

Bram smiled and shook his head.

"No, it's yours. I put it under your pillow last night."

"But, Bram, I put it under yours."

By this time Letizia had disentangled herself from the pillow and was sounding another tucket, so that she had to be smothered all over again with Nancy's pillow. And there was revealed another little box exactly like the first.

"Open it, muvver. Oh, do open it!" Letizia urged. "Perhaps there's choc-chocs inside."

"Strange," Bram exclaimed. "What's inside mine, I wonder?"

Nancy and he opened the two boxes. In each one was a silver key.

"Bram!"

"Nancy!"

"This is the key of my heart. Keep it always, my darling," he read in an awed voice.

"With this key you unlocked my heart," she read in equal awe.

They wished each other a merry Christmas, and with their eyes they vowed eternal love, those unlocked hearts too full for words, while Letizia blew such a resounding alarum on her trumpet that she fetched up Mrs. Pottage.

"Well now, fancy that! I heard her right downstairs in the kitchen. Well, it's real Christmas weather, and no mistake. Good morning, my beauty, and how are you?"

This to Letizia.

"Mrs. Porridge, Santy Claus brought me a dog and a lamb and a monkey and a rub-a-dub-dub and a wheedle-wheedle and a trumpet and a book and an orange and an apple and some sweeties and fousands of fings. And he came down the chiminy, and I wasn't a bit frightened."

Mrs. Pottage shook her head in delighted admiration.

"Did he come down head first or feet first?"

"Bofe," Letizia declared, after a moment's pause.

"You can't catch her out, can you? Why, she's as cunning as King Pharaoh," Mrs. Pottage chuckled, and with this she departed to fetch the morning tea.

Nancy was suddenly seized with a desire to go to Mass and take Letizia.

"I'll come too," Bram volunteered. "Now, don't discourage me."

It was true that Nancy always was inclined to discourage him from taking an interest in her religion. Not that she took such a very profound interest in it herself, to tell the truth. But she had a dread of people's saying that she had forced her husband to become a Catholic. He did at intervals bring up the subject of being received; but there never seemed to be time to take any steps in the matter when they were on tour, and when they were resting it seemed a pity to worry their heads about religion. However, that morning Nancy did not discourage Bram from accompanying her and Letizia to Mass.

Letizia was very full of her visit to the Crib, when she saw Mrs. Pottage again.

"And I saw the baby Jesus in his nightygown, Mrs. Porridge."

"You did?"

"Yes, and He was lying on His back and kicking His legs up in the air ever so high. And there was a moo-cow smelling Him."

"No, darling," her mother interrupted, "the moo-cow was praying to Him."

"Well, he was smelling Him too."

"You'd have to start walking the week before last to get in front of her," said Mrs. Pottage.

There was a letter from Nancy's father to greet with seasonable wishes, her and hers, and as a kind of Christmas present there was an extra flourish to his already florid signature. He had been engaged to play Sir Lucius O'Trigger in a production of *The Rivals* at a West End theatre, and he felt sure that this meant finally abandoning the provinces for London. There was, too, a letter from old Mrs. Fuller written by her companion.

> Lebanon House
> Brigham.
> Dec. 23rd, 1894.

Dear Bram,

I can no longer hold a pen, even to wish you a merry Christmas and a fortunate New Year, and as much to your Nancy and that unhappily named Letizia. Although I am indecently old—eighty-two—I ought still to be able to write, but I've had a slight stroke and I who once died to live now only live to die.

> Your loving
> Grandmother.

Besides these two letters there were a few cards from friends, but not many, for it is difficult to keep up with people's whereabouts on tour.

The Christmas dinner was entirely a small family affair, but only the more intensely enjoyed for that very reason. Mrs. Pottage was invited in to dessert, and also Mrs. Pottage's assistant, a crippled girl, who was imported to help in the household work on occasions of ceremony. Quite what help Agatha Wilkinson was no one ever discovered, for she could only move with extreme slowness and difficulty on a pair of crutches. Perhaps her utility lay in being able to sit quietly in a corner of the kitchen and listen to Mrs. Pottage's conversation, which increased in volubility, the more she had to do. There was a pineapple on the table, a slice of which the landlady emphatically declined.

"No, thanks, not for me. That's a thing I only eat from the tin. Raw, I'd sooner eat a pinecomb any day. Would you like to try a slice, Aggie?"

Agatha was too shy to refuse when Bram put a slice on her plate, and Mrs. Pottage watched with obvious gratification her fearful attempts to manipulate it.

"Ah, I thought she wouldn't like it. You needn't eat any more, Aggie, if it puts your teeth on the edge. Yes, it's my opinion if pineapples cost twopence apiece instead of ten shillings people might buy a few just to throw at strange cats. To scrape your boots on? Yes. To eat? No. That's my opinion about pineapples."

In the evening, when Letizia had been put to bed after a number of uproarious games in which Bram had surpassed even his own wonderful record as an animal impersonator, Mrs. Pottage came in as magnificent as a queen-dowager in black satin to ask if her lodgers would give her the pleasure of their company in the parlour.

"I've got a few friends coming in to celebrate Christmas. Mrs. Bugbird's here, and two of my unintendeds—Mr. Hopkins, the chandler—well, I thought I'd ask him, though he's no more addition to anything than a nought, which is what he looks like—and then there's Mr. Watcher. Yes, Watcher's a good name for him, for he watches me like a dog watches a bone. He and Mr. Hopkins can't bear the sight of one another. Well, I daresay there's a bit of jealousy in it, if it comes to that, just because I happened to refuse him before I refused Hopkins. His business is coal. Sells it, I mean. I don't think even Watcher would have had the nerve to propose to me if he'd have actually been a coalman. Oh, dear, oh, dear, who does marry coalmen, that's what I ask myself. Or sweeps, if it comes to that? And then there's Mr. and Mrs. Breadcutt, who's an inspector of nuisances for the London County Council. So, if you'll come in and join us, we shall be a very nice merry little party."

Though they were feeling rather tired, Bram and Nancy accepted the invitation, because Mrs. Pottage had been so kind to them and they knew she would be terribly disappointed if they refused. However, they stipulated that she must not persuade them to stay very late on account of the matinée, to which, they reminded her, she had promised to take Letizia to-morrow.

"Oh, I hadn't forgotten. In fact, I thoroughly enjoy a good pantomime. It's a pity Mrs. Bugbird's got to go and see her relations over in Putney, because that woman so loves a bit of fun and always laughs so hearty that she'd make any panto a success just by being there."

Mrs. Bugbird, who was in the parlour when Bram and Nancy walked downstairs, was built on an altogether larger scale than Mrs. Pottage. The latter was plump and for her age still remarkably buxom; but she was not noticeably too fat. On the other hand, Mrs. Bugbird's immense face crowned a really massive campanulate base. When she laughed, which was practically all the time, her little eyes kept bubbling up out of her cheeks and then apparently bursting as they were once more swallowed up by the rolls of fat. This likeness to bursting bubbles was accentuated by the drops of moisture that during her spasms of mirth kept trickling down Mrs. Bugbird's cheeks, so that she had from time to time to wipe them away with an extensive red silk handkerchief on which was printed in bright yellow a view of the Pool of London.

A feature of Mrs. Pottage's best parlour was one of those Victorian triple chairs, two of which were occupied by Mr. Hopkins and Mr. Watcher. This meant that they were practically sitting back to back, an attitude which did nothing to allay the rumour of their mutual lack of esteem. Sitting thus, with their polished bald heads, they looked like two boiled eggs in a china stand. No doubt, Mrs. Bugbird had perceived this ridiculous resemblance, for every time she threw a glance in the direction of the two rivals her eyes bubbled in and out with the rapidity of soda-water. The outward appearance of Mr. Breadcutt, the inspector of nuisances, bore no signs of his profession; indeed he looked as tolerant and as genial a man as one might expect to meet in a month. Perhaps the nuisances were ferreted out by Mrs. Breadcutt, an angular woman with a pair of intelligent, pink-rimmed eyes, who sat up on the edge of her chair like an attentive bull-terrier. The party was completed by Agatha Wilkinson.

"Well, now we're all here, what game shall we play?" Mrs. Pottage asked expansively.

"Kiss in the ring," Mr. Breadcutt suggested without a moment's hesitation. Whereupon Mr. Hopkins and Mr. Watcher both scowled, the one at the ceiling, the other at the floor, while Mrs. Bugbird rocked backward and forward in a convulsion of irrepressible mirth.

"George," said Mrs. Breadcutt sharply.

"Yes, my dear?"

"Behave yourself, even if it is Christmas. You ought to know better at your age than suggest such a game in a little room like this."

"That's just why I did suggest it," Mr. Breadcutt retorted. "I'd have a chance of catching Mrs. Pottage and helping myself to a good one."

Mr. Hopkins and Mr. Watcher turned simultaneously at this outrageous admission to glare at the inspector of nuisances. Unfortunately Mr. Hopkins turned his head to the left and Mr. Watcher turned his head to the right, so that their eyes met, and instead of glaring at Mr. Breadcutt they glared at each other.

"Well, I'm going to call on Mr. Fuller for a song," said Mrs. Pottage. She apologised later for thus dragging him into a performance on his night off. "But really," she said, "I thought Hopkins and Watcher was going to fly at one another. They looked like a couple of boxing kangaroos."

Bram obliged the flattered company with two or three

songs which Nancy accompanied on the ancient piano, the noise of which was the occasion of another apology by the hostess.

"More like teeth clicking than music, isn't it? Well, it hasn't really been used since the year dot excepting for a bookcase. It belonged to my dear old dad, and he only bought it to cover up a spot in the wall where the roof leaked. He couldn't bear music, the dear old man. When he was over seventy, he nearly got fined for squirting a syringe full of the stuff he washed his greenhouse with into the big end of a cornet and which a blind man was playing outside his house. Of course, as he explained, he wasn't to know the pore fellow was blind or he'd have spoke before he spouted. But *I'm* very fond of music, I am."

And to prove her sincerity Mrs. Pottage sang *Two Lovely Black Eyes,* a performance which so utterly convulsed Mrs. Bugbird that she fell off her chair, and sat undulating on the floor for nearly five minutes, until the united efforts of the male guests got her back again, when in order to deal with the moisture induced by such excess of mirth, she had to produce her reserve handkerchief, on which was printed a gruesome picture of the execution of Mr. and Mrs. Manning.

Then Nancy sang to Bram's accompaniment, after which Bram gave imitations of familiar animals to the intense pleasure of Mr. Breadcutt, who slapped his leg and declared he was a blooming marvel.

"George!" snapped his wife.

"Yes, my dear?"

"Don't swear!"

"Blooming isn't swearing."

"It's as near as not to be worth an argument," she said severely.

This caused Mr. Breadcutt to wink at Mr. Watcher, who thought he was winking at Mrs. Pottage and did not respond.

Then Mr. Hopkins tried to remember for the benefit

of the company what he assured everybody was a capital game that he often used to play at social gatherings twenty years ago.

"We all sit round in a circle," he began in a doleful voice. "Wait a minute, what do you do next? Oh, yes," he went on, as soon as he was sure that Mr. Watcher had been successfully isolated from Mrs. Pottage. "Now we all join hands." Perhaps the emotion of finding her plump hand firmly imprisoned in his own was too much for the ship-chandler, for he could not remember what was the next move. "Wait a minute," he implored, holding Mrs. Pottage's hand tighter than ever. "Don't move, and I'll remember in a jiffy. Oh, yes, I've got it! I knew I would! Somebody has to be in the middle of the circle. Mr. Watcher, perhaps you'd stand in the middle, will you?"

"Hadn't you better stand in the middle yourself?" the coal-merchant replied. "You thought of this game. We aren't guilty."

"Don't be so gruff, Watcher," said Mrs. Pottage sternly. "You've been sitting like a skelington at the feast ever since you arrived. Wake up and be a man, do."

Thus adjured Mr. Watcher unwillingly stood up in the middle of the circle.

"What's he do now, Hopkins?" Mrs. Pottage asked.

"I'm trying to remember. Oh, yes, of course, I know. I know. I know! He's blindfolded," Mr. Hopkins exclaimed in a tone as near to being cock-a-whoop as his low-pitched funereal voice could achieve.

"Mrs. B., you've got a nice big handkerchief. Tie Watcher up, there's a good soul," the hostess ordered.

Mrs. Bugbird in a gurgle of suppressed laughter muffled the coal-merchant's disagreeable countenance with her reserve handkerchief, from which his bald head emerged like one of those costly Easter eggs that repose on silk in the centre of confectioners' shops.

"Now what does he do, Hopkins?"

"Just a minute, Mrs. Pottage. I'm stuck again. No,

I'm not. I remember perfectly now. Turn him round three times."

This was done, and there was another pause.

"Well, what next?" everybody asked impatiently.

"That's just what I'm bothered if I can remember," said the chandler at last. "It's on the tip of my tongue too . . . but wait . . . yes, no . . . yes, I've got it . . . he asks . . . no, that's wrong, *he* doesn't ask anything, we ask *him* . . . Now what the juice is it we do ask him? . . . Don't say anything, because I'll remember in a minute . . . I'm bound to remember . . . You see, it's such a long time since I played this game that some of the rules . . ."

"Look here," Mr. Watcher's irate voice growled through the folds of the handkerchief, "if you think I'm going to stand here wrapped up like a Stilton cheese while you remember what game you played with Nore in the Ark, you're blooming well mistaken. And that's that."

"If you'd only have a morsel of patience, Mr. Watcher. I can't remember the whole of a big game all at once," protested the chandler, still clinging desperately to Mrs. Pottage's hand. "But I will remember it. It's on the tip of my tongue, I tell you."

"Well, what's on the tip of my tongue to tell you," shouted Mr. Watcher, "I wouldn't like to tell anybody, not in front of ladies." With which he pulled down the handkerchief round his neck and stood glaring at the other players with the expression of a fierce cowboy.

Mr. Breadcutt in order to quiet the coal-merchant proposed as a game familiar to everybody blind man's buff.

"Not me you don't blindfold again," said Mr. Watcher. "And if Mr. Hopkins starts in to try I'll blindfold him without a handkerchief."

"Well, what about a snack of supper?" suggested the hostess, who felt that the situation required a diversion.

And her supper was such a success that before it was over the two rivals were confiding in each other various

ways of getting the better of their common enemy, the
purchaser.

When it was time to adjourn again to the parlour, Bram
and Nancy begged to be excused from enjoying themselves any longer in Mrs. Pottage's company in view of
the hard day before them at the Theatre Royal.

"You've given us such a jolly Christmas, dear Mrs.
Pottage," said Bram.

"A lovely Christmas," Nancy echoed.

"Well, I'm sure I've enjoyed *my*self, and Mrs. Bugbird said she's never laughed so much in all her life as
what she did when Mr. Fuller was imitating them animals. 'Lifelike,' she said they was, and she spent her
girlhood on a farm, so that's a bit of a compliment coming
from her. Well, good night. Oh, dear, oh, dear, before
we know where we are we shall be seeing in the New
Year. I'm bound to say, what with one thing and another
life's full of fun."

CHAPTER X

THE PANTOMIME

"Now listen, Letizia, you're to be a very good little girl and do anything that Mrs. Pottage tells you without arguing," Nancy admonished her small daughter before she left Starboard Alley next morning to dress for the matinée.

"Can I take my lamb what Santy Claus gave me to the pantomine?"

"Yes, I daresay Mrs. Pottage will let you."

"And my dog? And my monkey? And my rub-a-dub-dub and my wheedle-wheedle and my . . ."

"No, darling, you can take the lamb, but the others must stay at home."

"I aspeck they'll cry," Letizia prophesied solemnly. "Because they guessed they was going to the pantomine."

"If she isn't a regular masterpiece," the landlady exclaimed. "Oh, dear, oh, dear! She's got an answer for every blessed thing. Listen, my beauty, we'll leave the rest of the menargerie to keep John company."

John was the canary, and fortunately this solution commended itself to Letizia, who seemed more hopeful for the happiness of the toys that were going to be left behind.

There is no doubt that the presence of Mrs. Pottage and Letizia contributed largely to the success of the Theatre Royal pantomime that afternoon. No false shame deterred Letizia from making it quite clear to the audience that it was her own mother who bearded the Demon King Rat in his sulphurous abode.

"Stop, ere you any viler magic potions brew,
For I declare such wickedness you soon shall rue."

"Muvver!" cried Letizia, clapping her hands in an ecstasy of welcome.

"Ush!" said a solemn and deeply interested woman sitting in the row behind.

"It *is* my muvver, I tell you," said Letizia, standing up on the seat of the stall and turning round indignantly to address the woman over the back of it.

"Of course, it's her mother," Mrs. Pottage joined in even more indignantly. "Nice thing if a child can't call out 'mother' in a free country without being hushed as if she was nobody's child."

The solemn woman took an orange out of a bag and sucked it in silent disapproval.

> "No use for you to raise the least objection,
>   Dick Whittington is under my protection,"

declared the Fairy Queen, waving her wand to the accompaniment of a white spot-light.

> "In vain you seek to make my plans miscarry,
>   For Dick his master's daughter shall not marry,"

declared the Demon King Rat, waving his sceptre to the accompaniment of a red spot-light.

"That man's bad," Letizia announced gravely.

If the traditional scene of alternate defiance of each other by the powers of Good and Evil had lasted much longer, she might have made an attempt to reach the stage and fight at her mother's side; but the Demon King Rat vanished down a trap and the Fairy Queen hurried off Left to make way for Cheapside.

"Why has faver got a red nose?" Letizia inquired, when Bram entered made up for Idle Jack. "I don't like him to have a red nose. My lamb what Santy Claus gave me doesn't like him to have a red nose."

Whereupon Letizia climbed up on the seat of the stall once more and turned her back on the stage in disgust.

"Would you mind telling your little girl to kindly sit

down," the solemn and deeply interested woman behind requested of Mrs. Pottage.

"This is my lamb what Santy Claus gave me," Letizia informed the solemn woman in her most engaging voice, at which the solemn woman turned to her neighbour and declared angrily that children oughtn't to be allowed into pantomimes if they couldn't behave theirselves a bit more civilised.

"Get down, duckie, there's a love," said Mrs. Pottage, who in spite of her contempt for the solemn woman could not but feel that she had some reason to complain.

"Well, I don't want to see faver with that red nose," objected Letizia, who thereupon sat down in her stall, but held her hands in front of her eyes to shut out the unpleasant aspect of her father in his comic disguise. However, Idle Jack did so many funny things that at last his daughter's heart was won, so that presently she and Mrs. Pottage were leading the laughter of the house.

Finally when Idle Jack emptied a bag of flour on the Dame, Letizia was seized by such a rapture of appreciation that she flung her lamb into the orchestra and hit the first violin on the head.

"Faver," she shouted. "I've frowed my lamb what Santy Claus gave me, and the wheedle-wheedle in the band has tooked him somewhere."

Bram came down to the footlights and shook his fist at his small daughter, an intimate touch that drove the house frantic with delight and caused the solemn woman to observe to her neighbour that she didn't know who did come to the theatre nowadays, such a common lot of people as they always seemed to be.

One of the features of pantomimes about this period was the introduction of a sentimental song, usually allotted to the Fairy Queen as having some pretensions to a voice, in the course of which a boy of about twelve, chosen no doubt from the local church or chapel choir, rose from his seat in the front row of the circle and an-

swered the singer on the stage, to the extreme delectation
of the audience.

The refrain of the song this year went:

> Sweet Suzanne,
> I'll be your young man,
> They've never made your equal
> Since the world began.
> Won't you take my name?
> For my heart's aflame
> For love of you,
> My pretty Sue,
> My sweet Suzanne.

and again:

> Your lips are red as rubies,
> Your eyes are diamonds rare,
> So while I have you,
> My lovely Sue,
> I'm as rich as a millionaire.

Why the Fairy Queen should suddenly enter and break
into this drivelling song was an unanswerable enigma,
and why a little boy in an Eton suit with a very white
collar and a very pink face should rise from the front
row of the circle and sing each verse over again, while
the Fairy Queen walked backward and forward with
one hand held to her apparently entranced ear, was an
equally unanswerable enigma.

At any rate Letizia thoroughly disapproved of the
anomaly. While all the women in the pit and gallery and
stalls and circle were exclaiming:

"Oh, isn't he a little love? Well, I declare, if he isn't
reelly lovely. Oh, do listen to the little angel," Letizia
was frowning. Then with great deliberation, unobserved
by Mrs. Pottage, who was languishing upon the sibilant
cockney of this detestable young treble, she stood up on
the seat and shouted:

"Muvver!"

The Fairy Queen, while still holding one hand to an entranced ear, shook her wand at her little mortal daughter. But Letizia was not to be deterred from the problem that was puzzling her sense of fitness.

"Muvver!" she shouted again.   *Why* is that boy?"

Then Mrs. Pottage woke from the trance into which the duet had flung her and pulled Letizia down again into a sitting posture.

"Duckie, you mustn't call out and spoil the lovely singing."

"I don't like that boy," said Letizia firmly.

"Yes, but listen."

"And my lamb what Santy Claus gave me doesn't like him."

"Hush, duckie, hush!"

"And I won't listen.   And I won't look, Mrs. Porridge."

"Come, come, be a good girl."

But Letizia struggled out of Mrs. Pottage's arms and retreated under the seat of the stall from which she did not emerge until this enigmatic interlude in the life of the Fairy Queen came to an end amid a tumult of applause from the profoundly moved audience.

Letizia failed to recognise her father when he came rushing on for the Harlequinade at the end of the Transformation Scene with the time-honoured greeting of "Here we are again!"   And when Mrs. Pottage told her who the clown was, she merely shook her head violently and reiterated "No, no, no, no, no!"

However, the Harlequinade itself thoroughly amused her, although she did not approve of the Harlequin's dance with her mother the Columbine.

"Who is that spotted man?" she asked.   "Why does he frow muvver up like that?   I don't like him.   I don't like his black face.   I won't let him frow up my lamb what Santy Claus gave me."

"Well, you threw it up yourself just now and hit the poor fiddle."

"Yes," Letizia acknowledged in a tone of plump contentment.

The Harlequinade came to an end with a wonderful trap-act, in which the Clown was pursued by the Policeman head first through one shop window, head first out through another, up a long flight of stairs that turned into planks just as they both reached the top, so that they both rolled down to the bottom and disappeared into a cellar. Out again and diving through more windows, whirling round doors without hinges, climbing over roofs, sliding down chimneys, until at last the Policeman's pursuit was shaken off and the Clown, after bounding up ten feet into the air through a star-trap, alighted safely on the stage whence, after snatching a basket that was hanging up outside a shop window, he began to pelt the audience with crackers while the orchestra stood up to play *God Save the Queen* and the curtain slowly descended on a great success at the Theatre Royal, Greenwich.

CHAPTER XI

THE END OF THE HARLEQUINADE

"I don't think you *were* a very good little girl," said Nancy reproachfully to her daughter when she was brought round to the dressing-room by Mrs. Pottage after the matinée.

"Yes, yes, yes, yes, yes," averred Letizia entirely impenitent. "My lamb what Santy Claus gave me saided I was a very good little girl. He saided 'Oh, Tizia, you *is* a good little girl!' "

The landlady beamed.

"There's one thing, she thoroughly enjoyed her little self, and so did I, I'm bound to say, even if we *was* a bit noisy."

"I'm afraid Letizia was very noisy indeed."

"Yes, but nobody minded two penn'orth of gin except a dismal-faced widow-woman sitting just behind us, and she'd had more than two penn'orth before ever she come out which is my opinion."

"My husband and I won't have time to dress and come home between the shows," said Nancy. "We're having some dinner sent in to us here. The curtain goes up again at seven, and it's nearly six now."

There was a tap on the door, and Bram, still in his clown's dress but without the tufted wig, peeped round the corner.

"Well, you're a nice one," he said to his daughter. "I nearly sent the policeman down to you."

"*Was* you that white man with a funny face?" Letizia asked incredulously.

"There you are, I told you it was your dadda," Mrs. Pottage put in.

"Yes," said Letizia, and in the tone of the affirmation a desire to admit frankly that she had been wrong was mingled with a slight resentment that Mrs. Pottage should have been right.

When Letizia had departed with the landlady, Bram and Nancy joined several other members of the company at a picnic meal. The talk was mostly of the pantomime, of how this song had gone and how that joke had got across, of whether it would not be wiser to cut this scene out altogether and shorten that one.

"Of course it'll play closer to-night," said one of the company. "And they'll be a little quicker with the changes. Or it's to be hoped they will."

"That limelight man is a bit of a jay," said the Demon King gloomily. "Would he follow me with that spot? Not he. And when I was singing my song, the fool was jigging it all over the stage like a damned rocket. His mate was better with you, Miss O'Finn."

"He was on me all right," Nancy allowed. "But he ruined the last verse of my first song by letting it fizz till I could have knocked him off his perch with my wand."

"I think our trap-act went great, old boy," said the Policeman to the Clown. "I've never known a trap-act go so smooth the first time. The house was eating it."

Bram nodded.

"Yes, it went all right," he admitted without enthusiasm. "But that star didn't seem to me to be working properly again. Which reminds me, I must get hold of Worsley and tell him to have a look at it."

"Who wants Worsley?" inquired the stage-manager, coming into the dressing-room at that moment.

"It was about that star-trap, old man," said Bram.

"Now, that's all right, old chap. Don't you worry. I've been down under the stage, and it's working to rights now. Lovely."

"I thought I wasn't coming through this afternoon," Bram grumbled.

"Why, you came up like a bird," Worsley assured him. "What are you talking about?"

"Yes, I know I *did* come up," Bram replied irritably, for he was feeling thoroughly tired. "But it did stick for a second or two, and you know what it would mean if I got caught."

"Oh, Mr. Worsley," Nancy exclaimed in a panic, "for God's sake see it's all right to-night."

"Now, don't you worry yourself, Miss O'Finn," the stage-manager begged. "Good Lord, you don't suppose *I* want to have an accident?"

"I wish you'd speak to that blasted limelight man about getting his red spot on me," said the Demon King. "He ruined every entrance I've got—and I haven't got too many."

The stage-manager decided that he should be happier elsewhere, and left the assembled diners.

"Have a drink, old man," somebody called after him. But Mr. Worsley suspected a *quid pro quo* and shouted back:

"Haven't time now, old man. I'll join you after the evening show. I've got to see the property man."

And they heard his voice go shouting along the corridors.

"Props! Props! Where the deuce is Props?"

"Poor old Mangel Worsley," said the Demon King, with a gloomy shake of the head. "He never ought to have gone in for panto. He's not up to it. He'd have done better to stick to Shakespeare. I saw his production of *Macbeth* for Wilson Forbes. Very pretty little show it was, too. Very pretty. But this sort of thing is too big for him altogether. He can't grasp the detail. Result? My entrances go for nothing. For absolutely nothing! It stands to reason, if a red spot-light's thrown Right Centre when I come on Down Stage Left it kills me dead. But that doesn't trouble Worsley, because he doesn't realise the importance of ensemble. He niggles, and it's a pity, because within limits he's quite a good stage-manager."

How full the Theatre Royal was that Boxing Night! And Morton's Theatre, the rival house, was just as full. People went to the pantomime even in days as near to us as the early nineties. They could not amuse themselves then by sporting with Amaryllis in the shade of a picture-palace while black-eyed heroes dreamed in profile during two hours of a monotonous reel or black-lipped heroines smeared their cheeks with vaseline and, intolerably magnified, blubbered silently at an unresponsive audience. The audience of the Theatre Royal that night was there to enjoy the performance, even though it lasted from seven o'clock till midnight. People went to the theatre in those days to see and to hear, to love and to hate. They were not sitting jam-packed in that reek of oranges and dust for the sake of cuddling one another. Nobody dressed up like a fireman came and squirted antiseptic perfumes over them. The odor of its own wedged-in humanity was grateful, an entity that breathed, cheered, laughed, and wept as one. The Grand, Islington, the Britannia, Hoxton, the Standard, Shoreditch, the transpontine Surrey, yes, and in those days Old Drury itself still defiant of change—all these theatres held people, not fidgety shadows gazing with lack-lustre eyes at a representation of fidgety shadows.

In spite of their fatigue the company played *Dick Whittington* that night at Greenwich with treble the vigour of the afternoon performance. Everything went better, in spite of the absence of Mrs. Pottage and Letizia. Even the limelight men managed to keep their beams steadily fixed on the object of their enhancement whencesoever he might enter, whithersoever he might move, wheresoever he might stand. The billows of the Demon King's bass rolled along twice as majestically. Nancy's song with the overwashed chorister in the circle earned a double encore. Principal boy, principal girl, dame, knockabout comedians, all gained the good-will of the house. But *the* success was Bram. After his first scene Idle Jack had only to appear on the stage to send the audience into a roar. The tritest line of dialogue was received as heavenly wit. The stalest piece of fooling was welcomed in a rapture.

"Darling, you are being so funny to-night," Nancy told him, when for a moment they found themselves side by side in the wings.

"I don't feel at all funny," Bram said. "In fact, it's because I'm feeling so tired and depressed off, I suppose, that I'm trying to cheer up by being extra funny on."

He squeezed her hand, and a moment later she heard the deep-voiced laughter of the house greeting another of his entrances.

Bram's success as Idle Jack that night was consolidated by his Joey. He was not just the traditional clown with wide red mouth, bending low in exaggerated laughter and treading always on hot bricks. There was something of the Pierrot in his performance. Not that he scorned tradition overmuch. The whole audience recognised him as the authentic Joey of their imagination; but he did contrive to be somehow the incarnate spirit of that London street much more essentially than the heavy-footed Harlequin, much more essentially than Columbine, whose short pink tarlatan skirt did not become Nancy's height, though she pirouetted on and off the stage gracefully enough. Pantaloon, too, was good, and the actor did manage to represent that hoary-headed ancient Londoner in his absurd Venetian disguise. But Bram was the ghost of old London itself—a London that was fast dying, though here in Greenwich it might seem to be as full of vitality as ever. It was the London of sweet lavender and cherry ripe, the London of hot cockles, of Punch and Judy shows and four-wheelers and lumbering knife-board omnibuses, of gas-lamps and queer beggars. Bram's incarnation of this vanishing city had that authentic whimsicality (the very term is nearly unintelligible now) of old cockney humour, an urban Puckishness as if for a while Robin

Goodfellow had tried to keep pace with the times and live in great cities. He made his audience feel that sausages were only strung together because it was more amusing to steal a string than a single sausage. His red-hot poker itself glowed with such a geniality of warmth as made the audience feel that everybody to whose seat it was applied was being slapped on the back in the spirit of the purest good-fellowship.

Nancy had flitted for the last time across that most fantastic yet so utterly ordinary street; and she paused in the wings for a moment, before going up to her dressing-room, to listen to the tumultuous laughter of the house at the great trap-act which was the climax of the Harlequinade. She saw Bram's white figure come diving through the shop window and safely caught by the scene-hands stationed on the other side. She saw the Policeman follow close upon his heels, and watched the pair of them chase each other round and round the revolving door. She heard the thunders of applause as the trick staircase shot the protagonists from top to bottom, and the still louder thunder when Bram appeared among the chimney-pots. Then she turned away and had just reached the door of her dressing-room when the corridors which had been echoing with the distant applause became suddenly still as death.

"I hope that husband of mine's not doing some particularly breakneck feat to thrill the Bank Holiday crowd," she said to the principal girl with whom she shared a room and who was by now nearly dressed. "What has happened?" Nancy repeated. This quiet was unnatural. A gust of overwhelming dread sent her hurrying back down the corridor, as she heard the agonised voice of Worsley crying:

"Ring down! Ring down! For the love of God, ring down!"

At the head of the stairs she met the Pantaloon, beardless, with startled eyes, who waved her back.

"Don't come down on the stage for a minute, Miss

O'Finn. There's been an accident. He was caught in the star-trap. The spring must have broken."

"Bram . . ."

He nodded, and burst into tears.

Nancy hurried past him toward the stage. Beyond the dropped curtain she could hear the murmur of the anxious and affrighted audience. Bram was lying beside the closed trap, the pointed sections of which were red.

"There isn't a doctor in the whole audience," Worsley was saying. "But several people have run to fetch one. How do you feel now, old man?"

Nancy pushed her way through the staring group, and knelt beside Bram, now unconscious, a bloody belt round his white dress, his head pillowed on the string of sausages.

"My precious one," she cried. "Oh, my precious one!"

His eyelids flickered at her voice, and his limp body quivered very faintly.

"A doctor will be here in a minute, Miss O'Finn," Worsley said.

"A doctor," she cried. "Damn you, damn you! A doctor! He told you the trap wasn't working properly. If he dies, it will be you that has killed him."

By now, several of the ladies of the company had joined the group round the prostrate clown.

"Hush, dear," said one of them, "don't say anything you may regret afterwards."

Nancy did not answer this pacific woman, but bent low over her husband.

"My precious one, my precious one."

The doctor came at last. When he had finished his examination, he shook his head.

"He is injured mortally."

"Dying?" Nancy whispered.

"He can hardly live many more minutes with these injuries. Has he any relations here?"

"I am his wife."

"My poor girl," said the doctor quickly. "I didn't realise that. But I couldn't have hidden the truth. He must lie here. He's unconscious. Even to move him to a dressing-room would probably kill him."

The group round the dying man moved away and left him alone with his wife and the doctor, on that silent bright unnatural stage.

"And is there nothing we can do?" she asked.

"Nothing, my poor girl. It is kinder to leave him unconscious and not try to revive him. He will suffer less."

But presently Bram's lips moved, and Nancy bending low to his mouth heard the dim voice speaking with a fearful effort.

"I'm dying—Nancy darling—I wish—I wish . . ."

The dim voice died away.

"Oh, my only love, my darling, what do you wish? Do you want to see Letizia?"

"No—no—better not—not kind for baby girls to see death—better not—better not—Mrs. Pottage very kind— kind and good—I wish—I wish . . ."

Again the dim voice was lost.

"What, my precious one? What do you wish?"

"Nancy—if things are difficult—we haven't saved much money—difficult—go to Caleb—too bitter about my people—too hard—faults on both sides—Nancy, kiss me once —quick—quick—I don't think I shall know soon if you kiss me. . . ."

She touched his cold lips with hers.

"Such a darling wife—always such a darling—very happy together—happy memories—your father's speech— yes, Caleb will look after you if things very difficult— give my love to grandmamma—always kind to me— happy memories—Nancy! Nancy! I wish—oh, my own Nancy, I do wish . . ."

The dim voice was lost in the great abyss of eternity that stretched beyond this fantastic ordinary street, beyond this silent bright unnatural stage.

"Sweetheart, what do you wish? What do you wish?"

But the Clown was dead.

CHAPTER XII

LOOKING FOR WORK

There was not much money left when the funeral expenses had been paid and Nancy had bought her mourning—those poor black suits of woe that in their utter inadequacy even to symbolise still less to express her grief seemed like an insult to the beloved dead. It was a desperate challenge to fortune to abandon the Greenwich engagement. But Nancy could not bring herself to the point of returning to the cast of the pantomime. That was beyond the compass of her emotional endurance. The management offered her a larger salary to play the Fairy Queen only, without appearing as Columbine; but she refused. The Employers' Liability Act did not exist at this date; and when the management suggested, as a reason for not paying her direct compensation, that the accident had already cost them dearly enough in the gloom it had shed over what promised to be a really successful production, Nancy's grief would not allow her even to comment on such a point of view. Bram was dead. People told her that she had a good case against the theatre. But Bram was dead. He was dead. He was dead. All she wanted was to leave Greenwich for ever, and when Mrs. Pottage offered her hospitality she refused.

"It's not pride, dear Mrs. Pottage, that prevents my staying on with you. You mustn't think that. It's simply that I could not bear to go on living alone where he and I lived together. I'm sure to find an engagement presently. I have enough money left to keep Letizia and myself for quite a little time."

"Well, don't let's lose sight of each other for good and all," said the landlady. "Let's meet some day and go

135

down to Margate together and have a nice sea blow. I've
got a friend down there—well, friend, I say, though she's
a relation really, but she is a friend for all that, a good
friend—well, this Sarah Williams has a very natty little
house looking out on the front, and we could spend a
nice time with her when she's not full up with lodgers.
I'd say 'come down now,' but Margate in January's a
bit like living in a house with the windows blown out
and the doors blown in and the roof blown off and the
walls blown down."

So, Nancy left Starboard Alley and went to live in
rooms in Soho, perhaps in the very same house where
more than a century ago Letizia's great-great-grand-
mother had been left with that cageful of love-birds and
the twenty pairs of silk stockings.

The houses in Blackboy Passage were flat-faced, thin,
and tall like the houses in Hogarth's "Night." At one end
an archway under the ancient tavern that gave its name
to the small and obscure thoroughfare led into Greek
Street. At the other end a row of inebriated posts for-
bade traffic to vehicles from Frith Street. The houses
had enjoyed a brief modishness in the middle of the
eighteenth century, but since then their tenants had gradually declined in quality while at the same time steadily
increasing in quantity. By this date nearly every one of
the tall houses had a perpendicular line of bells beside
its front door and a ladder of outlandish names. The
house in which Nancy found lodgings was an exception,
for all of it except the basement belonged to Miss Fewkes,
who was her landlady. Miss Fewkes was a dried-up little
woman of over fifty, with a long sharp nose, and raddled
cheeks so clumsily powdered as to give to her face the appearance of a sweet which has lost its freshness and been
dusted over with sugar. Incredible as it now might seem,
Miss Fewkes had had a past. She had actually been in
the Orient ballet once, and the mistress of several men,
each of whom was a step lower in the scale than his pred-
ecessor. From each of these temporary supporters she

had managed to extract various sums of money, the total of which she had invested in furnishing this house in Blackboy Passage, where for many years she had let lodgings to the profession. In spite of her paint and powder and past, Miss Fewkes wore an air of withered virginity, and appeared to possess little more human nature than one of her own lace antimacassars. Her thin prehensile fingers resembled the claws of a bird; her voice was as the sound of dead leaves blown along city pavements. Letizia disliked Miss Fewkes as much as she had liked Mrs. Pottage. Nor did Miss Fewkes like Letizia, whose presence in her lodgings she resented in the same way that she would have resented a pet dog's.

"I noticed your little girl's finger-marks on the bedroom-door this morning. Two black marks. Of course, as I explained to you, Miss O'Finn, I don't really care to have children in my rooms, but if I do take them in I rather expect that they won't make finger-marks. It's difficult enough to keep things clean in London, as I'm sure you'll understand."

Nancy would have left Miss Fewkes after a week if she had had to leave Letizia in her charge while she hung about in the outer offices of theatrical agents in Garrick Street and Maiden Lane. Fortunately, however, there were staying in the same house a Mr. and Mrs. Kino, who took a great fancy to Letizia and insisted on having as much of her company as they could obtain. Mr. Kino was the proprietor and trainer of a troup of performing elephants, which were then appearing at Hengler's Circus. Mrs. Kino, a large pink and yellow woman, had domestic ambitions and a longing for children of her own. Possibly her dependency on elephants had begotten in her a passion for diminutiveness. At any rate, until Letizia won her heart, she spent all her time in stringing beads for little purses. Even when she made friends with Letizia, the toys she always preferred to buy for her were minute china animals and Lilliputian dolls, for which she enjoyed making quantities of tiny dresses.

"Too large, duckie, much too large," was her comment when Letizia showed her the cargo of her Christmas stocking.

Miss Fewkes sniffed when she saw the china animals.

"Silly things to give a child," she said. "Next thing is she'll be swallowing them and have to be taken in a cab to the hospital, but, then, some people in this world go about looking for trouble and, when they get it, expect every one else to sympathise. Ugh! I've no patience with them, I haven't."

Nancy had found it impossible to persuade Letizia that she would never see her father again in this world.

"I aspeck he's only wented away," she insisted. "I aspeck he'll come back down the chiminy one night. My lamb what Santy Claus gave me saided he was perfickatally sure faver would come back down the chiminy one night. So, I fink we'd better leave the gas burning, don't you, because he wouldn't like to come back all in the dark, would he?"

Mrs. Kino was in the room when Letizia put forward this theory and with a dumpy hand she silently patted the black sleeve of Nancy, who had turned away to hide the tears.

Perhaps the kindest thing that fortune could have done for the young widow was to throw difficulties in the way of her obtaining an engagement. Had she found a "shop" immediately and gone out on tour alone after those happy years of joint engagements the poignancy of her solitude might have overwhelmed her. The battle for a livelihood kept her from brooding.

But it was a battle through that icy winter, with the little pile of sovereigns growing shorter and shorter every day and Nancy nearly starving herself that Letizia might lack nothing.

"Some people burn coal as if it was paper," Miss Fewkes sniffed. She did not know that every half-hundredweight meant no lunch for her lodger, and if she had, she would only have despised her for it.

"Nothing this morning, I'm afraid," the agent would say. "But something may be turning up next week. Two or three companies will be going out presently. Look in again, Miss O'Finn. I'm not forgetting you. You shall have a chance for the first suitable engagement on my books. Cold weather, isn't it? Wonderful how this frost holds. Good morning."

Down one long flight of draughty stone stairs in Garrick Street. Up another flight of tumbledown wooden stairs in Maiden Lane. Two hours' wait in an icy room with nothing to warm one but the flaming posters stuck on the walls.

"Ah, is that you, Miss O'Finn? I'm glad you looked in to-day. Mr. Howard Smythe is taking out *The New Dress*. Have you seen it? Capital little farce. There's a part that might suit you."

Any part would suit her, Nancy thought, for she was beginning to lose hope of ever being engaged again.

"Look in this afternoon, Miss O'Finn, round about three. Mr. Howard Smythe will be here then to interview a few ladies."

Down the long flight of tumbledown wooden stairs and out past the Adelphi stage-door into the Strand. What was the time? Half-past one. Mrs. Kino was taking Letizia to the circus. Not worth while to go home. She would find a tea-shop for lunch. A damp bun and a glass of London milk. A greasy marble table, and opposite a hungry-eyed clerk reading Gibbon's *Decline and Fall of the Roman Empire* while he eked out his bun and glass of milk. The waitress, who had nine warts on her fingers, flung down the skimpy bills with equal disdain for both these customers. Outside, the roar of the Strand on the iron-bound air. Inside, the rattle of plates and the harsh giggles of the waitresses. Outside, the grey frozen sky. Inside, leathery poached eggs and somebody arguing in a corner of the shop that he had ordered coffee.

"That is coffee," said the waitress, tossing her head.
"Is it? Well, I must have meant tea."

After lunch a walk along the Embankment to get warm.
Gulls screaming and quarrelling for the crusts that were
being flung to them. Wretched men and women freezing
on the benches. Plane-trees hung with their little black
balls that stirred not in this immotionable and icy air.
Back to Maiden Lane, and up the tumbledown wooden
stairs once more. Another endless wait in the cold ante-
room.

"Ah, good afternoon, Miss O'Finn. I'm sorry, but
Mr. Howard Smythe has filled up the vacancies in his
cast. But if you look in again next week, perhaps I
shall have something that will suit you."

"Anything will suit me," Nancy sighed.

"Ah, but you won't suit everything," the agent laughed.
"You're so tall, you know. The real tragedy queen, eh?
And managers do not want tragedy queens these days."

"Och, damn it, don't try to be funny," Nancy burst out.
"You know I'm not a tragedy queen."

"Sorry, I was only making a little joke."

"Well, after a month of agents in this weather one
loses one's sense of humour," Nancy replied.

At home Nancy found Letizia in a tremendous state
of excitement after her visit to the circus which had
concluded with an introduction to Mr. Kino's elephants.

"And I touched Jumbo's trunk, muvver, and it was all
hot. And he wagged his tail. And Mrs. Jumbo opened
her mouf as wide as that."

Here Letizia endeavoured to give an elephantine yawn
to illustrate her story.

"Yes, she took to my elephants," said Mr. Kino. "In
fact, I was nearly offering her an engagement to appear
with them."

Nancy laughed.

"No, I'm serious, Miss O'Finn. What do you say to
three pounds a week? And, of course, the missus and I
would look after the kid as if she was our own."

"Och, no, it's very sweet of you both, but I couldn't give her up like that."

"Arthur's joking about the performing part," Mrs. Kino put in. "He knows very well I wouldn't let her do any performing. But we would like to have her with us when we leave on Sunday week."

"You're leaving on Sunday week?" Nancy asked in alarm.

"Yes, we're going out on a long tour."

Nancy was terribly worried by the prospect of her fellow lodgers' departure. It would mean asking Miss Fewkes to look after Letizia while she was out. In her bedroom she counted over the money she had left. Only seven pounds, and out of that there would be this week's bill to pay. Things *were* getting desperate.

Until now Nancy had avoided meeting her father in London, because she felt that she could not bear the scene he would be sure to play over her widowhood. Her life with Bram was too real and wonderful for histrionics. But matters were now so serious that she could not afford to let her own intimate feelings stand in the way of getting work. Her father might be able to help her to an engagement. He might even be able to lend her a little money in case of absolute necessity.

So Nancy sent a note to the Piccadilly Theatre, where he was playing, and three days later she received an answer from an address in Earl's Court to say that owing to severe illness he had had to resign his part at the Piccadilly a week or two before. Would Nancy visit him, as he was still too unwell to go out?

"Mr. O'Finn?" repeated the slatternly girl who opened the door. "Can you see Mr. O'Finn? Who is it, please?"

"It's his daughter, Miss O'Finn."

The slatternly girl opened her eyes as wide as their sticky lids would let her.

"He's not expecting anybody this afternoon," she muttered.

"He may not be expecting anybody this afternoon,"

said Nancy sharply, "but his daughter is not exactly anybody. He has been ill and I want to see him."

The slatternly girl evidently felt incapable of dealing with this crisis, for she retreated to the head of the basement stairs, and called down:

"Mrs. Tebbitt, here's somebody wants to see Mr. O'Finn. Will you come up and talk to her, please?"

A sacklike woman with a flaccid red face and sparse hair excavated herself slowly from the basement.

"I understand my father has been very ill," Nancy began.

"Ill?" gurgled Mrs. Tebbitt breathlessly. "It's an illness a lot of people would like to die of. He's been on the drink for the last month. That's what he's been. He's drunk now, and in another hour or so he'll be blind drunk, because he's just sent out for another bottle of brandy. If you say you're his daughter and insist on seeing him, well, I suppose you'll have to, but his room's in a disgusting state and which is not my fault, for the last time the girl went up to give it a rout out he threw the dustpan out of the window and it hit a organist who was walking past—I know it was a organist, because he give me his card and said he'd lodge a complaint with the police, but we haven't heard nothing more since, but I've forbid the girl to touch his room again till he's sober, and which he won't be to-day, that's certain."

Nancy's heart was hardened against her father. In her present straits she could not feel that there was any kind of an excuse for behaviour like his.

"Thank you," she said coldly to the landlady. "Perhaps when he can understand what you're telling him you'll be kind enough to say that Miss O'Finn called to see him, but would not come up."

She turned away from the house in a cold rage.

In her bitterness she was tempted for a moment to accept the Kinos' offer to adopt Letizia and take her away with them on their tour. The worthlessness of her own father was extended in her thoughts to include all parents including herself. It would be better to abandon Letizia lest one day she might fail her as to-day her father had failed herself.

Then she saw Bram's whimsical face looking at her from the silver frame on her dressing-table, and she felt ashamed. She wondered again about that last unspoken wish of his. She had put out of her mind the idea of appealing to his brother to help in the guardianship of Letizia. But perhaps Bram had been really anxious that Letizia should heal the breach between them. Perhaps that had been his unspoken wish. He might have felt that she would be unwilling to ask a favour from his brother, and even with his dying breath have abstained from saying anything that she could construe into the solemnity of a last request, in case she should not like the idea of begging a favour from his relations. That would be Bram's way. Just a diffident hint, but nothing that could involve her too deeply.

That Monday evening Nancy paid Miss Fewkes her bill and stared at the few pounds that remained. Of course, she could carry on for a little while by pawning, but had she any right to imperil by such methods Letizia's well-being? Besides, now that the Kinos were going away, there was the problem of looking after Letizia during the day. At a pinch she could ask Mrs. Pottage to look after her for a week or two; but did not everything point to Brigham at this moment? Could she still have any pride after that account she had heard to-day of her father's degradation? No, her duty was clear. She would make one more round of the agents, and then if she was still without an engagement on Thursday, she would take Letizia to her husband's relations.

CHAPTER XIII

LEBANON HOUSE

Of all the great stations in the world Euston alone preserves in its Tartarian architecture the spirit in which the first railway travellers must have set out. So long as Euston endures, whatever improvements humanity may achieve in rapidity of travel and transport, we shall understand the apprehension and awe with which the original adventure must have filled the imagination of mankind. Mrs. Browning took to her bed in order to recover from the effects of a first view of Paddington Station; but Paddington is merely an overgrown conservatory set beside Euston, impressive in its way but entirely lacking in that capacity for permanently and intensely expressing the soul of an epoch, which makes Euston worthy of being mentioned in the same breath as St. Peter's, or the Pyramids of Gizeh, or even the sublime Parthenon itself. Not only does Euston express the plunge of humanity into a Plutonian era, a plunge more lamentable and swift than Persephone's from Enna in the dark chariot of Hades; but it peculiarly expresses within the lapse of a whole period the descent of the individual Londoner to the industrial Hell.

On an iron-bound day in early March the grimy portico of Euston might oppress the lightest heart with foreboding as, passing through to the eternal twilight of those cavernous and funereal entries, the fearful traveller embarks for the unimaginable North. The high platforms give the trains a weasel shape. The departure bell strikes upon the ear like a cracked Dies Iræ. The porters, in spite of their English kindliness, manage somehow to assume

144

the guise of infernal guardians, so that we tip them as we might propitiate old Charon with an obol or to Cerberus fling the drugged sop. St. Pancras and its High Anglican embellishments impress the observer as simply a Ruskinian attempt to make the best of both worlds. King's Cross is a mere result of that ugliness and utility of which Euston is the enshrinement. Paddington is an annexe of the Crystal palace. Victoria and Charing Cross are already infected with the fussiness and insignificance of Boulogne. Waterloo is a restless improvisation, Liverpool Street a hideous ant-heap. To get a picture of the spirits of damned Londoners passing for ever from their beloved city, one should wait on a frozen foggy midnight outside the portals of Euston.

Nancy may not have read Virgil, but her heart was heavy enough with foreboding when with Letizia, a tiny Red Riding Hood, she entered the train for Brigham on that iron-bound morning early in March. She wished now that she had waited for an answer to the letter announcing her visit. Visions of a severe man-servant shutting the door in her face haunted her. She tried to recall what Bram had told her about the details of his family life, but looking back now she could not recall that he had told her anything except his hatred of it all. And anyway, what could he have known of the present state of his family, apart from the sardonic commentary upon it in his grandmother's infrequent letters? It was twelve years since he had escaped from Lebanon House. His brother had been a boy of fourteen; his father was still alive then; his grandfather too; and that strange old grandmother, the prospect of meeting whom had kept Nancy from wavering in her resolution, was not bedridden in those days.

"Muvver," said Letizia, who had been looking out of the window at the Buckinghamshire fields, "I can count to fifteen. I counted fifteen moo-cows, and then I counted fifteen moo-cows again."

"You are getting on, aren't you?"

"Yes, I am, aren't I?" Letizia echoed, whereupon she burst into a chant of triumph, which caused an old gentleman in the opposite corner of the compartment to look up in some alarm over the top of his newspaper.

"Hush, darling, don't sing like that. You'll disturb the ladies and gentlemen who want to read."

"Why do they want to read?"

"To pass the time away."

"I would like to read, muvver."

Nancy produced her book.

"A cat sat on a mat. A fat rat sat on a mat," she proclaimed aloud.

"No, darling, if you're going to read you must read to yourself. The gentleman opposite isn't reading his paper aloud."

"Why isn't he?"

"Because it might worry other people and wouldn't be good manners."

"Is that gentleman good manners?"

"Of course, he has. Hush, darling, don't go on asking silly questions."

"When I make a rude noise with my mouf I put my hand up and say 'Pardon.'"

"Of course."

"Well, that gentleman maided lots and lots of very rude noises, and he didn't put his hand up to his mouf and say 'pardon.' Why didn't he, muvver?"

"Darling, please don't go on making remarks about people. It's not kind."

Letizia was dejected by this insinuation, and sat silent for a space. Then she cheered up:

"Muvver, if that gentleman makes a rude noise again, would it be kind for me to put up my hand to my mouf and say 'pardon'?"

Nancy thought that her daughter's present humour of critical observations augured ill for her success at Lebanon House, and she began to wish that she had left her behind in London.

"Listen, darling. I don't want you to be a horrid little girl and go on chattering when mother asks you to keep quiet. If you behave like this, your Uncle Caleb won't like you."

"If he doesn't like me, I won't like him," said Letizia confidently.

Nancy shook a reproachful head.

"Well, I shan't talk to you any more. In fact, I've a very good mind to leave you behind in the train when we get to Brigham."

"Where would I go?" Letizia asked, perfectly undismayed by this threat.

"I'm sure I don't know where you would go."

"I would ask a porter," Letizia suggested. "I would say, 'Please, Mr. Porter, where shall I go to?' and then he'd tell me, and I'd say, 'Oh, that's where I shall go, is it?'"

Suddenly a cloud passed across the mother's mind. It might be that to-morrow she would be travelling back through these same fields without her little girl. Ah, nothing that Letizia said could justify her in making mock threats of abandoning her in the train when in her heart was the intention of abandoning her in the house of that unknown brother-in-law. In swift contrition she picked Letizia up and kissed her.

"My sweetheart," she whispered.

Rugby was left behind, Lichfield in its frosty vale, the smoky skies of Crewe and Stafford. The country outraged by man's lust for gold writhed in monstrous contortions. About the refuse heaps of factories bands of children roamed as pariahs might, and along the squalid streets women in shawls wandered like drab and melancholy ghosts.

"Brigham, Brigham," cried the porters.

On the cold and dreary platform Letizia in her scarlet hood made the people turn round to stare at her as if she were a tropical bloom or some strange bird from the sweet South.

"Lebanon House?" the driver of the fly repeated in surprise. "Mr. Fuller's, do you mean, ma'am?"

And every time he whipped up the smoking horse his perplexity seemed to be writing on the grey air a note of interrogation.

Letizia drew a face on the mildewed window strap and another larger face on the window itself.

"Aren't you making your gloves rather messy, darling?" her mother enquired anxiously.

"I was droring," her daughter explained. "This teeny little face is Tizia." She pointed to the inscribed strap. "And this anormous big face is you." She indicated the window.

The horse must have been startled by the sound of Letizia's laughter which followed this statement, for it broke into a bony canter at the unwonted sound. A corpse chuckling inside a coffin would not have sounded so strange as the ripple of a child's laughter in this fly musty with the odour of old nose-bags and dank harness.

Looking out at the landscape, Nancy perceived a wilderness covered with sheds, some painted grey, some scarlet. A hoarding was inscribed in huge letters FULLER'S FIREWORKS. That must be the factory. Presently the fly began to climb a gradual slope between fields dotted with swings, giant-strides, and various gymnastic frames. Another hoarding proclaimed THE FULLER RECREATION PARK. Nancy did not think much of it. She did not know that Joshua Fuller might perhaps have swung himself into Parliament from one of those swings, had he only lived a little longer.

At the top of the slope the fly passed through a varnished gate, swept round a crackling semicircle of gravel between two clumps of frost-bitten shrubs, and pulled up before the heavy door of Lebanon House. Nancy looked in dismay at the grim stucco walls stained with their aqueous arabesques and green pagodas of damp. That the bright little form beside her could be left within those walls was beyond reason. Better far to flee this spot, and, whatever happened in London, rejoice that her baby was still with her. Yet perhaps Bram had really fretted over his separation from his family, perhaps in dying he had wished that Letizia might take his place in this house. Before she could be tempted to tell the driver to turn round, Nancy jumped out of the fly and rang the front-door bell. It was answered, not by that severe man-servant of her anxious prefigurations, but by an elderly parlour-maid, who must have been warned of her arrival, for she immediately invited her to step in. Nancy hesitated a moment, for now that she was here it seemed too much like taking everything for granted to send the fly away and ask the maid to accept the custody of her dressing-case. She had not liked to presume an inhospitable reception by arriving without any luggage at all, and yet, now that she saw her dressing-case standing on the hall chair, she wished she had not brought it. However, it would really be too absurdly self-conscious to keep the fly waiting while she was being approved. So, she paid the fare and tried not to resemble an invader, a thief, or a beggar.

"What is this house, muvver?" Letizia asked as they were following the elderly maid along the gloomy hall. "Is it a house where bad people go?"

"No, it's where your Uncle Caleb lives, and your two aunts——" Nancy broke off in a panic, for she simply could not remember either of their names. Were they Rachel and Sarah? This was serious.

"How is Mrs. Fuller?" she asked, in the hope that the elderly maid would feel inclined to be chatty about the health of the whole family and so mention the names of the two aunts in passing.

"Mrs. Fuller is the same as usual," said the maid.

"And Miss Fuller?" Nancy ventured.

"Miss Achsah and Miss Thyrza are both quite well." *What* was the name of the first one? The stupid woman had said it so quickly. However, she had got the

name of one.   Thyrza—Thyrza.   She must not forget
it again.

The elderly maid left Nancy and Letizia in a sombre
square room overcrowded with ponderous furniture and
papered with dull red flock.   On the overmantel was a
black marble clock with an inscription setting forth that
it was presented to Caleb Fuller, Esquire, by his devoted
employees on the occasion of his twenty-first birthday.
But did she not remember that Caleb had sacked all his
employees on that auspicious occasion?   Perhaps he had
not liked the gift, she thought with a smile.   Above the
clock hung a large steel engraving of what Nancy at first
imagined was intended to represent the Day of Judgment; but on examining the title she found that it was a
picture of the firework-display by Messrs. Fuller and Son
in Hyde Park on the occasion of the National Thanksgiving for the recovery of H. R. H. the Prince of Wales.

"Why does this room smell like blot-paper, muvver?"
Letizia inquired.

"Now, darling, I beg of you not to ask any more
questions at all.   Will you be kind to mother and do
that?"

Letizia wriggled one fat leg against the other for a
moment.

"Yes," she whispered at last resignedly.

"There's a pet," said Nancy, lifting her on a mahogany
chair, the seat of which was covered with horsehair.

"Ouch!" Letizia exclaimed, rubbing her leg.   "It's all
fistles, and where my drawses have gone away and left
a piece of my leg the fistles have bitten it.   Your drawses
don't go away and leave a piece of your leg.   So the
fistles don't bite you."

At this moment the heavy door opened quietly to admit
Caleb Fuller, a plump-faced young man with brown curly
hair and a smile of such cordial and beaming welcome that
Nancy's heart sank, for of course he would be delighted
to accept the responsibility of Letizia's upbringing.

"How do you do?   How kind of you to come and see

us," said Caleb. "So very kind. I can't say how much we appreciate it. You'll stay and have tea with us, won't you?"

"Thank you very much," said Nancy, wondering how on earth she was going to suggest what she had come all the way from London to suggest.

"You'll excuse our lack of ceremony? We're such simple people. I suppose you drove up from the station? And this is poor Bram's little girl, I suppose?"

Caleb's beaming expression had changed in a flash to one of extreme wide-eyed mournfulness.

"Will you give your Uncle Caleb a kiss, my dear?" he asked in smugly sentimental accents.

"No, fank you," Letizia replied, evidently supposing that she was behaving extra well in refusing so politely.

Nancy could not bring herself to reprove her daughter's disinclination. She felt that, if she had been a little girl of Letizia's age, she should not have cared to kiss this very old young man.

Caleb turned on his smile to dispose of the rebuff.

"Let me see, how old is she?"

"Five next July."

"Can she talk much?"

"I'm afraid she can talk a great deal too much," Nancy laughed. "Being with grown-up people all the time has made her a very precocious little girl, I'm afraid."

She was wondering how she could manage to keep the conversation trained on Letizia until she could muster up the courage to ask her brother-in-law the favour she desired.

"I think it's such a pity to let children grow up too soon," Caleb sighed in a remote and dreamy tone that trembled like the vox humana stop with the tears of things. "I like all little things so much; but I think people and animals deteriorate when they grow big. I had a dear little cream-coloured kitten, and now that lovely little kitten has grown into an enormous hulking cat and spends all its time in the kitchen, eating. I noticed when I was going through the household books that we were getting extra fish, so I went into the matter most carefully, and do you know . . ." The horror of the story he was telling overcame Caleb for a moment, and he had to gulp down his emotion before he could proceed. "Do you know I found that they were actually buying special fish for this great cat?" His voice had sunk to an awe-struck whisper. "It came as a terrible shock to me that such a pretty little tiny kitten which only seemed to lap up a small saucer of milk every now and then should actually have become an item in the household expenditure nowadays. . . . Of course," he added hastily, "I told the cook she had no business to give it anything except scraps that couldn't be used for anything else. But still . . ." Caleb allowed his narrative to evaporate in a profound sigh.

"Bram spoke of you just before he died," Nancy began abruptly.

"How very kind of him," Caleb observed, reassuming quickly that expression of devout and wide-eyed sentimentality, though in the tone of his voice there was an implication of the immense gulf between Bram's death and his own life.

"He seemed to regret the breach between himself and his family," she continued.

"It was always a great grief to us," Caleb observed. He was still apparently as gently sympathetic; yet somehow Nancy had a feeling that behind the wide-eyed solemnity there was a twinkle of cunning in the grey shallow eyes, a lambent twinkle that was playing round the rocky question of what she was leading up to, and of how he should deal with any awkward request she might end by making.

"He was anxious that I should bring Letizia to see you all," Nancy pressed.

There was a reproach in her brother-in-law's gaze that made her feel as if she were being utterly remorseless in her persistency. Nevertheless, Caleb turned on quite easily that cordial welcoming smile.

"I'm so glad," he murmured from the other side of the universe. "I don't think tea will be long now."

"Oh, please don't bother about tea," she begged.

Caleb beamed more intensely.

"Oh, please," he protested on his side. "My aunts and I would be very much upset indeed if you didn't have tea. And to-day's Thursday!"

Nancy looked puzzled.

"I see I shall have to let you into a little family secret. We always have a new cake on Thursday," he proclaimed, smiling now with a beautifully innocent archness. Turning to Letizia he added playfully, "I expect *you* like cakes, don't you?"

"I like the cakes what Mrs. Porridge makes for me," Letizia replied.

"Oatmeal cakes?" Caleb asked in bewilderment.

"Letizia," her mother interrupted quickly, "please don't answer your uncle in that horrid rude way. Mrs. Pottage was our landlady at Greenwich," she explained.

Caleb looked coldly grave. He disapproved of landladies with their exorbitant bills.

"You must find it very unpleasant always being robbed by landladies," he said.

"Bram and I were very lucky usually. We met far more pleasant landladies than unpleasant ones."

Nancy paused. She was wondering if she should be able to explain her mission more easily if the subject of it were not present.

"I wonder if Letizia's aunts would like to see her?"

"Oh, I'm sure they would," Caleb answered. "We'll all go into the drawing-room. I'm sure you must be wanting your tea."

"If we could leave Letizia with her aunts, I would like very much to talk to you for a minute or two alone."

Caleb squirmed.

"Don't be anxious," Nancy laughed. "I'm not going to ask you to lend me any money."

"Oh, of course not," he said with a shudder. "I never thought you were going to do that. I knew Bram would have explained to you that I really couldn't afford it. We have had the most dreadful expenses lately in connection with the factory. I have had to lock up several thousand pounds."

He made this announcement with as much judicial severity as if he had actually condemned the greater part of his fortune to penal servitude for life.

"Yes, it must be horrible to have a lot of money that can't behave itself," Nancy agreed.

Her brother-in-law regarded her disapprovingly. He resented few things more than jokes, for he objected to wasting those ready smiles of his almost as much as he hated wasting his ready money.

"Well, shall we go into the drawing-room?" he asked, trying to make his guest feel that merely to lead her from one room to another in Lebanon House was giving her much more than he would give many people for nothing.

"Are those aunts?" Letizia exclaimed in disgusted astonishment when she was presented to the two drab middle-aged women with muddy faces and lace caps who, each wearing a grey woollen shawl, sat on either side of a black fire from which one exiguous wisp of smoke went curling up the chimney.

"Yes, those are your aunts, darling," said Nancy, hoping that Letizia's generic question had not been understood quite in the way that it was intended. "Run and give them a kiss."

There must have been a note of appeal in her mother's voice, for Letizia obeyed with surprising docility, even if she did give an impression by the slowness of her advance that she was going to stroke two unpleasant-looking animals at the invitation of a keeper. Then it was Nancy's turn to embrace the aunts, much to the amazement of her daughter, who exclaimed:

"You kissed them too! Was you told to kiss them?"

"May I leave Letizia with you while I finish my talk with Caleb?" Nancy asked her aunts.

Caleb looked positively sullen over his sister-in-law's pertinacity, and he was leading the way back to what was apparently known as the library, when the elderly maid appeared with the tea. He beamed again.

"You *must* have tea first. I'm sure you *must* be wanting your tea. I was telling—er—Nancy about our Thursday cake, Aunt Achsah."

Caleb's face was richly dimpled by the smile for which the family joke was responsible, and at which Aunt Achsah and Aunt Thyrza tittered indulgently. Nancy was saying over in her head the name of the elder aunt so that she should be able to remember it in future. Then she gazed round in depression of spirit at the curtains and upholstery and wall-paper, all in sombre shades of brown, and at the bunches of pampas-grass, dyed yellow, blue, and red, which in hideous convoluted vases on bamboo stands blotched the corners of the room with plumes of crude colour. Could she leave Letizia in this house? Would Bram really wish it?

Aunt Achsah and Aunt Thyrza had by now wound themselves up to express the sorrow that they felt convention owed to Nancy.

"He was a wild boy and a great anxiety to us," Aunt Thyrza sighed. "But we were very fond of him."

"It nearly killed his poor father when he took to the stage," Aunt Achsah moaned. "He had such a beautifully religious bringing-up that it seemed particularly dreadful in his case. Of course, we do not believe that there may not be some good men and women on the stage, but all the same it was terrible—really terrible for us when Bram became an actor."

"But didn't you have a sister who went on the stage?" Nancy asked.

The two drab women stared at her in consternation. How did this creature know the story of the lost Caterina? Why, their mother must have told Bram. The shameful secret was a secret no more.

Caleb knitted his brows, and his granite-grey eyes gleamed. So, this was the woman's game. Blackmail! This was why she wanted to talk to him alone. He would soon show her that he was not the kind of man to be frightened by blackmail. As a matter of fact, Caleb himself, who had only heard when he came of age about the shameful past of his Aunt Caterina, had been much less impressed by the awfulness of the family secret than his aunts had expected.

"Yes, we did have a sister who went on the stage," Aunt Thyrza tremulously admitted. "But that was many, many years ago, and she has long been dead."

Nancy was merciful to the aunts and forbore from pressing the point about the existence of good people on the stage. She was not merciful, however, to Caleb when tea came to an end and he showed no sign of adjourning with her to the library.

"Are you sure you won't have another piece of cake? Do have another piece of cake," he begged, turning on the smile almost to its full extent. That he could not quite manage the full extent was due to the irritation this obtrusive young woman's pertinacity was causing him.

"No, indeed, I really couldn't," said Nancy, donning a bright little smile herself as a cyclist hopes his oil-lamp will avail to protect him against the dazzling onrushing motor-car. "Letizia, darling," she added firmly. "I'm going to leave you here with Aunt Achsah and Aunt Thyrza for a little while. You will be good, won't you?"

"But I'd like to stroke the puss-cat."

"The cat?" Aunt Achsah exclaimed. "What cat?"

"The puss-cat what that man was talking about to muvver," Letizia explained.

"The cat isn't allowed in the drawing-room," Aunt Thyrza said primly.

"Why isn't he? Does he make messes?"

The two aunts shuddered. It was only too sadly evident that the stage had already corrupted even this four-year-old child.

"Cats live in kitchens," Aunt Achsah laid down dogmatically.

"Well, can I go to the kitchen, muvver?" Letizia asked. "Because I would like to see the puss-cat. I fink puss-cats are much, *much* nicer than aunts."

"No, darling, I want you to stay here," and with this Nancy hurried out of the room, followed reluctantly by her brother-in-law.

When they were back in the library, which, now that she had a clue to its status, Nancy perceived did contain half-a-dozen bound volumes of the *Illustrated London News,* three or four books of religious reading, and a decrepit Bradshaw, she came straight to the point.

"Caleb, times are rather bad for theatrical business, and . . ."

"Business is bad everywhere," Caleb interrupted. "Of course, you know that I am engaged in manufacturing fireworks? My brother no doubt has told you that. Trade has never been so bad as it is this year, and only recently an Order in Council has made it illegal to use chlorate of potash with sulphur compounds. That is a very serious matter indeed for firework manufacture. Indeed, if it had not been for our discovery that aluminium can be successfully used for brightening our colour effects, I don't know what *would* have happened to the business. Luckily I was one of the first, if not *the* first manufacturer to realise the advantages of aluminium, and so I had already ceased to use chlorate of potash with sulphur for quite a long time, in fact, ever since as a boy of twenty I found myself practically in sole charge of our factory. My brother's desertion of his father twelve years ago ruined all my chances. I was getting on so splendidly at school. I was winning prizes for Latin and Scripture and all kinds of subjects, and my masters were so enthusiastic about my education. But when I was only fifteen, my father said to me: 'Caleb, you can either go on with your school work or you can give up school and enter the business at once on a small salary.' It was a hard choice, but I didn't hesitate. I gave up all my schoolwork, because after my brother's desertion I felt it was my duty to enter the business. And I did. You don't know how hard I've worked while my brother was amusing himself on the stage. But I don't bear his memory any grudge. Please don't think that I'm criticising him, because of course I wouldn't like to say anything about one who is no longer with us. I only want you to understand that my position is by no means easy. In fact, it's terribly difficult. So, though I would be happy to lend you lots of money, if I had any to spare, I'm sure you'll understand that, with all the expenses I've been put to over this Order in Council and changing my factory and one thing and another, it simply isn't possible."

"I'm not asking you to lend me any money," Nancy said, as soon as her brother-in-law paused for a moment to take breath. "But Bram when he was dying . . ."

"Oh, please don't think that I don't sympathise with you over my brother's death. It was a shock to us all. I read about it in the local paper. I'd had a little trouble with the proprietor over our advertisements, so he printed all about Bram being a clown in great headlines. But in spite of the shocking way he died like that on the stage, I showed everybody in Brigham how much upset we all were by asking for the Recreation Ground to be closed for two whole days. So please don't think we weren't very much shocked and upset."

"Bram, when he was dying in my arms," she went on, "told me if I was ever in difficulties to go to you, because he was sure that you would want to help me."

"Yes, that's just the kind of thing my brother would say," said Caleb indignantly. "He never cared a straw about the business. He hated the factory. He always had an idea that money was only made to be spent."

"I don't think that Bram expected me to borrow any money from you," said Nancy. "But he thought that you might care to assume the responsibility of bringing up Letizia. He thought that she might be a link between him and his family."

"Bring up Letizia?" Caleb gasped. "Do you mean, pay for her clothes and her keep and her education?"

"I suppose that is what Bram fancied you might care to do. I would not have come here to-day, if I had not believed that I owed it to his child to give her opportunities that her mother cannot give her. Please don't think that I want to lose Letizia. It has cost me a great deal . . ." her voice wavered.

"But you could have told me what you wanted in the letter, and that would have saved you your railway fare," said Caleb reproachfully.

"I didn't mean the money it cost. I meant the struggle with my own feelings."

"I think it would be wrong of me to try and persuade you to give up your child," said Caleb solemnly. "I wouldn't do it, even if I could. But I can't. You must remember that I still have my old grandmother to keep. Of course, she's bedridden now, and she can't waste money as she used to waste it, for she was shockingly extravagant whenever she had an opportunity. But even as it is she costs a great deal. I have to pay a nurse-companion; and the doctor *will* come once a week. You know how ready doctors always are to take advantage of anybody in a house being ill. They just profit by it," he said bitterly. "That's what they do, they just profit by illness. And besides my grandmother, I have to pay annuities to my two aunts. I'm not complaining. I'm only too glad to do it. But I'm just telling you what a load of domestic responsibilities I have on my shoulders already, so that you can appreciate how utterly impossible it would be for me to do anything for my brother's little girl. Well, you heard what I told you about that cat, and if I can't afford the extra amount on the household books for a cat, how can I possibly afford what a child would cost? I'm only so distressed you should have gone to the expense of coming all this way to find out something that I could have told you so well in a letter. I can't imagine why you didn't write to me about this child. You do see my point of view, don't you? And I'm sure that you would rather not have your little girl brought up here. The air of Brigham is very smoky. I'm sure it wouldn't be good for children."

"Well, that's that," said Nancy. "I've done what Bram asked me to do, but I'm just dazed. I just simply can't understand how you and Bram came out of the same womb."

Caleb winced.

"Of course, I know that you do talk very freely on the stage," he said deprecatingly. "But I wish you wouldn't use such words in this house. We're simply provincial people, and we think that kind of expression rather unpleasant. I daresay we may appear old-fashioned, but we'd rather be old-fashioned than hear a lady use words like that. I'm afraid, by what you just said, that you haven't really understood my point of view at all. So, I'm going to take you into my confidence, because I do want you to understand it and not bear me any ill-will. My motives are so often misjudged by people," he sighed. "I suppose it's because I'm so frank and don't pretend I can do things when I can't. So I'm going to give you a little confidence, Nancy." Here Caleb beamed generously. "It's still a secret, but I'm hoping to get married in June, and of course that means a great deal of extra expense, especially as the lady I am going to marry has no money of her own."

"I hope you'll be happy," Nancy said.

"Thank you," said Caleb in a tone that seemed to express his personal gratitude for anything, even anything so intangible as good wishes, that might contribute a little, a very little toward the relief of the tremendous weight of responsibility that he was trying so humbly and so patiently to support. "Thank you very much."

Nancy was wishing now with all her heart that she

had not been so foolish as to bring that dressing-case with her. She only longed now to be out of this house without a moment's delay. She wished too that she had not dismissed the fly, for it would be impossible to carry the dressing-case and Letizia all the way to the railway station. Here she would have to remain until another fly could be fetched.

"There's a good train at half-past seven," said Caleb, who was observing Nancy's contemplation of her dressing-case on the hall-chair. "If you like, I'll telephone to the hotel for a fly to be sent up. But I'm afraid I shall have to ask you to excuse me from waiting any longer. I have rather a lot of work to do this evening. I'm trying to save expense wherever I possibly can," he added with a martyr's ecstatic gaze toward a lovelier world beyond this vale of tears.

"Oh, please don't trouble to wait an instant. I'll go back to the drawing-room."

"Yes, there's a fire in there," Caleb observed, it seemed a little resentfully.

At this moment a neat young woman with bright intelligent eyes came down the stairs.

"Excuse me, Mr. Fuller, but Mrs. Fuller would like Mrs. Bram Fuller and her little girl to go up and see her."

Caleb's face darkened.

"But surely it's too late for Mrs. Fuller to see visitors? Besides, Mrs. Bram Fuller wants to catch the seven-thirty train."

"It's only half-past five now," said Nancy eagerly. "And I should not care to leave Brigham without seeing Letizia's great-grandmother."

In her disgust at Caleb she had forgotten that there was still a member of this family who might compensate for the others.

"Mrs. Fuller will be very annoyed, Mr. Fuller, if she doesn't see Mrs. Bram Fuller and her little girl," the young woman insisted.

"Very well, nurse, if you think it's wise," Caleb said.

"But I hope this won't mean an extra visit from the doctor this week."

The bright-eyed young woman was regarding Caleb as a thrush regards a worm before gobbling it up.

"It would be extremely unwise to disappoint Mrs. Fuller. She has been counting on this visit ever since she heard yesterday that Mrs. Bram Fuller was coming to Brigham."

"My poor old grandmother works herself up into a great state over every domestic trifle," Caleb said angrily. "It's a great pity an old lady like her can't give up fussing over what happens in the house."

Nancy went into the drawing-room to rescue Letizia from her aunts.

"Good-bye—er—Nancy," said Aunt Achsah. "I hope you won't think that I am intruding on your private affairs if I say to you how grieved both your Aunt Thyrza and myself are to find that our poor little grand-niece apparently knows nothing whatever about our Heavenly Father. We do hope that you will try to teach her something about Him. Of course, we know that Roman Catholics do not regard God with the same reverence and awe as we do, but still a forward little girl like Letizia should not be allowed to remain in a state of complete ignorance about Him. It's very shocking."

"Oh, I do so agree with my sister," Aunt Thyrza sighed earnestly.

"Good-bye, Aunt Achsah. Good-bye, Aunt Thyrza," said Nancy. "Come along, Letizia."

And the way her little daughter danced out of the room beside her mother exactly expressed what she wanted to do herself.

CHAPTER XIV

LETIZIA THE FIRST

"Mrs. Fuller has been so excited ever since the letter came to say that you would pay a visit to Lebanon House," the nurse stopped to tell Nancy at the head of the stairs, before showing the way along the landing to the old lady's room.

"Are we going to see more aunts, muvver?" Letizia anxiously inquired.

"No, darling, you're going to see dear father's grannie whom he loved very much; and he would like you to love her very much too."

"Well, I will love her," Letizia promised.

"You must remember that *your* name is Letizia and that *her* name is Letizia. You were christened Letizia because father loved his grannie. And remember she is very old and that's why you'll find her in bed."

"Will she be like Red Riding Hood's grannie?" Letizia asked.

"Perhaps she will be a little."

"But a naughty wolf won't come and eat her?" Letizia pressed on a note of faint apprehension.

"Oh, no," her mother assured her. "There are no wolves in this house."

Was it a trick of the gathering dusk, or did the bright-eyed young woman raise her eyebrows and smile to herself at this confident reply?

Nancy had never been so much surprised in her life as she was by the aspect of old Mrs. Fuller's room. The old lady, wrapped in a bed-jacket of orange and yellow brocade and supported by quantities of bright vermilion cushions, was sitting up in a gilded four-post bed, the curtains and valance of damasked maroon silk and the canopy sustained by four rouged Venetian *amorini* with golden wings. Over the mantelpiece was a copy of Giorgione's "Pastorale." Mirrors in frames of blown glass decorated with wreaths of pink glass rosebuds and blue glass forget-me-nots hung here and there on the white walls, the lighted candles in which gave the windowpanes such a bloom in the March dusk as is breathed upon ripe damsons. Bookcases on either side of the fireplace were filled with the sulphur backs of numerous French novels. On a mahogany table at the foot of the bed stood a green cornucopia of brilliantly tinted wax fruits that was being regarded with slant-eyed indifference by two antelopes of gilded wood, seated on either side.

Of course, Nancy had known that old Mrs. Fuller was different from the rest of the family; but this flaunting rococo bedroom made a sharper impression of that immense difference than could all the letters to her grandson. It was strange, too, that Bram should never have commented on this amazing room, set as it was in the heart of the house against which his boyhood had so bitterly revolted. In her astonishment at her surroundings she did not for the moment take in the aspect of the old lady herself; and then suddenly she saw the dark eyes of Bram staring at her from the middle of those vermilion cushions, the bright eyes of Bram flashing from a death's head wrapped in parchment. She put her hand to her heart, and stopped short on her way across the room to salute the old lady.

"What's the matter?" snapped a high incisive voice.

"Oh, you're so like Bram," cried Nancy, tears gushing like an uncontrollable spring from her inmost being, like blood from a wound, and yet without any awareness of grief, so that her voice was calm, her kiss of salutation not tremulous.

"Might I lift my little girl on Mrs. Fuller's bed, nurse?" she asked.

"Don't call her nurse," the old lady rapped out. "This

ain't a hospital. It's only that sanctimonious ghoul Caleb who calls her nurse. She's my companion, Miss Emily Young. And why should the wretched child be lifted up to see an old bogey like myself?"

"I think she'd like to kiss you, if she may," said Nancy.

"Yes, I *would* like to kiss you," said Letizia.

The old woman's eyes melted to an enchanting tenderness, and, oh, how often Nancy had seen Bram's eyes melt so for her.

"Lift her up, Emily, lift her up," said Mrs. Fuller.

Miss Young put Letizia beside her and the old woman encircled the child with her left arm. The other hung motionless beside her.

"I'm not going to maul you about. I expect your aunts have slobbered over you enough downstairs. Just give me one kiss, if you want to. But if you don't want to, now that you're so close to my skinny old face, why, say so, and I shan't mind."

But Letizia put both arms round her great-grandmother's neck and kissed her fervidly.

"And now sit down and tell me how you like Lebanon House," she commanded.

"Is this Lebbon House?"

The old woman nodded.

"I like it here, but I don't like it where those aunts are. Have you seen those aunts, grannie?"

"I made them."

"Why did you make them, grannie? I don't fink they was very nicely made, do you? I don't fink their dresses was sewed on very nicely, do you?"

"You're an observant young woman, that's what you are."

"What is azervant?"

"Why, you have eyes in your head and see with them."

"I see those gold stags," said Letizia, pointing to the antelopes.

"Ah-ha, you see them, do you?"

"Did Santy Claus give them to you? He gived me a

lamb and a monkey and lots and lots of fings, so I aspeck he did."

"I expect he did too. But they're antelopes, not stags."

"Auntylopes?" Letizia repeated dubiously. "Will Santy Claus put gold aunts in your stocking at Christmas?"

"*Mon dieu,* I hope not," the old lady exclaimed. "So you like antelopes better than aunts?"

"Yes, I do. And I like puss-cats better. And I like all fings better than I like aunts."

"Well, then I'll tell you something. When Santa Claus brought me those antelopes, he said I was to give them to you."

Letizia clapped her hands.

"Fancy! I fought he did, grannie."

"So, if you'll take them into the next room with Miss Young, she'll wrap them up for you while I'm talking to your mother."

"How kind of you to give them to her," said Nancy, from whose eyes the silent tears had at last ceased to flow.

"Letizia darling, say 'thank you' to your kind grannie."

"*Senza complimenti, senza complimenti,*" the old woman muttered, "The pleasure in her eyes was all the thanks I wanted."

"I aspeck they won't feel very hungry wivout the apples and the pears," Letizia suggested anxiously.

"Of course they won't, darling," her mother interrupted quickly.

"You'd better wrap up some of the fruit as well, Emily," said the old lady with a chuckle.

"No, please . . ." Nancy began.

"Hoity-toity, I suppose I can do what I like with my own fruit?" said the old lady sharply. "Draw the curtains before you go, Emily."

When Letizia had retired with Miss Young, and the gilded antelopes and a generous handful of the wax fruit, the old lady bade Nancy draw up one of the great Vene-

tian chairs. When her grandson's wife was seated beside
the bed, she asked her why she had come to Brigham.

Nancy gave her an account of her struggles for an
engagement and told her about Bram's death and that
unuttered wish.

"He may have worried about your future," said the
old lady. "But it was never his wish that Letizia should
be brought up here. Never! I know what that wish
was."

"You do?"

"He was wishing that he had become a Catholic. He
used to write to me about it, and I'm afraid I was discouraging. It didn't seem to me that there was any point
in interrupting his career as a clown by turning religious
somersaults as well. I'm sorry that it worried his peace
at the last, but by now he is either at rest in an eternal
dreamless enviable sleep or he has discovered that there
really is a God and that He is neither a homicidal lunatic,
nor a justice of the peace, nor even a disagreeable and
moody old gentleman. I used to long to believe in Hell
for the pleasure of one day seeing my late husband on the
next gridiron to my own; but now I merely hope that, if
there is another world, it will be large enough for me to
avoid meeting him, and that, if he has wings, an all-
merciful God will clip them and put him to play his harp
where I shan't ever hear the tune. But mostly I pray
that I shall sleep, sleep, sleep for evermore. And so
young Caleb objected to bring up my namesake? By
the way, I'm glad you've not shrouded her in black."

"I knew Bram wouldn't like it," Nancy explained.

"I loved that boy," said the old lady gently. "You
made him happy. And I can do nothing more useful than
present his daughter with a pair of gilded antelopes."
Her sharp voice died away to a sigh of profound and
tragic regret.

Nancy sat silent waiting for the old lady to continue.

"Of course, I could have written and warned you not
to ask young Caleb for anything," she suddenly began

again in her high incisive voice. "But I wanted to see
you. I wanted to see Letizia the second. I *must* die
soon. So I didn't attempt to stop your coming. And, as
a matter of fact, you've arrived before I could have written to you. No, don't hand your child over to young
Caleb, girl. Just on sixty-six years ago my mother
handed me over to old Caleb. I suppose she thought that
she was doing the best thing for me. Or it may have
been a kind of jealousy of my young life, who knows?
Anyway she has been dead too long to bother about the
reason for what she did. And at least I owe her French
and Italian, so that with books I have been able to lead
a life of my own. Letizia would hear no French or Italian in this house except from me. And even if I could
count on a few more years of existence, what could I
teach that child? Nothing, but my own cynicism, and
that would be worse than nothing. No, you mustn't hand
her over to young Caleb. That would be in a way as
wrong as what my mother did. Your duty is to educate
her. Yes, you must educate her, girl, you must be sure
that she is taught well. She seems to have personality.
Educate her. She must not be stifled by young Caleb
and those two poor crones I brought into this world.
It would be a tragedy. I had another daughter, and I
was not strong enough in those days to secure her happiness. Perhaps I was still hoping for my own. Perhaps
in trying to shake myself free from my husband I did not
fight hard enough for her. She ran away. She went
utterly to the bad. She died of drink in a Paris asylum.
Caterina Fuller! You may read of her in raffish
memoirs of the Second Empire as one of the famous
cocottes of the period. If my mother had not married
me to Caleb, I daresay I should have gone to the bad
myself. Or what the world calls bad. But how much
worse my own respectable degradation! It was only after
Caterina's death that I ceased to lament my prison. It
was as if the sentient, active part of me died with her.
Thence onward I lived within myself. I amused myself

by collecting bit by bit over many years the gewgaws by which you see me surrounded. They represent years of sharp practice in housekeeping. The only thing for which I may thank God sincerely is that I wasn't married to young Caleb. I should never have succeeded in cheating him out of a penny on the household bills. I should never have managed to buy a solitary novel, had he been my accountant. I should have remained for ever what I was when I married, raw, noisy, impudent, scatterbrained, until I died as a bird dies, beating its wings against the cage. Educate Letizia, educate her. I wish I had a little money. I have no means of getting any now. I had some, but I spent it on myself, every penny of it. Don't despair because you've not had an engagement since Christmas. It's only early March. *Mon dieu,* I haven't even a ring that you could pawn. But I don't worry about you. I'm convinced you will be all right. Easy to say, yes. But I say it with belief, and that isn't so easy. I shall live on for a few weeks yet, and I know that I shall have good news from you before I die."

All the while the old lady had been talking, her face had been losing its expression of cynicism, and by the time she had finished it was glowing with the enthusiasm of a girl. It was as if she had beheld reincarnate in little Letizia her own youth and as if now with the wisdom of eighty-three years she were redirecting her own future from the beginning. Presently, after a short silence, she told Nancy to search in the bottom drawer of a painted cabinet for a parcel wrapped up in brown paper, and bring it to her. With this she fumbled for a while with her left hand and at last held up a tunic made apparently of thick sackcloth and some fragments of stuff that looked like a handful of cobwebs.

"The silk has faded and perished," she murmured. "This was once a pair of blue silk tights. I wore them when I made my descent down that long rope from the firework platform. It was a very successful descent, but my life has perished like this costume—all that part of

it which was not fireproof like this asbestos tunic: Take
this miserable heap of material and never let your daughter make such a descent, however brightly you might
plan the fireworks should burn, however loudly you might
hope that the mob would applaud the daring of her performance, however rich and splendid you might think the
costume chosen for her. Yes, this wretched bundle of
what seemed once such finery represents my life. Wrap
it up again and take it out of my sight for ever, but do
you, girl, gaze at it sometimes and remember what the old
woman who once wore it told you a few weeks before she
died."

There was a tap at the door, and the elderly parlour-
maid came in to say that the fly for which Mr. Fuller
had telephoned was waiting at the door.

"Do you mean to say that Mr. Fuller hasn't ordered
the brougham to take Mrs. Fuller to the station?" the
old lady demanded angrily.

"I think that the horse was tired, ma'am," said the
elderly maid, retreating as quickly as she could.

"I wish I had my legs. I wish I had both arms," the
old lady exclaimed, snatching at the small handbell that
stood on the table at the left of the bed, and ringing it
impatiently.

Miss Young brought Letizia back.

"Emily, will you drive down with my visitors to the
station? I shan't need anything for the next hour."

It was useless for Nancy to protest that she did not
want to give all this trouble. The old lady insisted. And
really Nancy was very grateful for Miss Young's company, because it would have been dreary on this cold
March night to fade out of Brigham with such a humiliating lack of importance.

"Good-bye, little Letizia," said her great-grandmother.

"Good-bye, grannie. I've told my auntylopes about
my lamb and about my dog and about all my fings, and
they wagged their tails and would like to meet them very
much they saided."

On the way to the station Miss Young talked about nothing else except Mrs. Fuller's wonderful charm and personality.

"Really, I can hardly express what she's done for me. I first came to her when she was no longer able to read to herself. I happened to know a little French, and since I've been with her I've learnt Italian. She has been so kind and patient, teaching me. I used to come in every afternoon at first, but for the last two years I've stayed with her all the time. I'm afraid Mr. Fuller resents my presence. He always tries to make out that I'm her nurse, which annoys the old lady dreadfully. She's been so kind to my little brother too. He comes in two or three times a week, and sometimes he brings a friend. She declares she likes the company of schoolboys better than any. She has talked to me a lot about your husband, Mrs. Fuller. I thought that she would die herself when she heard he had been killed like that. And the terrible thing was that she heard the news from Mr. Fuller, whom, you know, she doesn't really like at all. He very seldom comes up to her room, but I happened to be out getting her something she wanted in Brigham, and I came in just as he had told her and she was sitting up in bed, shaking her left fist at him, and cursing him for being alive himself to tell her the news. She was calling him a miser and a hypocrite and a liar, and I really don't know what she didn't call him. She is a most extraordinary woman. There doesn't seem to be anything she does not know. And yet she has often told me that she taught herself everything. It's wonderful, isn't it? And her room! Of course, it's very unusual, but, do you know, I like it tremendously now. It seems to me to be a live room. Every other room I go into now seems to me quite dead."

And that was what Nancy was thinking when the dismal train steamed out of Brigham to take Letizia and herself back to London, that melancholy March night.

CHAPTER XV

THE TUNNEL

The only other occupant of the railway-carriage was a nun who sat in the farther corner reading her breviary or some pious book. Letizia soon fell fast asleep, her head pillowed on her mother's lap, while Nancy, watching the flaring chimneys in the darkness without, was thinking of that old lady who had flared like them in the murk of Lebanon House. After two hours of monotonous progress Letizia woke up.

"Muvver," she said, "I fink I've got a funny feeling in my tummy."

"I expect you're hungry, pet. You didn't eat a very good tea."

"It was such a crumby cake; and when I blowed some of the crumbs out of my mouf, one of those aunts made a noise like you make to a gee-gee, and I said, 'Yes, but I'm *not* a gee-gee,' and then the plate what I was eating went out of the room on a tray."

"Well, I've got a sponge cake for you here."

Letizia worked her way laboriously through half the cake, and then gave it up with a sigh.

"Oh, dear, everyfing seems to be all crumbs to-day."

"Try some of the lemonade. Be careful, darling, not to choke, because it's very bubbly."

Letizia made a wry face over the lemonade.

"It tastes like pins, muvver."

The nun who overheard this criticism put down her book and said, with a pleasant smile, that she had a flask of milk which would be much better for a little girl than lemonade. She had, too, a small collapsible tumbler, from which it would be easier to drink than from a bottle.

"Is that a glass, muvver?" Letizia exclaimed. "I was finking it was a neckalace."

"Thank Sister very nicely."

"Is that a sister?" Letizia asked incredulously.

The various relationships to which she had been introduced this day were too much for Letizia, and this new one seemed to her even more extraordinary than the collapsible metal tumbler. Nancy explained to the nun that they had been making a family visit to hitherto unknown relations in Brigham, to which the nun responded by saying that she, too, had been making a kind of family visit inasmuch as she had been staying in Lancashire at the mother house of the Sisters of the Holy Infancy.

"Right out on the moors. Such a lovely position, though of course it's just a little bleak at this time of year."

She had laid aside her pious book and was evidently glad to talk for a while to combat the depression that nocturnal journeys inevitably cast upon travellers in those days before corridors were at all usual in trains. In those days a railway compartment seemed such an inadequate shelter from the night that roared past in torrents of darkness on either side of it. The footwarmers, glad though one was of them, only made the chilly frost that suffused the upper portion of the carriage more blighting to the spirit. The dim gaslit stations through which the train passed, the clangour of the tunnels, the vertical handle of the door which at any moment, it seemed, might become horizontal and let it swing open for the night to rush through and sweep one away into the black annihilation from which the train was panting to escape, the saga of prohibitions inscribed above the windows and beneath the rack which gradually assumed a portentous and quasi-Mosaic significance—all these menacing, ineluctable impressions were abolished by the introduction of the corridor with its assurance of life's continuity.

Nancy told the nun that she was a Catholic, and they talked for a time on conventional lines about the difficulty of keeping up with one's religious duties on tour.

"But I do hope that you will go on trying, my dear," said the nun.

The young actress felt a little hypocritical in allowing her companion to presume that until this date she had never relinquished the struggle. Yet she was not anxious to extend the conversation into any intimacy of discussion, nor did she want the nun to feel bound by her profession to remonstrate with her for past neglect. So instead of saying anything either about the past or the future, she smiled an assent.

"You mustn't let me be too inquisitive a travelling companion," said the nun, "but I notice that you're in deep mourning. Have you lost some one who was very dear to you?"

"My husband."

The nun leaned over and with an exquisite tenderness laid her white and delicate hand on Nancy's knee.

"And you have only this little bright thing left?" she murmured.

Letizia had been regarding the nun's action with wide-eyed solemnity. Presently she stood up on the seat and putting her arms round her mother's neck, whispered in her ear:

"I fink the lady tied up with a handkie is nice."

"You have conquered Letizia's heart," said Nancy, smiling through the tears in her eyes.

"I'm very proud to hear it. I should guess that she wasn't always an easy conquest."

"Indeed, no!"

"Letizia?" the nun repeated. "What a nice name to own! Gladness!"

"You know Italian? My husband's grandmother was Italian. I often wish that I could speak Italian and teach my small daughter."

"What is Italian, muvver?" Letizia asked.

"Italian, Letizia," said the nun, "is the way all the people talk in the dearest and most beautiful country in the world. Such blue seas, my dear, such skies of velvet, such oranges and lemons growing on the trees, such flowers everywhere, such radiant dancing airs, such warmth and sweetness and light. I lived in Italy long ago, when I was young."

Nancy looked up in amazement as the nun stopped speaking, for her voice sounded fresh and crystalline as a girl's, her cheeks were flushed with youth, her eyes were deep and warm and lucent as if the Southern moon swam face to face with her in the cold March night roaring past the smoky windows of the carriage. Yet when Nancy looked again she saw the fine lines in the porcelain-frail face, and the puckered eyelids, and middle-age in those grave blue eyes. In Italy, then, was written the history of her youth, and in Italy the history of her love, for only remembered love could thus have transformed her for a fleeting instant to what she once was. At that moment the train entered a tunnel and went clanging on through such a din of titanic anvils that it was impossible to talk, for which Nancy was grateful because she did not want Letizia to shatter the nun's rapture by asking questions that would show she had not understood a great deal about Italy or Italian. Presently the noise of the anvils ceased, and the train began to slow down until at last it came to a stop in a profound silence which pulsed upon the inner ear as insistently as a second or two back had clanged those anvils. The talk of people in the next compartment began to trickle through the partition, and one knew that such talk was trickling all the length of the train, and that, though one could not hear the words through all the length of the train, people were saying to one another that the signals must be against them. One felt, too, a genuine gratitude to those active and vigilant signals which were warning the train not to rush on through that din of anvils to its doom.

And then abruptly the lights went out in every single

compartment. The blackness was absolute. People put up windows and looked out into the viewless tunnel, until the vapours drove them back within. Now down the line were heard hoarse shouts and echoes, and the bobbing light of the guard's lamp illuminated the sweating roof of the tunnel as he passed along to interview the engine-driver. In a few minutes he came back, calling out, "Don't be frightened, ladies and gentlemen, there's no danger." Heads peered out once more into the mephitic blackness, and the word went along that there had been a break-down on the line ahead and that their lighting had by an unfortunate coincidence broken down as well. Everybody hoped that the signals behind were as vigilant as those in front and that the red lamps were burning bright to show that there was danger on the line.

"I aspeck the poor train wanted a rest, muvver," said Letizia. "I aspeck it was sleepy because it was out so late."

"I know somebody else who's sleepy."

"P'r'aps a little bit," Letizia admitted.

"Dear me, she *must* be tired," her mother said across the darkness to the nun. "Well, then, put your head on my lap, old lady, and go right off to sleep as soon as ever you can."

For some time the two grown-ups in the compartment sat in silence while the little girl went to sleep. It was the nun who spoke first.

"I wonder whether it will disturb her if we talk quietly? But this utter blackness and silence is really rather dispiriting."

"Oh, no, Sister, we shan't disturb her. She's sound asleep by now."

"Does she always travel with you when you're on tour?" the nun asked.

"Until now she has. You see, my husband only died at Christmas and we were always together with her. I am a little worried about the future, because I can't afford to travel with a nurse and landladies vary and of course she has to be left in charge of somebody."

"Yes, I can understand that it must be a great anxiety to you."

Nancy thought how beautiful the nun's voice sounded in this darkness. While the train was moving, she had not realised its quality, but in the stillness now it stole upon her ears as magically as running water or as wind in pine-tree tops or as any tranquil and pervasive sound of nature. In her mind's eye she was picturing the nun's face as it had appeared when she was speaking of Italy, and she was filled with a desire to confide in her.

"That is really the reason I've been to Brigham," Nancy said. "I thought that I ought to give my husband's relations the opportunity of looking after Letizia. Not because I want to shirk the responsibility," she added quickly. "Indeed I would hate to lose her, but I did feel that she ought to have the chance of being brought up quietly. My own mother died when I was very young, and my father who is on the stage allowed me to act a great deal as a child, so that really I didn't go to school till I was over twelve, and it wasn't a very good school, because I was living in Dublin with an aunt who hadn't much money. Indeed I never really learnt anything, and when I was sixteen I went back to the stage for good. I'm only twenty-four now. I look much older, I think."

"I shouldn't have said that you were more than that," the nun replied. "But how terribly sad for you, my dear, to have lost your husband so young. Many years ago before I became a nun I was engaged to be married to a young Italian, and he died. That was in Italy, and that is why I still always think of Italy as the loveliest country and of Italian as the most beautiful language. But you were telling me about your relations in Brigham."

Nancy gave an account of her visit, and particularly of the interview with Letizia's great-grandmother.

"I think the old lady was quite right. I cannot imagine that bright little sleeping creature was intended to be brought up in such surroundings. Besides, I don't think it is right to expose a Catholic child to Protestant influences. Far better that you should keep her with you."

"Yes, but suppose I cannot get an engagement? As a matter of fact, I have only a pound or two left, and the prospect is terrifying me. I feel that I ought to have gone on acting at Greenwich. But to act on the very stage on which my husband had died in my arms! I couldn't. I simply couldn't have done it."

"My dear, nobody would ever dream of thinking that you could. It's cruel enough that you should have to act on any stage at such a time. However, I feel sure that you will soon get an engagement. Almighty God tries us in so many ways—ways that we often cannot understand, so that sometimes we are tempted to question His love. Be sure that He has some mysterious purpose in thus trying you even more hardly. Nobody is worth anything who cannot rise above suffering to greatness of heart and mind and soul. Do not think to yourself that a foolish old nun is just trying to soothe you with the commonplaces of religious consolation. To be sure, they are commonplaces that she is uttering, but subtleties avail nothing until the truth of the great commonplaces has been revealed to the human soul. Our holy religion is built up on the great commonplaces. That is why it is so infinitely superior to the subtleties of proud and eccentric individuals as encouraged by Protestantism. What a long time we are waiting in this darkness! Yet we know that however long we have to wait we shall sometime or other get out of this tunnel."

"Yes, but if we wait much longer," said Nancy, "I will have another problem to face when we get to London, for I will never dare arrive back at my present landlady's too late."

"I can solve that problem for you, at any rate," said the nun. "I shall be met at Euston by a vehicle, and I know that our guest-room is free to-night. So don't let your night's lodging worry you."

After this they sat silent in the darkness for a long time. The presence of the nun filled Nancy with a sense of warm security and peace of mind. Gradually it seemed to her that this wait in the tunnel was a perfect expression of the dark pause in her life, which, beginning with the death of Bram, had ended in her visit to Brigham. A conviction was born in her brain, a conviction which with every minute of this immersion in absolute blackness became stronger, that somehow the presence of the nun was a comforting fact, the importance of which was not to be measured by her importance within the little space of the railway-carriage, but that the existence of this nun was going to influence the whole of her life, which must soon begin again when the train emerged from the tunnel. The curtain would rise once more upon the pantomime, and, whatever the vicissitudes that she as the heroine of it might have to endure, there would always be a Fairy Queen waiting in the wings to enter and shake her silver wand against the powers of Evil. It was very childish and sentimental to be sitting here in the dark dreaming like this, Nancy kept telling herself; but then once more the mystery of the tunnel would enfold her as one is enfolded by those strange half-sleepy clarities of the imagination that flash through the midway of the night when one lies in bed and hopes that the sense of illumination that is granted between a sleep and a sleep will return with daylight to illuminate the active life of the morning. Her thoughts about the nun reassumed their first portentousness; the comparison of her own life to a pantomime appeared once more with the superlative reality of a symbol that might enshrine the whole meaning of life. Then suddenly the lights went up, and after a few more minutes the train was on its way again.

Nancy was glad indeed on arriving at Euston toward two o'clock of a frore and foggy night to drive away with

Sister Catherine in the queer conventual vehicle like a covered-in wagonette with four small grilled windows. To have argued with Miss Fewkes about her right to enter the tall thin house in Blackboy Passage at whatever hour she chose would have been the climax to the Brigham experience.

The Sisters of the Holy Infancy were a small community which was founded by one of several co-heiresses to a thirteenth-century barony by writ, dormant for many centuries. Instead of spending her money on establishing her right to an ancient title Miss Tiphaine de Cauntelo Edwardson preferred to endow this small community and be known as Mother Mary Ethelreda. The headquarters of the community were at Beaumanoir where Sister Catherine, the right-hand of the now aged foundress, had been visiting her. This was a Lancashire property which had formerly been held by Miss Edwardson's ancestors and repurchased by her when she decided to enter the religious life. In London the house of the community was situated in St. John's Wood where the Sisters were occupied in the management of an extremely good school. There was a third house in Eastbourne which was used chiefly as a home for impoverished maiden ladies.

Sister Catherine was head-mistress of St. Joseph's School, and it was there that she took Nancy and Letizia from Euston. The porteress was overjoyed to see her, having been working herself up for the last two hours into a panic over the thought of a railway accident. The white guest-room was very welcome to Nancy after the fatigue of this long day, so long a day that she could not believe that it had only been fifteen hours ago that she set out from Euston to Brigham. She seemed to have lived many lives in the course of it—Bram's life as a boy with his brother, old Mrs. Fuller's eighty years of existence, Sister Catherine's bright youth in Italy, and most wearingly of all, Letizia's future even to ultimate old age and death. And when she did fall asleep she was travelling, travelling all the time through endless unremembered dreams.

In the morning Letizia greatly diverted some of the nuns by her observations on the image of the Holy Child over the altar, which was a copy of the famous image of Prague.

"Muvver, who is that little black boy with a crown on His head?"

"That is the baby Jesus, darling."

"Why is He dressed like that? Is He going out to have tea with one of His little friends?"

Nancy really did not know how to explain why He was dressed like that, but hazarded that it was because He was the King of Heaven.

"What has He got in His hand, muvver? What toy has He got?"

"That's a sceptre, and a thing that kings hold in their hands."

"Are you quite sure that He is the baby Jesus, muvver?" Letizia pressed.

"Quite sure, darling."

"Well, I don't fink he is. I fink he's just a little friend of the baby Jesus, who He likes very much and lets him come into His house and play with His toys, but I don't fink that little black boy is the baby Jesus. No, no, no, no, no!" she decided, with vigorous and repeated shakes of the head.

Nancy was sorry when they had to leave St. Joseph's School and return to Blackboy Passage.

"I fink here's where the little friend lives," Letizia announced.

"Oh, darling, you really mustn't be so terribly ingenious. You quite frighten me. And what am I going to do about you next week when the dear Kinos will be gone?"

CHAPTER XVI

BLACKBOY PASSAGE

As Nancy had anticipated, Miss Fewkes was more than doubtful about her ability to keep an eye on Letizia while her mother was haunting the offices of theatrical agents.

"I'm not really at all used to children," she sniffed angrily. "Supposing if she was to take it into her silly little head to go and jump out of the window? There's no knowing what some children won't do next. Then of course you'd blame *me*. I've always been very nervous of children. I could have been married half-a-dozen times if I hadn't have dreaded the idea of having children of my own, knowing how nervous they'd be sure to make me."

"I wondered if perhaps Louisa might be glad to keep an eye on her, that is, of course, if you'd let me give her a little present. It probably won't be for more than a week." It certainly wouldn't, Nancy thought, at the rate her money was going, for she could not imagine herself owing a halfpenny to Miss Fewkes. And even that little present to Louisa, the maid-of-all-work, would necessitate a first visit to the nearest pawnbroker.

"Louisa has quite enough to do to keep her busy without looking after the children of my lodgers," the landlady snapped.

Poor Louisa certainly had, Nancy admitted to herself guiltily, at the mental vision of the overworked maid toiling up and downstairs all day at Miss Fewkes's behest.

"I don't see why you don't take her out with you," said the landlady acidly.

"Oh, Miss Fewkes, surely you know something of theatrical agents!" Nancy exclaimed. "How could I possibly drag Letizia round with me? No, I'll just leave her in my room. She'll be perfectly good, I'm sure. And while we are on the subject of room, Miss Fewkes, will you let me know how much you will charge me for the bedroom only, as I shan't be wanting the sitting-room after this week."

"Oh, but I don't particularly care to let the bedroom by itself," Miss Fewkes objected. "I haven't another bedroom vacant, and what use would the sitting-room be to anybody by itself? Perhaps you'd prefer to give up both rooms?"

Nancy hesitated. Then she plunged.

"Certainly, Miss Fewkes. I really wanted to give them up some time ago. They're very expensive and very uncomfortable, and not overclean."

"Well, I shan't argue about it, Miss O'Finn," said Miss Fewkes haughtily. "Because I wouldn't soil my lips by saying what I think of a person who behaves like you do. But I do know a little about the prerfession, having been in it myself, and if you *are* what you pretend to be, which I don't think, all I can say is the prerfession has changed for the worse since my day."

With this she snapped out of the room, as a little wooden cuckoo snaps back into his clock.

Nancy sat down and wrote to Mrs. Pottage.

> 5 Blackboy Passage,
> Soho.
> Friday.

DEAR MRS. POTTAGE,

I'm rather worried what to do with Letizia while I am looking for work. I wonder if you'd look after her for a week or two? I have a very unpleasant landlady here who hates children, and so I must get a new room until I find an engagement. Don't ask me to come to Greenwich too, because, dearest Mrs. Pottage, I simply couldn't. But Letizia's different, and if you wouldn't mind having her with you for a little while it would be such a weight off my mind. You must please charge me whatever you think is fair. I haven't the least idea, so I must leave that to you. I leave here on Monday, and if you will let me know by then what time will suit you I will bring Letizia to Greenwich station, if you'd be kind enough to meet us. I haven't told Letizia herself that she may be going to stay with you, because I don't want to disappoint her if you can't manage it, and of course I will perfectly understand if you can't.

Yours affectionately,
NANCY O'FINN.

Nancy felt more cheerful when she had posted this letter.

Early on Sunday morning the Kinos left Blackboy Passage.

"You won't change your mind at the last minute and let us take the kid?" Mr. Kino asked.

Nancy shook her head.

"It would be a weight off your shoulders, wouldn't it?" he pleaded.

"Yes, but it would be a terrible weight on my mind," said Nancy. "Dear Mr. Kino, I couldn't let her be adopted, I couldn't really."

Yet when the Kinos had gone, and Nancy was sitting by the window, listening to the church bells and to the occasional footsteps of people clinking along the frozen Sabbath streets and to the emptiness of Soho without the distant roar of traffic, she began to wonder if she ought not to have accepted the Kinos' offer. She tried to make up her mind to put on her things and take Letizia to the late Mass in the Soho Square church; but the dejection reacted on her energy, and she felt incapable of getting up from her seat, of doing anything except stare out of the window at the grey March sky or look with a listless resentment at Miss Fewkes's pictures of girls in sunbonnets cuddling donkeys over gates or of girls in furs feeding robins in the snow. She even lacked the energy, when the morning had passed and it was nearly two o'clock, to ring and ask when Miss Fewkes proposed to serve dinner. And when dinner did arrive, with everything cooked so badly as to make it nearly inedible, she did not feel that she could be bothered to protest.

"Muvver," said Letizia, "why has my gravy got spots of soap in it?"

"Because it's getting cold, my dear. So eat it up quickly before it gets any colder."

"But, muvver, when I put it into my mouf, it all sticks to the top of it and won't come off."

"Don't go on grumbling, there's a good little girl. If you don't like it, don't eat it."

"Well, I won't," said Letizia decidedly.

A rice-pudding, which tasted like a dry sponge wrapped up in old leaves, caused Letizia many sighs before she could swallow even a mouthful, and some bananas which looked as if the greengrocer had tried to reshape them after they had been driven over by the traffic of Covent Garden all day, did nothing to help matters. As for the coffee, it might have been smeared on a boy's fingers to stop him from biting his nails, but it was never meant to be drunk.

One of the reasons for Miss Fewkes's perpetual bad temper was an inclination on the part of visitors to the lower basement of the house to ring Miss Fewkes's bell and so fetch her downstairs unnecessarily to open the front door. This being the second Sunday of the month, Louisa had been allowed to go out, and Miss Fewkes was in her tiny little bedroom in the roof of the house when her bell rang twice. The idea of going all the way downstairs only to find that a visitor had arrived for the people in the basement did not appeal to the little woman. So she opened the bedroom window and, peering out over the sill, perceived upon the steps below an exceedingly bright cerise bonnet belonging to what was apparently a respectable middle-aged woman.

"Who are you ringing for?" Miss Fewkes called down in her rasping voice.

The cerise bonnet bobbed about for a while until at

last it discovered from what window it was being addressed, when it looked up and shouted back:

"What's it got to do with you who I'm ringing for? If you're the servant here, just you come down and open the door the same as what I would if anybody rung my front bell."

"Do you want Mr. and Mrs. Blanchit?" Miss Fewkes called down. "Because if you do, it's the broken bell by the area gate and kindly ring that."

"Do I want who?" the cerise bonnet shouted back.

"Mr. and Mrs. Blanchit!"

"No, I don't, you saucy old outandabout! What next are you going to ask? You just come down and open the door the same as I should myself."

Miss Fewkes slammed her window down and left the cerise bonnet on the steps. After ringing about a dozen times, it went down the steps again and standing in the middle of the pavement shouted "Hi!" several times in rapid succession. A small boy blowing a mouth-organ stared at the cerise bonnet for a moment, stopped his tune, and asked it if it had lost anything.

"What 'ud I be staring up at the top story of a house for, you saucy little image, if I'd have lost anything— unless I'd dropped my umbrella out of a balloon, and which I haven't? . . . Hi!"

On hearing the cerise bonnet begin to shout again, the small boy put the mouth-organ in his pocket and looking up in the air shouted "Hi!" too. Two little girls dragging behind them a child of doubtful sex smeared with barley sugar stopped to gaze, and then three more small boys arrived on the scene and proceeded to augment the duet of "Hi!"

A policeman, who had been lured from Dean Street into Blackboy Passage by the noise, inquired of the cerise bonnet what its need was.

"Can't you get into your house, mum?"

"No, I can't. I want to visit a lady friend of mine who lives at 5 Blackboy Passage, and when I rung the

bell a female like a potted shrimp poked her head out
of a top-floor window and asked me if I wanted Mr. and
Mrs. Blanchit."

"Mr. Blanchit lives at number five," one of the small
boys volunteered. "Down in the basement, he lives."

"Well, what's that got to do with you, you pushing
little eel? I don't want the man. I want to see my lady
friend."

"Perhaps you've got the wrong number," the policeman suggested.

"Wrong number be . . . well, I won't say what I was
thinking, because it doesn't always do."

It was at this moment that Letizia, who had been trying
vainly for an hour after dinner to make her mother play
with the gilded antelopes, decided to look out of the
window.

"Muvver! Muvver!" she shouted, clapping joyful
hands. "I can see Mrs. Porridge in the street, and she's
talking to a policeman."

Nancy jumped up, and ran to the window.

"Why, so it is! Dear, dear Mrs. Pottage! I'll go
down and open the door."

"There you are!" Mrs. Pottage exclaimed triumphantly
to the policeman after she had embraced Nancy. "Didn't
I tell you my lady friend lived here?"

The policeman strode off with a good-natured smile:
the small boy took the mouth-organ out of his pocket
and, after watching the policeman safely through the
archway of the Tavern, resumed his interrupted tune.
The two little girls, without looking to see if the sugar-
smeared neutral was ready to be dragged on again, moved
forward on their way. The three other small boys discovered a new method of wearing out boots and set off
to practise it. Mrs. Pottage and Nancy retired into
Number Five. Blackboy Passage was once more abandoned to its Sabbath emptiness and silence.

"Well, you do live in a Punch and Judy show and no
mistake," Mrs. Pottage declared, as she followed Nancy

up the stairs, the jet bugles of her best bonnet tinkling and lisping as she moved.

"My landlady doesn't like being called down to open the door; and the girl's out," Nancy explained.

"Landlady you call her? Skylady I should call her. That is if I called her a lady at all, and which I most certainly never shouldn't not if I lived to be as old as Methussalem."

Letizia was waiting at the head of the stairs to welcome Mrs. Pottage, into whose outspread arms she flung herself in a rapture of welcome.

"Mrs. Porridge! Mrs. Porridge!"

"My heart's jool!"

"Oh, Mrs. Porridge, where have you been? I didn't know where you could be, and I went to a circus and touched an ephelant on his trunk and it was all hot and I saw a little friend who the baby Jesus liked and I saw my big grannie and the wolf didn't eat her at all and I saw two aunts and they smelt all funny like the inside of a dirty-cloves basket and we had rice-pudding for dinner and it sticked my teef togevver, and I've got two golden auntylopes and they eat apples made of soap."

"My good gracious, if you haven't been going it," Mrs. Pottage declared, with a critical glance round the sitting-room of the lodgings. "Poky! Very poky! And not at all clean. Why, that grate don't look as if it had been swept since the fire of London, and, oh, dear, oh, dear, just look at the dust on those pictures! If a water pipe burst in this house you'd have weeds growing on the frames. Well, I suppose I haven't got to tell you who I've come to fetch?"

Nancy smiled.

"I knew you wouldn't fail me."

"Yes, but wait a minute. I didn't at all like the tone of that letter you wrote me."

Nancy looked worried.

"Not at all I didn't like it. Yes, I see myself sending in a bill for that blessed infant's keep. Why, you might as well ask me to charge you for the sun shining in at your windows."

Nancy saw that she had genuinely hurt the good soul by mentioning money in connection with Letizia's visit.

"Dear Mrs. Pottage, you could hardly expect me to plant her down on you without at least offering to pay, but I won't offend you by arguing further. You know exactly how I feel about your kindness, my dear soul."

"Kindness be . . . oh, dear, now that's twice in the last half hour I've nearly said that word. It comes of keeping company with Mr. Currie. Let me see, you won't have heard of him, because he's only been courting me since I gave the go-by to Watcher and Hopkins. He's a very hasty-tempered man, and his language *is* a bit of a coloured supplement. Mrs. Bugbird passed the remark to me I'd really have to mind my p's and q's, and I said it wasn't my p's and q's I had to look out for, it was my b's and d's. Of course, Mrs. Bugbird herself didn't mind. Oh, no, she's a very broad-minded woman. In fact her father, so she's often told me, used to preach regularly at street corners against any kind of religion at all. But I shan't keep this Currie hanging around much longer. No, he gets me into bad habits, and the next time he proposes marriage will be the last. Besides, even if I liked *him,* I don't like his business which is fried fish. Fancy me in a fried-fish shop for the rest of my life! Why, I'd sooner marry an engine driver and live in a railway station. Well, an engine driver did propose to me once. But I saw he had the habit of driving too much, and that would never have suited me. Why, even of a Sunday afternoon he wasn't happy if he couldn't walk me round Greenwich Park at sixty miles an hour. I remember once just for a joke I started whistling the same as an engine might, and everybody stopped and begun staring, and which made him a bit annoyed. In fact he thought I was touched in my head, and that Sunday was his last. Well, he's the only one of all my many who didn't wait for me to say 'no' defi-

nite, but went and hooked it himself. And going back
to the subject of my language this last month, it wouldn't
do at all if Letichia's coming home with me, so I think
I'll drop him a p.c. and not wait for the third time of
asking."

"Am I coming home with you, Mrs. Porridge?" Letizia asked, clapping her hands.

"You're coming home with me this blessed afternoon
just as soon as your dear ma's packed up your tiddlies.
Your friend Mrs. Bugbird will be popping in, and we'll
have a sprat tea together. And dear Aggie Wilkinson's
dancing about on her pore crutches, because you're coming home to your Mrs. Porridge." She took Nancy
aside, and continued in a lower voice. "I read between
the lines of your letter, dearie, and I knew you didn't
want to come near Greenwich. So I just skipped into
my Sunday best and come along to fetch her. She can
stay as long as you like. I'd say she could stay for ever.
Only she wants a better bringing-up than what a woman
like me could give her."

"Oh, but I'm sure to get an engagement very soon,
Mrs. Pottage, and then of course she'll go on tour again
with me. I wouldn't have bothered you now, if I hadn't
thought you'd be glad to have her for a while, and if I
hadn't wanted to leave these rooms as soon as possible."

"And I don't blame you. I'd sooner live in a dustbin.
But where are you going when you leave here?"

"Oh, I shall find somewhere to-morrow. I'm so glad
you did come to-day for Letizia. It will make it ever so
much easier for me. The only thing I'm worrying about
is the luggage."

"Well, why don't you let me take what luggage you
don't want down to Greenwich, and then when I bring
you Letichia, I can bring you your luggage at the same
time. There's no sense in travelling a lot of luggage
round with you like a peacock's tail. We can just pop
what you don't want into a four-wheeler and take it
to London Bridge."

Nancy hesitated. She was wondering if she had enough money left to pay the cab now, and Miss Fewkes's bill to-morrow morning. However, if she hadn't, she could visit the pawnbroker early and pledge some odds and ends, so she decided to accept Mrs. Pottage's offer.

"Now who's going to fetch the four-wheeler?" Mrs. Pottage wanted to know when the packing was finished. "Shall I give a holler to Her Landladyship upstairs?"

"Ask Miss Fewkes to fetch a cab?" Nancy exclaimed. "Why, she'd . . ." Words failed her to express what Miss Fewkes would do.

"But what *is* this Miss Fewkes?" demanded Mrs. Pottage indignantly. "Three ha'porth of nothing from what I could make out of her. Still, rather than create a row on a Sunday afternoon I'll go and fetch the four-wheeler myself. I'll stand in Shaftesbury Avenue till one comes along. There's one thing, the police won't be so likely to take me for a kerbstone fairy as what they would Lady Fewkes. Oh, dear, oh, dear! Well, I'm bothered if some people nowadays don't give theirselves as much airs as if they was Margate, Ramsgate, and Brighton all rolled into one."

In about ten minutes Mrs. Pottage returned, followed by a burly old cab-driver in a dark blue beaver coat with treble capes and a shiny bowler hat.

"I've brought a most obliging driver along with me," she proclaimed. "The first cab I got, the fellow wouldn't leave his horse at the corner to come and help down with the luggage. Afraid of his horse, he said. 'I suppose you're afraid it'll fall down and never stand up again if you left go of the reins?' I said. 'Never heard of a horse running away, I suppose,' he answers back very sarcastic. 'What?' said I, 'that pore skelington run away? Why, it couldn't walk away. It might fade away, yes. And if it didn't run away of itself, I'm sure nobody wouldn't ever run away *with* it. Not even a cats meat man, and they'll run away with anything as looks a little bit like flesh and blood. But that horse of yours don't.

That horse of yours looks more like a clothes-horse than a real animal. Only I'd be very afraid to hang a towel on its back for fear it might break in half under the weight.' And with that I walked on and found this driver who's been most obliging, I'm sure."

The cabman touched his hat in acknowledgment of the flattery, and asked which piece they wanted down first.

But now a greater obstacle to the departure of the luggage than an unwilling cab-driver presented itself, for Miss Fewkes appeared, her tow-coloured hair elaborately done as it always was on a Sunday afternoon to resemble a brand-new yacht's fender from which state it gradually wore away during the stress of the week.

"And what is the meaning of this?" she demanded, folding her arms.

Nancy explained why her luggage was going away this afternoon.

"Then perhaps you'll pay my weekly bill, Miss O'Finn, before you remove your boxes?" said Miss Fewkes.

"My bill will be paid to-morrow morning before I leave."

"Yes, but I'm not in the habit of permitting my lodgers to remove their luggage until their bills are paid," Miss Fewkes insisted.

Mrs. Pottage gasped.

"Well, of all the impudence I ever did hear! Well, I passed the remark to the policeman that you looked like a potted shrimp, but shrimp sauce is more what you ought to be called."

"It's easy to see what *you* are," Miss Fewkes spat out venomously. "The sort of woman *you* are is plain to any one who's sharp and has eyes."

At this point, the burly cab-driver, who was evidently afraid of being involved in this feminine dispute, retired downstairs until the matter was settled.

"It is easy to see what I am," Mrs. Pottage agreed. "Because I'm a decent-made woman. But it's far from

easy to see what you are, let me tell you, very far from
easy, because you aren't as big as a second helping of
underdone mutton at an eating-house. You *may* have
eyes. So's a needle. You *may* be sharp. So's a needle.
And I wouldn't care to look for you in a haystack any
more than what I would a needle, and that's the solid
truth I'm telling you. You asked for it, ma'am, and now
you've had it, and if you'll kindly stand on one side you
won't get carried out with the luggage like a speck of
dust off of your own dusty banisters."

"This luggage don't leave my house before my account's been settled," Miss Fewkes shrilled. "Not if I
have to fetch in a policeman to you."

"Fetch a policeman?" Mrs. Pottage jeered. "Well, for
a woman who looks like last night's buttonhole or a
sucked sweet as a kid's spat out on the pavement, you've
got a tidy nerve."

Nancy thought that it was time to interfere, because
she did not want Letizia to be frightened by the quarrel.

"I'm quite willing to pay your bill, Miss Fewkes, if you
suspect that I'm trying to give you the slip," she said.

"Not at all," Mrs. Pottage interposed. "It's beyond
reason giving in to such as she. Let her call this policeman we've heard so much about, and it's my opinion he'll
laugh in her face, that is if he could tell it *was* her face,
which I don't think."

"You vulgar, impertinent woman," Miss Fewkes ejac-
ulated.

"Yes, thank goodness I *am* a woman," Mrs. Pottage
retorted. "And thank goodness you can reckonise me as
such, which is more than what I could reckonise you,
not if I was looking at you with two telescopes at once.
Why, if I was you I'd be afraid to go out alone in case
I got took by a showman for a performing flea. It's a
nine days' wonder you never got pecked up by a sparrow;
but there, I suppose even a sparrow knows what isn't
good for him."

To what heights of invective Mrs. Pottage might have

risen was never to be known, because Nancy insisted on paying Miss Fewkes her bill, which enabled her to retreat to her own room and cease to oppose the departure of the luggage.

"But there, perhaps it's as well," conceded Mrs. Pottage. "Or I *might* have been tempted to say something a bit rude."

With the aid of the good-natured cabman the luggage was put on the four-wheeler; and an hour later Nancy waved farewell to Letizia and her hostess at London Bridge Station.

CHAPTER XVII

THE TWO ROADS

On Monday morning with a lighter heart than she had known for many weeks Nancy left Miss Fewkes. She had ten shillings and a few odd coppers when she stepped out of the tall thin house in Blackboy Passage, carrying her dressing-case in her hand; but she had not to worry about Letizia at present, and the removal of this anxiety had revived her confidence in being soon able to get a "shop." Meanwhile, she had to find a cheap room somewhere. This proved to be much less easy than she had expected. At first all the owners of the houses announcing apartments seemed to regard her with equal suspicion.

"I don't keep the kind of room you want," said one.

"I wouldn't mind taking you in myself," said another. "But my husband don't like having women in the house."

"If you're looking for gay rooms," said a third with brutal directness, "you'd better try the other side of Oxford Street. You won't find anything to suit you round here. We have to be too careful of the police."

When at last Nancy did reach a quarter where landladies appeared less dismayed by the prospect of letting to a single woman, she found that the most exorbitant prices were asked in every house.

"Two pounds a week for a bedroom only," said one. "Or if you have a latchkey, three pounds."

"But why should I pay a pound a week for a latchkey?" Nancy asked in astonishment.

"Well, if you have your own latchkey, I shouldn't make any extra charge for the gentlemen you brought home. Otherwise I'd have to charge you five shillings a head."

Nancy laughed.

"But I don't want to bring gentlemen home with me. I'm on the stage," she explained.

The stolid countenance of the woman with whom she was negotiating did not change its expression.

"If you don't want to bring men back, you don't want a room in my house."

With this she slammed the door in Nancy's face, obviously annoyed at the waste of her time.

Another landlady was quite distressed by the suggestion that Nancy should have a bedroom for ten shillings a week.

"A nice-looking girl like you doesn't want to come down to that," she exclaimed. "You trust your luck a bit, my dear. Why don't you take my two nice rooms on the ground floor and cheer up? They've always been lucky rooms to girls like you. The last one who had them got off with a wine-merchant somewhere up North, and he's fitted her out with a lovely little flat of her own. He only comes up to London for a day or two every month, so she has a nice easy time of it. I'm sure I don't know whether it's me or my rooms, but certainly I've seen a lot of luck come the way of girls like you."

At last after a peregrination of various apparently economical quarters Nancy found a tiny garret at the top of a tumbledown house in Unicorn Street, which joined Red Lion Square to Theobalds Road. This was the third time in succession that she had taken lodgings in a thoroughfare for foot passengers only, and superstition began to suggest a hidden significance in this collocation. The third time? It might be from here that she would discover the main thoroughfare of her future life.

Unicorn Street was dark and narrow, and the upper portions of several of the houses overhung the pavement so far as almost to meet. These relics of London before the Great Fire had by this date already been condemned, although they were not actually pulled down for another ten years. The majority of the shops belonged to second-hand booksellers, whose wares seemed as tattered and decrepit as the mouldering old houses above. Their trade was mostly done from shelves outside the shops containing books labelled at various prices from one penny to a shilling. There were of course other books inside, but these were usually stacked anyhow in tottering heaps and simply served to replenish the shelves and boxes on the contents of which, when the weather allowed it, seedy men of various ages browsed slowly, humping their backs from time to time like caterpillars when they thought they had caught sight of a rarity. Mr. Askin, the owner of the shop high above which Nancy found her cheap room, resembled the English idea of an elderly German professor before the war destroyed that pleasantly sentimental conception. His lanky white hair hung over his collar like greasy icicles; he wore blue glasses, carpet slippers, and a frock coat; he even smoked a long china pipe. The prospect of seeing his shop pulled down to make way for blocks of eligible offices did not disturb him, because he had made up his mind that within two years he was going to be drowned. As he apparently never moved a yard away from his shop, Nancy was puzzled by this confident belief, and ventured to ask him on what it was based.

"Have you studied the effects of the moon?" he inquired contemptuously.

Nancy admitted that she never had.

Whereupon he put his forefinger against his nose and said very solemnly:

"Then don't meddle in what you don't understand. If I say I'm going to be drowned before two years are out, then it means I've studied the question and come to my own conclusions and resigned myself to what must be. And that's that, isn't it? So try and not talk so silly, young lady."

Mr. Askin had bought enough books, according to his calculations, to outlast him and leave a trifle over for his widow. These had at one time filled every room in the house; but as soon as they were sold the empty rooms were furnished with a few odds and ends and let. The top stories were now completely void of books, which was how Nancy managed to rent one of the garrets in the roof for the sum of seven shillings a week. The other garret was inhabited by Maudie Pridgeon, the Askins' maid-of-all-work, who could not do enough for Nancy once she heard she was a real actress.

"Oh, Miss O'Finn," she begged. "I wonder if you'd be kind enough to hear me recite *The Lighthouse-Keeper's Daughter* some afternoon, and tell me if I've got a chance to get on the stage myself. It's the dream of my life. I may not be a Sarah Burnhard or an Elling Terry, but it's in me, Miss O'Finn. I feel shore it's in me. Sometimes I feel I could burst with what's in me. I was afraid it might be wind for a time after I'd been reading about some medicine or other. But it ain't, Miss O'Finn, it's acting. It is reelly. So some time, when we have a moment to ourselves, I do wish you'd hear me recite and give me a bit of good advice. And of course I can rely on you not to say a word to Mrs. Askin about my ambishing or she might pass some nasty remark about it. She never moves out of the back room behind the shop herself, and she'd never believe as I might be a star hiding my light under a bushel."

The reason why Mrs. Askin never moved out of that back room was her profound conviction that all men were thieves, and collectors of old books the greatest. So, day in day out, she sat in a flocculent armchair which at night was turned into her bedstead, watching with a suspicious eye the behaviour of prospective customers. She was a dark unwieldy woman with a hairy chin, a profusion of tufted moles, and what was almost a heavy moustache. It was agreed when Nancy took the garret that she was not to expect any cooking to be done for her; and when she saw the Askins' meals being prepared in that back room and Mr. and Mrs. Askin and Maudie each eating a disgusting plateful balanced on different heaps of incredibly dusty books, she did not regret the arrangement. She managed to make her own garret fairly clean; and though it was perishingly cold up there under the ancient roof, though the bed was hard and the rats scampered round inside the raw-boned plaster walls, she had the satisfaction of feeling perfectly sure that nowhere in London could she be lodged more cheaply. The solitude of the long, long evenings when she used to go to bed at eight o'clock in order to keep warm was immense; and yet she liked it, for she seemed, high up in this garret, to be as near to Bram as she could reach on earth. There was no blind to the decayed window of the dormer and, blowing out her candle, Nancy used to lie for hours staring out at the tawny London sky, while beneath her pillow Bram's watch was always ticking, his watch that she had never allowed to run down. And once in sleep he held her in his arms, and once she woke with his kisses warm upon her lips; but mostly when she dreamed of that beloved lost one it was of running with him along endless platforms to catch fantastic and unattainable trains, and of acting with him in nightmare plays without having studied the part in which she was being suddenly called upon to appear. Meanwhile, it seemed that the tangible and visible world was fast dissolving into an unstable dream when Nancy, after three weeks of pawnshops and agents' offices and of apparently being as far away as ever from any engagement, was persuaded by Maudie to hear her recite *The Lighthouse-Keeper's Daughter* and was asked at the end of it to advise her about a dramatic future.

"I think you said it very well, Maudie," Nancy assured the little maid, whose cheeks were flushed and whose eyes were flashing with excitement. "But I must really advise you to give up all idea of the stage as a profession. Look at me. I am an experienced actress and yet I can't get an engagement. I've been trying ever since January, and now it's nearly April. All the managers say I'm too tall; and you know, Maudie dear, you're just as much the other way, aren't you? You and I want special parts written for us, that's the trouble."

The little maid's eyes filled with tears.

"Oh, Miss O'Finn," she sobbed, "you've been and gone and shattered my life's ambishings with them words. You see, when I'm reciting I feel as if my head was going through the ceiling, but of course what you feels and what you is ain't the same, is they? Still, it's always the darkest hour before the dawn, they say, and I've still got my young man. When I see him on Sunday night I'll tell him as I've given up my life's ambishings, and he can start saving up for merridge as soon as he likes. It's broke *my* heart, but he'll be happy. He was always afraid he'd lose me, Miss O'Finn. He never could believe I'd remain a simple milkman's wife when I become famous, and on'y last week he let a lovely double-bed go by because he didn't want to have it on his hands and me out of his reach."

A few days after Nancy had destroyed Maudie's dramatic ambitions she received a letter from Mrs. Pottage.

> 3 Starboard Alley,
> Greenwich.
> April 1st

MY DEAR MRS. FULLER,   !

Its' a nice day to choose to write a letter to any one but there you won't get it till April 2nd so you won't think any one's sending you a live mouse or any silly joke like that. Well, here we are as well as we can be thank God—Letitsha is in the pink there's no doubt about it and so am I but this is not what I am writing about. Last week we had the *Lights of Home* company at the Royal and Mr. Plimmer who was acting in it was lodging with me and this week they finished and he's staying on with me because he says he's never been so comfortable in his life but he's took a great fancy to Letitchia and that's a fact—He raves about her and I won't say I'm surprised because she's been on the Top of her Form and making us all laugh fit to Bust. Mrs. B. says she's laughed a lot in her life and which is a fact but she don't think she ever laughed so much as what she has this week. She split her stays one afternoon—They went off like a Cannon—Talk about a royal Salute—And Mr. Plimmer says she's a born actress and ought to be on the boards without delay—well, he's taking out a company himself in a drama he's written something after the stile of *East Lynne* well about the same as far as I can see only a bit more East in it from what I can make out and he wants Letissia for the child and you for the Mother. He'll write plenty of stuff for her because he says She'll Knock Them. Well, I'm bound to say I think she will and Mrs. B's convinsed of it: So I gave him your address and he's going to pop up to London to-morrow if you'll make arrangements to be in I've given him your address. What a voice that Kid has he said to me Mrs. Pottage. Good God it would reach to the back row of the gallery in any theatre. Well I hope this'll be the end of all your troubles and which I think it will dearie—

Letitsia sends her love and so do I and I hope this is an end of all your worries even if it is April Fools Day. Mrs. B. sends all the best and so do I.

Your loving old
JOHANNA POTTAGE.

Here was a most unmistakable turning out of this long lane, Nancy thought, a turning at so sharp an angle that the prospect of taking it alarmed her imagination, so far did it seem likely to lead Letizia and herself away from the direction in which Bram and she had been travelling together. Nancy's mind went back to her own appearance at the age of six in *Green Bushes*. Her mother was no longer alive to witness that first performance of a squeaky-voiced little boy in the old-fashioned melodrama, of which she could remember nothing except the hazy picture of the heroine dressed in a Fenimore Cooper get-up as she came running down the bank, gun in hand. Her father had made arrangements for her to live with the baggage man and his wife during that tour. She had liked Mr. Ballard, a big fat man with a very much waxed moustache, but little Mrs. Ballard with her cold hooked nose, pink and half-transparent at the tip, had been antipathetic. She could see her now sighing and sewing all day. If Letizia did go on the stage as a child, she should not act away from her mother at any rate. It would always have to be a joint engagement.

Maudie interrupted Nancy's pictures of the past by coming up to say that a gentleman was down in the shop and wanted to see her.

"I didn't know if you'd have liked me to have brought him up here, Miss O'Finn? I hope I done right in asking him to wait a minute in the shop?"

"Good gracious, yes, Maudie! He couldn't come up here. I'll be down very soon."

Nancy looked at the card: *Rodney Plimmer. "Custody of the Child" Company*. Evidently that was the play he was presently going to take out on tour. Nancy put on her hat and coat, for if she was going to talk business with Mr. Plimmer they would certainly have to talk elsewhere than in Unicorn Street.

The actor was turning over the pages of one of Mrs. Askin's tattered folios when she came down into the shop.

"Now don't tell me you've got another appointment, Miss O'Finn," he said. "I've been hoping you would come out to lunch with me."

"Oh, no, I haven't any appointment, and I'll be delighted to lunch with you."

"Capital! Then, if you're ready, shall we wend our way toward some little place where we can talk far from the madding crowd?"

There was nothing remarkable about Mr. Plimmer's appearance. The clean-shaven face, the full mobile lips, the tendency toward sleekness, the suggestion that his clothes were being worn with a little too much of an air, the moist impressionable eyes, all these traits were sufficiently familiar to Nancy among the men of her profession.

"Now, have you any prejudices on the subject of restaurants?" Mr. Plimmer inquired with rich voice and elaborate manner.

"None whatever."

"You don't pine for music and such like gaieties?"

She shook her head.

"Then, let me see." He paused with such dramatic abruptness in the middle of the pavement that an errand-boy who was just behind bumped into his broad back. "Why don't you look where you're going, my lad?" he asked with exaggerated dignity.

"Why don't you look where you're stopping?" the errand-boy retorted and hurried on, whistling indignantly.

"Self-possession is nine points of the law," said Mr. Plimmer. "By the way, that's not bad, eh, Miss O'Finn? I think I'll note that down as rather a good line." He took out a small pocket-book, and entered the remark. "A word in the hand is worth two in the head," he observed with a smile; and as he did not bother to enter this line under the other Nancy supposed that he used it frequently.

"Then, let me see," said Mr. Plimmer, returning to the original attitude which had provoked this diversion. "I have it! Kettner's. You've no prejudice against Kettner's?"

"None whatever. I've never been there," Nancy replied.

"Never been to Kettner's? Oh, then of course we must go to Kettner's. No music at Kettner's. And if there's one thing I hate it's chops and sonata sauce."

Mr. Plimmer blinked his moist eyes as if he were dazzled by the brilliancy of his own wit.

"And now what about a hansom?"

The drive from the corner of Theobalds Road to Kettner's was a strain on Nancy, because Mr. Plimmer was evidently extremely nervous in hansoms and talked all the time of the close shaves he had had when driving in them. If ever their driver showed the least audacity in passing another vehicle, Mr. Plimmer would draw in his breath with a hiss, or put his hand out over the apron as if he would seize the too urgent horse by the tail and stop his going too fast. However, Kettner's was reached in safety, and Mr. Plimmer was no sooner on the pavement than he recovered all his suave composure so that he entered the restaurant with the air of knowing exactly where to go and what to order, whenever he should choose to eat in London.

"They know me here," he whispered to Nancy. "Ah, good morning, Gaston."

The waiter who had just placed the menu before him looked slightly astonished at being thus addressed; but he was too urbane to put his client out of countenance by pointing out, as Nancy felt sure he could have pointed out, that his name was not Gaston.

"Now, let me see, what is it I always have here?" said Mr. Plimmer.

"Will you take ze table-d'hôte lunch, sare?" the waiter suggested.

"Oh, you recommend that, do you? Let me see . . ."

The waiter began to translate rapidly the meaning of the various items, so rapidly that Mr. Plimmer did not even have time to say "cheese" instead of "fromage."

"Gaston always makes himself responsible for my lunch here," he explained to his guest. "He knows my tastes, and you can be sure he's going to give us something special."

The waiter, having taken the order for the table-d'hôte, returned with the wine list.

"Ah-ha, now this will take a bit of thought," said Mr. Plimmer. "Let me see now. Let—me—see. White or red wine, Miss O'Finn?"

Nancy chose white.

"What woman ever chose red?" he laughed romantically. "Now let—me—see. What's the number of that Chambertin I usually drink here, Gaston?"

"Number 34 is a very nice wine, sare."

"That's it! That's it! A bottle of 34. Extraordinary, isn't it, the way these fellows remember every customer's likes and dislikes?" he observed to Nancy when the waiter had retired to fetch the wine. "It must be quite a year since I was in Kettner's, and yet he remembered which was my particular tipple. But of course I always tip him well. Oh, yes, old Gaston has good reason to remember my tipple."

Mr. Plimmer winked solemnly to indicate that the pun was intentional.

After a little more talk about the advantages of establishing a personal relationship with waiters if you wished to fare well at restaurants, Mr. Plimmer came to business.

"I think our excellent old landlady Mrs. Pottage has already written to you something of what I wanted to talk about. The fact is, Miss O'Finn, I have been completely subjugated by your little girl. And what an actress! I don't know if you've met Mrs. Pottage's friend with the queer name?"

"Mrs. Bugbird?"

"Just so. Well, your daughter's imitation of Mrs. Bugbird is simply marvellous. She has genius, that child. And genius is not a word that one uses lightly in our profession. No, Miss O'Finn, it is a word that one uses with caution, with extreme caution. But I don't mind telling you that during the last week I have been staggered by her possibilities."

"I'm afraid she comes of precocious parents," said Nancy. "My husband went on the stage when he was only sixteen, and I made my first appearance ten years earlier. In my case, I'm afraid that such early promise was fatal."

"I'm sure you do yourself an injustice," said Mr. Plimmer. "You are feeling discouraged at the moment. It is not to be wondered at. But I venture to think that the proposal I am going to make to you will open a brighter vista. How do you find the wine?"

"Delicious," said Nancy, who might as well have been drinking water, so little was she aware of her glass.

"It is good, isn't it? I'm bound to say Gaston never

lets me down. I don't know if Mrs. Pottage told you that the occasion of my finding myself under her hospitable roof was my engagement with the *Lights of Home* company. A queer old-fashioned melodrama, one at which we are tempted to laugh nowadays. But I accepted the engagement with a purpose. One is never too old to learn, in our profession. I wanted to get the feeling of the audience for melodrama. Of course, in my early days I played a good deal in melodrama, but during the last ten years I have been mostly on tour with London successes. Last year, I had an idea for an original play, and while I was resting I embodied my wandering fancies in tangible shape. I have written, Miss O'Finn, what I do not hesitate to call the finest domestic drama of our time, *The Custody of the Child*. A striking title, eh? The subject is, as you may guess, divorce, but treated, I need hardly say, in a thoroughly pleasant manner. I abominate these modern plays—Ibsen and all that kind of thing. Thank goodness, the great majority of our countrymen are with me there. We don't want that kind of raking in muckheaps. No, the moment that the British drama forgets that it is founded upon British family life, the British drama is dead. I hope you agree with me?"

Nancy supposed that he was more likely to stop talking if she agreed with him than if she argued with him. So she nodded her head in emphatic approval.

"I knew the mother of that child must be an intelligent woman."

"Surely you haven't been discussing the present state of the drama with Letizia?" said Nancy.

Mr. Plimmer laughed solemnly.

"Not exactly. But, by Jove! that child would be quite capable of discussing it. She'd talk a great deal more sense about it than most of these confounded dramatic critics. Don't speak to me about dramatic critics, Miss O'Finn. They disgust me. I can't bring myself to speak about them. I regard dramatic critics and wife-beaters as the most contemptible beings on earth. By what right does a man who knows no more about acting than a graven image set himself up to criticise people who do? There he sits in the front row of the stalls with last night's shirt and a perpetual sneer—but don't ask me to go on talking about such rascals. My gorge rises against them. I despise them. I regard them with contempt and aversion. I wish you hadn't brought up this topic, Miss O'Finn. I can't even enjoy Gaston's excellent lunch when I think about dramatic critics. It's their ignorance that is so appalling, their ignorance, their lack of taste, their dishonesty, their . . . but, no, I cannot speak about them! Do let me pour you out another glass of wine."

"You were telling me about your play, Mr. Plimmer."

The actor-author mopped his brow, and after reviving himself with a few mouthfuls of food was able to continue.

"This play of mine, Miss O'Finn, might seem to bear a superficial resemblance in the main theme to *East Lynne*. But it is only very superficial. Until the excellent Mrs. Pottage to whom I read it said that the great scene in the third act reminded her of a similar scene in the dear old-fashioned drama at which we have all wept in our day, I confess that even this superficial likeness had not struck me. However, Mrs. Pottage was right. There undoubtedly is a faint resemblance. But what of that? Did not somebody or other, some great writer whose name escapes me for the moment, say that there were only six original plots in the world? After all, it's the treatment that counts. But let us be practical. I did not invite you out to lunch to hear me discuss abstract theories of art. At the end of this month *The Custody of the Child* will be presented for the first time on any stage at the Prince of Wales' Theatre, Leeds. Will you and your daughter accept what I am tempted to call the two leading parts? I have engaged an excellent young actor for the husband—Clarence Bullingdon. Do you know him? No? He's very sound. My own part is a comparatively small one. Well, I didn't want to give the critics a chance of saying that I had written a play to show off my own acting."

"But would I suit the part?" Nancy asked.

"Exactly what I require. You might have served as the model for my inspiration."

Nancy wavered. The last thing she had intended was to allow Letizia to act. Yet, would it hurt her so much to be acting with her mother?

"What salary are you suggesting, Mr. Plimmer?"

"I had allotted five pounds a week to your part, Miss O'Finn, but if your little girl will appear with you, I am prepared to double that."

Ten pounds a week! It was as much as she and Bram had ever earned together, and a good deal more than they had earned sometimes. It would be madness to refuse. Besides, work was necessary if she was not to break down under this anxiety. Yet Letizia was very young to be acting.

"What time would my little girl be finished?" she asked.

"Ah, you're thinking of her bedtime. Well, of course, she would be late. In fact, her scene in the last act is the crux of the whole play. But surely she could lie down every afternoon? We shall only have one matinée in the week."

"You are tempting me, Mr. Plimmer. And yet I don't really think I ought to let my little girl act. Couldn't you engage me at five pounds a week without Letizia?"

The actor shook his head.

"Candidly, that would be a bit awkward, Miss O'Finn. The fact is that I have already half promised your part elsewhere, and if it were not for your little girl I should not care to break my word."

"But I wouldn't like to keep another girl out of the part," said Nancy quickly.

"That is being quixotic—unnecessarily quixotic; and

quixotic, dear lady, rhymes with idiotic. No, the other lady would perfectly understand my point of view in doing anything within reason to obtain the services of a good child actress in a play where so much, everything, in fact—depends on that child actress. I understand from Mrs. Pottage that you have been out of an engagement for some time, Miss O'Finn, and you will pardon me if I say that I judged from your lodgings that you are perhaps not in too healthy a financial condition. I am willing if you accept the engagement for your daughter and yourself to pay you half-salary until we open at Leeds. Come, I think I have shown how really anxious I am to have your little daughter."

"I'll let you know to-night," Nancy began.

"No, no, don't wait till to-night. Say 'yes' now. Come, give me your purse and I'll put your first week's salary inside and post you the contract to-night."

There was sixpence-halfpenny in that purse, and to-morrow, Nancy thought, her last brooch would have to go to the pawnshop. After that there would only be a few dresses, and then Bram's watch must go and perhaps even her wedding-ring. It would be madness to refuse. She pushed her purse toward Mr. Plimmer.

"All right. Consider us engaged," she sighed.

The actor was frankly delighted. He ordered a fresh bottle of Chambertin and talked for another half-hour enthusiastically about his play and the success that Letizia was going to make. But Nancy could not be merry. She was wondering what Bram would have said about Letizia's acting. The people in the restaurant faded out of sight; the noise of knives and forks died away; the conversation sank to less than a whisper, to less than the lisp of wind in grass. There stood Bram in the entrance, his eyebrows arched in a question, his eyes half-laughing, half-critical, his lips pursed. It seemed to Nancy that she rose from her seat and cried out to him; but in that instant the people in the restaurant reappeared and the noise of talk and plates was louder than ever. There was no Bram in the entrance of the restaurant, no Bram anywhere in the world.

Mr. Plimmer offered to drive Nancy to Unicorn Street; but she refused and bade him good-bye outside Kettner's. She wanted to be alone, and finding herself in Soho she thought that she would look in at her late lodgings and inquire if there were any unforwarded letters waiting for her, not that she expected any, but it might be that somebody had written to her at that address. It would be cheerful to find a letter from the Kinos. The Kinos? Ah, but it was not the same thing. It was quite another matter for Letizia to act in the same play as her mother.

Miss Fewkes was ungracious when she opened the door to her late lodger. She had not let any of her rooms since the Kinos and Nancy went away.

"There was a letter and a parcel came for you some days ago, but I don't know if I can find them. If you'd have left your address I could have forwarded it on. But I'm too busy to keep an eye on stray letters kicking about and getting in the way when I'm dusting."

However, in the end she found what turned out to be a postcard from Mrs. Kino sending messages from herself and her husband. The parcel was a set of Japanese boxes, one inside the other down to the last one which was hardly bigger than a pin's head. These were for Letizia to play with.

There was nothing about Miss Fewkes that invited one to stay and gossip with her. So Nancy went away with her post, and as she did not want to visit Blackboy Passage again she left her address behind her in case any more letters did happen to come.

That night Nancy lay awake for a long time, puzzling over the wisdom and morality of the step she had taken. Was it due to selfishness? Was it due to her own desire to be at work again? At work! At work again! No longer to lie here night after night, staring out of the curtainless window at the tawny London sky, her heart sick for his arms about her. The evenings might not be so long when she was working again. There would be indeed the poignancy of once more treading boards that he and she had trod together; there would be the agony of seeing again the familiar platforms along which he had run with cups of tea for her; there would be continuous reminders of what she had lost. Reminders? What reminders were needed to make more empty this empty world? At work again! At work! Every week a new town. Always something to distract her from this eternal ache, some poor little futile change, but still change —change and work. Was it very selfish of her to sacrifice Letizia to her own need? Very wrong and very selfish? Yet even from a practical point of view, surely it was right to take this money when she had the chance? She could not leave Letizia with Mrs. Pottage indefinitely. To refuse an offer like this while she accepted the old landlady's charity would put her in such a humiliating position. Bram surely would not blame her. He would remember what had happened when she went to his brother, and she would know that she had tried to put her own feelings on one side. It made such a difference to open her purse and hear the crackle of that five-pound note when she put in her hand to find a penny for the bus-conductor. It was as comforting and warm as the crackling of a fire in wintertime.

"Oh, my darling," she cried toward the stars that were visible again at last after that unending black frost, "my precious one, I don't think I have any more courage left. I can't live alone any longer and wonder what I shall have to pawn of ours next."

In the morning Maudie came in with two letters. The first envelope she opened held the contract from Mr. Rodney Plimmer with a note asking her to sign it and return to him at Greenwich. The handwriting on the outside of the second, which had been forwarded from Blackboy Passage, was unfamiliar, and the postmark showed that it was a week old. Miss Fewkes must have thought yesterday that she had lost it, and had therefore said nothing about it. It was lucky that she had called at her old lodgings. Or was it so lucky? The unfamiliar writing filled Nancy with foreboding, and her heart beat very fast as she tore open the envelope.

> St. Joseph's School,
> Sisters of the Holy Infancy,
> 5 Arden Grove,
> N. W.

> Annunciation B. V. M.

DEAR MRS. FULLER,

After our talk in the train two weeks ago I wrote to the Reverend Mother about you and your little girl. Unfortunately she has been laid up with a bad chill, so that only to-day I have had her answer. She gladly authorises me to offer you the protection of the Holy Child for little Letizia. This would mean that the Community will be utterly responsible for her education until she reaches the age of eighteen. I do not know of course if you will be willing to let her come to us so young. I did not speak to you on the subject, because I did not want to make any kind of half-promise without the authority of the Reverend Mother. We should perfectly understand your not wanting to lose her yet a while, and we shall be willing to accept the care of her at any time during the next three years. But if I may advise you, I think you would do right to send her to us now. You will not consider me too narrow-minded if I say that life on tour with all sorts of changing influences, some good and some perhaps bad, is not the best early influence for a little girl, especially an intelligent and forward little girl like yours. However, this you must decide for yourself. Of course, she will have a very good education, and by being relieved of all financial responsibility you will be able to save money for her when she leaves us.

Will you let me know what you decide? We are ready to take her immediately. I have thought a great deal about you this fortnight, dear child, and I humbly pray to Almighty God that He will give you His grace to choose what is best for yourself and for your little girl.

> Yours affectionately in J. C.
> SISTER CATHERINE.

Here was another wide turning out of that long lane, every bit as wide and important as the first, but leading in exactly the opposite direction.

Nancy looked at the contract from Mr. Plimmer and at the letter from Sister Catherine. Why was she hesitating which road to take? Was it the dread of parting with Letizia? A little. Was it the thought of the disappointment of Mr. Plimmer, who with all his absurdity had appreciated Letizia and thus endeared himself to her mother? A little. Was it the fancy that Mrs. Pottage might be hurt by the rejection of an offer that she would have supposed so welcome? A little. Or was it cowardice about her own immediate future? That most of all. It was the dread of tempting fortune by a refusal of this engagement. It was the dread of sending back that comfortably crackling five-pound note and having to pawn her last brooch before she could even pay for the registered letter in which it ought to be sent. It was dread of the tawny London sky louring at her through that curtainless window, of tumbledown wooden stairs in Maiden Lane and weary stone steps in Garrick Street, of seeing her wedding-ring appraised by a pawnbroker's thick and grimy fingers, of loneliness, eternal, aching loneliness. There recurred the picture of that old lady framed by vermilion cushions, and the sound of her high thin voice repeating, "Educate your child. Educate her." There came back the old lady's confident interpretation of her grandson's unuttered wish. Whatever the cost, Bram would surely choose the convent. Nancy was once more in that silent tunnel, listening to Sister Catherine's voice plangent with the echoes of her passionate fled youth. She remembered how deeply fraught with significance that conversation had seemed. And the impulse that had drawn her footsteps to Blackboy Passage to inquire for letters she did not expect? Who should dare to say it was not Bram himself who had guided her thither? So that between Letizia and the future offered her stood nothing except her mother's cowardice.

Nancy took her brooch to the pawnbroker's and raised upon it the sum of fifteen shillings and sixpence. Of this she spent a shilling in sending this telegram.

Sister Catherine
    5 Arden Grove.
      N. W.

Your letter just received gratefully accept your kind offer will call and see you this afternoon

NANCY FULLER.

Then she bought a registered envelope and slipped the five-pound note inside it with a letter of apology to Mr. Plimmer.

Fourteen shillings and threepence in the world, but Letizia was safe. She found a Catholic church and spent the odd coppers lighting three penny candles to Our Lady of Victories.

CHAPTER XVIII

TRIENNIAL

As if fortune had had no other object in view but the trial of Nancy's character by adversity, she had no sooner handed over Letizia to the care of the Sisters than she secured an engagement with a bloodthirsty melodrama called *The Lights of Paris,* in which she toured what were called the "number two" towns for many, many weeks. Her part was very different from the one Mr. Plimmer had offered her. Instead of the unhappy young mother reconciled in the last act to a forgiving husband she was to be a dark-eyed adventuress, all ostrich plumes and swishing silk petticoats, whose diabolical support of the villain earned groans and hisses from every audience and whose death at last in the very sewer where she had plotted to drown the heroine was greeted with acclamation. However, what did the part matter? She was earning four pounds a week, out of which she was managing to save half. And what did these dreary manufacturing towns matter? There was less temptation to spend money in them. Or the dull company of second-rate actors and actresses? There was small encouragement to waste her money in buying clothes to impress them. Blackburn, Bury, Bolton, St. Helens, Oldham, Rochdale, Preston, Wigan, Warrington, Widnes, Halifax, Huddersfield, Hartlepool, Gateshead, Sunderland, South Shields. Rain and smoke and blight and the stench of chemicals. The clatter of clogs every morning and every afternoon when the women were going to and from their work in the factories. Soot and puddles. Murky canals slimed always with a foul iridescence. Sodden shawls and wet slates. Infinite ugliness, dawns and days and dusks cinereous, eternal infestivity, and ceaseless monotone. No vivid colour anywhere except occasionally in the gutters a piece of orange-peel and on the sweating walls the posters of the tawdry melodrama in which she was playing. It was good to think of Letizia far from these drizzling and fumid airs.

In November the *Lights of Paris* company visited Brigham where for several years now a theatre had stood actually on the site of the original tabernacle of the Peculiar Children of God. On making inquiries about the present state of Lebanon House, Nancy heard that old Mrs. Fuller had died about five months earlier. When Letizia went to school at the convent, Nancy had written and told the old lady; but she had never received an answer to her letter. She did not feel at all inclined to visit Caleb or the aunts, and although she found out where Emily Young was living she did not succeed in meeting her, Miss Young being away that week. Nancy was wondering if her news about Letizia had pleased the old lady, when the following week at Birkenhead she had a letter from Miss Young.

22 Rosebank Terrace,
Brigham.
November 20th, '95.

DEAR MRS. FULLER,

I was so disappointed to miss you during your stay in this dreary place, but I was away on a visit to some cousins in Macclesfield. I wrote to you when Mrs. Fuller died, but I was afraid as I never heard from you that the letter failed to reach you. I sent it to the address from which you wrote last April about your little girl. Mrs. Fuller had just had a second stroke, and I'm not sure that she understood what I was reading to her. Still, I fancied that I noticed an expression in her eyes that looked as if she had understood and was glad. She was really unconscious though until she died in May just before Mr. Caleb Fuller was married. I miss her dreadfully, and Brigham seems duller every day. You are lucky to be on the stage and able to travel about from one place to another. Life here is simply beastly. I'm trying to get a place as secretary to somebody and have been working hard at typewriting and shorthand. I hope I shall succeed. I hate Brigham more every moment of the day. I do hope that we shall meet somewhere again. Wishing you all good luck.

With kind regards. I am,

Yours sincerely,
EMILY YOUNG.

Nancy smiled when she read of the envy her career inspired, smiled when she thought of Blackburn, Bury, Bolton, St. Helens, Oldham, Rochdale, Preston, Wigan, Warrington, Widnes, Halifax, Huddersfield, Hartlepool, Gateshead, Sunderland, and South Shields.

The following Sunday the *Lights of Paris* company found themselves in Warrington, and after Benediction at a little tin mission-church Nancy saw the priest and arranged for Masses to be said for Letizia's great-grandmother. It was not so much the spiritual satisfaction she derived from the fulfilment of this pious duty as the feeling that somehow or other Masses said in this tin church for the repose of that strange old woman's soul would express her personality in the immense void of eternity as effectively as on earth she had expressed herself with those vermilion cushions and Venetian mirrors. She had defied in her own creative world the overwhelming nonentity of Lebanon House, just as on the walls of her room Giorgione's "Pastorale" had defied the meanness of contemporary existence, prevailing with colour against time itself. Now let beauty and compassion rise from the smoke of Warrington to sustain her soul.

There was no opportunity that December to go South and spend Christmas with Letizia; but Nancy was gratefully surprised by an invitation from Mother Mary Ethelreda to visit the convent at Beaumanoir on the moors of northern Lancashire, whence she could easily return in time for the matinée at Burnley on Boxing Day. The drive through the cold upland air, the quiet and seemliness of the conventual life, the dignity of the aged

Mother Superior, the whiteness and candlelight within, the snow and starshine without, all united to compose Nancy's mind so that when she returned to the theatre she moved in a dream, like one who has voyaged from afar and whose body has arrived while the spirit still lingers on the way. Looking out of her window that night, she fancied that the stars high above the smoke of Burnley were jingling like silver bells, so much nearer seemed they since her visit to the Convent of the Holy Infancy at Beaumanoir on the wintry moors. And she knelt down to thank Almighty God that Letizia's youth was clear and bright, remote and crystalline as one of those stars ringing down notes of harmonious light upon the discordant gloom in which her mother wandered.

It was June before Nancy saw Letizia. They spent a month together in the cottage where she was born among the Kentish cherry orchards. The pinks smelt just as sweet along the garden paths as then. There were not fewer roses nor less honeysuckle in the high hedges of the lanes. The haycocks threw shadows quite as far across the shaven leas, across the green-glowing gold-bloomed leas. And when Letizia was tucked away in her old cot and Nancy sat by the lattice, poring upon the perfumes of the evening, there were just as many ghost moths dancing upon the dusky air of the garden, fluttering with the old fantasmal passion above the spiced and sombrous flowers. But in no lane and in no lea, behind no hedge, across no brook, at the end of no garden path was Bram, who in this same month six years ago was everywhere. Yet, in spite of the poignancy of remembered joys that she could never know again, Nancy was very happy during her holiday. Letizia was as diverting as ever, with her long tales of school, as definite in her likes and dislikes and as quick to express them.

At the end of the month the long-promised stay with Mrs. Pottage at Margate was accomplished, and Nancy noted with a little pang for the way Letizia was getting older that she no longer called her old friend Mrs. Porridge, just as now she always said "mother" instead of "muvver."

"Well, they haven't starved her at this convent," the old landlady declared after she had embraced Letizia and presented her cousin, Mrs. Williams, the pleasant and hospitable woman in whose house they were to stay. "I was very doubtful about the idea when you settled to put her in this convent, because I've always had a horror of nuns, and which is why I've never been to see her. I know I read a story once about a pore girl they bricked up, and it gave me the horrors to that extent it was weeks before I could go down into the cellar and fetch up a scuttle of coal. But the child's looking a regular nosegay. What do they give you to eat, duckie?"

"Oh, we have breakfast and dinner and tea and supper, and a glass of milk at eleven," Letizia said.

"You do?" Mrs. Pottage exclaimed. "Oh, dear, oh, dear, they regular gormingdise you! I've got it all wrong about nuns. I suppose it's the name that sounds so empty. But certainly I fancied if you had two slices of dry bread and a glass of water you thought you'd done well for one day."

"Mrs. Pottage, when shall we go paddling?" Letizia asked persuasively.

"Paddling?" said Mrs. Pottage. "You surely don't expect me to go paddling?"

"Well, of course you must paddle," Letizia exclaimed. "Don't you know we're at the seaside?"

"But if I take off my shoes and stockings and pull up my skirts they'll think the British Museum's broken loose," said Mrs. Pottage. "You haven't seen my legs, duckie. Talk about marble columns. Well, my legs would make a marble column look like a knitting-needle. Besides, supposing I got my toe bit off by a kipper?"

The next morning, armed with several baskets of strawberries and a large green-lined gingham umbrella,

Mrs. Pottage set out with Nancy and Letizia to savour the delights of Margate beach.

"Fine weather for a sail, mum," said one of the longshoremen.

"Yes, but you'd be the one that was sold," Mrs. Pottage retorted.

"Nice day for a row, mum," suggested another longshoreman. "A shilling the first hour, and sixpence every hour afterwards."

"Who do you think I am?" Mrs. Pottage demanded. "Grace Darling? No, thanks, young man, I'd sooner spend the money on winkles."

It was such a jolly week at Margate. Although Mrs. Pottage was never lured into a boat, she was persuaded by Letizia into paddling; and when she found herself with the water round her knees she was so much amused by the ridiculous sight she must be making of herself that she became as helpless with laughter as her friend Mrs. Bugbird did and sat down with such a tremendous splash that every child on the beach came running in her direction at the rumour that an elderly woman had been seized by a ferocious shark. Letizia was so much amused by the spectacle of Mrs. Pottage sitting down in the sea and remaining there helpless with laughter that she sat down herself, whereupon several other little girls and boys followed her example, to the consternation of their nurses who had to fling down their novelettes and hurry to the rescue. Yes, it was a jolly week at Margate, a week of sitting on the sun-baked sands and eating strawberries, of paddling and visiting the camera obscura, of listening to Negroes and Pierrots, of digging castles and buying shrimps for tea, of exploring the mysterious marine underworld of the pier, of wild rides on donkeys and sedate drives in goat-carriages, of sweets and paperbags and asphalt promenades. But it came to an end very quickly. Mrs. Pottage went back to Greenwich. Letizia went back to the convent. Nancy went on tour again to play the adventuress in another melodrama.

And for another two years she played adventuresses, rustling her silk petticoats, hissing defiance through her clenched teeth, and smoking with amazing effrontery the cigarettes that in those days indicated on the stage a woman dead to shame. Nor did she catch more than an occasional glimpse of Letizia during that time, because she managed to fill up the summers of both 1897 and 1898 by acting in stock seasons at northern theatres, where for one week during the illness of the leading lady she had an opportunity of showing what she could do with parts like Rosalind, Viola, and Lady Teazle. But the next week she was playing the colourless Celia, the tiresome Olivia, and the prototype of the modern adventuress, Lady Sneerwell. Yet even these parts only lasted for the two reputed fine months of the year. By the middle of July she was once more immersed in monotonous villainy, measuring her success not by the applause but by the groans and hisses of the unsophisticated audiences for whose entertainment she kept the hero and the heroine apart until the very end of the fifth act. Her salary was still four pounds a week; but every week she was still able to save half. There was over £200 for Letizia in the bank when in the autumn of 1898 Nancy secured an engagement in the provincial tour of a popular musical comedy to sing a contralto part with a good song in each of the two acts and, what interested her much more, a salary of five pounds a week. It was while she was with this company that she met John Kenrick.

CHAPTER XIX

NANCY'S CONTRALTO

The acquaintance began in Bristol by Nancy's finding a letter waiting for her at the stage-door on the second evening.

> Royal Severn Hotel,
> Bristol,
> Oct. 11. Tuesday aft.

DEAR MISS O'FINN,

Business having brought me to Bristol, I found myself at the Princess's Theatre last night, and I want to tell you how very much I enjoyed your performance of the Baroness —a difficult and ungrateful part in an absurd production. But apart from your acting I was tremendously struck by your voice. If it were well trained, I don't hesitate to say that you might go very far indeed in grand opera. Good contraltos are so rare, and good contraltos who can act are simply not to be found except in the unusual atmospheric conditions set up by a blue moon. To show my genuine enthusiasm, although my business in Bristol is at an end, I am staying on another night in order to give myself the pleasure of hearing you sing a second time. And will you set the seal upon the pleasure by joining me at supper in my hotel after the performance? I will call for your answer before going in front. Don't concern yourself about "clothes." Such a supper as I can offer you will not be worthy of a grand toilette.

> Yours very truly,
> JOHN KENRICK.

Nancy was not used to getting letters of appreciation from the front of the house. Adventuresses of the type that she had been playing did not attract the susceptible pen. She really hardly knew how to reply. At the same time it was pleasant to be told nice things about one's voice and one's acting. She reread the letter. Rather an affected way of writing, she decided, when she came to the remark about the blue moon. Still, the affectation of the host was not sufficient reason to decline supper with him. Grand opera? The man was mad. Grand opera? Did he know anything about grand opera? It might be interesting to go out to supper. After all, if he turned out to be an idle bore she was not bound to see any more of him. Business might detain him in Bristol; but she never would, if he were tiresome. Nancy borrowed a piece of notepaper from the stage-door keeper and wrote a brief acceptance of the stranger's invitation.

"I've got off with an impresario," she told the lady who shared her dressing-room.

"With a what, dear?"

"Or a Lothario. I'm not quite sure yet," Nancy laughed.

"Have I put too much black on my left eyelid?" the other asked intensely. "It looks a bit smudgy, doesn't it?"

"You're not much interested in my young man," said Nancy in mock reproach.

"I'm sorry, dear. I was so fussed by this gard-awful liquid-black I bought last week at Cardiff."

"Perhaps it was coal," Nancy suggested.

"Oh, you don't think it is really!" exclaimed her companion. "Oh, whatever shall I do? My god, if I wasn't a perfect lady I could say something." Whereupon Miss Pamela Fitzroy proceeded to express her opinion of Cardiff chemists and of the liquid-black they supplied to poor actresses, in very strong language indeed. "What were you saying, dear?" she stopped suddenly to ask Nancy. "Weren't you saying something about getting off with a foreigner? You watch him, that's my advice. I had a Spanish boy following me round last tour when I was with the *Fun of the Fair* crowd, and what I went through, my dear! He'd only

got to look at me, and I'd feel like ringing the nearest
fire-alarm. And then he got jealous and took to walking
up and down outside the stage-door and glaring at all
the men of the company. Of course it used to amuse
them, and they'd whistle *Toreador* or whatever the song
is. In the end, however, he ran out of money and got
pinched for passing a dud cheque at Bradford."

"But my young man isn't a foreigner," said Nancy.

"Damn and blast this liquid-black," swore Miss Pamela
Fitzroy.

With the consciousness that somebody in front was
interested in her Nancy sang her two songs better that
night than she had ever sung them. She was feeling so
much excited over the prospect of going out to supper
while she was dressing after the performance that,
though she knew she was being ridiculous, she simply
could not resist saying to Miss Fitzroy:

"I felt in voice to-night. I really enjoyed singing."

"That's right," her companion replied indifferently.
"A short life and a merry one. Do you know, dear,
I think I've put on weight. My corsets! I believe I'll
have to give up drinking Guinness. They say it's fatten-
ing. What a shame! Still, I don't want to get too fat.
Men don't really like massive women nowadays. I
wonder why. My dear old mother says they got had
so often when women used to wear crinolines that they
took to thin women in self-defence. You ought to meet
my dear old mother. She's such a naughty old thing.
You know, a real good sport. Weren't you saying you
were going out to supper with a fellow in front, dear?
Have a good time, and say 'champagne' in a firm voice.
Don't let him think he can get away with Sauterne, or
you'll find yourself going home on the last tram instead
of in a cab. You want to watch these fellows in the
provinces. They think an actress will give them a season
ticket for paradise on a bottle of lemonade and two ham
sandwiches."

Nancy's admirer was waiting for her outside the stage-door. He was a tall dark clean-shaven man with a heavy chin and large deep-set eyes. The impression of his size was accentuated by the long double-breasted overcoat he was wearing. His voice was deep and sympathetic in spite of his rather sombre appearance.

"So kind of you to accept my casual invitation," he murmured. "Come along, I've a decrepit vehicle waiting for us outside the front of the theatre."

The dining-room of the Royal Severn Hotel did not succeed any better than most provincial hotels in suggesting an atmosphere of nocturnal gaiety. The two waiters looked as if they had been dragged out of bed by the hair of their heads in order to attend to the wants of the unreasonable beings who required to be fed at this unnatural hour. Most of the tables suggested that they would welcome more cheerfully the eggs and bacon of the morning breakfast than the lobster mayonnaise of supper. The very flowers in attendance appeared heavy with sleep and resentful at not being allowed a night's repose with the other table decorations that were piled upon one of the sideboards like wreaths upon a coffin. Half the room was in twilight, so that the portion of it that was lighted was so uncomfortably bright as to seem garish. At one end two members of the chorus were trying to make a pair of youthful hosts feel at their ease by laughter that sounded as thin as broken glass.

"I'm sorry to inflict this atmosphere of gloom upon you," said Mr. Kenrick. "Let's try to dissipate it in a bottle of champagne. I did my best to order a special supper, but my efforts were regarded with suspicion by the management. Your fellow performers over there seem to be enjoying themselves. Touring with them must be rather like travelling with an aviary of large and noisy birds."

"Oh, but they're such dears," Nancy exclaimed, in arms against any criticism of her fellow players.

Mr. Kenrick put up a monocle and looked across at

the group for a moment. Then he let it fall without comment.

"You sang better than ever to-night," he said gravely.

Nancy felt that she simpered.

"I'm in earnest, you know. What are you going to do about it?"

"My voice?"

He nodded.

"What can I do?"

"You could have it trained."

"But, my dear man, do you realize that I'm twenty-eight? Rather late in the day to be cultivating operatic ambitions."

"Not at all when the voice is as good as yours, and if you go to the right man."

"And where is he to be found?"

"Naples."

Nancy laughed.

"It's like a fairy-story where the poor heroine is set an impossible task by the wicked stepmother. How do you think I could afford to go to Naples?"

"That's just what I wanted to discuss with you," said Kenrick.

"But wait a moment," Nancy interrupted. "I have a little girl."

"What has that got to do with training your voice?"

"Why, this. Every penny that I can save I am saving for her. She is in a convent now, and when she leaves school in another twelve years I want her to have a voice and be able to afford to pay for its training. I want her to have everything that I lacked. I would be wrong to spend the money I have saved in building castles in Spain for myself."

"But, my dear woman, if in another twelve years you are an operatic star of some magnitude you'll be able to do much more for your daughter than you could with what you'll save as a provincial actress between now

and then. But forgive me; you speak of a little girl.
You have a husband then?"

"My husband is dead. He died nearly four years
ago."

Kenrick nodded slowly.

"And—forgive my bluntness—you have no other en-
tanglements?"

She flushed.

"My marriage was never an entanglement . . . and
if you mean 'am I in love with anybody now?' why,
no, I could never love anybody again."

"That's a sad remark for twenty-eight. A woman's
grande passion usually happens when she is thirty-three."

"Mine won't," said Nancy obstinately.

"I shouldn't dare the God of Love," Kenrick warned
her. "Remember, he's a mischievous boy and nothing
gives him greater delight than to behave as such. Never
dare a boy to climb an apple-tree or Cupid to shoot his
arrows in vain. You offered him a fine target by that
remark of yours. But don't let's begin an argument
about love. It's your voice I want to talk about. Surely
you must realise that you possess a contralto of the finest
quality?"

"I thought it was a fairly good natural voice," Nancy
admitted. "But I certainly never supposed it was of the
finest quality."

"Not only have you a marvellous voice, but you can
act. Very few contraltos can act. On the operatic stage
they usually sound like governesses who have drunk a
little too much at a fancy-dress ball."

"Rather voluptuous governesses usually," Nancy
laughed.

"Yes, but with the healthy voluptuousness of women
who have been eating plenty of the best butter and
drinking quarts of the richest cream. You would be
different."

"I hate to be rude," Nancy said. "But do you know,

it always seems to me such a waste of time to talk about impossibilities. Perhaps I've no imagination. I'll talk as long and as earnestly as you like about the best way of travelling from one town to another, or of any of life's small problems, but to discuss which seaside resort in the moon would be the jolliest place to spend one's holidays surely isn't worth while."

"But why is your appearance in opera so remote from any prospect of being realised?"

"I've told you, my dear man," said Nancy impatiently. "I have planned my life so that my small daughter may have what I could not have. To indulge my own ambitions at her expense would be wrong. I can't pretend that I'm denying myself much, because, to be honest, until I had your letter I had never contemplated myself as an operatic star. I knew I had an unusually good contralto voice. I knew that I could act as well as most women and a good deal better than some. Your letter was a pleasure, because it is always a pleasure to feel that one has interested somebody. I am grateful to you for inviting me out to supper and saying nice things about my possibilities. But now let's talk of something else, for you'll never infect me with any ambition to do anything that could risk my ability to do what I can for my daughter, just by acting quietly in the provinces as I am acting at present."

"Listen to me, Miss O'Finn," said Kenrick earnestly. "I am a business man. That is my inheritance from a hard-working father. But I have one passion, and that is not business. My passion is the opera; my dream is to make enough money to be able to help the opera in England. But I am rich enough to do something for the individual artist, and I beg you to let me help you. Let me guarantee you what you would usually earn on the provincial stage. Let me pay for your lessons. The *maestro* I want to teach you is an old friend of mine. If at the end of six months he tells me that you are not the finest contralto of the time, why, then you can go back to your

life on tour.   At the worst you will have spent six
months in Italy to gratify the whim of an eccentric business man whose dreams are all of art.   At the best you
will be able to do what you like for your daughter in
another ten years, and long, long before that.   We'll not
talk about it any more to-night.   Go home and sleep over
my proposal.   Think over it for a week.   I must be back
in town to-morrow.   If at the end of a week you feel
that you can risk six months in Italy to have the world
at your feet, send me a line, and I will pay into your
account the necessary funds.   You can leave this absurd
company when you like."

"Och, I would have to give a fortnight's notice," said
Nancy quickly.

Kenrick smiled.

"Very well, give your fortnight's notice.   To-day is
the eleventh.   If you settle by next Saturday that will
be the fifteenth.   On the first of November you can quit
the fogs and be on your way to Naples.   It will probably
be fine weather.   It usually is about then in the south
of Italy."

"You seem to have made up your mind that I'm going
to accept your generosity," Nancy said.

"There is no generosity in gratifying one's own desires," Kenrick observed.   "But if you have any feelings of pride on the subject, why, you can pay me back
when your position is secure."

"But why, really, are you doing this?" Nancy asked,
looking deep into the eyes of her host.

"Really and truly because I believe you have a great
voice and may become a great singer, and because if
you did I should get as much satisfaction from your
success as if I had a voice and were a great singer myself," he replied.

The thin laughter of the chorus-girls at the other end
of the room commented upon this grave assertion.   The
waiter put up a grubby hand to hide a yawn.

When Nancy woke next morning she felt like the heroine of an Arabian Nights tale who has been carried half across Asia by a friendly djinn. But when she called at the theatre for her letters, the following note was a proof that she had not been dreaming:

> Royal Severn Hotel,
> Bristol.
> October 12.

DEAR MISS O'FINN,
  Do think very hard over our talk last night. You can't lose anything by my offer; you may gain a very great deal. In fact, I am positive that you will. Let me know your decision at my London address, 42 Adelphi Terrace, and I will get into communication with Maestro Gambone, and fix up your lessons. I suggest you live at an Italian *pensione* in Naples. The more Italian you can learn to speak, the better you will sing it. I'll find out a good place.
  Good luck to you.
> Yours sincerely,
> JOHN KENRICK.

It was a fine October day of rich white clouds and rain-washed blue deeps between. A faint haze bronzed the lower air and lent the roofs and chimneys of the city a mirrored peace, a mirrored loveliness. Nancy wandered down by the docks and in contemplation of the glinting masts tried to find an answer to the riddle of her future. Suppose her voice turned out to be less good than he had supposed? Well, that would be his bad judgment. But had she the right to accept money from a stranger in the event of failure? It would be his own fault if she proved a failure. It was a serious matter to leave a company in which she had expected to be playing until next summer. What would Sister Catherine say? Nancy remembered what Sister Catherine had said about Italy that night they met in the train. Sister Catherine would never be the one to blame her. She took Letizia's letter out of her bag and read it through again.

St. Joseph's School,
5 Arden Grove,
N. W.
Sunday.

MY DEAR MOTHER,

I hope you are very well. I am learning Italian with Sister Catherine. It is very nice. I know twenty-two words now and the present indicitive of "I am." I like it very much. We have a new girl called Dorothy Andrews. She is very nice. She is eight and a half years old, but she is not so big as me. I must stop now because the bell is ringing for Vespurs and Benedicsion.   Your loving

LETIZIA.

She was safe for so many years, Nancy thought. Would it be so very wrong to embark upon this adventure?

That night, when she was singing the first of her two songs, she tried to imagine that the piece was *Aïda* and that she was Amneris.

"If I get a genuine encore," she promised herself, "I'll write to him and accept."

And she did get a most unmistakable encore.

"Your songs went very well to-night, dear," said Miss Fitzroy grudgingly. "Had you got any friends in front?"

The next day Nancy wrote to John Kenrick and told him that she was going to accept his kind offer, and that on Sunday, October 23rd, she should be in London.

He telegraphed back: *Bravo will meet train if you let me know time.*

But she did not let him know the time of her arrival at Paddington, for she thought that there was really no reason why he should want to meet her train. Somehow it made his interest in her seem too personal, and Nancy was determined that the whole affair should be carried through on the lines of the strictest business. Besides, she would be staying at the convent, and it would be so exciting to learn her first words of Italian from Letizia.

CHAPTER XX

St. Joseph's School was a pleasant early Victorian house with white jalousies encircled by a deep verandah of florid ironwork. The garden, even for the spacious northwest of London, was exceptionally large, and like all London gardens seemed larger than it really was by the contrast between its arbours and the houses entirely surrounding them. There was a mystery about its seclusion that no country garden can possess, and one could imagine no fitter tenants of its leafy recesses than these placid nuns and the young girls entrusted to their tutelage. It seemed that in all those fortunate windows of the houses which overlooked through the branches of the great lime-trees this serene enclosure there must be sitting poets in contemplation of the pastoral of youth being played below. The flash of a white dress, the echo of a laugh, the flight of a tennis-ball, the glint of tumbling curls, all these must have held the onlookers entranced as by the murmur and motion and form and iridescence of a fountain; and this happy valley among the arid cliffs of London bricks must have appeared to them less credible than the green mirages in desert lands that tease the dusty eyelids of travellers.

"I'm glad you have a friend of your own age," Nancy said to Letizia, when the morning after her arrival they were walking together along the convent avenue strewn with October's fallen leaves.

"Well, she's not a very great friend," Letizia demurred.

"But I thought you wrote and told me that she was so very nice?"

"Well, she is very nice. Only I don't like her very much."

"But if she's so very nice, why don't you like her?"

"Well, I don't like her, because she *is* so nice. Whenever I say, 'Let's do something,' she says, 'Oh, yes, do let's,' and then I don't want to do it so much."

"Darling, isn't that being rather perverse?"

"What's 'perverse,' mother? Do tell me, because I'm collecting difficult words. I've got thirty-eight words now, and when I've got fifty I'm going to ask Hilda Moore what they all mean, and she's twelve and it'll be a disgusting humiliation for her when she doesn't know. And that'll be simply glorious, because she thinks she's going to be a yellow-ribbon presently."

"But don't you want to be a yellow-ribbon?"

"Oh, I don't think it's really worth while. Evelyn Joy who's much the nicest girl in the school has never been a ribbon. She said she couldn't be bothered. She's frightfully nice, and I love her one of the best six people in the world. She can't be bothered about anything, and most of the girls are always in a fuss about something. Dorothy Andrews only wants to do what I want, because she thinks she ought to. Fancy, she told me she simply longed to be a saint. And she said if she died young she'd pray for me more than anybody, and I said, 'Pooh, St. Maurice is *always* praying for me and he wears armour and is very good-looking, so there's no need for you to die young.' And then she cried and said when she was dead I'd be sorry I'd been so cruel."

Nancy thought that Letizia was not less precocious than she had always been, and she wondered if she ought to say anything to Sister Catherine about it. She decided that Sister Catherine was probably well aware of it and, not being anxious to give her the idea that she was criticising the wonderful education that the nuns were giving her little daughter, she resolved to say nothing.

She did, however, discuss with Sister Catherine her

own project to go to Italy and have her voice trained; and she was much relieved when it was approved.

"It would be wrong not to avail yourself of such an opportunity," the nun exclaimed. "Even if it involved breaking into your own savings, I should still urge you to go; but there seems no likelihood of that, and there is no reason why you shouldn't accept this Mr. Kenrick's offer. I'd no idea that you had a wonderful voice, and how delightful to be going to Italy. Do sing for us one evening at Vespers before you go. Sister Monica would be so pleased, and we shall all enjoy it so much. We shall feel so grand."

"But I'm just as much astonished to hear that I've got this wonderful voice as you are," Nancy said. "Nobody ever told me I had, until this fairy prince arrived in Bristol."

"Ah, but I think people are always so afraid to think anybody has a good voice until somebody else has established the fact for them," Sister Catherine laughed. "It was just a piece of good luck that you should be heard by somebody who understood what good singing is. . . . I'm glad you think dear little Letizia is looking so well. She is a great treasure, and we are all very proud of her. She has so much personality, and I'm doing my best to let her keep it without spoiling her."

"I'm sure you are," Nancy said. "And och, I wish I could ever tell you how grateful I am to you."

"There is no need of words, dear child," said the nun, smiling. "You prove it to us all the time. I heard from the Reverend Mother yesterday, and she inquired most affectionately after you."

That afternoon Nancy went to Mr. Kenrick's flat in Adelphi Terrace. He was so kind that she reproached herself for having refused so brusquely to let him meet her at Paddington.

"Well, it's all arranged with Maestro Gambone. He's really the kindest old man, though he may seem a little fierce before you know him. Should he, on hearing your voice, decide it's not worth training, you'll have to forgive me for rousing your ambitions and let me see you through any difficulties you may have about getting another engagement in England. I have taken a room for you with some people called Arcucci who have a *pensione* in the Via Virgilio which is close to Santa Lucia. Arcucci himself was a singer; but he lost his voice through illness, poor chap. He never earned more than a local reputation at the San Carlo Opera House; but he is full of stories about famous singers, and you'll get the right atmosphere from him. His wife is a capable and homely woman who will make you as comfortable as Neapolitans know how, which, to tell the truth, is not saying much."

While her patron was speaking, Nancy was gazing out of his study window at the Thames and letting her imagination drift down on the fast-flowing ebb with the barges that all seemed like herself bound for some adventure far from this great city of London. Away on the horizon beyond Lambeth the domes of the Crystal Palace sparkled in the clearer sunshine. Even so, on an horizon much farther south than Sydenham flashed the elusive diamonds of success and fame.

"Tuesday is no day to set out on a journey," said Kenrick. "So, I've taken your ticket for Wednesday. You'll leave Paris that night from the Gare de Lyon in the Rome express, and you'll be at Naples on Friday afternoon."

He went to a drawer in his desk and took out the tickets.

"Good luck," he said, holding Nancy's hand.

She was again the prey of an embarrassment against which she tried hard to struggle, because it seemed to smirch the spirit in which she wanted to set out. This constraint prevented her from thanking him except in clumsy conventional phrases.

"Now, will you dine with me to-night?"

She wanted to refuse even this, but she lacked the

courage; in the end she passed a pleasant enough evening, listening to her host expatiate upon the career for which he assured her again and again she was certainly destined. He wanted her to lunch and dine with him on the next day too; but she pleaded the urgency of shopping and packing and her desire to see something of her daughter.

"Very well then," he said, as he put her into a hansom outside Verrey's where they had dined. "I'll be at Victoria on Wednesday morning."

Nancy was glad to be jingling back to St. Joseph's, alone with her dreams in the sharp apple-sweet air of the October night.

The next day Mrs. Pottage arrived to say good-bye and help Nancy with her shopping. By now she had long been an institution at St. Joseph's, where her conversation afforded the most intense delight to the nuns.

"Well, when you wrote you was off to Italy I was in two minds if I wouldn't suggest coming with you. I don't know what it is, whether I'm getting old or ugly or both, but I've not had a single proposal for eighteen months. I suppose it means I've got to be thinking of settling down and giving some of the younger ones a chance. Well, take care of yourself in Italy, and don't eat too much ice-cream. Funny thing, I-talians should eat so much ice-cream and yet be so hot. There was an opera company came to Greenwich once, and the tenor who was an I-talian stayed with me. 'Well,' I said to myself, 'what he'll want is plenty of macaroni and ice-cream.' He looked a bit surprised, I'm bound to say, when I give it him for breakfast on the Sunday morning, but I thought he was only surprised at any one knowing his tastes so well. But, will you believe me, when I give it him for dinner again, he used language that was far from I-talian, very far. In fact, I never heard any one swear so fluent in English before or since. It quite dazed me for the moment. But we got on all right as soon as I found he liked good old roast beef. He gave

me two passes for the Friday night, and Mrs. Bugbird
and me thoroughly enjoyed ourselves. The opera was
called *Carmen* and Mrs. B. thought it was going to be
all about them, and when she found it was actually the
name of a woman she laughed herself silly. Every
time this Carmen came on she'd whisper to me, 'a good
pull up,' and then she'd start off shaking like a jelly.
But there, she's very quick to see the radiculous side of
anything, Mrs. Bugbird is. Well, good-bye, dear, and
take good care of yourself. You know your old Mrs.
Pottage wishes you all the best you can wish for yourself."

Sister Catherine had repeated her request that Nancy
should sing to them, especially as it was the feast of All
Saints. So after practising with Sister Monica, who had
charge of the music, she sang Mozart's motet *Ave
Verum Corpus* at Benediction amid the glowing candles
and white chrysanthemums of the little chapel.

"Mother, you don't often sing in church, do you?"
Letizia asked.

"Didn't I sing well?" said her mother with a smile.

"Yes, I expect you sang very well, but I thought it
was a little loud, didn't you? Sometimes it sounded like
a man singing. I think you ought to be careful and not
sing quite so loud, mother."

Luckily the nuns themselves enjoyed Nancy's rich
contralto a great deal more than did their pupils. The
warmth of femininity spoke to their hearts of something that they had lost, or rather of something that
most of them had never won. It was easy to understand
and sympathise with the readiness of the nuns to turn
away for a few minutes from the austere ecstasies of
Gothic art to worship some dolorous "Mother" of
Guido Reni. A flush had tinged their cheeks so virgin-
ally tralucent, as if a goblet of water had been faintly
suffused by a few drops of red wine.

Kenrick was at Victoria to see Nancy off next morning. Just as the train started, she leaned out of the

window of her compartment and exclaimed breathlessly:

"Please don't think me ungrateful. I do appreciate tremendously what you are doing for me. Really, I do."

His long, sombre face lit up with a smile, and he waved his hand as Nancy withdrew from London into the train again.

France dreamed in a serenity of ethereal blue. In the little wedding-cake cemeteries black figures were laying wreaths of immortelles upon the graves. Nancy remembered with a pang that it was All Souls' Day and reproached her cowardice for not having laid flowers on Bram's grave at Greenwich before she left England. The bunch of carnations with which Kenrick had presented her became hateful to hold, and she longed to throw it out of the window. She would have done so, if two English old maids had not been regarding her curiously from the other side of the compartment, the one above her Baedeker, the other above the *Church Times*. Why should elderly English women travelling abroad look like butterfly-collectors?

"*Parlez vous anglaise?*" said one of them to the ticket-collector, nodding her head and beaming as if she were trying to propitiate an orang-utan.

"Yes, I spik English, madame," he said coldly after punching the tickets.

The other elderly lady congratulated her companion upon the triumphant conversation.

"He undoubtedly understood perfectly what you were saying, Ethel."

"Oh, yes, I think we shall get along capitally after a time. I was always considered very good at French in my schooldays, and it's just beginning to come back to me."

Her ambition had been kindled by her success with the first ticket-inspector. With the next one who invaded the compartment she took a line of bold and direct inquiry.

"*Paris, quand?*"

The inspector stared back, indignation displayed upon his countenance.

"Comment?"

"Non, quand," said the elderly lady.

The inspector shrugged his shoulders and slammed the carriage-door as he retired.

"That man seemed rather stupid, I thought, Ethel."

"Most stupid," the ambitious Ethel emphatically agreed.

Nancy felt thankful that Letizia would be taught French properly. Sister Catherine had already suggested to her that when she was twelve she should be sent for three years to a convent in Belgium with which the Sisters of the Holy Infancy had an arrangement of exchanging pupils. Nancy had been a little alarmed at first by the prospect of sending Letizia abroad all that time; but after these two absurd Englishwomen she felt no trouble was too great and no place too far and no separation too long that would insure Letizia against talking French like them in public.

But presently Nancy was too much occupied with her own problems—transferring herself and her luggage from one station in Paris to another, finding out how the *wagon-lit* toilet arrangements worked, how to reply to the Italian examination of baggage in the Mt. Cenis tunnel, and how to achieve the change at Rome into the Naples train—either to criticise anybody else or even to dream and speculate about her own operatic future.

Then Vesuvius loomed above the russet orchards and dishevelled vines on the left of the railway. Nancy suddenly remembered that when she and Bram were first married he had one day said how much he should like to visit Naples with her. He had told her that he had seen a picture of it when he was a boy and of what a thrill it had given him. Now here it actually was, and he was not by her side to behold it. Here Naples had been all these years, and he had never seen it.

Time heals many wounds; but in some he makes a deeper gash every year with his inexorable scythe.

CHAPTER XXI

CLASSIC GRIEF

Nancy was lost at first in the *pensione* to which Kenrick had entrusted her. The bareness of it seemed to reflect the bareness of her own mind amid the unmeaning sounds of a strange tongue. During the first week she felt that she should never, stayed she in Naples for years, acquire a single word of Italian, and the week after she was convinced that she should never be able to say anything more than the Italian for "yes," "no," "please," "thanks," "good night," "good morning," and "bread." For a fortnight she was so completely stunned by the swarming rackety city that she spent all her spare time in the aquarium, contemplating the sea-anemones. The stories of great singers with which Signor Arcucci was to have entertained her leisure seemed indefinitely postponed at her present rate of progress with Italian. She should have to become proficient indeed to follow the rapid hoarseness of that faded voice. Meanwhile, she must wrestle with an unreasonable upside down language in which *aqua calda* meant hot water and not, as one might suppose, cold. Nancy cursed her lack of education a hundred times a day, and an equal number of times she thanked Heaven that Letizia already knew twenty-two Italian words and could say the present indicative of the verb "to be." Signora Arcucci was a plump waxen-faced Neapolitan housewife who followed the English tradition of supposing that a foreigner would understand her more easily if she shouted everything she had to say about four times as loud as she spoke ordinarily. She used to heap up Nancy's plate with spaghetti; and, as Nancy could not politely excuse herself from eating any more, she simply had to work her way through the slithery pyramid until she felt as if she must burst.

Nor did Maestro Gambone do anything to make up for the state of discouragement into which her unfamiliar surroundings and her inability to talk had plunged her. Nancy found his little apartment at the top of a tall tumbledown yellow house that was clinging to the side of the almost sheer Vomero. He was a tiny man with snow-white hair and imperial and jet-black eyebrows and moustache. With his glittering eyes he reminded her of a much polished five of dominos, and when he wanted anything in a hurry (and he always did want things in a hurry) he seemed to slide about the room with the rattle of a shuffled domino. Although his apartment stood so high, it was in a perpetual green twilight on account of the creepers growing in rusty petrol tins that covered all the windows.

"You speaka *italiano,* madama?" he asked abruptly when Nancy presented herself.

"No, I'm afraid I don't."

"*Allora come canta?* How you singa, madama?"

"I only sing in English at present."

"What musica you havva?"

Nancy produced the stock-in-trade of ballads, which the maestro fingered like noxious reptiles.

"*E questo?* Anna Lowrie *o qualche nome indiavolato. Probiamolo. Avanti!*"

The little man sat down at the piano and was off with the accompaniment on an instrument of the most outrageously tinny timbre before Nancy had finished deciding that he was not so much like a domino as a five-finger exercise.

"*Eh, avanti!*" he turned round and shouted angrily. "What for you waita, madama? *Di nuovo!*"

In the green twilight of this little room hanging over the precipitous cliff above the distant jangling of Naples

Nancy could not feel that Maxwellton Braes had ever existed. She made a desperate effort to achieve an effect with the last lines.

> "And for bonnie Annie Laurie
> I would lay me down and dee."

There was a silence.

Then the *maestro* grunted, twirled his moustache, rose from the piano, and sat down at his desk.

"Here I writa when you come," he said. *"A rivederla e buon giorno."*

He thrust the paper into Nancy's hand and with the same gesture almost pushed her out of his apartment. The next thing of which she was conscious was walking slowly down the Vomero in the honey-coloured November sunshine and staring at the hours and days written down upon the half-sheet of notepaper she held in her hand.

So the lessons began, and for a month she wondered why she or anybody else should ever have suffered from a momentary delusion that she could sing. She knew enough Italian by that time to understand well enough that Maestro Gambone had nothing but faults to find with her voice.

"Have I made any progress?" she found the courage to stammer out one morning.

"Progresso? Ma che progresso? Non sa encora camminare."

Certainly if she did not yet know how to walk she could not progress. But when should she know how to walk? In her halting Italian Nancy tried to extract from the *maestro* an answer to this.

"Quanda camminerà? Chi sa? Forse domani, forse giovedì, ma forse mai."

Perhaps to-morrow, perhaps on Thursday, but perhaps never!

Nancy sighed.

When she got back to the *pensione* she sat down and wrote to her patron.

> Pensione Arcucci,
> Via Virgilio 49.
> Napoli.
> Dec. 8.

DEAR MR. KENRICK,

I really don't think it's worth your while to go on paying for these singing lessons. Maestro Gambone told me to-day that I might never know how to sing. I'm sure he's disgusted at my slowness. I've been having lessons for a month now, and he has had ample time to judge whether I'm worth his trouble. He evidently thinks I'm not. It's a great disappointment, and I feel a terrible fraud. But I'm not going to reproach myself too bitterly, because, after all, I would never have thought of becoming a singer if you hadn't put it into my head. So, next week I shall return to England. I'm afraid your kindness has been . . .

Nancy put down her pen. Her struggles with Italian seemed to have deprived her of the use of her own tongue. She could not express her appreciation of what he had done for her except in a bread-and-butter way that would be worse than writing nothing. For all the sunlight flickering on the pink and yellow houses opposite she felt overwhelmed by a wintry loneliness and frost. And then she heard coming up from the street below the sound of bagpipes. She went to the window and looked out. Two men in heavy blue cloaks and steeple-crowned felt hats, two shaggy men cross-gartered, were playing before the little shrine of the Blessed Virgin at the corner of the Via Virgilio an ancient tune, a tune as ancient as the hills whence every year they came down for the feast of the Immaculate Conception to play their seasonable carols and grave melodies until Christmastide. Nancy had been told about them, and here they were, these—she could not remember their name, but it began with "z"—these *zamp* something or other. And while she stood listening by the window she heard far

and wide the pipes of other pious mountaineers piping
their holy ancient tunes. Their bourdon sounded above
the noise of the traffic, above the harsh cries of the
street-vendors, above the chattering of people and the
clattering of carts and the cracking of whips, above the
tinkling of mandolins in the barber-shops, sounded remote and near and far and wide as the bourdon of bees
in summer.

The playing of these pipers calmed the fever of
Nancy's dissatisfaction and seemed to give her an assurance that her failure was not yet the sad fact she was
imagining. She decided to postpone for a little while
her ultimatum to Kenrick and, tearing up the unfinished
letter, threw the pieces on the open brazier, over which
for so many hours of the wintry days Signor Arcucci
used to huddle, slowly stirring the charcoal embers with
an iron fork and musing upon the days when he sang
this or that famous part. He was out of the room for
a moment, but presently he and his Signora, as he called
her, came in much excited to say that the *zampognieri*
were going to play for them. The pipers in the gim-
crack room looked like two great boulders from their
own mountains, and the droning throbbed almost un-
bearably in the constricted space. When everybody in
turn had given them a lira or two, they acknowledged
the offerings by presenting Nancy as the guest and
stranger with a large wooden spoon. She was taken
aback for the moment by what would have been in
England the implication of such a gift. Even when she
had realised that it was intended as a compliment the
omen remained. She could not help wondering if this
wooden spoon might not prove to be the only gift she
should ever take home from Italy. Nevertheless, the
zampognieri with their grave carols healed her fear of discouragement, and during the next fortnight Maestro Gambone on more than one occasion actually praised her singing and found that at last she was beginning to place her
voice somewhat more approximately where it ought to be

placed. It was as if the fierce little black and white man
had been softened by the spirit of Christmas, of which
those blue-cloaked pipers were at once the heralds and the
ambassadors with their bourdon rising and falling upon
the mandarin-scented air. Absence from home at this
season did not fill Nancy with sentimental regrets. Since
Bram died Christmas had not been a happy time for her,
so intimately was its festivity associated with that dreadful night at Greenwich four years ago. She welcomed
and enjoyed the different atmosphere of *Natale,* and after
so many grimy northern winters these days of turquoise,
these dusks of pearl and rose, these swift and scintillat-
ing nights.

On the anniversary of Bram's death she drove out to
Posilipo and sat on a rock by the shore, gazing out
across the milky cerulean waters of the bay. For all the
beauty of this classic view she was only aware of it as
one is aware of a landscape by Poussin or Claude, about
whose vales and groves and gleaming temples no living
creature will ever wander. The dove-coloured water that
lapped the rock on which she sat, the colonnade of dark-
domed pines along the brow of the cliff, Ischia and Capri
like distant castles of chalcedony, Vesuvius in a swoon
of limpid golden air—all without Bram was but a vanity
of form and colour. The thought of how easily he might
have been preserved from death afflicted her with a madness of rage. Indifference to the beauty of her surroundings was succeeded by a wild hatred of that beauty,
so well composed, so clear, so bland, and so serene. But
for the folly of one incompetent and unimaginative fellow man he might have been sitting beside her on this
rock, sitting here in this murmurous placidity of earth
and sea and sky, gazing out across this crystalline ex-
panse, his hand in hers, their hearts beating together
where now only his watch ticked dryly. Nancy longed
to weep; but she could not weep in this brightness. Yet
she must either weep or fling herself from this rock and
sink down into the water at her feet, into that tender

water with the hue and the voice and the softness of a dove. She let a loose stone drop from her hand and watched it sink to the enamelled floor of the bay. How shallow it was! She should never drown here. She must seek another rock round which the water swirled deep and indigo-dark, water in which a stone would flicker for a few moments in pale blue fire and be lost to sight long before it reached the bottom. Nancy left the rock where she had been sitting and tried to climb upward along the cliff's edge in search of deep water at its base. And while she climbed her clothes became scented by the thickets of rosemary. There appeared to her distraught mind the image of Bram as Laertes and of the actress who had played Ophelia saying to him, *"There's rosemary, that's for remembrance."* She herself had been understudying the Queen and had been standing in the wings to watch how the mad-scene was taken. She could see the expression of mingled horror and pity on Bram's face, as he took the sprig of rosemary from his sister's hand. *Pray, love, remember.*

"Bram," she cried aloud in an agony of repentance. "I didn't mean it. I'm not really mad. I won't drown myself. I won't really."

Then she flung herself face downward among the bushes of rosemary and wept. For an hour she lay hidden from the sun in that bitter-sweet grey-green gloom of the cliff's undergrowth until at last her tears ceased to flow and she could stand up bravely to face again the future. More lovely now was the long sweep of the Parthenopean shore, more lucid the wash of golden air, richer and more profound the warm wintry Southern peace; and she standing there among the rosemary was transmuted by the timelessness of her grief into a timeless figure that might haunt for ever that calm and classic scene.

The last sunset stain had faded from the cloudy cap of Vesuvius, and the street-lamps were already twinkling when Nancy got back to Naples. She went into a church, and there in a dark corner prayed to be forgiven for that brief madness when she had wished to take her life. She sat for a long while, thinking of happy times with Bram, soothed by the continuous coming and going of poor people to visit the Crib, all lit up at the other end of the church. She knelt once more to beg that all that was lost of Bram's life might be found again in his daughter's; and her ultimate prayer was as always for strength to devote herself entirely to Letizia's happiness.

Thus passed the fourth anniversary of the Clown's death.

CHAPTER XXII

SORRENTO

Two days after her visit to Posilipo Nancy came back from her singing-lesson to discover John Kenrick at the *pensione*.

"I found that I could get away from England for a few days," he announced. "And I thought I'd come and ascertain for myself how you really were getting on."

"Very badly," Nancy told him.

"So your last letter implied. But Gambone always errs on the side of discouragement. I'm going to have a chat with him on the way back to Bertolini's. Will you dine with me there to-night? Or, no, wait a minute. I'll come down and fetch you, and we'll eat at a more native restaurant and go to the opera, or are you tired of the opera?"

Nancy had to confess that she had not yet been to San Carlo.

Kenrick was astonished.

"I couldn't very well go alone, and I haven't had anybody I could ask to go with me," she explained.

"You've been feeling lonely," he said quickly. "And you're looking a bit overstrained. Has Gambone been working you too hard?"

"I doubt if he thinks I'm worth working very hard," said Nancy.

"Nonsense! I'm going to find out exactly what he does think about your voice and your prospects. I wager you'll be pleasantly surprised to hear what a great opinion he has of you."

Kenrick left her soon after this, and then Nancy realised how terribly lonely she had been ever since she came

248

to Naples. A few weeks ago she would have been vexed
by the arrival of her patron. It would have embarrassed
her. It might even have made her suspect him of ulterior
motives. But his arrival now was a genuine pleasure,
and if only he came away from Maestro Gambone with
good news of her progress, she should be happier than
she had been for months. Even an unfavourable report
would be something definite, and in that case she could
return to England immediately. Loneliness in beautiful
surroundings was much harder to bear than fellowship in
ugliness. To go back to playing adventuresses in the
black country would have its compensations.

When Kenrick returned to take her out to dinner,
there was a smile on his sombre face. He put up his
monocle and looked at Nancy quizzically.

"You're a nice one!"

"What's the matter? What have I done?"

"I thought you told me you weren't getting on?"

"I didn't think I was."

"Well, Gambone says you're a splendid pupil, that
you work very hard, that you have a glorious natural
voice, and that if he can keep you another six months
he'll guarantee you an engagement at San Carlo next
autumn. What more do you want?"

Nancy caught her breath.

"You're joking!"

"I'm not indeed. I was never more serious."

"But why didn't he say something to me?"

"Gambone is a Neapolitan. Gambone is a realist.
About women he has no illusions. He thinks that the
more he beats them the better they'll be. He only told
me all this after exacting a promise not to repeat it
to you for fear you would be spoilt and give up working
as well as you're working at present. I reproached him
with not having looked after you socially, and he nearly
jumped through the ceiling of his apartment."

" 'She is here to work,' he shouted. 'She is not here
to amuse herself.' 'But you might at least have man-

aged to find her an escort for the opera.' And I told him
that you had not yet visited San Carlo. *'Meno male!'*
he squealed. I presume your Italian has at least got as
far as knowing that *meno male* means the less harm
done. *'Meno male* that she has not filled her head with
other people's singing. She has enough to do with her
practising, enough to do to learn how to speak and pro-
nounce the only civilised tongue that exists for a singer.'
I told him that you had been lonely, and what do you
think he replied? 'If she's lonely, let her cultivate carnations. *Garofani!'* he yelled at the top of his voice.
'Believe me, my good sir, carnations are a thousand
times more worth while than men and ten thousand times
more worth while than women.' 'Even good contraltos?'
I laughed. *'Sicuro!* Or sopranos, either,' the old villain
chuckled."

"Well, in some moods I would agree with him," Nancy
said.

"Anyway, whatever the old cynic may say, he has a
profound belief in your future. When he was ushering
me out of his apartment . . ."

"Oh, he ushered you out?" Nancy laughed. "He always pushes me out."

"He would! But listen, he took my arm and said, with
a twinkle in his bright black eyes, 'So you heard her sing
and knew she had a voice?' I bowed. *'Siete un conos-
cente, caro. Felicitazioni.'* "

The opera played at San Carlo that night was *La
Traviata.* Nancy, not oppressed by the sound and sight
of a contralto singing and acting far better than she
could ever hope to sing and act, thoroughly enjoyed it.
The Violetta was a delicate and lovely creature so that,
even if her *coloratura* did lack something of the finest
quality and ease, her death was almost intolerably moving. Alfredo was played by an elderly tenor into whose
voice the *vibrato* of age had already insinuated itself.
He was, however, such a master of all the graces that
neither his appearance nor the fading of his voice seemed

to matter a great deal. In compensation for an elderly
tenor, the heavy father was played by a very young
barytone with a voice of glorious roundness and sonor-
ity. Kenrick was much excited by this performance and
phophesied for this new singer a success all over Europe
as round and sonorous as his voice. He declared that
he had never heard Germont's great aria "Di Provenza"
given so well.

After the performance they went to supper at one of
the popular restaurants near the opera house, where
Kenrick discoursed upon the æsthetic value of *La
Traviata.*

"It's the fashion to decry it as a piece of tawdry and
melodramatic sensationalism, but to my mind it fulfills
perfectly Aristotle's catharsis."

"That sounds reassuring," Nancy laughed. "But I'm
afraid I don't in the least understand what it means."

"Aristotle found an æsthetic value in the purging of
the emotions. Well, at the end of *Traviata* we are left
with the feeling that music could not express more completely the particular set of emotions that are stirred by
the story of Alfredo, Violetta, and Germont. No critic
has ever done justice to the younger Dumas's *Dame
aux Camélias* either as a novel or as a play. Yet both
they and the opera founded upon them have a perennial
vitality so marked as almost to tempt me to claim for
them an eternal vitality. The actuality of *Traviata* is so
tremendous that on the first night of its production in
Venice it was a failure because the soprano playing Violetta was so fat as to revolt the audience's sense of fact.
This seems to me highly significant. You cannot imagine an operatic version of, let us say, *Wuthering Heights*
being hissed off the stage because the Heathcliff revolted
any audience's sense of fact. Now *Wuthering Heights*
much more nearly approximates to melodrama than *La
Dame aux Camélias.* The pretentious spiritualism with
which a sordid tale of cruelty, revenge, and lust is decked
out cannot hide from the sane observer the foolish parody

of human nature presented therein. It has been acclaimed as a work of tragic grandeur and sublime imagination as if forsooth grandeur of imagination were to be measured by the remoteness of protagonists or plot from recognisable life. Let us grant that *Traviata* exhibits a low form of life——"

"Or a form of low life," Nancy interposed.

"No, no, don't make a joke of it! I feel seriously and strongly on this subject," Kenrick averred. "But a live jelly-fish is a great deal more marvellous and much more beautiful than a stuffed lion. Nothing really matters in a work of art if it lacks vitality. I would not say that *Wuthering Heights* lacked all vitality, but its vitality is slight, indeed it is almost imperceptible except to the precious and microscopic taste of the literary connoisseur. The vitality of *La Dame aux Camélias* is startling, so startling indeed as to repel the fastidious and academic mind just as a don would be embarrassed were his attentions solicited by a gay lady outside the St. James's Restaurant. The trouble is that the standards of criticism are nearly always set up by the middle-aged. *La Dame aux Camélias* is a book for youth. We have most of us lived not wisely and not well in our youth, and middle-age is not the time to judge that early behaviour. Let it be remembered that the follies of our youth are usually repeated when we are old—not always actually, but certainly in imagination. An old man should be the best judge of *La Dame aux Camélias*. Well, if that is a vital book, and just because of its amazing vitality, a great book, *Traviata* is a great opera, because, unlike that much inferior opera *Aïda,* it is impossible to imagine any other music for it. All that could be expressed by that foolish dead love, all the sentimental dreams of it, all the cruelty of it, and the sweetness and the remorse, all is there. We may tire of its barrel-organ tunes, but we tire in middle-age of all youth's facile emotions. We can scarcely imagine ourselves, let us say, waiting two hours in the rain for any woman. We should be

bored by having to find the chocolates that Cleopatra preferred, and we would not escort even Helen of Troy to
the nearest railway station. But fatigue is not neces-
sarily wisdom, and so much that we reject in middle-age
is due to loss of resiliency. We cannot react as we once
could to the demands of the obvious excitement. We
are, in a word, blasé."

Nancy felt that she was rushing in like a fool, but she
could not sit here and watch Kenrick blow away all argument in the wreaths of his cigarette smoke. She had to
point out one flaw in his remarks.

"But when I said that I would never love again and
implied that I knew what I was talking about, because
I was twenty-eight, you warned me that a woman's most
susceptible age was thirty-three."

"Thirty-three is hardly middle-age," said Kenrick. "I
was thinking of the chilly forties. Besides, you can't
compare women with men in this matter. The old saw
about a woman being as old as she looks and a man as old
as he feels is always used by women as an illustration
of the advantage of being a man. As a matter of fact,
the advantage lies all the other way. It is so much easier
to look young than to feel young. A woman is never too
old to be loved. You can hardly maintain that a man is
never to old to love. I doubt if a man over thirty ever
knows what love means."

"Och, I never heard such a preposterous statement,"
Nancy declared. "Why, think of the men who cherish
hopeless passions all their lives."

"For my part I can never understand a man's cherishing a hopeless passion," he declared. "I should feel so
utterly humiliated by a woman's refusal of her love that
my own passion would be killed by it instantly. And the
humiliation would be deepened by my knowledge of
woman's facility for falling in love, which is, of course,
much greater than a man's, as much greater as her fas-
tidiousness and sensitiveness are less. To be refused by
a woman, when one sees on what monstrous objects she

is prepared to lavish her affection, seems to me terrible. Equally I do not understand why a woman, who after her childhood so rarely cherishes a hopeless passion that will never be returned, is always prepared to cherish the much more hopeless passion of continuing to love a man after he has ceased to love her. I suppose it's because women are such sensualists. They always regard love as a gratification of self too long postponed, and they continue to want it as children want broken toys and men fail to give up smoking. The famous women who have held men have held them by their infinite variety. Yet the one quality in a lover that a woman finds it hardest to forgive is his variety."

"Och, I don't agree at all," Nancy declared breathlessly. "In fact I don't agree with anything you've said about love or men or women. I think it's a great pity that you have let yourself grow middle-aged. You wouldn't be able to have all these ideas if you were still capable of feeling genuine emotion. I'm not clever enough to argue with you properly. No woman ever can argue, because either she feels so strongly about a subject that all her reasons fly to the wind, or, if she doesn't feel strongly, she doesn't think it worth while to argue and, in fact, finds it a boring waste of time. But I feel that you are utterly wrong. I know you are. You're just wrong. And that's all there is to be said. My husband had more variety than any man I ever knew, and I loved his variety as much as I loved every other single one of his qualities."

There were tears in her big deep-blue eyes, the tears that always came to them when she spoke of Bram, and flashing tears of exasperation as well, at being unable to defeat her companion's cynicism, for all his observations seemed to her to be the fruit of a detestable and worldly-wise cynicism, the observations of a man who has never known what it was to suffer or to lose anything in the battle of life.

"Forgive me if I spoke thoughtlessly," said Kenrick.

"I get carried away by my tongue whenever I go to an opera. Operas stimulate me. They are the *reductio ad absurdum* of art. I seem always to get down to the bedrock of the æsthetic impulse at the opera. We are deluded by a tragedy of Æschylus into supposing that art is something greater than it is, something more than a sublimation of childhood's games, something comparable in its importance to science. In opera we see what a joke art really is. We know that in the scroll of eternity the bottle-washer of a great chemist is a more conspicuous minuscule than the greatest artist who ever shall be."

"I think I'm too tired to listen to you any longer," Nancy said. "I really don't understand anything you're talking about now, and even if I did I feel sure I wouldn't agree with you."

Kenrick laughed.

"I plead guilty to being a chatterbox to-night. But it was partly your fault. You shouldn't have sat there looking as if you were listening with such intelligence. But let's leave generalisations and come to particulars. Gambone says a little holiday will do you good."

"I don't believe you," Nancy laughed. "Maestro Gambone never indulged in theories about his pupils' well-being. I simply don't believe you."

"Yes, really he did. I asked him if he did not think that you would be all the better for a short rest, and he agreed with me. Now, why don't you come to Sorrento with me and see in this New Year that is going to be your *annus mirabilis?*"

Nancy looked at him quickly.

"You're thinking of the proprieties? There are no proprieties at Sorrento. You want a change of air. I promise not to talk about art. We'll just take some good walks. Now don't be missish. Treat me as a friend."

Yet Nancy still hesitated to accept this invitation. She had no reason that she could express to herself, still less put into words. It was merely an irrational presentiment that she should regret going to Sorrento.

"Why don't you answer?" he pressed.

"I was only wondering if it was wise to interrupt my lessons," she told him lamely.

"But you wouldn't lose more than a couple. We shan't be away more than five days. I've got to be back in London by the fifth of January."

"All right. I'd really love to come if Gambone won't think I'm being lazy."

Kenrick drove her back to the Via Virgilio, and next morning they took the boat for Sorrento.

They stayed in an old sun-crumbled *albergo* built on one of the promontories, the sheer cliff of which had been reinforced by immense brick arches raised one above another against its face, so that the soft tufaceous rock, which rather resembled rotten cheese, should not collapse and plunge *albergo,* tangled garden, and pine-dark promontory into the inky blue water two hundred feet below. Sorrento looks north, and the proprietor of the *albergo,* a toad-faced little man with sandy hair and a food-stained frock coat much too large for him, suggested that his new guests would be more comfortable at this season in rooms with an aspect away from the sea. The south aspect of the *albergo* formed three sides of an oblong, and the doors of all the rooms opened on a balcony paved with blue and green porcelain tiles and covered with the naked grey stems of wistaria, the convolutions of which resembled the throes of huge pythons. The view looked away over orange groves to the Sorrentine hills, and particularly to one conical bosky peak on which the wooden cross of a Camaldolese congregation was silhouetted against the sky. In the garden below the balcony tazetta narcissus and China roses were in bloom. There were not many other guests in the *albergo,* and these were mostly elderly English and American women, all suffering from the delusion that Italy was the cheapest country on earth and from a delusion of the natives that all English and Americans were extremely wealthy.

Kenrick apologised for bringing Nancy to the *Albergo*

del Sole rather than taking her to one of the two fashionable hotels.

"But we can always go and feed at the Tramontano or the Victoria," he pointed out. "And there's a charm about this tumbledown old place. I was here once ten years ago and always promised myself a return visit. Of course, Winter is not the time to be in Sorrento. It's not till the oranges come into their glory, about Easter, that one understands the raptures of the great men who have visited this place. The fascination of Sorrento is a stock subject with all the letter-writers of our century."

"Och, but I would much rather be staying here," Nancy assured him. "I think this place is so attractive."

"It would be more attractive in Spring when the creamy Banksia roses are in blossom and hung with necklaces of wistaria. It is a little melancholy now. Yet the sun strikes warm at midday. I've told them to make up a roaring fire of chestnut logs in your room."

"They've certainly done so, and it's as cosy as it can be."

"I only hope the weather stays fine for our holiday," said Kenrick, putting up his monocle and staring an appeal to the tender azure of the December sky.

And the weather did stay fine, so that they were able to drive or walk all day and escape from the narrow walled alleys of Sorrento, alleys designed for summer heats, when their ferns and mosses would refresh the sun-tired eye, but in Winter damp and depressing, soggy with dead leaves.

On the last day of the old year they climbed up through the olives until they reached an open grassy space starred thick with the tigered buff and mauve blooms of a myriad crocuses, the saffron stamens of which burned like little tongues of fire in the sunlight.

"Forgive the melancholy platitude," said Kenrick, "but I am oppressed by the thought of our transience here, and not only our transience, but the transience of all the tourists who sojourn for a while on this magic coast. The song of a poet here is already less than the warble of a passing bird; the moonlight is more powerful than all the vows of all who have ever loved in Sorrento; no music can endure beside the murmur of the Tyrrhenian. 'Here could I live,' one protests, and in a day or two the railway-guide is pulled out, and one is discussing with the hotel porter how to fit in Pompeii on the way back to Naples. Ugh! What is it that forbids man to be happy?"

"Well, obviously most of the people who visit Sorrento couldn't afford to stay here indefinitely," said Nancy, who always felt extremely matter-of-fact when her companion began to talk in this strain.

"Yes, but there must be many people like myself who could."

"Some do."

"Ah, but not in the right way. They dig out a house-agent and inspect eligible villas and behave exactly as if they were moving from Bayswater to Hampstead, which in fact they are. I don't want to adjust these surroundings to myself. I want to become an integral part of them. I should like to stay on in the *Albergo del Sole* without writing letters or getting letters. I should like to be sitting here when these crocuses have faded, and the grass is wine-stained by anemones or silvery with asphodels. I should like to watch the cistus petals fluttering to the hot earth, and to lie for hours listening to the cicali, lie and dream all through the Summer as still and hot as a terra-cotta shard, lie and dream until the black sirocco whips the orchards and spits into my face the first drops of autumn rain. But if I had to make arrangements for my business and explain that my nerves required a long rest, all the savour would be taken out of my whim. Oh, *dio,* I am as full to-day of yearnings for the *au delà* as a French symbolist, or a callow German who sees the end of his *Wanderjahre* looming."

All the way back to the town Kenrick walked along beside Nancy in a moody silence. She felt that perhaps she had been too discouraging, and just before they emerged from the last of the olives she put a hand on his arm and said:

"Will it do anything to console you if I tell you how perfectly I have enjoyed these days here? I'm not an eloquent person, Mr. Kenrick."

"Oh, for heaven's sake call me John. Haven't you noticed I've been calling you Nancy all this time?"

"I'll try to call you John," she promised. "But it's terribly hard for me to call people by their Christian names. I'm not an eloquent person . . . John. In fact, I'm sort of tongue-tied. But surely you must realise what you've done for me."

He stopped abruptly and looked into her eyes.

"Have I really done much?"

"Why, you know you have. You know you have. I was a touring actress without an idea of ever being anything else, and you've given me the chance to be something much more than that."

"That's all I've managed to do?" Kenrick asked.

"Isn't it enough?"

He seemed to be striving either to say something or not to say something, Nancy did not know which. Then he shivered.

"Come along, it's beginning to turn chilly as the sun gets behind the hills. Let's go and have a fashionable tea at the Victoria, and book a table for to-night."

After dinner they sat in the lounge and watched the sophisticated *tarantella* that was splashed on the tourists three times a week as from a paint-pot of gaudy local colour. Followed luscious songs and mandolinades, and shortly before midnight the *capo d'anno* procession arrived to sing the song of the New Year. It was accompanied by a band of queer primitive instruments; but the most important feature of the celebration was a bay-tree, which was banged on the floor to mark the time of the rhythmical refrain throughout the song's many verses.

Everybody drank everybody's else health; the elderly
English and American women twinkled at the inspiration
of an extra glass of vermouth; all was music and jollity.

The moonlight was dazzling when Kenrick and Nancy
left the hotel, the air coldly spiced with the scent of man-
darins. He proposed a walk to shake off the fumes, and,
though she was feeling sleepy after a long day in the
open air followed by the long evening's merrymaking,
Nancy had not the heart to say that she would rather go
home to bed. They wandered through the alleys now in
darkness, now in a vaporous sheen of grey light, now full
in the sharp and glittering eye of the moon. The naked
arms of the walnut-trees and figs shimmered ashen-pale.
Here and there a gust of perfume from the orange-
groves waylaid them to hang upon its sweetness like
greedy moths. After twenty minutes of meandering
through these austere blazonries of argent and sable
they turned back toward the *albergo* and followed their
shadows away from the soaring moon, their little shadows
that hung round their feet like black velvet, so rich
seemed they and so substantial upon the dusty silver of
the path.

All was still when they reached the *albergo,* and the
porcelain tiles of the balcony were sparkling in the moonshine like aquamarines.

"Good night," said Nancy, pausing in the doorway of
her room. "And once more a happy New Year!"

Kenrick stood motionless for an instant. Then he
stepped forward quickly into the doorway and caught
Nancy to him.

"You can't say good night like this," he gasped.

She struggled to free herself from the kiss he had
forced upon her. In her physical revolt against him the
lips pressed to hers felt like the dry hot hide of some
animal.

"Let me go! Let me go!" she choked. "Och, why
are you doing this and spoiling everything?"

In escaping from his arms Nancy had gone right into

her room. Kenrick followed her in and, shutting the door behind him, began to plead with her.

"Let me come and sit in here for a while. I won't try to kiss you again. Let's pull up a couple of chairs to the fire and talk."

"Och, do go away," Nancy begged. "There's nothing to talk about now, and it's late, and I feel so unhappy about this."

All the time she was talking she was searching everywhere for the matches to light the lamp and illuminate with its common sense this mad situation created by moonshine and shadows and flickering logs.

"You've surely realised that I've been madly in love with you ever since I saw you at Bristol?" he demanded.

Nancy found the matches and lit the lamp. Then she turned to face Kenrick.

"Of course I didn't realise it. Do you suppose I would have let you pay for my singing-lessons and all this, if I'd thought you were in love with me? I see it now, and I could kill myself for being so dense. And me supposing it was all on account of my fine voice! Och, it's too humiliating. Just an arrangement between you and Gambone, and me to be so mad as to believe in you."

"Now don't be too unjust, Nancy," he said. "You have a fine voice, and even if you turn me down as a lover I'm still willing to see you through with your training."

"I thought you knew so much about women," she stabbed. "You don't really suppose that I'd accept another penny from you now?"

"Why not?"

"Why not? Well, I won't ever be your mistress, and since it was the hope of getting me for your mistress that made you send me out here—you can't deny that, now, can you?—well, since it was that and I can't oblige, you don't suppose I'll accept your charity?"

"But I tell you I do think you have a fine voice, and

so does Gambone. I swear to you he does. This hasn't been a trick to get you out to Italy, and nothing else; though it would be absurd to pretend that I'd have done what I did for you for *any* woman with a fine voice."

"Why couldn't you have told me there was a price attached? It wasn't fair of you to let me come out here without knowing that."

Nancy was on the verge of breaking down; but she knew that if she cried Kenrick would take the opportunity of such weakness to attempt a reconciliation, and she was determined to finish with him for ever to-night.

"I suppose it wasn't," he admitted. "But you must remember that I didn't know you then as I know you now, and perhaps I assumed that you were like most women, for I swear most women would have realised that I was in love."

"But it's such a damnable way of being in love!" Nancy exclaimed. "If you loved me, how could you think that I'd pretend such innocence? To make myself more interesting? Well, I suppose if you go through life judging women by your own ideas about them, you *would* have discovered by now that all of them were frauds."

"Listen, Nancy," Kenrick said. "Is it because you don't love me that you refuse me as a lover? Or is it because of the conventions? Would you marry me, if I could marry you?"

"Do you mean if I weren't an actress?" she said, blazing.

"No, no," he replied impatiently. "For God's sake don't talk like that. What on earth difference could that conceivably make? I can't marry you, because I'm married already, and because my wife would die rather than divorce me. But would you marry me?"

"No, never in this world! I won't be your mistress, because I don't love you, and even if I did love you a little, I wouldn't be your mistress, because I could never love you as much as I loved my husband and I wouldn't do anything to hurt his child and mine."

"Are you sure you don't love me? Are you sure the second and more sentimental reason isn't the true one?"

"I'm so far from loving you," she declared, "that I couldn't even hate you. Now perhaps you'll go away and leave me alone? Remember what you said the other night in Naples about cherishing hopeless passions? Or was that just all nothing but beautiful talk?"

"Why don't you love me?" he asked.

"I told you once that I could never love anybody again. You had a theory about that, I remember. Now do go away, and leave me alone."

"Forgive me, Nancy."

"I'll forgive you if you let me know to a farthing what you've paid for me from the moment I left London."

"That's not forgiveness," he said. "You needn't be cruel. After all, it's not unforgivable to love a woman. I loved you from the beginning. I haven't just taken advantage of moonlight to indulge myself. At least, let me continue paying for your lessons. I'm going back to England at once; I'll promise not to worry you any more. Do, Nancy, please do let me see you through!"

She shook her head.

"I couldn't."

"You're sacrificing yourself for pride."

"It's not entirely pride," she said. "There's pride in it, but it's—oh, I can't explain things as you can. Please tell me what I've cost you. I have enough, I think, to pay you back."

"I won't accept it," he declared. "And for no reason whatever can you prove to me that I ought to accept repayment. I persuaded you to leave your engagement. You believed in my sincerity. And I was sincere. I think it's wrong of you to give up your singing. But I know it's useless to argue about that with you. What I have paid is quite another matter, and I simply refuse to accept repayment. If you can't even succeed in hating me, you've no right to ask me to do something for which I must hate myself."

"Yes, but you only used my voice as an excuse for the rest," Nancy argued. "Your main thought in getting me out to Italy was to make me your mistress. Apparently I must have given you the impression that your trouble was worth while. Yet when you invited me to come with you to Sorrento on this holiday, why did you ask me to treat you as a friend? As a matter of fact, the idea that you wanted to make love to me did pass through my mind, but you drove away the fancy by the way you spoke, as if you knew that I suspected your reasons and wanted to reproach me for my nasty mind. Did you or did you not expect that I would give myself to you here?"

"It was here that I first thought that you were growing fond of me," Kenrick said evasively. "I can tell you the exact moment. It was yesterday afternoon when you put your hand on my arm."

"I *was* growing fond of you. But not in that kind of way," she said. "Naturally I was growing fond of you. You had, as I thought, done a great deal for me. I was grateful; and when you seemed depressed I wanted to comfort you."

"Nancy, let's cut out to-night and blame the moon." She shook her head.

"I can't. I know myself too well. Just to give you pleasure because I owe you a great deal, I would like beyond anything to cut out to-night and go on with my singing. But the moment I was alone I'd begin to fret. I haven't enough confidence in my success as a singer. For one thing, now that you've told me that you were attracted to me personally at Bristol I feel that you've thought my voice better than it is. Suppose at the end of another five or six months Gambone shouldn't consider me worthy of being pushed along? I'd have nothing to fall back upon. I'd have failed myself and my daughter and you, artistically, and I'd have failed you in the only way that might compensate you for that failure."

"But if the risk is mine and I'm willing to accept it, why must you worry?"

"It's no good. I know myself. I know that I couldn't endure taking your money under those conditions."

"But you aren't seriously proposing to give up your lessons and leave Naples simply because I've told you that I'm in love with you?"

"Yes, yes, I am. I'm going back to-morrow."

"But how will you explain your sudden return to your friends?"

"I haven't so very many friends to bother about. But I shall tell those I have that my voice wasn't good enough to make it worth while going on."

Kenrick flung himself into a chair and poked the logs savagely.

"You make me feel such a clumsy brute," he groaned. "Can't I find any argument that will make you change your mind?"

"None."

"But at any rate you aren't serious about paying me back the trifling sum I've spent on you?"

"I am indeed."

"Nancy, I've taken my disappointment fairly well; you can't deny that. I beg you to be kind and not insist on this repayment. I promise not to inflict myself or my hopes upon you. I'll do anything you tell me, if only you'll be generous over this. Your only motive for repaying me can be pride. Use your imagination and try to realise what it will mean for me if you insist. I do love you. I might have pretended that the magic of this night had turned my senses for a moment, but by being sincere I've ruined any hope I had for the future. My dream is shattered. Be generous."

He looked so miserable, hunched up over the fire, that Nancy fought down her pride and agreed to accept as a present what he had already done. She was inclined to regret her weakness a moment later, when she saw that her surrender went far to restore Kenrick's optimism about their future relations. He began to talk about the beauty of Italy in the Spring, of the peach blossoms in March and the orange-groves in April. The mistake was in having sent her out in Winter. In Spring she must think over everything and come out again. And so on, and so on until Nancy could have screamed with exasperation at his inability to comprehend the finality of her decision.

It was nearly two o'clock before Kenrick left Nancy's room. The stress of argument had chased away her fatigue; but in Kenrick's new mood she did not dare stand on the balcony and pore upon the hills of Sorrento floating like islands in that sea of moonshine. He was capable of supposing that she had changed her mind and of expecting the fulfilment of his passion. The fire had died down to a heap of glowing ashes. The room was heavy with the smoke of Kenrick's incessant Macedonian cigarettes. So this was the end of Italy. Yet she did not feel more than a twinge or two of sentimental regret for the loveliness of earth and sea and sky that she was deliberately abandoning. She had the happiness of knowing that she had been true to herself. A dull, a bourgeois virtue perhaps for a rogue and a vagabond; but Nancy, knowing all that she now wanted from life, did not feel sorry for that self to which she had been true.

Three days later Italy seemed as far away as paradise, when the cliffs of England loomed through a driving mist of dirty southerly weather.

CHAPTER XXIII

CŒUR DE LION

It seemed as if fortune was anxious to compensate Nancy for the sudden shattering of her operatic dreams. The very first agent to whom she went on her return to London greeted her with something like acclamation.

"Why, Miss O'Finn, I am glad you've looked in this morning. Mr. Percy Mortimer"—the agent's harsh voice sank to a reverential murmur—"Mr. Percy Mortimer has had some difficulty with the lady he engaged to play rather an important part in his new play at the Athenæum, and his secretary wrote to me to ask if I would send some ladies to interview him with a view to his engaging one of them. He requires a tall dark lady of some presence, and of course with the necessary experience. This would be a splendid opportunity for you, Miss O'Finn, if you happened to please Mr. Mortimer."

"Naturally I should like nothing better than to be at the Athenæum," said Nancy in a voice that was nearly as full of awe as the agent's.

"It isn't so much the salary," he pointed out. "In fact, Mr. Mortimer does not believe in paying very large salaries to the actors and actresses who are supporting him. He thinks—and he is undoubtedly right—that to have one's name on the programmes of the Athenæum is the equivalent of several pounds at most of the other London theatres.

"Now, don't talk too much about it before Mr. Mortimer has even seen me," Nancy begged.

"He'll be at the Athenæum this afternoon at half-past three. I'm only sending along two other ladies. And I think you're just what he wants."

Mr. Percy Mortimer was something more than a great figure of the London stage; he was an institution. Everybody agreed that should Her Majesty decide to create another theatrical knight Percy Mortimer was undoubtedly the one she would select for the accolade. The prime cause of his renown in England was that if there was ever any question of choice between being an actor or a gentleman he would always put good breeding before art. This was held to be elevating the drama. If by chance the public disapproved of any play he produced, Percy Mortimer always apologised before the curtain on the first night and laid the blame on the author. Two or three years before this date he was acting in a play by a famous dramatist who became involved in a sensational and scandalous lawsuit. Percy Mortimer did not take off the play. He owed something to art. But he paid his debt to good breeding by expunging the author's name from the playbills and the programmes.

Nancy had to pass the vigilance of various chamberlains, constables, and seneschals before she reached the Presence, a handsome man with a face as large and smooth as a perfectly cured ham.

"Miss O'Finn?" he inquired graciously, with a glance at her card. "Of Irish extraction, perhaps?"

She nodded.

"A part is vacant in my new play," he announced. "The public is anxious to see me in historical drama, and I have decided to produce Mr. Philip Stevens's *Cœur de Lion*. The vacant part is that of a Saracen woman who has escaped from the harem of Saladin. It is not a long part, but it is an extremely important part, because the only scene in which this character appears is played as a duologue with myself."

Mr. Mortimer paused to give Nancy time to appreciate what this meant.

"Here is the script," he said. "Perhaps you will read me your lines?"

Nancy took a deep breath and dived.

"Thank you, Miss O'Finn," said Mr. Mortimer. "One of my secretaries will communicate my decision to your agent in the course of the next twenty-four hours."

He pressed a bell, which was immediately answered by a chamberlain to whom was entrusted the task of escorting Nancy back into the commonplace of existence.

And the very next day when Nancy, who was staying at St. Joseph's, went to her agent, she was offered the part at a salary of £5 a week.

Not only was *Cœur de Lion* a success with the critics, who hailed Mr. Philip Stevens as the morning-star of a new and glorious day for England's poetic drama; but it was a success with the public. This, of course, made the critics revise their opinion and decide that what they had mistaken for a morning-star was only a fire-balloon; but the damage was done, and English criticism suffered the humiliation of having praised as a great play what dared to turn out a popular success. One or two papers actually singled out Nancy's performance for special commendation which, considering that the part did not look difficult and that she played it easily and naturally, betrayed astonishing perspicacity for a dramatic critic. She found pleasant rooms in St. John's Wood, quite close to the convent. Kenrick made several attempts to see her, and on one occasion waited for her outside the stage-door. She begged him not to do this again as it might involve her dismissal from the Athenæum, because one of Mr. Mortimer's ways of elevating the English drama was to make it an offence for any of the ladies of his company to be waited for outside the stage-door.

For three months everything went well for Nancy except that the expense of London life was a constant worry for her, although she tried to console herself with the thought that she had already saved a certain amount of money, and that after her success in *Cœur de Lion* she might expect to get a larger salary in her next London engagement. Otherwise she was happy.

Then one night early in April she was informed by the stage-door keeper that a gentleman who would not leave his name had been inquiring for her private address. Nancy supposed that it was Kenrick again; but the stage-door keeper remembered him well. This was a much older gentleman with curly white hair who was quite definitely a member of the profession.

"Of course, I didn't give him your address, miss. But if he calls again, what shall I say?"

It was her father. What should she say? Nancy's conscience had touched her from time to time for the way she had let her father drop out of her life ever since that day he had failed her so badly. She did not know if he was acting in London or in the provinces, or if he was not acting anywhere. His name had never been mentioned all these months of touring. On no railway platform had she caught a glimpse of him as two "crowds" passed each other during long Sabbath journeys. He might have been dead. And now here he was in her path. What should she say?

"Ask him to leave his address, will you? And say that I will write to him."

If her father dreaded another such a disastrous visit as the one she paid him four years ago, he need not leave his address. If, however, he did leave it she would have time to ponder what response to make.

Michael O'Finn did not call again at the stage-door of the Athenæum, but two or three days after this his daughter received a letter from him at the theatre.

544 Camberwell Road, S. E.
2:30 P.M. Sunday, April 17, 1899.

MY BELOVED DAUGHTER,

How many times since last we met have I picked up my pen, how many times have I laid it down again with a groan of paternal despair! That you had reason to complain of me I will not deny. My head is bowed before your just and natural ire. But the sight of your name—your dear, dear name—although you share the second portion of it with that least worthy of God's creatures, your wretched father—the sight of your name, I repeat, in the cast of *Cœur de Lion* watered with hope the withered plant that in happier days and in the glory of his blossoming prime gave that tender shoot to the world, which is your sweet self.

I will not attempt to condone my fault. I will not attempt it, I say. At the moment when I should have been standing upon the doorstep of that humble habitation in which I sojourned for a space to welcome you with open arms and tears of joy, I was, owing to a combination of unfortunate circumstances, prone upon my bed in the first-floor front. I have not to warn you, my child, against the evils of drink, because in you glows the pure and temperate soul of your beloved mother. At the same time I should lack all the noble instincts of paternity if I did not remind you that "virtue cannot so inoculate our old stock but we shall relish of it." That being so, do not allow yourself to be tempted by even a solitary glass of champagne. Water, pure, wholesome, pellucid water is the natural element of a being like yourself. But to come to the point of this letter. Two years ago, weary of being "a walking shadow, a poor player that struts and frets his hour upon the stage," I longed to be "heard no more." I was at that time lodging in the house from which I write this despairing epistle. In a moment of folly I proposed to link myself in matrimony with my landlady's daughter. The wretched woman accepted my hand. The Tragic Muse would be rendered dumb by the task of painting my misery ever since that inauspicious day. Ay, even Melpomene herself would stammer. One word, one word alone can indicate a dim and shadowy outline of my existence, and that one word is Hell.

You will observe that I have resumed after a blank. That blank I wish to draw over my life for the last two years. But I have now reached a lower depth, a gloomier abyss, where in addition to all my other ills the spectre of famine looms above me. The wolf is scratching at the door. In a word, unless somehow or other I can raise the sum—a bagatelle for a Crœsus or a Rothschild, for me a burden heavier than Atlas bore—the sum of £158. 14s. 3½d. within the next week, I and my wife and my mother-in-law will be in the street. I do not for an instant imagine that you yourself have such a sum handy. You are like your father only a poor stroller. But it has occurred to me that you might be acquainted with some fortunate individual who could advance you this amount to save your father from destitution in company with the two least attractive companions that can be imagined for such an existence.

I beg that you will not attempt to visit me. Since I gave up brandy, this house appears to me as what it undoubtedly is—a mercenary hovel. Yet I am "fain to hovel me with swine and rogues forlorn in short and musty straw." In a word, I am better off in 544 Camberwell Road than "to be exposed against the warring winds, to stand against the deep dread-bolted thunder."

My beloved Nancy, do your best for me. Overlook my failings and come to my aid.

> "Dear daughter, I confess that I am old;
> Age is unnecessary; on my knees I beg
> That you'll vouchsafe me raiment, bed, and food."

These words addressed by the hapless Lear to his unnatural daughter Regan I take from their context and utter to one who has ever been a Cordelia.

To that most wretched of earth's creatures

Her

FATHER.

Nancy was not deluded by the laboured rhetoric of this letter. She understood that her father's need was serious. She had the money that would relieve him. She must send it immediately. To be sure he had failed her four years ago, but had she not allowed her bitterness to make her unnatural? Was she not to blame a little for this disastrous later phase of his career? Oh, yes, more than a little. Moreover, that money in the bank, since her break with Kenrick, had never lain there comfortably. It had never seemed to belong to her as genuinely as once it did. The sum her father required so gravely was more than Kenrick could have spent on that Italian adventure of hers. She took out her cheque-book and sat down at the table. Or should she go and see him in Camberwell? She read her father's letter again. No, it was clear he did not want her to be a spectator of his wretchedness. But at least she could invite him to her rooms—yet could she? That would mean talking about Letizia, and perhaps he would want to see her. Was it very heartless of her not to want him to see Letizia? After all, he had not suggested visiting her. She would send him this money and she could decide later what she should do.

Nancy received a long and emotional letter of thanks, in which her father said that he was feeling very low, but that without doubt her rescue of him from the desperate position in which he had been plunged would rapidly restore him to health. Meanwhile, he begged her again not to dream of visiting him in Camberwell. When the warm weather began in May he would come and see his beloved daughter.

But when the warm weather came in May, Nancy read an obituary in *The Era* of that ripe old actor, Michael O'Finn, a fine comedian and a tragic actor of no mean ability.

CHAPTER XXIV

DECENNIAL

Cœur de Lion suffered from cardiac depression in the heat of July and ceased to beat half-way through the month. Although Mr. Percy Mortimer offered Nancy a part in his autumn production, he did not offer her a higher salary. Not only had she been unable to save a penny in London; she had had to draw heavily on what remained of her savings when she had paid her father's debts. No doubt, if she stayed on at the Athenæum she should gradually establish herself as a London actress, but should she ever save any money? She felt that she lacked the temperament to become a star. Even if she had had the consuming white-hot ambition, she did not possess the necessary personality. For one thing she was too useful an actress. She would always be given parts that were difficult to fill, obviously. She would never establish herself as the one actress who could play one particular kind of part. Nevertheless, to refuse a good part in the forthcoming production at the Athenæum was not an easy thing to do. Another conspicuous success would mean a rise of salary for the next production and, were there nothing for her at the Athenæum, she might surely count on a good engagement at another theatre. Then there was Letizia in London, and it *was* so jolly to be able to see her almost every day. She seemed to grow more amusing and interesting and adorable all the time. There were many years yet before she should be wanting that money to launch her on whatever career she chose. Would she choose the stage? Probably. Plenty of personality there. With the natural sense of the theatre she must inherit from both sides she would stand a splendid chance of becoming a really renowned actress. But what a much greater chance she would stand if she were not hampered by the urgent need of a livelihood. Not that Nancy intended her daughter to be aware of her amateur status. If she chose to be an actress, she should begin under the impression that there was not a farthing between herself and starvation in the event of failure. But once she secured a London engagement, why, then the money to dress herself, the money to be able to turn up her nose at a small salary, the money to flick her fingers in the face of any manager—— But Letizia's début was a long way off yet. She might not choose the stage; and was it risking so much for her mother to stay on and enjoy the amenity of acting in London?

Nancy was on the point of settling for the autumn with Mr. Mortimer when an actor with whom she had played in two provincial companies before Bram's death offered her £7 a week to go out on tour with him in a repertory of Robertson's plays—£7 a week in the country was the equivalent of £10 a week in town. Nancy flung away any hope of fame, flung away the amenity of the London stage, flung away the pleasure of seeing Letizia every day, and became once more a strolling player, wandering the next ten years up and down the length of England, in and out of Wales, over to Ireland, and across the border into Scotland. She never sang any more except at festive gatherings to celebrate some Bohemian occasion; but if she sang no more on the stage, neither did she play another adventuress. Her engagements were nearly always with number one companies for number one towns. Having once achieved £7 a week, she never acted again for less, and without stinting herself too much or denying herself a month's rest she managed to put by £100 every year.

Until Letizia was twelve she was allowed to spend the summer holidays with her mother, who was, of course, always on tour in August, so that Letizia had plenty of

experience of theatrical life in her impressionable childhood. At the age of eleven she fell very much in love with
a good-looking actor of forty-five, a member of the company with which her mother was touring. At first Nancy
was amused by this precocious passion and had many jokes
about it with Mr. Bernard Drake, the object of Letizia's
adoration. But when, notwithstanding the bracing air of
Blackpool, Letizia began to grow thin and pale and hol-
low-eyed and altogether thoroughly love-sick, Nancy became anxious about her health and begged Drake not
to encourage her little daughter by any kind of "let's
pretend." The next week the company was playing at
Douglas, and Letizia was no better in spite of all sorts
of amusements and thrills that included a personal introduction by Mr. Drake to several freaks then being
shown at one of the halls by the sea for which Douglas
was famous in those days.

"What *is* the matter, Letizia? Aren't you enjoying
your time with me?"

They were sitting among the heather beyond the town,
looking at the calm sea and the curve of the long *marina.*

"Oh, yes, I'm enjoying myself terribly," said Letizia
in woebegone accents. "Only, in another month I shall
have to go back to school."

"But the holidays aren't half over yet," her mother
pointed out.

"No, not yet," Letizia sighed. "But they *will* be over."

"Would you like to invite Mrs. Pottage to come and
stay with us next week—no, next week is Llandudno and
Rhyl—the week after at Hastings?"

"No, thank you, mother. She'll only laugh all the time
at everything."

"Letizia, do not be so ridiculous. It's only during the
last fortnight that you've not been laughing at everything
all the time yourself."

"I don't think I shall ever laugh again," Letizia
groaned.

"Why on earth not?"

"Because I want so dreadfully to be grown up."

"Well, you can't go on moping for the next seven years, my dear."

"Will I be grown up in seven years?" Letizia asked, brightening. "That isn't so very long, is it? I'm more than half-way already. . . . Mother?" she resumed.

"Yes?"

"When does a bearded lady begin to grow a beard? I couldn't suddenly become a bearded lady, could I, when I was grown up?"

"Of course not, you noodle."

"You're quite sure?" Letizia pressed.

"Positive."

"The bearded lady was very nice when I shook hands with her," said Letizia pensively. "But I wouldn't much like to kiss her if I was a man, would you?"

"Not at all," Nancy declared with a grimace.

"Mother?"

"What now?"

"Do you think she'd mind if I asked her if she had any bits of beard when she was eleven?"

"No, darling, I don't want you to meet those freaks again. I can't think why Mr. Drake ever introduced you to them. It was very naughty of him."

Letizia turned a pale and reproachful face to her mother.

"I think Mr. Drake is the nicest man who ever lived," she proclaimed solemnly. Then in a voice that strove to to be nonchalant, she asked how old he was.

"About forty-five."

"Mother?"

"Still another puzzle for poor me?"

"Is fifty-two frightfully old for a man to be?"

"Very old indeed."

"Too old to marry?"

"Much too old," said Nancy decidedly.

Letizia uttered a sigh of unutterable despair, and in spite of everything that her mother could do, in spite of a boisterous visit from Mrs. Pottage to Hastings, she remained in a state of gloom all through the summer holidays. Moreover, Sister Catherine wrote to Nancy half-way through the next term that she was so worried about Letizia's health that she thought it would be wise if she went to Belgium early in the New Year, as London did not seem to be suiting her. Nancy wondered if she should say anything about her unfortunate passion for a middle-aged actor, but decided that it might give a wrong impression to the nuns and kept silence. She was glad she had, when soon after Letizia's arrival in Belgium she received a letter full of excitement and good spirits. The sickness of love was evidently cured. But that it could endure so long at the age of eleven made Nancy a little anxious about her daughter's emotional future.

Four years passed while Letizia was at school in Belgium. There were changes among the Sisters of the Holy Infancy. Mother Mary Ethelreda died and was laid to rest in the soil which her ancestors had held long ago by the sword. Sister Catherine was elected mother-superior. Sister Rose became head-mistress of St. Joseph's. There were no changes in Nancy's existence apart from the change every week from one town to another. She never heard of Kenrick nowadays. He had passed out of her life as if he had never been. Mrs. Pottage was growing old, and for the first time since Bram's death Nancy visited Starboard Alley to celebrate the old lady's seventieth birthday.

Aggie Wilkinson was there looking now almost as old as Mrs. Pottage and in some respects a good deal older, though she was still alluded to by her mistress as if she were in short skirts.

"Pore little thing, it does her good to get about a bit on those crutches of hers. She likes a jollification as much as I do myself. She's been helping me with the birthday cake, and which I don't mind telling you is a proper mammoth and no mistake. It 'ud make Mong Blong look like a fourpenny lemon-ice."

Mrs. Bugbird was there, and Nancy thought that she too looked a proper mammoth, so much fatter had she grown with the years.

"It's to be a nice cosy little party," Mrs. Pottage announced. "In fact we're all here now except one."

With this she winked at Mrs. Bugbird, who shook with her accustomed laughter, though she was now so immense that she could scarcely fall off any chair, and not very easily fall off a sofa.

Nancy gratified her hostess by displaying a great deal of curiosity about the missing guest.

"He's my one and only left," Mrs. Pottage said. "No, I'm joking. He isn't what you'd call a suitor at all. In fact, he wouldn't suit anybody. He's just a nice quiet old fellow called Hayhoe who likes to pop in of a evening and smoke his pipe in my kitchen. He's been in Australia all his life, and when he come home again he found all his friends and relations was dead and buried. So the pore old boy's a bit lonely, and he enjoys himself telling the tale to me about Australia, and which seems to me from what I can make out of it a much larger place than what you'd think. And on Sunday to pass the time he blows the organ. He says that's the only way he can go to church without missing his pipe, though whether because the organ has pipes and to spare or because he's for ever puffing at the bellows I never could rightly make out. He's entertained Mrs. B. and I a lot this last winter, and he's very handy with a hammer and nails. In fact, we call him the jumping kangaroo among ourselves. Hush, here he comes."

Perhaps Mr. Hayhoe was abashed by the presence of a stranger, for he certainly did not jump about at all that afternoon, but sat small and silent in a corner of Mrs. Pottage's room until he was called upon to help cut the cake, which he did with the air of performing a surgical operation.

"Well, I shall certainly do my best to live a bit longer," Mrs. Pottage declared when she was responding to the good wishes of her guests, "for the longer I live, the more I enjoy myself. Oh, dear, I do wish I'd have been a month or two younger though, and then Letitsia could have been with us this afternoon. She *has* been away a time. Talk about Brussels sprouts, she *will* be a Brussels sprout by now, and no mistake. You mark my words, Mrs. Bugbird, that child'll come home a walking maypole."

And certainly Letizia did seem the most enormous creature to her mother when they met again, with her skirts half-way between her knees and her ankles and her dark-brown wavy hair in a tight pigtail.

"Fancy, having a flapper for a daughter," Nancy exclaimed.

"I know, isn't it too perfectly beastly, mother. I hope Sister Rose will let me fluff my hair out again. After all, I'm only just fifteen, and I don't want to be grown up before I need be. But I don't expect she will. She was always the strictest of the lot. I can't *think* why they made her head-mistress of St. Joseph's."

Sister Rose felt that it was her duty to try and quell some of Letizia's exuberance, and throughout the next year Nancy was getting letters from her daughter about "rows." With all her strictness Sister Rose seemed much less capable than Sister Catherine of keeping her pupils in order; or perhaps it was that Letizia was now one of the big girls and consequently involved in much more serious escapades than those of the juniors. Then came the most tremendous row the school had ever known, according to Letizia.

> St. Joseph's School,
> Sisters of the Holy Infancy,
> 5 Arden Grove,
> N. W.,
> May 15, 1906.

DARLING MOTHER,

There's been the most frightful row, and it looks as if one or two of us will get the boot. I don't think I shall because I'm not in up to the hilt. But it's all very thunderous, and Reverend Mother has been sent for to deal with matters. What happened was this. You know the backs of the houses in Stanwick Terrace look down into our garden? Well, one of the girls—I'll mention no names because a deadly system of espionage has been instituted—we'll call her Cora which sounds an evil and profligate name. Cora met a youth, well, as a matter of fact, he's not such a youth, because he's left Cambridge. So he must be about 22. Cora met him during the Easter Hols, and was most fearfully smitten. So they arranged to correspond. In fact she considers herself engaged to him. Which of course is piffle, because she's only sixteen. She asked me to be one of her confidantes now, and later on a bridesmaid, and get hold of her notes. Oh, I forgot to say that this youth lives in Stanwick Terrace. So, he used to put them under a flower-pot on the garden wall. But the silly idiots weren't content with notes. They found that they could easily signal to one another from their rooms, and they arranged a code. Two candles in the window meant "My darling, I love you madly"; and all that sort of piffle. Cora used to work her messages with the blind, and I and Joan Hutchinson, the other girl who shares a room with her, got rather fed up with her pulling the blind up and down in a passionate ecstasy. So I said, "Why don't you go out and talk to him over the garden wall? We'll let you down with a sheet, which will be rather a rag." As a matter of fact that's just what it was; because the beastly sheet busted, and there was poor Cora dancing about by the light of the moon in a nightgown and a mackintosh. Sister Margaret, who has apocalyptic visions every night, thought Cora—oh, I'm sick of calling her by a false name, and anyway if some stuffy old nun does open this and read it, well, I hope she'll enjoy it. I do hate espionage. Don't you? We've only had it here since Sister Rose succeeded to the throne. Well, Sister Margaret was looking out of her window just as the sheet busted and dropped Enid Wilson—that's the girl—down into the garden. She at once thought it was a miracle, and rushed to Sister Monica who sleeps in the next room and banged on her door and said, "Oh, sister! Our Lady has just descended into the garden." Tableau vivant! There's a picture for you! Of course Joan and I were simply in fits. Anyway there's the most terrific row on that the school has ever had. Enid is convinced that she's going to be expelled. Investigations by the authorities have discovered all about her darling Gerald. Apparently one of the gardeners found a note and gave it to Sister Rose. Joan Hutchinson and I are in pretty well to the hilt for letting Enid out of the window, and so at any moment you may receive a curt note from Reverend Mother to say that I am incorrigible and please accept delivery.

Heaps of love,

Your sinister child

LETIZIA.

That's what Sister Rose thinks I am. She said to me, "I cannot help thinking, Letizia, that you have played a very sinister part in this sorry affair."

Nancy immediately wrote a stern letter to Letizia, reproaching her for not appreciating what the nuns had done for her, and by the same post she wrote to Mother Catherine, pleading for a lenient view of what she assured her was really more a thoughtless prank than a serious and premeditated piece of naughtiness.

Perhaps Mother Catherine decided that Sister Rose's methods tended to make her pupils rebel against them by outrageous behaviour. At any rate, Sister Rose went to take charge of the house at Eastbourne and rule the indigent maiden ladies provided for therein. Sister Perpetua came down from Beaumanoir to be head-mistress; and there were no more letters from Letizia about rows, for Sister Perpetua, like Mother Catherine, was never strict for the sake of strictness, but wise and holy and human.

That year Nancy was acting in the North, so she spent Christmas at Beaumanoir with Mother Catherine. Snow was lying thick on the moors when she arrived. It reminded her of that Christmas eleven years ago when Mother Mary Ethelreda was still alive.

Mother Catherine had changed very little with passing

time. Her tranquil azure eyes had lost none of their
fiery compassion, none of their grave and sweet com-
prehension. By half-past three when Nancy arrived at
the convent a dusk heavy with unladen snow was creeping
over the moor, and the candles were already lighted in the
Reverend Mother's parlour.

"I have been so distressed over Letizia's behaviour,"
said Nancy. "I cannot think what happened to her last
spring."

"Don't upset yourself about her, my dear child,"
Mother Catherine replied, patting Nancy's hand. "She
is quite herself again now, and in any case it was really
nothing more than the normal exuberance of youth.
Frankly, I am pleased to find her relatively much younger
now than she was before she went to Belgium."

"But I was so shocked at her apparent ingratitude,"
Nancy sighed.

Mother Catherine shook her head.

"She is not ungrateful. You must remember that she
has been at school many, many years now. I can easily
understand that St. Joseph's must be seeming irksome,
and that is one of the reasons why I am glad to have this
chance of talking over with you a plan that is in my
mind. I must tell you that dear Mother Mary Ethelreda
left the Community very well endowed, and there is a
fund set apart for the benefit of any girls who show
any kind of artistic promise. They are to be helped to
achieve their ambition, no matter what it may be. As
you know, Letizia has definitely made up her mind to go
on the stage . . ."

"She has not said so to me," Nancy interrupted.

"Well, that of course is just what you would expect.
Parents and teachers must always expect to be suddenly
confronted with the inexplicable reserve of the young.
Just as she wrote you a full account of that foolish business with Enid Wilson and Joan Hutchinson, so she has
given me her confidence about her career. I fancy that

the instinct to entrust a secret to an outsider is a normal one. You would be expected to regard her theatrical hopes with a professional eye just as I should be expected to regard her escapades with a professional eye."

Nancy nodded her agreement with this.

"Very well," Mother Catherine went on, "if Letizia is going on the stage it is important that she should now concentrate on deportment, elocution, dancing, singing, and all the graces that will adorn her vocation. Another of our pupils longs to paint, and another who shows signs of having a really lovely voice wishes to become a singer. I propose to send these three young cousins of the Muses for a couple of years to Italy with a *dame de compagnie*. Thus each one will be able to study what will most help her afterwards."

"To Italy!" Nancy exclaimed.

"I don't think Letizia will ever have a voice as good as her mother's," the nun said, with a smile. "And that reminds me, will you sing *Adeste Fideles* for us at the midnight Mass?"

"Oh, I never sing nowadays," Nancy replied, the tears standing bright in her eyes at the thought of the delight that was in store for that little daughter—a walking maypole now perhaps, but still so much her little daughter.

"But you must sing for us," Mother Catherine insisted. "We want to hear your voice roll out above our thin notes. It is so dreadful, this news that the French Government has forbidden midnight Mass in any of the French cathedrals or churches this year. What woes that wretched country is calling down upon itself! It will hearten us to hear your voice singing that wonderful old hymn."

Nancy felt that it would sound like affectation to refuse after this, and into her voice at midnight she put all the triumph, all the gladness, all the gratitude in her mother-heart.

So, for the next two years Letizia was writing home to England the most absorbing accounts of Rome, where she and her companions spent most of their time, though on different occasions they visited all the famous cities of Italy. While up and down the length of England, in and out of Wales, over to Ireland, and across the border into Scotland wandered her mother.

CHAPTER XXV

THE COMMON CHORD

Nancy was considerably startled when Letizia at the age of nineteen entered the chorus of the Vanity Theatre. She had old-fashioned ideas about the dignity of her profession, and the chorus of the Vanity did not appeal to her as a worthy or suitable medium for the début of an actress who wanted to take her career seriously.

"Oh, but it's so reassuring, mother," Letizia exclaimed. "Can't you understand how reassuring it is not to be chosen for your talents, but simply, solely, and entirely for your looks?"

"Yes, but the girls in the Vanity chorus are such a mixed lot. And I don't like their outlook on life. It's nearly always hard, mercenary, and, well, to speak quite frankly, my dear child, immoral."

"I'll be the shining exception," Letizia vowed.

"Ah, yes, it's all very well to say that. But you'll soon be liable to take your tone from your surroundings, and become like the rest of them. Dear, it's no use for me to pretend that your engagement at the Vanity is anything but a dreadful disappointment to me after your education, because it is—a dreadful disappointment."

"Mother, try to believe I know what I'm doing. I'm not proposing to remain a Vanity girl. But the Vanity chorus is just what I require after such a careful bringing up. It will cure all the prunes and prisms of convent life; it will give me poise; and it will teach me the way of the world, of which at present I'm really hopelessly ignorant. I'm only just nineteen, and I must look fairly nice already or Mr. Richards would never have engaged me."

Nancy contemplated her daughter. She had not turned

out so tall as she gave promise of being when she came back from Belgium. She was a full inch and a half shorter than her mother, and much, much slimmer. She had the fine Oriano profile with her mother's vivid complexion and rich blue eyes ringed with a darker sapphire, and her mother's deep-brown wavy hair. Yes, she certainly did look "fairly nice." But still, the Vanity chorus —it was a disappointment. Nancy had made up her mind that Letizia should begin her stage experience by going out on tour with some sound Shakespearian or Old Comedy company. She would not earn much in the way of salary, but that would teach her how to be careful with money. And then after a couple of years of knocking about the provinces and playing all sorts of parts she could concentrate upon getting a London engagement and setting out to be famous. Now without taking anybody's advice Letizia had gone off and interviewed John Richards and been engaged by him for the Vanity chorus. It was obvious that she could not live on her salary in such surroundings, which meant that her mother must give her an allowance if she was to be protected against the difficulty of trying to live up to a standard beyond her means without being exposed to temptation. And Nancy did grudge her savings being drawn upon to maintain a position in the Vanity chorus. However, the harm was done, and she was too wise to offer any more opposition for fear of making Letizia decide out of contrariness that the Vanity chorus was the end of an actress's ambition. So, she offered her an allowance of £20 a month and put off on tour with a determination to save an extra pound a week from her own salary of £7. Of course, she never told Letizia that her allowance was being drawn out of her mother's savings, but let her understand that it had been left for that purpose by her father.

The memory of Lettie Fuller and her short swift career upon the Vanity stage, bright and light as the dance of a butterfly through the hours of a Summer morning, should still be so fresh in the minds of play-goers that there is a kind of embarrassment in writing about it. Anyway, Lettie Fuller was our Letizia, and in the years 1910 and 1911 she was the spirit of youth and London as no doubt to-day that elusive and lovable spirit is incarnate in some other young woman. Peace and beauty and fortune attend her and all those who do adore her!

Letizia had not been six months in the chorus before she attracted the attention of John Richards by some imitations she gave at a supper party at which, most un-usually for him, he was present. If John Richards's eyes seemed exclusively occupied with the personal appearance of the young women who adorned his theatre, they were not on that account blind to talent. He asked who the good-looking girl was, remembered now that he had en-gaged her himself, was informed that she came of the-atrical stock, and made a note on his cuff that she was to be given an important understudy. Letizia's luck held. The lady who played the part she was understudy-ing was taken ill at Brighton one Saturday afternoon; and that very night John Richards, who happened to pay one of his periodical visits to the back of a box in order to be sure that his company was not letting the show down by slackness, witnessed Letizia's performance. He turned to his companion, and asked what he thought of her.

"I think she's a marvel."

"So do I," said John Richards.

Yet he did not mention a word to Letizia about having seen her. In fact, neither she nor any of the company knew that the Guv'nor was in front, for these visits to his theatre were always paid in the strictest secrecy. However, when in July the musical comedy for the au-tumn production was ready for rehearsal, John Richards offered Letizia a part with three songs that were likely to take London by storm, if the actress knew how to sing them.

Nancy was acting in Leicester the week that Letizia's telegram arrived with its radiant news of the luck her birthday had brought. She went into the church where twenty-one years ago she and Bram were married, and there she lighted every candle she could find to Our Lady of Victories. The pricket blazed with such a prodigality of golden flames in the jewelled sunlight that the old woman who was cleaning out the pews came up to find out if this extravagant stranger was a genuine devotee.

"It's all right," Nancy told her. "I was married in this church twenty-one years ago, and I am thanking Heaven for happiness after much sorrow."

The old cleaner smiled so benignly that Nancy gave her half a crown and begged for her prayers. Then she sought out the priest, and asked him to say Masses for the soul of Letizia's great-grandmother and for herself a Mass of thanksgiving, and still another Mass for the intention of the Sisters of the Holy Infancy. She gave him, too, alms for the poor of his parish, and then going home to her lodgings she knelt beside her bed and wept the tears of unutterable thankfulness, those warm tears that flow like outpoured wine, so rich are they with the sunshine of the glad heart.

Letizia's first night was on the ninth of September. Her mother decided to give up her autumn engagement, and trust to finding something later on when the supremely important date was past. She did not want to worry Letizia during her rehearsals; but her experience might be of service, and she ought to be near at hand. Nancy stayed at her old rooms in St. John's Wood which she had chosen originally to be near Letizia at school in the days when she herself was a London actress. Perhaps if she could have mustered up as much excitement about her own first night in London, she might have been famous now herself instead of merely being favourably

known to a number of provincial audiences. Yet how
much more wonderful to be the mother of a famous
daughter in whose success she could be completely absorbed without feeling the least guilt of egotism.

The piece that Autumn at the Vanity was only one of
a long line of musical comedies between which it would be
idle to attempt to distinguish; the part that Letizia played
was only one of many similar parts, and the songs she
sang had been written over and over again every year for
many years; but Lettie Fuller herself was different. She
was incarnate London, and this was strange, because
she had neither a cockney accent nor, what was indeed
unexpected on the musical comedy stage, a mincing su-
burban accent. She did not open big innocent eyes at
the stalls and let her underclothes wink for her. She
neither pursed her lips nor simpered, nor waggled her
head. But she was beautiful with a shining naturalness
and an infectious vitality; and, as Mrs. Pottage told her
mother, she was as fresh as a lilac in Spring.

The old lady—the very old lady, for she was now
seventy-five—was sitting with Nancy in the middle of
the stalls. Nancy thought that she would be less nervous
there than in a box, and it would be easier for Letizia
not to be too much aware of her mother's anguished
gaze.

"Well, I'm sorry she's gone and had herself printed
Lettie Fuller," said Mrs. Pottage. "Because I'd made
up my mind that before I died I *would* learn how to spell
Letitsia, and I brought my best glasses on purpose so
as I could see the name printed as it should be. And then
she goes and calls herself Lettie, which a baby-in-arms
could spell. And Mrs. Bugbird and pore Aggie Wilkinson was both very anxious to know just how it was spelt,
so they'll be disappointed. I only hope Mrs. B. will
reckonise her when she comes on, because she won't
know who she is from Adam and Eve in the programme."

"Is dear old Mrs. Bugbird here?" Nancy exclaimed.

"Of course she's here—*and* pore Aggie Wilkinson, of

course. Why, they wouldn't have missed it for nothing. It's only to be hoped that Mrs. B. don't fall over in the excitement. She's in the front row of the upper circle, and if she did come down she'd about wipe out the front six rows of the pit. Still, I daresay Aggie will hook one of her pore crutches in the back of Mrs. B's bodice which is bound to bust open in the first five minutes. The last time she and me went to the theatre she looked more like a tug-of-war than a respectable woman before the piece was over."

"The overture's beginning," Nancy whispered, for people were beginning to turn round and stare at the apple-cheeked old lady who was talking so volubly in the middle of the stalls.

"So any one can see by the airs that conductor fellow's giving himself. Why band-conductors should be so cocky I never *could* fathom. It isn't as if they did anything except wave that blessed bit of wood like a kid with a hoopstick. It's the same with bus-conductors. They give theirselves as many airs as if they was driving the blessed bus itself. That's it, now start tapping," she went on in a tone of profound contempt. "Yes, if he dropped that silly bit of wood and got down off that high chair and did an honest night's work banging the drum, perhaps he might give himself a few airs. Ah, now they're off, and depend upon it that conductor-fellow thinks, if he stopped waving, the band would stop playing, and which of course is radicalous."

The overture finished. The first bars of the opening chorus were being played. The curtain rose.

"There she is! There she is!" Mrs. Pottage gasped when from the crowded stage she disentangled Letizia's debonair self. "And don't she look a picture, the pretty jool!"

When the moment came for Letizia to sing her first song, her mother shut her eyes against the theatre that was spinning before them like a gigantic humming-top. It seemed an hour before she heard Letizia's voice ring-

ing out clear and sweet and cool across the footlights.
She saw her win the hearts of the audience until they
were all turned into one great heart beating for her.
She heard the surge of her first encore, and then she
might have fainted if Mrs. Pottage had not dug her
sharply in the ribs at that moment.

"Did you hear what that old buffer in front of us
said?" Mrs. Pottage whispered hoarsely.

"Something nice about Letizia?" she whispered back.

"He said he was damned if she wasn't the best girl
John Richards had found for years. And how I didn't
get up and kiss the blessed top of his bald head I'm bothered if I know."

The curtain fell on the first act, and the loudest applause was always for Letizia.

"Oh, she's knocked 'em," Mrs. Pottage declared.
"She's absolutely knocked 'em. But she's lovely! And,
oh, dear, God bless us both, but how she did remind me of
her pore father once or twice."

The old lady fumbled for Nancy's hand and squeezed
it hard.

"Well, I don't mind saying she's made me feel like
a girl again," Mrs. Pottage went on after a moment or
two of silence. "Every sweetheart I ever had come into
my mind while she was singing that song. You know!
It was like riding on the top of a bus in fine weather
when they've just watered the streets and the may's
out in flower and you say to yourself there's no place
like dear old London after all and begin to nod and dream
as you go jogging along, thinking of old faces and old
fancies and the fun you've had years ago."

The curtain rose on the second act, and with every
line she said and with every note she sang Lettie Fuller
became nearer and dearer to her audience that night.

Once, after a sally had been taken up by the house in
roars of laughter, Mrs. Pottage exclaimed to Nancy:

"Hark! did you hear that? That was Mrs. Bugbird's
laugh above the lot. Oh, I'd reckonise that laugh if I

was in my coffin. You mark my words, she'll be whooping in a moment. That's always the way it gets her. But pore Aggie'll pat her back if she whoops *too* hard."

In spite of the encores—and Letizia always won by far the loudest and most persistent of them—the curtain fell at last on another thundering Vanity success.

"Bravo, bravo, my beauty!" Mrs. Pottage stood up to shout when Letizia took her call. Lots of other people were standing up and shouting, so her enthusiasm was not so very conspicuous. Nancy felt too weak with emotion to stand up herself, and sank back in a pale trance of joyful relief.

"There's Mrs. B.!" Mrs. Pottage suddenly exclaimed. "And if she claps much louder, she'll clap herself out of that new dress of hers for good and all. And when she gets out in the Strand she'll be run in to Bow Street if she isn't careful. She's the most excitable woman I ever *did* know."

At last the audience consented to let the performers retire, and a few minutes later Nancy held Letizia in her arms.

"Darling mother, was I good?"

"Darling child, you were perfect."

"And where's Mrs. Pottage?" Letizia asked. "Did she think I was good?"

"The dear old soul's waiting to be invited into your dressing-room."

"Mrs. Pottage! Mrs. Pottage!" Letizia cried, hugging the old lady. "You're coming back to supper with me, aren't you?"

"Oh, no, duckie. I've got Mrs. Bugbird and pore Aggie Wilkinson waiting to go back to Greenwich. We're all going to take a cab to London Bridge."

"Oh, but they must both come to supper too. They must really. I'll get a car to drive you home. You *must* all come. I won't be long dressing."

And, if it was possible for Nancy to feel any happier that night, it was when her little daughter showed that success had not made her heedless of old simple friends.

The very next day Nancy went round to see her agent.

"You don't mean to tell me you want to get another engagement at once, Miss O'Finn? Why, I should have thought you would have wanted to stay and enjoy your daughter's success. It was wonderful. What notices, eh? By Jove, it's refreshing nowadays to hear of anybody clicking like that."

"Oh, no, I've rested quite long enough," Nancy said. "I want to be off on tour again as soon as possible."

The agent looked at his book.

"Well, I'm awfully sorry, Miss O'Finn, but I don't believe there's anything just at the moment that would suit you." He paused. "Unless—but, no, of course, you don't want to play that line of parts yet."

"What line?"

"Why, Charles Hamilton is losing Miss Wolsey who has been playing Mrs. Malaprop, Mrs. Hardcastle, etc., with him for the last fifteen years."

"You mean the old women?" Nancy asked.

"Quite—er—quite."

"I would like to be with Charles Hamilton," she said pensively. "And at forty it's time to strike out in a new line of parts."

"Well, he's playing at Croydon this week. If you would consider these parts, why don't you go and see him? It's a pleasant company to be in. Forty-two weeks, year in year out, and of course he occasionally has a season in London. Nothing but Shakespeare and Old Comedy."

Nancy did not hesitate. Now that her daughter was safely launched it was time for her to be settling down. She went back to her rooms and wrote a long letter to Mother Catherine about Letizia's triumph. Then she wrote to Charles Hamilton for an interview. She went to Croydon, interviewed him, and a fortnight later she was playing with him at Sheffield—Mrs. Candour in *The*

School for Scandal on Monday, the Nurse in *Romeo and
Juliet* on Tuesday, Mrs. Malaprop in *The Rivals* on Wednesday, Mistress Quickly in *The Merry Wives* on Thursday, nothing on Friday when *Twelfth Night* was per-
formed, but on Saturday Mrs. Hardcastle in *She Stoops
to Conquer* at the matinée and at night once more the
Nurse in *Romeo and Juliet*.

Nancy no longer worried over her increasing tendency
to increasing portliness, and she never regretted joining
Charles Hamilton's company, which now that Mrs. Hunter-Hart had retired represented the last stronghold of
the legitimate drama in Great Britain. So long as Charles
Hamilton went out on tour she determined to tour with
him. The habit of saving so much out of her salary
every week was not given up because Letizia was secure;
indeed she saved more each week, because now that she
had taken to dowagers she could afford to ignore the
changes of fashion which had made dressing a problem
so long as she was competing for parts with younger
women.

And then Letizia Fuller after enchanting London for
a year abandoned the stage for ever in order to marry
the young Earl of Darlington.

The following letter to her mother explained her
reasons:

> 125 Gordon Mansions,
> Gordon Square,
> W. C.
> Sept. 15.

MY DARLING DARLING MOTHER,

In a few days you will read in the papers that I am engaged to be married to Lord Darlington. I haven't said anything to you about this before, because I wanted to make up
my own mind entirely for myself. He proposed to me first
about two months ago, and though I loved him I wondered
if I loved him enough to give up the stage. You don't know
how much I was enjoying being loved by the public. That's

what I wondered if I could give up, not the ambition to become a great actress. But I've come to the definite conclusion that I'm not really so very ambitious at all. I think that simple happiness is the best, and my success at the Vanity was really a simple happiness. It was the being surrounded by hundreds of jolly people, every one of whom I liked and who liked me. But I don't think I should ever want to be a wonderful Lady Macbeth, and thrill people by the actress part of me. I'm not really acting at the Vanity. I'm just being myself and enjoying it.

Of course, people might say that if marriage with an earl is simple happiness then simple happiness is merely social ambition. But I assure you that unless I loved Darlington I would not dream of marrying him. He's not very rich, and apart from the pleasure of being a countess it's no more than marrying any good-looking, simple, country squire. The only problems for me were first to find out if I loved him as much as I loved the public and being loved by them, and secondly to know if he would agree that all the children should be Catholics. Well, I do know that I love him more than I love the public and I do know that I want his love more than I want the love of the public. And he agreed at once about the children.

Thanks to you, darling, I'm not likely to seem particularly out of place in my new part. Perhaps it's only now that I realise what you've done for me all these years. You shall always be proud of me. I do realise too what dear Mother Catherine and the nuns have done for me. I'm writing to her by this post to try to express a little of my gratitude.

Darling mother, I'm so happy and I love you so dearly.

Your own

Letizia.

Three days later, the engagement of the beloved Lettie Fuller gave the press one of those romantic stories so dear and so rightly dear to it. Two days after the announcement Nancy received from Caleb Fuller a letter addressed to her care of Miss Lettie Fuller, at the Vanity Theatre.

The Towers,
Lower Bilkton,
Cheshire.
Sept. 18, 1911.

MY DEAR NANCY,

I've been intending to write to you for a long time now to invite you and Lettie to come and stay with us. But this new house which I have just built has taken longer to get ready than I expected. It's situated in very pretty country about fifteen miles from Brigham, and my architect has made a really beautiful miniature castle which everybody admires. I presented dear old Lebanon House to the Borough of Brigham to be used as an up-to-date lunatic asylum which was badly required in the district.

Trixie and I do so very much hope that you and Lettie will come and stay with us and spend a quiet time before the wedding takes place, of which by the way we have read. You haven't met Trixie yet, and it's always such a disappointment to her. But I'm sure you'll understand what a mess we've been in with building. I want you to meet Norman too. Do you know, he's fifteen. Doesn't time fly? He's at Rossall, and I've made up my mind to give him the chance his father never had and let him go to the University.

Are you interested in gardening? Trixie is a great gardener and spends all her time with her roses. Now, I think I've given you most of our news, and we are waiting anxiously to hear you are going to give us the pleasure of your visit. Poor Aunt Achsah and Aunt Thyrza are both dead. I would have sent you a notice of the funerals if I had known your address.

With every good wish for your happiness and for the happiness of dear little Lettie,

Your affectionate brother-in-law,

CALEB FULLER.

To this Nancy sent back a postcard:

Hell is paved with good intentions, Caleb!

It is tempting to prolong this with an account of Letizia's wedding and to relate what Mrs. Pottage wore at it and what she said when Lord Darlington kissed her good-bye, before he and Letizia set out on their honeymoon. It is tempting to dwell on the wit and the beauty of Letizia Darlington and still more tempting to enlarge upon her happiness. But she and her husband belong too much to the present to be written about and this tale of over eighty years is already too long. Yet, one more letter must be printed.

> C/o Charles Hamilton's
> Shakespeare-Sheridan Company.
> Princess's Theatre,
> Bristol.
> Dec. 3, 1913.

DARLING LETIZIA,

I'm so overjoyed you're glad to have a second little boy, though I hope you'll have a little girl soon. You are a dear child to want me to give up acting and settle down with you at Vipont for the rest of my life. But you know, I am still comparatively young, only 44, and from every point of view I think it is better that I should go on acting. I am very happy with Mr. Hamilton, and the life on tour suits me. Moreover, it amuses me to feel that one day I may have quite a nice little nest egg for this new little boy who will be a younger son, and I know that Vipont requires all the money you've got to keep it up properly. God bless you, my darling, and let me go on acting quietly in this very pleasant old-fashioned company which is more like a family party than anything else.

My dear love to all of you.

> Your loving
>
> MOTHER.

And up and down the length of England, in and out of Wales, over to Ireland, and across the border into Scotland Nancy O'Finn still wandered.

THE END